DRAWN FROM LIFE

DRAWN

from LIFE

a novel

Sarah P. Blanchard

Drawn from Life

Copyright © 2024 by Sarah P. Blanchard

Cover design by Sarah P. Blanchard and GetCovers; AdobeStock images

All rights reserved. No part of this book may be reproduced, stored or transmitted in any form or by any means, electronic, mechanical, photocopying, recording, scanning or otherwise, without written permission from the publisher, except in the case of brief quotations embodied in critical articles and reviews. It is illegal to copy this book, post it to a website, or distribute it by any other means without permission.

Sarah P. Blanchard asserts the moral right to be identified as the author of this work.

Designations used by companies to distinguish their products are often claimed as trademarks. All brand names and product names used in this book are trade names, service marks, trademarks, and registered trademarks of their respective owners. The publishers and the book are not associated with any product or vendor mentioned in this book. None of the companies referenced within the book have endorsed the book.

This book is a work of fiction. Names, characters, places, and incidents either are products of the author's imagination or are used fictitiously.

First Printing, March 2024
Eagle Ridge Farm
ISBN: 979-8-218-33228-0

For Phil and Rich,
my Hōkūleʻa and Hōkūpaʻa

ONE

Thursday, November 18, 2015 - 2:00 a.m.

"Really, Em. You're being such a drama queen, all that moaning and groaning. It's not like you're dying. You saw the X-rays, it's just a little crack."

Lucy risked a glance away from the wet road to frown at her cousin Emma, huddled beneath a blanket in the passenger seat. "And, FYI, your shirt's buttoned all crooked. You look like a sad-ass refugee."

A gust of wind rocked the car. Sucking in her breath, Lucy tightened her grip on the wheel and braked. She hunched forward, squinting past thrashing wipers into inky blackness. Seeking a glimpse of slick pavement through the downpour.

Woozy with painkillers, preoccupied with tracking rain streaks on the side window, Emma blinked herself halfway into focus and organized a response.

"Next time," she began slowly. "Next time I break a bone…I'll dress better. I'll be dressed. No more…" She thought a bit. "No more posing nudely. Nudidity? Posing nude."

Lucy scowled. "You don't mean that, right? You can't stop sitting for me. I need you, Em. You're my abso-fucking-lutely best model, always have been." Her eyes flicked from the road to Emma. "You're kidding, right? Hey, Mouse. I *said* I was sorry."

Nudidity, Emma thought. There's a fun word. Who used to say that?

Radar O'Reilly, that's who. On *M.A.S.H.*, her dad's favorite show. She should call. Let him know she was okay. The broken collarbone was nothing, they'd still be there for Thanksgiving.

Call her dad, she amended. Not Radar O'Reilly. And not right now because it was like two in the morning.

Belatedly, Emma caught up to Lucy's words and worry. "But posing for you is dangerous. You saw it, right? That easel attacked me." She frowned. "And my name's not Mouse. I hate that nickname. You should use my real name."

The pain meds were doing a fine job of blurring everything except the mesmerizing swipe of the wipers. Emma rolled her head back toward the side window, careful not to jostle her left arm in its sling.

Lucy found the interstate's on-ramp and accelerated, risking a skid.

Emma wanted to say something about the perils of excessive speed on slippery mountain roads, but then she felt the Subaru's all-wheel-drive take hold and the moment was gone. The words weren't lining up correctly anyway.

Lucy exhaled loudly and relaxed her grip on the wheel. "That doctor said you'll be just fine, Em, all healed up in a week or two. So no one needs to know about this, right?"

Emma considered that. "I'll need an extension from Panetta. I've got a paper due Friday, the day after tomorrow. No, tomorrow. Today's Thursday already, right?"

"I'll call Panetta," Lucy assured her. "What's your topic? Never mind," she added quickly. "This is just me, faking an interest. I'm sure it's totally mind-numbing."

"The Roles of Women…" Emma frowned in concentration. "…in Sub-Saharan Village…Economies? …Maybe."

"Yeah, boring as fuck." Lucy swapped dismissal for persuasion. "Don't worry, I'll tell Panetta you got a doctor's note. But no one else needs to know. Right?" Fingers twitched on the wheel. "This is adulting one-oh-one, Em. We don't need to run to Daddy or Uncle Jerry with every little boo-boo, right? We solve our own fucking problems. Pinky-swear, okay?"

Only Lucy would say fucking and pinky-swear in the same breath.

Through the rain and inky darkness, Emma saw the flash of an exit sign and the lights of what might be a gas station. She wanted to remind her cousin about the Subaru needing gas but instead she fell asleep.

She woke to the crunch of tires on gravel and the growl of the Outback downshifting as it began the sharp climb to their cabin. On the car's instrument panel, the GET GAS NOW light glowed red.

A small panic jolted Emma upright. "Lucy, the gas—" She gasped as a sharp pain knifed her left shoulder.

Lucy scowled, her face inches from the windshield as she navigated a hairpin turn through the downpour. The wipers were slapping frantically now, running on high. At the second switchback, she slowed to a crawl and snapped on the high beams.

"Stupid headlights." One hand left the wheel to scoop back a shock of white-blond hair. "They're fucking useless! I can't see anything."

"Go back to low beams," Emma forced the words through clenched teeth. "It won't reflect off the rain as much."

"Really?" Lucy snapped. "Do you want to drive?"

Emma bit back a response.

Yes I do, but no I can't. What if we run out of gas? No one else drives this road, we're still half a mile from home—

Her right hand flew to the grab handle as the Subaru fishtailed on loose gravel and thumped into a pothole. She caught her lower lip between her teeth and braced both feet against the floor. Pain shot again through her shoulder.

Five minutes later, they pulled into the nearly invisible clearing at the end of the old logging road. The Outback sputtered its last fumes and died, sliding a little sideways in the mud.

At least the cabin's lights were still on.

Lucy offered Emma a weak grin, the silver stud in her lower lip glinting in the dashboard's glow before she switched off the ignition.

"Made it, Mouse. Easy-peasey."

They stumbled through blasts of cold rain to the porch, strewn now with slick wet leaves. Inside, Lucy slammed the door against a blast of wet wind as Emma dropped her wet blanket on the floor and toed off her muddy shoes.

Rain drummed hard on the cabin's metal roof. We're okay now, Emma thought as Lucy helped her peel off wet jeans and socks. In a few hours it would be daylight. When the rain ended Lucy could take their other car, Emma's Miata, to get gas for the Subaru. Everything would be fine.

As Emma tried to figure out how to lie on her right side while holding an icepack on her left shoulder, Lucy's "easy-peasey" tickled Emma's memory. One of her mother's favorite phrases. What other platitudes would Kit Gillen provide now?

It's not a problem unless you make it a problem, Emmie. A warm blanket and a hot cup of tea, that's all you need. Let Lucy do the hard stuff. She'll take care of you like she always does.

Except Emma's mother was gone forever and there was nothing easy-peasey about life with Lucy.

***

Emma at nineteen liked to study root causes. What factors precipitated the Great Depression? Which innovation motivated a barter economy to transition to a monetary system? How did she end up with a hairline crack in her collarbone?

The physics of that was simple: The crossbar of Lucy's easel collided with Emma's clavicle. Force plus velocity plus trajectory. But what was the propelling force, Lucy's frustration with that damned art project or the disturbing text from Maggie, Lucy's mother? Probably both.

Like all juniors in Silvermill College's School of Art, Lucy was required to produce a capstone project, a major work worthy of exhibition at the end of the fall semester. She'd proposed creating a three-dimensional self-portrait, a life-sized plaster sculpture that she would then destroy during the gallery show.

Lucy had a theme and a title, Genesis and Catharsis. She knew what Catharsis would look like, a multimedia video extravaganza—with strobe lights, clashing cymbals, maybe cannon fire—during which she'd sledgehammer her plaster self into smithereens.

But Genesis was proving tricky. She'd begun with typical Lucy-style enthusiasm, creating detailed drawings that exaggerated her own angular features—aquiline nose, wide shoulders, sharp hips. Plus all the body art, the ink and metal ornaments.

The timeline required her to complete a frame of wood and chicken wire by Thanksgiving, but she'd spent all of October and half of November changing her mind about the perfect posture to express The Full Essence of Lucy. Nude, of course, but what then? Spreadeagled on a concrete slab or draped on a tree limb? Emerging from the ground as a hellish demon or crouching like a hungry spider? She loved Louise Bourgeois' arachnid *Maman* at the National Gallery in Ottawa, but wouldn't a spider be too derivative?

Emma suggested a Lucy-piñata, suspended from a tree branch like a naked paratrooper or a flying zombie. Just joking, she added, but Lucy liked the idea. She just couldn't decide what should spill out of the Lucy-zombie-piñata when she destroyed it on camera. Condoms, maybe.

After months of listening to Lucy's indecision, Emma was done contributing feedback. *You're going to smash it anyway,* she wanted to say. *Just get it done.*

On the afternoon before the hospital trip—Wednesday, a week before Thanksgiving—they'd come home early from classes. Emma retreated to her bedroom to work on her economics paper while Lucy sat in front of the television, sketchpad in hand, to draw warrior poses from *Game of Thrones* freeze frames.

A little before six p.m., Lucy dragged her big A-frame easel into the center of their front room and set it up beside the fieldstone fireplace.

"Please, Em, I need you to pose. Twenty minutes, that's all. I've got it narrowed down to three concepts. It won't take long."

Emma stifled a sigh. The economics paper needed her full attention but Lucy sounded desperate. She set aside her laptop and pulled off her sweatshirt because posing for Lucy usually meant posing nude.

"Twenty minutes," Emma agreed. "Then dinner. I'm holding you to that. How about Norah Jones?"

They'd agreed years earlier that the model chooses the music. To the opening notes of "Sunrise," Emma draped her jeans and underwear neatly over the sofa and stood naked on the braided rug in front of a dark window.

"I need your hair up," Lucy reminded her.

Emma gathered her heavy curls, wrestling the mass of hair into a thick bird's nest and securing it with an elastic band above her neck. A few russet strands always escaped, springing away from her head in defiance of hairdressing and gravity.

At Lucy's direction, Emma eased into a warrior pose with feet planted wide and hands clutching an imaginary broadsword over a shoulder.

Beneath the music she heard a light rain peppering the windows, the beginning of a storm moving through the mountains. She shuddered a little, imagining the cold rain against her skin.

"Puh-leese, Em," Lucy coaxed. "Hold it just a little longer. I've really got to get this done. Bring that left leg forward a bit."

By the time the first sketch was completed, all the blood had left Emma's arms. Twenty minutes came and went, but Lucy kept sketching and coaxing.

"Hang on, Em. I've almost got it. Five more minutes."

Then it was five more in a new position and five more after that, until Lucy forgot to ask and Emma forgot to protest.

Norah Jones ran out of songs. The only sounds now were the rain and Lucy's frustrated mutterings as she dragged a floor lamp around the room and repositioned her easel. Nothing was working. She blamed gloomy lighting, paper-curling humidity, and Emma.

"Jeez, Mouse. That pose is so static. You're just standing there like a freaky little rodent. I need you fierce and powerful. Be a dragon queen."

Emma steeled herself, not for the pose but for what would happen next. There'd be swearing and foot-stomping, sketches ripped to shreds. Eventually Lucy might produce something brilliant, but the process was always fraught with drama.

"Just fucking try," Lucy growled. "Come on, Mouse. You've got to look like me."

Emma remembered Rodin's nude study of Jean d'Aire, a bronze sculpture at the art museum in Raleigh. One of Auguste Rodin's besieged *Burghers of Calais*, the massive figure stood in defiance and despair, fists clenched at his side as he prepared to sacrifice himself to an invading army.

Worth a try.

"How about this? From the Rodin garden." Emma turned away and imagined herself large and powerful. Knees locked, fists coiled, jaw clenched.

Lucy's scowl evaporated. "Oh! Yes. Can you get more weight on your right leg? Like you're stepping into death. Keep your back arched, show those biceps. That's awesome!"

But it wasn't awesome, it was impossible. Emma was six inches shorter and ten pounds heavier than Lucy, all soft curves where Lucy was hard bone and muscle. Emma didn't have biceps.

She couldn't be a body double for her Valkyrie cousin and she really couldn't be the nine-foot-tall statue of a desperate, naked Frenchman. Five minutes later, her arms began trembling. When her right calf cramped, she collapsed on the sofa and folded herself into a blanket.

"Sorry, Lucy, I can't do this. You took pictures of the Rodins. Can't you just look at those?"

"No, I can't! I deleted those stupid photos and now there's no time!"

She tore the Emma-burgher sketch off her easel and ripped it in half. Crumpled the pieces and tossed them into the cold fireplace. Threw herself into a chair and buried her face in her hands.

"It's a fucking disaster," she groaned.

"Let's take a break," Emma coaxed. "We can go back to it after dinner."

She pulled on her clothes and began ladling chili from the pot on the stove while Lucy sulked on the sofa. Emma hesitated over a bottle of red wine, then poured a scant half glass for Lucy. She corked the bottle and tucked it away in a cupboard.

Food brought Lucy back to life. She ate hunched over the table, spoon in one hand and phone in the other, alternating between eating and swiping through a dating app. Left, left, left. She snort-laughed derisively and kept swiping.

They finished the chili just before eight, when Lucy's phone pinged with a text.

TWO

"Fucking spam." Lucy frowned. Her finger hovered over the delete icon.

She paused. "What—? It's my mother. But it's someone else's phone." She swiped rapidly, her frown deepening. "Shit! Really? She says she's moving again. Leaving New Haven, going back to Stanstead."

Lucy was born in Stanstead, Quebec, just north of Vermont.

Emma set their empty bowls in the sink. "When's she leaving? After Thanksgiving?"

"Now! *Right now.*" Lucy's face pinched in dismay, then fury. "This is so fucking *stupid*. She says I can't call her back because the phone she's using belongs to someone named Brad. Who the hell is Brad? She's left Hartford, she's literally on a bus. But she's heading *north*, not south. They're almost at the border and now they've lost the cell signal. *Fuck.*"

"North?"

"Canada! Quebec!"

"But she'll be back for Thanksgiving, right?"

Lucy threw her phone. It skidded off the table, bounced on the braided rug, and came to rest against a leg of their saggy old sofa. Being closer, Emma retrieved it and placed it back on the table.

Lucy jumped to her feet and began pacing between the fireplace and kitchen sink.

"Shit shit shit! My *fucking* mother. She can't *do* that! They'll stop her at the border. She can't get a work visa, she can't get a job. If she sneaks in, she'll get deported. Again."

"Why's she going?"

"Who the fuck knows?"

"I'm sorry." Emma couldn't offer a hug, she'd be flung off. "Last time you talked, she was clean, right? Six months sober?"

Lucy continued pacing. "This is *Maggie* we're talking about, remember? No fucking way she's still clean. And she's the one who said oh, let's get everyone together for Thanksgiving at the family farm." She mimicked a saccharine wheedling. "We've got things to talk about, she said. To celebrate, because Maggie's sober. She swore she's getting her life together, everything's turning around. Yeah, no." She resumed pacing.

"Maybe—"

"Fuck that shit. She's disappeared again and I'm *done* with her."

"But we'll still have Thanksgiving. Dad and Jerry are flying down on Tuesday."

Lucy paused to glare at Emma. "You don't get it! She was supposed to ask Jerry—" She broke off abruptly. "Fuck it. Let's go somewhere. I'm sick of hanging out here."

Emma knew if they drove the twenty miles into Asheville, Lucy would head for a bar. Emma, always the designated driver, would have to drive them home through the storm.

"Let's not, okay?" Emma hated to beg so she aimed for logic. "Your tank's almost empty. Do you really want to stop for gas tonight, in this rain? Besides, I've got work to do."

Lucy flopped onto the sofa and threw her head back to stare at the ceiling. Emma waited a beat, then opened her textbook.

A minute later, Lucy shot back onto her feet and strode to her easel. "Okay, let's finish this stupid drawing. You offered, remember? After dinner, you said."

Emma sighed. She marked her book with a paper napkin and shed her clothes again.

Lucy poked through her box of charcoals. "You know, Em, in the whole fucking world you're the only one who understands me. The only one who puts up with me when I get crazy."

Emma couldn't claim to understand Lucy but she suspected the last part was true. No one else tolerated her cousin's tantrums and sarcasm. But was that a strength or a weakness?

Lucy positioned a wooden chair near the window. "Nothing hard, Em, I promise. Just sit and stare at the window, okay? And pull the band off your hair. Let it hang loose, or whatever it wants to do." She switched off the overhead light and dragged her easel across the floor, bringing it closer to Emma. Now the only light came from a small desk lamp on the kitchen table.

"Shake your head again, Em. Your hair, it's wild." Lucy pulled a wool blanket off the sofa. "Here, drape this over your shoulders. Maybe I'll add some fabric for texture. Rags, or wet seaweed. Remember that exhibit in Montreal, with the kinetic fabric that moved to music? A skirt started fluttering when I sang to it. That's what I need."

Emma groaned inwardly. Another concept, another complication. But if Lucy was feeling inspired instead of frustrated, she'd go along with it. "Thanks for the blanket, it's getting chilly. Maybe you could light a fire."

"When it's raining? No, it'll just make the room smokey. Besides, the wood's all wet."

It was Lucy's turn to bring in logs from the woodpile by the porch.

Emma pulled the blanket closer, thinking she should've kept her clothes on. How many years had she been posing for Lucy's art? She couldn't remember the first time. Before kindergarten, certainly.

Cousins with no other siblings, they were only a year apart in age. They'd been thrown together since childhood by circumstances and their family's collective need to cope with Lucy's mercurial mother.

Whenever motherhood—or life in general—overwhelmed Maggie, Emma's small rural home in eastern Connecticut became Lucy's refuge. The doorbell would ring, usually late at night. There were whispers or raised voices, sometimes tears. A shadowy figure handed over a backpack and nudged a sullen Lucy through the door.

Emma's mother Kit or father Frank always folded Lucy into an unreciprocated hug and exclaim, "Look, Emmie. Here's Lucy, she's staying with us for a night or two, maybe a week. Isn't that wonderful? We can always make room for Lucy."

The night or the week frequently stretched to a month or longer, depending on where Maggie had gone and why. Rehab, jail, drugs, a new boyfriend, alcohol, a halfway house, drugs again, jail again. Frank's sister always vowed to return for her daughter, as soon as she got her act together.

Each time, Emma set aside her toys and offered Lucy a fresh box of crayons or markers. The girls learned to co-exist through a shared interest in art. Their talents emerged early: Lucy's artistic skills, Emma's ability to follow and admire.

Lucy especially loved the gritty messiness of charcoal. She often used both hands, holding a drawing stick in her right and a blending stump or eraser in her left. If the work went well, she'd swap the blunt stick for a thin piece of burnt grapevine or a white highlighter. She was her own toughest critic, though, and most drawings were abandoned halfway. Sheets of sixty-pound Strathmore crumpled on the hearth made excellent fire starters.

Now Lucy paused, scowling. "I've got the lighting right, but the composition is flat. It needs depth." She pointed her charcoal at Emma, accusing. "You're easy to sketch, Em, but hard to draw. I want myth and mystery, but you're all saints and serenity. No depth."

Emma tried to speak without moving. "What did I do? Was I shivering? I'm trying to hold still but it's cold."

Half of her body was covered by the blanket, the other half exposed. She felt goosebumps and nipples rising, probably not the look Lucy was looking for. "How about a Mona Lisa smile? That's mysterious."

"Stop that, Mouse," Lucy muttered. "Don't move. And stop mocking me."

Emma flinched. "Sorry. I'm not mocking. I'm—"

"No stupid Mona Lisa face."

There was a *snap* and Lucy groaned. "Shit. I need a new stick." She rummaged through her box. When she resumed sketching, the strokes came hard and rough, like a rake scraping concrete.

"Em," Lucy demanded, "why don't you ever get angry? I'm trying to put some emotion into this drawing but you aren't giving me anything."

Time to shut this down, Emma thought. *Get up, get dressed, get warm.*

But she remained in her chair, distracted by the sight of her own reflection in the window. Floating in darkness, framed by an exuberant mane of curls, her face looked blank and inconsequential. The mask of an artist's manikin.

"Okay, if you can't do anger, try shame." Lucy was drawing now with quiet, carefully controlled strokes. "Think of something shameful. Like that asshole in seventh grade, what was his name? The boy who grabbed you behind the bleachers." Her voice softened with memory. "Remember how he got you down, shoved his hands under your shirt?"

Emma's goosebumps vanished in a flush of heat.

Lucy was prompting pain like it was a friendly bit of nostalgia. "Remember what that felt like? Show me that feeling. I want to draw that." She continued amiably, "Then remember how glad you were when I hauled him off you. Remember what I did to him? You were so scared, you were crying. But I saved you, right?"

"That's not fair—" The blanket slipped to the floor as Emma leaped to her feet. Naked and not caring, she spun to face her cousin. "I'm done—"

Lucy kept drawing, apparently unconcerned that her model had broken the pose. "Okay, so give me something else then. How about some random time when you really screwed up. No, fuck that, I forgot, the Mouse never screws up. Oh, I know! How about grief? That could work. Remember when your mother asked you to go skiing with her? But you said no. So she went alone, and then she died."

Lucy stepped back from the easel to inspect her work. Shook her head, sighed, and added as an afterthought, "I loved skiing with your mother. If I was there, I'd have gone. Then maybe she wouldn't have died."

The casual cruelty took Emma's breath. "No!" she choked out.

She bit down hard on her lower lip and forced her words past the tang of blood. "You don't get to use my grief for whatever this is."

Lucy resumed drawing, but now her strokes came quick and angry with a fresh violence that threatened to tear the paper. She remained silent.

Face wet with tears, Emma retrieved the blanket from the floor and fumbled it around her torso. From long habit, she sought conciliation. "Lucy, I'm sorry about your mother running off again. But what you're doing right now, it's a mind-fuck. Don't dump all your shit on me."

Emma, who seldom swore, had captured Lucy's attention. The scrape of charcoal stopped.

"Much better, Mouse. You're actually defending yourself." A pause. "This is exhausting."

What's exhausting? Emma wondered. *Drawing me, or bullying me?* How could she defuse her cousin's anger?

"I can't be the angry one," she said finally. "That's your job, Lucy. Remember the summer you turned twelve? Uncle Jerry said you acted like you were the Director of Outrage and Fury. He said it's my job to stay calm, to balance your anger. We're yin and yang, that's why we're friends."

Suddenly Lucy was standing way too close, pushing the fury into Emma's face. "Yin and yang? Friends? Shit, that's it? That's what you think we are?"

Emma pulled her blanket tighter and fought the instinct to retreat. "Sorry. How about—"

Lucy spun back to her easel. "Sit down, Mouse! I'm not done. And do *not* say besties," she spat, "or something equally fucking stupid, like BFFs or soul sisters. Superficial crap."

"No, I mean— I don't know! Fam? Tribe? Blood sisters? What would *you* call us, Lucy?"

The second piece of charcoal broke and Lucy's face twisted in rage. She grabbed the easel with both hands and heaved it.

Charcoals and sketchpad rattled to the floor as the easel's wooden crossbar smacked Emma's left collarbone. Too startled to cry out, she crumpled to her knees on the bare floor. Whimpering, gasping for breath, she clutched her left arm tight against her breasts.

Lucy's rage evaporated. Begging forgiveness, she guided Emma to the sofa and rushed to fill a plastic bag with crushed ice. She helped Emma dress and guided her through a cold drenching rain into the Subaru, then drove ever so carefully down their treacherous mountain road with the car's headlights reflecting nothing but slanting rain and the black forest.

In the emergency room, Emma sat for three hours on a hard plastic chair. She dripped melted ice and hot tears while Lucy swore at the hospital staff. Shortly before one a.m. on Thursday morning, a burly ER nurse in wrinkled teal scrubs took X-rays.

"You've got lots of bruising but only a small crack in the clavicle," he said. "You're going to have swelling and pain, but you don't need surgery."

He taped her shoulder to immobilize it and showed them how to fasten a sling and a clavicle brace. "This will take the pressure off. Ice it every two or three hours, if possible, for the first twenty-four. Don't try to use it at all for three days. Then you can swap the sling for just the brace so you'll have a little mobility in that arm. Really, you just gotta leave it alone to heal. In a week or two it should feel a lot better and then you can get a referral for PT."

When he handed Emma a prescription, Lucy scoffed. "Hah. Percocet? That's not strong enough."

The nurse spoke to Emma but kept a wary eye on Lucy. "Follow the directions. There's enough for three or four days, no refills. Then if you still need something for the pain, try acetaminophen or ibuprofen or a combo. This is an opioid, so don't even think about driving until you're off it. Got that?"

THREE

Late Thursday morning, as Emma dozed under a quilt in her painkiller blur, Lucy paced the front room and sometimes the front porch, swearing at the weather.

Forecasters were predicting eight to ten inches of rain, maybe more, before it all cleared out, which might be today or Friday or Saturday. Hard to tell, because the storm was stalled right over them.

They were stuck. The Subaru was out of gas, and Emma's Miata couldn't be driven in weather like this. The convertible was prone to skidding on gravel and ice, it bottomed out on every pothole, and its canvas top was in tatters.

Emma knew her twelve-year-old, pearl white sports car with its temperamental clutch and sticky parking brake was completely unsuited for these Appalachian mountain roads. So why did she keep it? Because it was her pride and joy. Her seventeenth birthday present. The talisman that her father hoped would lend a touch of cool-kid status to his shy, unpopular daughter.

Emma didn't care about status but she loved the car and agonized over the care she couldn't give it here. The Miata should be residing safely in a warm garage, not stuck beneath a frayed blue tarp in the freezing mud where falling tree limbs could punch holes in its burgundy roof.

Which was what happened two weeks earlier, when a widowmaker broke off a half-dead pine tree and ripped down through the canvas top, leaving a hole that Emma could fit her head through.

No, she and Lucy weren't going to drive the Miata in this cold downpour.

The storm continued all day Thursday. By mid-afternoon, Lucy changed the timeline from Thursday to Friday for the getting-gas expedition, and added groceries to the list because they'd run out of milk and bread. Declaring an attack of cabin fever, she binge-watched *Game of Thrones* without even pretending to work on her capstone project.

That evening, Lucy thawed a cheese pizza and topped it with a leftover slice of deli turkey, which reminded Emma about Thanksgiving.

"Lucy, have you told Dad or Uncle Jerry about Maggie? That she's not coming for Thanksgiving."

"Not my job. It's her information, she can tell them."

"But Jerry's planning to pick her up at the bus station. I'll call him."

Lucy scowled. "Leave it." Her irritation simmered, rising like a stench.

Emma offered a compromise. "I'll text my dad."

"Whatever. But don't mention your shoulder."

On Friday, it rained harder. Emma abandoned the icepack and began staring at her books, not quite able to concentrate but unwilling to quit trying. She roused herself sufficiently to suggest that Lucy call a few of her friends, see if someone could bring them a gallon of gas for the Subaru.

Lucy brushed her off. "Who's even left? Everyone's gone for Thanksgiving. They're all ghosting me. We're fine, I'll get gas tomorrow. Besides, I'm busy."

Finally annoyed with her own procrastination, Lucy dragged a roll of wet chicken wire from the porch into the front room. She unrolled several yards of wire and began wrestling with tin snips, cutting the unwieldy wire into chunks that she twisted into ragged, tortured shapes.

On Saturday the rain let up for an hour, then fell harder. Emma called three gas stations near Asheville but all were short-handed and too busy to deliver gas. Was she serious? On the weekend before Thanksgiving? One manager told her his own tanks were empty, too. Another informed her that running out of gas in your own yard didn't qualify as an emergency. Another said he could send someone out but not until Monday.

The rain finally stopped on Sunday afternoon.

At three-thirty, Lucy pulled on her best Mountain Girl outfit—sheepskin jacket, a feedstore logo cap, paint-stained jeans, and hiking boots—and slopped through the shoe-sucking muck to the side yard where the Miata sat beneath its tarp.

"Hey Em," she called. "Hurry up. It's fucking freezing out here." She yanked off the tarp and kicked rocks over the blue plastic to anchor it against a freshening breeze.

Paused on the porch, Emma leaned over the railing and squinted at broken clouds. The air was thick with the smell of dead leaves, the rotting debris field of autumn. Shivering, she tugged her jacket a little tighter over the clavicle brace, an arrangement of padded straps that immobilized her left shoulder.

"Em, I need your keys." Lucy reached for the driver's door handle. She skidded in the mud and nearly fell. "Whoops!" She grabbed the Miata's side mirror and erupted in giggles. "No worries, I meant to do that."

Emma frowned. "Don't break my car." She hesitated. Lucy was not a giggler. And was she slurring her words? "Maybe we should wait a little longer," she added. "Can you hear the stream? It's really loud. There's been so much rain, it's probably flooding the road."

"So let's get going. It's almost four—"

Emma remained on the porch. "It'll be dark before we get back. And there'll be a hard freeze tonight."

"No shit, weather girl." More giggling from Lucy. "Yeah, it's cold. Let's go." She fumbled her hands into leather gloves.

Emma was now fairly certain that Lucy was drunk.

Waiting for the rain to stop, they'd scrounged lunch from an olive jar and a bag of stale taco chips. Lucy popped open a beer. Only one beer, or more? Emma should have paid closer attention, but she'd taken her last Percocet at noon and was planning an afternoon nap.

Now, watching her cousin stumble through a puddle, Emma wondered if she should ride along to caution Lucy's driving. Or, third option, maybe her collarbone had healed enough so she could drive her own car. She flexed her left elbow. The ache had definitely eased, but how would she manage the stick shift?

"Hey," Lucy called, "where's the gas can?"

"Under the porch. But there's kerosene in it."

It was Lucy who'd put lamp oil in the gas can.

"Well," Lucy said. "I'll buy another one. But we still need shopping bags." She slogged back to the porch, trailing mud up the steps and through the front door.

Frowning, Emma shivered again and watched a swirl of dead leaves tumble across the yard. Even in good weather, driving these steep mountain roads required planning and energy. She was having serious regrets, not for the first time, about her decision to share off-campus housing with Lucy. Though she wasn't sure how much regret she should assign to the house, and how much to her housemate. Probably fifty-fifty.

Lucy found the furnished cabin six months earlier at the end of her sophomore year at Silvermill College, in the beautiful month of May when the Appalachians were at their most alluring. The craigslist ad sounded wonderful: gorgeous views, two bedrooms, a cathedral-ceilinged front room with a big fireplace, a satellite dish for TV and wi-fi.

The old hunting lodge clung to a west-facing ledge of granite halfway up Bishops Knob, a sparsely populated mid-sized peak eight miles east of campus and twenty miles northwest of Asheville. Their front porch offered a spectacular view of graduated peaks rising to a blue-gray skyline that stretched fifty miles west into Tennessee. Summer and early fall were warm and breezy, the woods full of birdsong and every shade of green. By mid-November, though, storms began to batter the cabin with sleet and freezing rain. The raw winds blew smoke back down the chimney and set the windows rattling.

Now it was four days before Thanksgiving and most of the trees were bare. From their front porch, Emma had a clear view of the narrow access road that climbed, switchback by switchback, from the shadowy cove below.

Their neighbor's boy Billy was walking along the road. Nine or ten years old, a small child with big dark eyes and tangled black hair, to Emma he always seemed a little feral. In warmer months he usually went shirtless, wearing only dirty gym shorts and falling-apart sneakers. She'd met him back in late May, when his bare shoulders and thin chest were spotted with insect bites and old scabs.

Saying hello had startled him into a wary silence. When he did speak, the words came out in a jumble.

"That's a Carlina wren," he whispered in an up-country drawl. "A male. They got this three-noter, kinda like a whistle…whistle. Like sayin 'teakettle teakettle teakettle' but faster. I'm Billy," he added, "but I ain't sposed to be out. Don't tell no one you seen me….seen me."

He'd repeated the last words in a whispery, near-silent echo. Blushing, he clapped a hand over his mouth and vanished, leaving her to wonder why a child his age was alone in the forest mid-morning on a school day.

Now, on this late-November day, Billy wore a too-small jacket and frayed jeans, better than shirtless but still not adequate for the cold.

Shivering in sympathy, Emma watched from the porch as he ducked behind a boulder in the woods below. A blue van appeared on the gravel road, crawling downhill. It disappeared around a steep curve without stopping.

Emma recognized the van. The driver, Billy's mother Chrissy, lived with her four young kids in the only other home on their road, a rusty single-wide trailer set in a weedy clearing a quarter-mile downhill. The yard in front of the trailer was landscaped with abandoned toys, dead appliances, and a torn *Thank You Jesus* banner hanging from a walnut tree. Whenever Emma drove by, she waved to whoever was in the yard: Chrissy or the kids or an unknown man who seemed to be forever dismantling a pickup. Only Billy ever waved back, and only if he was alone.

Other than Emma's Miata and Lucy's Outback, Chrissy's van was the only vehicle that regularly traveled their road, a one-lane dirt track winding for two steep miles up from Chickapay Crossroads, a junction distinguished by a stoplight and a small dollar store with erratic hours.

The old loggers' path was optimistically labeled a "private drive" on county maps. In passable shape at the bottom, by the time it reached their cabin it was no more than a pair of wheel ruts with ragwort and thistles growing in the center. On the rare occasion when two vehicles met, one had to nudge against the uphill bank or reverse into a slightly wider space where one of the game trails branched off.

Mail trucks and Uber drivers did not come to their cabin. Letters and packages were dropped at the dollar store. After every storm, the ruts grew deeper, the potholes wider. Lucy's car was the obvious choice for driving on their miserable excuse for a road but today they'd have to take the low-slung, skid-prone Miata with the ripped ragtop.

And who was more fit to drive?

Emma thought again about Lucy's giggles. Maybe her cousin was high instead of drunk. Or both high and drunk?

Lucy often stashed cannabis in the cabin. A tin of high-octane gummies in her sock drawer, a baggie of buds in the medicine cabinet. She was too careful—usually—to risk a DUI. One ticket, one warning, and Uncle Jerry would yank everything: tuition, rent, car insurance, even her car. Lucy frequently drank and got high, but only when she could rely on Emma to drive.

Could Emma drive today? She'd taken the Percocet four hours ago. The familiar fuzzy-brain feeling was wearing off and surely she'd be okay now, right?

Lucy emerged from the cabin waving a pair of Trader Joe's shopping bags. "Found them. But I need your keys." She clumped down the steps.

Emma followed. "I don't think it's safe—"

Lucy exhaled sharply. "Oh for fuck's sake, Em, get real. Your car's perfectly fine to drive now the rain's stopped."

"I'll drive."

"What? You can't drive, you're wearing that brace. How will you shift it? *Keys*, Em." She tugged at the driver's door. "Fuck, it's locked."

"No, it's not."

Lucy yanked harder and the door popped open. She swayed and lurched back, scrambling to keep her feet.

Emma frowned. "Lucy, you're trashed."

"No, I'm not. I'm fine." Lucy folded herself down into the driver's seat and snort-laughed. "Shit, the seat's forward! Your legs are so freakin short."

Emma felt her throat close. Why couldn't she just say it? *Get out of my car, Lucy. You aren't fit to drive.*

There was a sharp *thunk* as Lucy found the adjustment lever and the seat shot to its farthest-back position. She fastened her seatbelt and pulled the door shut. Planting her hands on the wheel at ten and two, she grinned at Emma.

"Okay, Mouse, I'm ready. Get in if you're coming. Or hey, stay home and nurse that broken wing. Leaves more room for groceries. You can't carry much anyway."

Faced with the fact of Lucy buckled into the driver's seat, Emma climbed in on the passenger side, awkwardly reaching across with her right hand to latch the seatbelt. "Did you adjust the mirrors? The parking brake's sticky, remember? You've got to pull it up really hard to set it."

"I *know*." She smacked the steering wheel with both hands. The grin was gone, replaced by a thin snarl. "You tell me that. Every. Single. Fucking. Time."

"I just wanted to remind you—"

"Hey, Mouse, you know what?" Lucy unsnapped her belt. "I've changed my mind. I'm staying home. You can drive your own fucking car."

She scrambled out, leaving the driver's door ajar but stopping a few yards away with her back to the car, fists clenched at her side and feet braced in the mud.

Like the Burgher of Calais, Emma thought, *filled with fury and despair.* "Lucy, I know you're angry about Maggie. I didn't mean—"

Lucy spun to face Emma. "Fuck Maggie. She's screwed up everything. You have no fucking idea—"

"You're right. I have no idea." Emma flexed her left arm again. Could she drive? The shoulder was stiff but not sore. She'd be extra careful not to spin her wheels on the wet gravel. Stay in first gear through the switchbacks, avoid the washouts. If her left arm wasn't up to holding the wheel while she changed gears, she'd steady it with a knee like she'd seen Lucy do.

But what if the pain returned, or she injured her shoulder again?

"Come on, Lucy," Emma said. "Yeah, it's my car. I should drive. But I need you to come, too. Maybe you're right, maybe it will hurt too much and I won't be able to manage the gears. I'll probably need you to drive home, anyway. Please."

Emma dropped the keys in the cupholder and unbuckled her seatbelt.

FOUR

First came a slow tilt, the heavy rumble of rocks and earth. A hollow place opened in Emma's gut, like the imminent drop of a roller coaster but much, much worse.

Then came a long slide and a sickening first flip.

Everything accelerated, spinning and tumbling until the cold sky and black earth smashed together. Rocks trees metal, shrieking and grinding.

She heard a child scream. Children? Maybe it was her own voice, high and shrill.

The earth filled her ears, nose, and mouth. She smelled leaf mold, wild grapes, and blood.

Darkness arrived then, cold and silent. She was alone for a long time.

The copper taste of fear rose like bile in her throat then because everything shameful was moving closer, soon to be lying beside her in the freezing rubble.

People were dying and it was all her fault.

FIVE

September 21, 2023

Squinting against the afternoon sun, Chaz stabbed his narrow-bladed shovel into damp red clay, carving clean the sides of a new post hole. Only eight more and he'd be done with the digging. The Kubota's power auger worked fast but you still had to get down in the dirt to get the depth right. He wanted it done right.

He hefted a six-foot post from the dwindling stack on the tractor's front pallet fork. As the post thudded into place, he glanced back along the plumbline stretched above a row of twenty identical holes. Ten feet apart, two feet deep, ten inches wide. From each hole a post tilted upward, waiting to be spirit-leveled into straightness and set in slushy concrete. After the concrete set, he'd use the tractor to stretch the hundred-foot rolls of woven wire tight against the posts and pound in staples. Last, he'd hang gates and string two strands of solar-powered electric wire around the outside.

Coyotes weren't getting into *this* sheep pasture.

Chaz felt lucky, landing this summer job on Miz Emma's farm. He was used to the heat and sweat, the afternoon showers that came down hard and sudden from massive thunderheads above the mountains. He was proud of the muscles he'd grown and the callouses he'd earned by clearing trails, bucking hay bales, and digging post holes. He especially liked driving the big Kubota tractor and running the attachments with the cool-sounding names: cutterbar, disc mower, rotary rake, hay tedder, haybale spike.

What he didn't like was the damn insects. Mosquitoes and deerflies in the woods, greenbottles and hummingbird-size horseflies in the fields. Gnats and chiggers everywhere.

And ticks, hiding everywhere in the grass. Holding out their shitty little legs to grab on and bury their bloodsucking mouthparts into you.

The stingers were the worst. White-face hornets defending their paper nests in the weeds, yellow jackets that rose up from holes in the ground like the spawn of Satan.

His kid sister Jessie called them all yellow stripey things, a stupid name because it made hornets sound the same as the bees in the flower gardens at Miz Buckner's, where his sister Jessie still lived. She claimed she could pet the bumblebees, if she moved slow and talked gentle.

Yeah, no. Nobody'd find Chaz petting a bee. Which was why he kept a can of twenty-foot wasp spray in the Kubota's cupholder, and two more cans under the seat of his pickup.

Chaz's hatred of wasps and hornets went way back. The September he'd started first grade, Ma told everyone she was deathly allergic to yellow jackets so her kids must be too. Ma said if any of them got stung they'd swell up and die. She'd come up with this weird homemade bug-repelling stuff made from what she called her medicinals, plants she grew beside their skanky old trailer. Lavender, rosemary, marigolds, garlic. Chaz definitely remembered the garlic.

Ma crushed the leaves and roots of everything. Mixed it with cider vinegar and strained the mess through a piece of flannel shirt, then wiped it on everyone's skin. Soaked their clothes and make him drink it, too. That way, she said, the medicinals would come right out through his skin.

Bless her heart, what a flippin smelly mess he'd been. Jessie, too, but she was too young for school back then so she didn't care so much.

First grade was hell. He spent the first couple months slumped down at his desk like the loser-kid he was, oozing garlic. Other kids called him Stinkpot and worse, and beat him up every day. The teachers wrinkled their noses and backed off.

It wasn't until the first frost in November that Ma quit using that evil stuff. Then she got a new boyfriend so that kept her busy and when spring came she'd traded those foul medicinals for quartz crystals to hang around their necks. He didn't stink of garlic any longer but the damage was done, and he was forever known as the weird loser who smelled like a shithouse.

Chaz had never once been stung by a yellow jacket and neither had Ma or Jessie, as far he knew, but a dozen years later the stench of garlic still turned his stomach.

His buddy Darren, who'd signed up with the Army three days after graduation, told him there's way better stuff now to keep the bugs off. During his first Sunday evening phone call from boot camp, Darren jumped right into complaining about the weather and the insects.

"It's not even summer yet and everything sucks, man. Humidity's so bad it feels like y'all are breathin through a wet-wipe. Heat's awful. They call black-flag when it's gonna be over ninety. Then they haul us out of bed extra early, like three-thirty A-fucking-M, to do our five-miler before sun-up. And the bugs. We got every kinda bug like back home, but bigger. Palmetto bugs, a fancy name for roaches, but these're the size of baseballs. Plus fire ants that sting like bitches. They build big mounds in the sand in the middle of our ropes course, and we have to crawl through 'em. Jesuschrist, I miss the mountains."

Darren sounded proud, though. Like it was all *his*, the hot muggy weather, the fire ants, the monster roaches. So when Darren lowered his voice like he was giving out classified information, Chaz listened.

"The army's got a secret weapon. They treat our fatigues with this kick-ass chemical to keep bugs away. Per-meth-reen. It works good on ticks. They can't have us gettin sick from Lyme ticks, so all our clothes have this stuff in it. Doesn't work on fire ants, though."

"What's it smell like?"

"No smell at all. They say it's made of flowers, like those yellow mums the feed store sells. It's real sick shit."

Chaz googled on a library computer and learned that anybody could buy permethrin, not just the U.S. Army. The stuff was developed years earlier, right nearby in Greensboro. So much for Darren's secret weapon.

Chaz put the information to good use. Every morning, he covered himself with as much permethrin-treated clothing as possible. Today he wore a greasy green John Deere ball cap, a denim shirt streaked with brown paint, once-white crew socks permanently tinted orangey pink from the red clay soil, and khaki cargo pants salvaged from Goodwill. The only items that wouldn't take a permethrin bath were his steel-toed work boots, his work gloves, and his mirrored shades.

He knew the shades gave him a raccoon-faced tan but he didn't care because he needed something to hide behind while he worked on Miz Emma's farm and kept watch. No one notices the farmhand, right? But out here in the fields all day, he almost never saw Miz Emma. He needed a job closer to where she hung out. Summer was almost over and he had to find a new job anyway. He still had his part-time gig stocking shelves at Aldi, but he needed something full-time.

Now he leaned over the warm steel of the Kubota's fender and retrieved his water bottle from the seat. He really wanted a cigarette, but he was trying to ration himself. Not go cold turkey, just cut back a bit. His next job might have him working someplace where they wouldn't let him smoke.

He'd started smoking on his tenth birthday when Ma's boyfriend Gordy dared him to light up. Ma was so mad she'd kicked Gordy out for a whole week. Chaz was glad about that part. He'd have quit the smokes, period, if that mean SOB disappeared for good. But then Gordy came back with a box of Ma's favorite pink wine and she forgave him.

Thinking about Gordy always made the hairs on his arms prickle.

Ma forgave Gordy but she kept laying into Chaz like a nutter whenever she caught him with tobacco breath or, freakin hockey sticks, an actual cigarette.

"A nasty habit! Nasty!" she'd yell. Then she'd launch a full-on rampage, ripping open his backpack and rooting through his closet on a search-and-destroy mission for the demon tobacco. He got better at stealing smokes and hiding them, but then she died a few months later and it didn't matter anymore.

Now, slouched against the side of the tractor, long fingers crinkling the sides of a flimsy water bottle, Chaz worked his mouth around her words. *A nasty habit, a nasty habit, a nasty habit.*

He hated how words got stuck in his head when something bothered him. He broke the brain-stutter this time by balling a fist and smacking his thigh, hard, with the knuckles. The jammed-up words faded and he was able to think again. He needed his head clear to think about getting a new job.

He'd seen a job posting at the big barn, the art gallery or the studio or whatever they called it. General handyman. Painting and carpentry, fixing things. And lots of moving stuff around because that's what artists did, right? Always rearranging things. Setting up classrooms, changing out light fixtures, building display cases. Putting up pictures, taking them down, plastering the nail-holes, more painting.

When the art center held their events he could park cars in the hayfield. Maybe even help with security, setting up cameras and alarms. Him and Darren took a Zoom course on that, last winter. Darren said it was a total waste of time, because he only wanted to learn how to put up his deer cams in the woods. Which turned out to be super simple. But Chaz liked learning about all of it, the networking and the different devices.

He'd have to dress better for a job at the art barn. In black, because that's what artists wore. He'd need to check out the county's clothing closet and the Goodwill. Toss the old dirt-stained crew socks and buy new black ones.

With that job, he'd be in the middle of everything. There'd be girls, too, students from the high school and the community college. He saw them each afternoon when he stopped by the machine shop to refuel the tractor or drop off his tools.

He didn't want to think too much about the girls because they probably wouldn't look at him anyway. If he spoke to one or tried to catch her eye, she'd toss her hair in that way they had. They'd whisper to each other and cut side-eyes at him, then shake their heads and walk away.

They always knew, didn't they? That he'd been a nobody, just a bounced-around foster kid. Clumsy and left-handed and too small, until suddenly he wasn't. He'd grown four inches the summer he turned twelve and four more the following year and suddenly none of the county's hand-me-downs fit his long arms and big feet. Most kids his size got recruited for the high school basketball team, but foster kids don't get asked because who'd give them a ride home after practice?

After he graduated last May, he'd moved into a farmworker's single-wide trailer in a tomato field. He left Miz Buckner's with two cardboard boxes of clothes, his old pickup, and the money he'd saved from working at Aldi. His thousand dollars seemed like a lot until he went looking for a cheap place to live. The county still gave him six hundred a month for rent but that would end when he turned twenty-one.

Case workers were always asking him, "So what's your future plans, Chaz?" He always said, "Workin hard, stayin out of trouble." Which didn't say a thing about the future but seemed to be enough of a plan for them.

He also planned to stay close to Miz Emma, but he wasn't going to tell anyone about that. He didn't fully understand it himself.

Done with his break, Chaz began mixing concrete. He poured dry quickset into each posthole, slopped in water from the tank on the back of the Kubota, and straightened each post with a spirit level. Then he bungee-corded his tools onto the pallet skid and throttled up the tractor.

A glance at the late-afternoon sky told him the evening would be clear and dry. He'd clean up a bit and head for Arby's or the new Taco Bell. Pick up dinner and a six-pack, drive to the creek, park in his spot under the hemlocks. Eat, drink a couple beers, listen to music and watch the cars go by.

Working all summer on the farm, he'd come to recognize the usual people and their rides. Miz Emma's was his favorite, a late-model Jeep Trailhawk, forest green. Miz Weingardt, who managed the art center's sales gallery, drove a big old Suburban, useful for hauling around people and paintings. Mister Bell, one of the teachers, had a nice silver Lexus. Mister Jacobs, the old ponytailed dude who'd hired him for the summer, drove an ancient black Sentra with rusty bumpers and a bad muffler, usually spattered with mud. No wonder that guy always went home alone.

Chaz had memorized the art center's schedule, too. It was posted online where he could check it every Sunday afternoon on the library computer. There were after-school art classes for kids, and daytime classes for everyone else. Landscape painting, photography, watercolors. And every Thursday evening at seven-thirty there was a figure drawing class.

Chaz liked to sketch little drawings of cars and spaceships. He wondered if a person could just show up for the Thursday night class, or if you had to register and pay first and maybe prove you were a real artist before they let you in. That was also on his list of things to find out.

SIX

Dear Chrissy, I'm so sorry...

Emma set her pen aside and frowned.

September twenty-first, the autumn equinox. She still had two months to work on her annual letter, but the end of summer always got her thinking early about what she needed to say. The first five words were easy because they were always the same, but the rest got harder each year. What could she write that hadn't already been said in the previous seven years? All her words were horribly inadequate.

She'd brought pen and paper into the art center's supply closet, hoping something more would come to her among the crayons and cleansers, but ten minutes of after-dinner contemplation on a hard metal chair hadn't produced a single clear thought.

If only her mother were here. Kit Gillen always knew the right thing to say. Emma ached every day for the loss of her.

Emma knew she was revisiting the older grief to avoid thinking about the letter. Now her Seiko wristwatch told her it was six-forty so she stood and slipped the paper into the pocket of her faded blue kimono. Tightened the sash, left the closet, and walked barefoot and alone across the wooden planks of the barn's great hall.

In the office doorway, she paused to rub the toes of one bare foot against the opposite ankle, gently scratching an insect bite and thinking about the sound of the words she wanted before she tried saying them.

"Hey, Jonah. Can you find me some bag propellors?"

She wanted her voice to flow smoothly. Knew it was hopscotching, not flowing, because that's what it usually did.

A big-shouldered man with a happy-walrus mustache and a sparse gray ponytail, Jonah Jacobs pushed his chair back from the desk. Frowning slightly, he removed steel-rimmed glasses to rub the bridge of his nose.

His hesitation meant he needed a minute to interpret her request. Emma sighed. She'd meant bug repellant, but what had she said? Propellant? Maybe prophylactic or proprietary or something else.

"I'd find it myself," Emma added slowly, "but I think it's bee hinder...behind...your compacter."

The furrows on his high forehead deepened, telling Emma at least one of those words, too, was wonky. Her former therapist—now her colleague—spent years wading through her stumbles and word salads, performing a sort of verbal triage. He'd learned to gently correct the truly bizarre scrambles and let the minor hiccups slide. If he tried to point out every malapropism, her brain's speech center would short-circuit in frustration. Then she'd freeze and quit speaking.

Jonah took his time, settling his wire-rims back into place and rummaging through the clutter behind his iMac. He found two cans of insect repellent wedged between a stack of sketchpads and a canvas bag stuffed with his camera lenses.

He tapped an ear with a thick finger, suggesting a correction. "Maybe trade columbine for computer screen?"

She wrinkled her brow and practiced, silently mouthing *computer screen.*

Jonah held up both cans and peered at the labels. "Mosquitoes or houseflies?"

"Moss-keepers. The green can. It's got peep."

Another ear tap. "Moss-keepers? Maybe mosquitoes. With DEET."

She glanced away and raised her left hand to her hair, tugging forward a curtain of russet curls. *Slow down,* she reminded herself. *Sound it out, think it then say it. One syllable at a time, dammit.*

"Moss-kee-toes....DEET."

"Nailed it." He nodded. "But you know, I hate it when you use this stuff."

"It works."

"Yeah. Don't use too much, okay? Don't spray it in your eyes, and don't drink it. The label says drinking it will make you vomit or give you seizures."

She gave him the eye-roll he wanted. "I wasn't plant...plan-ning to drink it. I'll just let the seas...sei-zures...manage them-selves." She added a smile to tell him she wasn't offended by his reference to seizures.

Remembering the paper in her pocket, she pulled it out and dropped it into the trash basket. "First draft. Trying to start early this year."

Jonah's chair creaked, protesting his bulk as he swiveled back to the desk and peered at his screen. "You've got plenty of time. Just say what's on our mind."

"Same as last year. Nothing's changed."

He had no response to that so he nodded at the insect repellant. "Maybe you should go out on the deck to spray that thing. Then no one else has to breathe it." Meaning him, because no one else had arrived yet.

He said it casually but she heard his voice go a bit southern, a sure sign of his concern. It was the way he'd turned "thing" into "thang." Jonah Jacobs had tried for five decades to flatten his accent, a blend of North Carolina piedmont fused with an undertone of eastern Mediterranean. His parents emigrated from Lebanon when Jonah was six, fleeing the civil war in 'seventy-five. The mixed inflections of his speech tended to return at the end of a long day. She liked this about him, not only that he worried about her but that his voice sometimes betrayed his worry. Emma's voice betrayed her every day.

"Okay." She pretended a confidence she didn't feel. "The deck, sure. I'll stand ... upwind so I don't breathe it...either."

His round shoulders relaxed a little. He resumed tapping at his keyboard, dark eyes and gray mustache going down and up again, inspecting class schedules and lists of art supplies. "You're sounding pretty good, actually. New meds?"

"Fake it 'til you make it." Smoothly delivered because she'd practiced. He turned to stare.

"Sorry. Too...perky?"

"The words were fine but you sounded a little jokey. Sort of silly, which isn't you."

Her eyes filled. "I'm trying, Jonah. If I can't joke, I'll go flat."

He'd been her therapist in the early days so he knew what *going flat* meant. Hiding in the closet, sobbing, yanking at her clothes, chewing on her lower lip and inner cheeks until her mouth swelled and she tasted blood. *Going flat* hadn't happened in two years but it was still a possibility.

"I'm sorry," he said. "You sure you're up for this tonight?"

"You know it helps me be…vis-i-ble. Not a ghost."

"I know." He hesitated and added, "We've got a full house, so it will be a bit crowded. We may have someone new, this woman from Canada who's trying to decide about joining the co-op. I invited her to stop by, if she can get here on time."

Emma nodded vaguely, a little distracted. Thinking about how she'd agreed to do that simple thing, walk out on the deck to spray the bug repellant. Six months earlier, she couldn't have gone alone onto the deck, or any high place. She never knew how she'd feel or what she'd do in high places. Freeze, scream, fling herself over the edge.

She wanted to focus now on something concrete so she looked at the aerosol can in her hand. Good old reliable Deep Woods Off, thirty percent DEET. She'd need it on this warm, humid evening. At both ends of the barn, the big double doors were open wide to catch the mountain breezes. Every gnat and mosquito would find her bare skin like a heat-seeking missile.

She certainly couldn't spray herself here in the art center's cramped, windowless office. Floor-to-ceiling cabinets filled one wall; along the other side, two computer workstations sat cheek-by-jowl with full bookshelves above. A pair of office chairs took up most of the floor space in the middle.

The office had an entrance at each end like a tiny-home shotgun house. The front door opened off the barn's central hall, the back door—two doors, really, an inner wooden one and an outer screen door—led to what they called the balcony, a six-foot-wide boardwalk that wrapped around the back of the barn. It led to the much larger main deck and patio where there were tables and chairs and bright market umbrellas.

Tonight, the inner rear door was propped open with a doorstop, a football-sized chunk of rose quartz. A light afternoon breeze drifted through the screen door to play with the papers on Jonah's desk.

Emma squeezed behind his chair on her way to the deck, bare feet treading carefully on the worn scrap of green carpet. As she worked her way past bookshelves and a tripod, she remembered something she'd practiced earlier.

"Your pontoon's come loose. Your hair's gone…feral, like it's fried…steel wool."

This time his hesitation was brief and came with a grin. "Feral was fine. But—pontoon? For ponytail?"

"Pontoon's better than…poon-tang." She couldn't resist a small smile. She'd worked hard on that one, speaking into her phone's voice-recording app and listening to the playback. Turning flubs into puns.

Jonah's caterpillar eyebrows arched appreciatively as he reached up to tighten his thin gray ponytail. "Nice one. Maybe I should do a man-bun."

"You need…more to…work with." The words emerged slowly but fumble-free, a small victory over her brain's wayward speech center.

She'd spent ten months in speech therapy re-training her vocal cords to form basic sounds, and another six months to conquer simple words and short sentences. She'd conquered one-syllable words and could manage most of the two-syllable ones, if she spoke slowly. Anything longer required deliberate, sound-by-sound concentration and lots of practice with a voice recorder for playback. Only then would she have a chance of matching actual speech to the words that formed in her brain.

The small sense of victory she'd earned by teasing Jonah evaporated as Emma latched the screen door behind her. Her heart quickened. She paused, facing the closed door and clutching the aerosol can. A breeze flirted with the hem of the kimono and she focused for a moment on that.

At her back was the deck railing and beyond that was air, a vast space of air, with sharp rocks below. It was too terrifying to look at and too fascinating not to. She needed to wait.

She heard late-summer cicadas whirring crescendos in the trees and smelled the delicious odor of warm oak rising from the planks beneath her feet. Remembering the mantra about feet, she flexed her toes and planted her heels. Concentrated on the important work of inhaling and exhaling.

Become heavy, grounded and balanced. Feel the solid floor beneath your feet. That's where your breath comes in, through your feet and up into your belly. Where your courage comes in.

She could let go of the doorknob now, so she did that. Keeping her right shoulder close to the barn wall, trailing her fingertips along its rough siding, she observed the grain of the worn gray wood and planned her path. It was perhaps five yards along the narrow boardwalk to the southwest corner of the barn. There the deck widened into the patio, where she could step away from the abyss.

Ten steps, that was all. She could do it in ten steps.

Emma took the tenth step. Exhaling, she placed the spray can on a round wooden table and sank into a chair. Waiting for her pulse to slow, she gazed above the barn's weathered walls to its new roof, a bright red carapace of glossy metal.

Think of that, she told herself. *Reconstruction and rebirth.*

The massive building was a hundred feet long and a hundred years old. Built by Emma's ancestors into the side of a ridge, the bank barn had three levels that took advantage of the slope. On the high-ground side, giant sliding doors opened directly from the front yard into what had been the farm's warehouse, a soaring space of post-and-beam scaffolding and rough-cut rafters. Inside, along the side walls, two sets of stairs gave access to the lofts above. Below the main floor, livestock once sheltered at the bottom of the slope in the rock-walled cellar.

The barn's twelve-by-twelve timbers were hewn from American chestnut and the floor was made of yellow pine, built to bear the weight of mules, wagons, and tractors. But over the decades, the once-prosperous Gillen farm fell on hard times. The family moved away, leasing the land to a local farmer.

Then Emma's uncle Jerry inherited the farm and decided to restore the barn. Repurposed as an art and education center, the main floor now held an office, restrooms, classrooms, a central exhibit hall, and a sales gallery. The second-story haylofts became studios and a darkroom.

An outdoor junkyard of broken tractors and rusted tools became space for a sculpture garden and a multi-level deck. Emma helped with its design, envisioning the deck as the perfect venue for *plein aire* workshops and garden-party weddings. The view was magnificent but the deck itself was terrifying.

At the back of the barn, the narrow walkway was cantilevered over empty space. Forty feet below was a rock-strewn hill pasture with nothing but air between the deck and death. The deck had railings, of course. The top rail was constructed of cedar planks bolted to sturdy posts, all reassuringly solid. But the "rails" below that were metal cables. Thin and nearly invisible.

It's very secure, her father the engineer explained. *Very secure, everything safe and done to code. See? Ten cables, four inches apart. No one can slip through.*

But it looks so flimsy, she thought.

We're installing the very best in invisible railing, the builder assured her. *Wherever you sit or stand, you'll have an unobstructed view of the mountains. It's like the railing isn't even there.*

Exactly.

The county building inspector was impressed with the construction and signed off on everything, including the invisible deck railing.

Now sitting safely on the lower part of the deck, with her back against the wall of the barn, Emma risked a look over the hillside pasture to the hazy blue mountains.

On the road below, light from the setting sun glinted off a white pickup. She stood, raising a hand to shade her eyes from the sun as she watched its progress through the trees. The truck approached the fork, where a left turn would take it into the village of Bracken Falls and then south to the interstate. A right turn would bring it here, over the narrow bridge at Wilbur's Cove Creek and up the hill to Stonefall Art Center.

It was only ten of seven. The studio session wouldn't start for another forty minutes.

The truck turned left, heading toward the village. Not coming here, then. Its brake lights flashed briefly before it disappeared around a bend in the road.

Waiting on the deck as the sky darkened, Emma wondered idly about their new co-op applicant. She wasn't concerned, exactly, but you never knew what to expect from someone new. Artists could be brilliant, generous, unpredictable, catty, territorial, laid back, volatile, sweetly compassionate. Domesticated, uncultivated, or anything in between.

Stonefall's co-op concept was simple: Offer artists their own studios. Give them marketing support, administrative infrastructure, and a place to exhibit. In return, members shared costs and labor, and paid a commission on sales of their work. To join the co-op, a candidate had to demonstrate talent, commitment, and a willingness to share their work with the community. A membership committee vetted new applicants to be sure they'd do their part: work in the gallery, attend meetings, offer studio tours, and sweep the floors.

Every so often, Jonah asked Emma if she'd like to join the membership committee but her answer was always no. She was happy in her role as office manager and bookkeeper. Managing budgets, balancing accounts. Answering the phone as little as possible, communicating mostly by emails and texts.

And she could be their model. Holding a pose for the figure drawing sessions required no voice at all.

But a new co-op member meant a new round of introductions and explanations. *This is Emma, who speaks very slowly and sometimes says the wrong word. Just ask her to write it down if you don't understand.*

Now the sky was darkening to charcoal, splashed with lingering streaks of coral. Fireflies flashed their come-hither codes in the woods. On the deck and along the garden walkways, pathway lights flicked on to illuminate stairs and landings. Emma smelled wild grapes, honeysuckle, and new-mown hay on the evening breeze.

She checked her watch again. Ten after seven, time to get ready. She slipped out of the kimono and draped it neatly over a chair. Naked now except for her watch, she planted one foot on the chair and eased into a runner's stretch.

She felt an ache flare below her right hip. Not a knife blade of pain, just a warning twinge, so she pushed into a hamstring stretch. A physical therapist—one of many—explained how a ligament was catching sometimes on the metal pin near the top of her femur. Nothing to worry about; the compound fracture healed years ago.

On to torso stretches. Left-right, forward-back, holding the rail now but ignoring the sheer drop beyond. She curved her spine cautiously, exploring the limits of the fused vertebrae in her lower back. More hardware there, plates and screws holding the bones in place.

She finished her warm-up and took inventory. All the parts—flesh and bone and metal—seemed to be cooperating well enough tonight. She occasionally walked with a slight limp but that was to be expected because her right leg was half an inch shorter than her left. The doctors told her to wear orthotic inserts in her shoes but tonight she was barefoot and lopsided. Who ever heard of a nude model wearing orthotics?

She looked down at her scarred right thigh with clinical detachment. How long before the surgeons' warranty would run out? She was only twenty-seven. What would her body be like at Jonah's age, fifty-five? Or her father's, sixty-one?

Emma picked up the can of bug spray and stepped away from the table. She closed her eyes, held her breath, and sprayed as much of her body as she could reach. She leaned back against the rough wall of the barn and felt the breeze dry her bare skin.

Through the trees, the headlights of two cars brightened the road below. They paused at the fork, then turned right. The first arrivals.

Emma wrapped her kimono around her and tied the sash. Loosened and ruffled her hair, finger-combing the curls over the long scar by her left temple. A useless habit. Her wild mane would go wherever it wished.

Emma returned to the office as Jonah was shutting down his computer.

She set the insect repellent on his desk. "That new person. What's her background?"

Jonah found his notes. "Lyssa Morales. She was doing ceramics in Calgary. Mostly hand-built vessels, not wheelwork. She took some classes at Riz-Dee last year." He meant RISD, the Rhode Island School of Design. "Graphic design and video compositing. No degree. I think she just took a few online classes."

"Good school." This was like saying MIT or Harvard was a good school. RISD was prestigious, selective, and expensive. "But clay and video? We don't have studios for those."

"She says she's been away from her art for a while and wants to get back to basics. Draw and paint, do some figure studies."

"She doesn't need to join the co-op for that. Just sign up for classes."

Jonah shrugged. "Testing the waters, I guess. She's getting divorced. Says she wants to move somewhere warmer than Calgary, which is pretty much anywhere. She discovered Asheville a month ago and loves the 'vital art scene' and the 'awesome mountain vibe.'" She saw our flyer in Margo's." He crooked thick fingers into air quotes. "That 'cute little café'."

"Margo spits in your coffin if you call her place cute."

Jonah smiled and touched his ear.

Emma's brow wrinkled. "What?"

"Coffin for coffee. Good one."

"I meant that," she insisted. "Coffin."

"Sure you did." He glanced at his watch. "It's time." A pause. "You're still good? You remember this wasn't my idea."

Jonah said this every time she offered to model. "Yes," she said. "Part of my mind…full…ness work."

"I wouldn't call it mindfulness."

She shrugged, let it go. They'd talked about this repeatedly and he wasn't her therapist anymore.

Jonah left the office and headed across the central hall to the classroom. Emma trailed behind, stopping at the supply closet to pick up two white bath towels and a yoga mat.

The classroom was a 30x60 white-walled space with built-in cabinets and sinks and a line of tall, north-facing windows. A dozen people busied themselves, moving easels and small tables into a rough semicircle. In the center was a wooden stool on a two-foot dais.

Acknowledging no one, Emma walked toward a shoji screen set just inside the door. She unbuckled her watch and tucked it into a kimono pocket, then slipped off the robe and draped it over the screen. Wearing only a light gloss of sweat and mosquito repellent, she picked up her towels and yoga mat and threaded her way through easels and artists to stand on the dais.

Transformation time. Bookkeeper to artists' model.

SEVEN

Emma arranged one towel over the stool and dropped the other on the floor. The room hummed with settling-down activity, the rustle of sketchpads and easels. Jonah adjusted the angle of a tripod floor lamp. To ensure privacy, he taped a sheet of brown paper over the glass in the classroom door. The paper bore a message in black marker, clearly visible from outside:

> FIGURE SESSION
> DO NOT DISTURB

Emma sat on the stool, listening to the soft twang of a slack-key guitar floating from speakers on the back wall. She usually preferred chamber music, Mozart or Shostakovich, but tonight she'd wanted summer to linger so she'd borrowed an album from Jonah, a mix of slack-key guitar pieces by a group named Hapa. The haunting, key-changing melodies and chants seemed a good fit for the warm evening.

"Okay, people," Jonah said. "We're tight on space tonight so please, find your spot and stay there. Anyone still have their cellphone? Turn it off, please, and drop it in the basket by the door."

He paused. No one moved. "Our model will change position frequently to give you plenty of opportunity for different angles and foreshortening. We'll start with quick warm-ups, a dozen sixty-second gesture poses. Then we'll do a few at five minutes and finish up with some longer studies, twenty-five minutes each. There's a five-minute break every half hour. If you need to talk to me, let's step into the hall so we don't bother the others." He set the timer on his watch. "Here we go."

The co-op's new applicant was officially a no-show.

Emma began with a stop-action posture, as if caught in the act of striding forward with arms swinging. She heard the rapid shoosh and scritch of drawing tools on newsprint and cartridge paper, everyone working quickly to get their impressions on paper before she changed position. There was no time to work on composition or detail or value; the goal was to capture the paused moment as they reduced her body to simple geometric shapes and sweeping lines.

Jonah's timer pinged. She turned her back to the group. Same pose, different angle.

Short gesture poses had to be dynamic and expressive, like movement interrupted. She shifted next to a warrior pose borrowed from last winter's yoga classes.

Another ping, another pose. From warrior one to warrior two, modified with a twist of the torso, then frozen in place for half a minute.

Ping, change again. Ping. Ping. She went down on one knee, leaned on the stool, raised both arms to the ceiling. As she held each brief pose, she planned the next so she could move, re-balance, and settle quickly into stillness.

Every intensely focused face in this group was familiar to Emma. At front and center was Felicia Weingardt, their gallery manager and *plein aire* workshop leader. Mid-forties, Black and Baltimore-born, Felicia possessed the compact grace of a gymnast and the steely force of an inner-city high school counselor, both of which she'd been. Not quite five feet tall, she was the only person in the room who made Emma feel tall.

At the very back of the room towered Harris Felton. Tanned, muscled, nearly a foot and a half taller than Felicia, he looked like Hollywood's idea of an ironworker, which he was. Harry approached drawing like a contact sport, wielding fat charcoal sticks in wild, sweeping lines on oversized sketchpads. An auto mechanic in his day job, he attracted many women and some men like yellow jackets to a food truck, despite the persistent presence of black grease under his fingernails and a suspicious wife at home.

Tonight, Emma detected the odor of patchouli and noticed damp comb lines in Harry's wavy brown shoulder-length hair. He'd begun to care about hair and showers after his metalwork sculptures began capturing notice in the local art world—much to the dismay of his wife, who'd thought she was marrying a regular working guy, not a newly popular artist.

Ping, change. Emma sat on the stool again with her head flung back and her hands gripping the seat behind her butt, body arched as far back as her fused spine allowed. She felt the warmth of Jonah's tripod spotlight on the length of her torso, breasts to pubis. The pose wasn't erotic, she hoped, just a tensioned stretch to bring the ribcage into sharp relief.

To Emma's left was Simon Bell, a quiet, slightly built Aussie transplant. He was the head graphics designer for a video game company he'd started three years earlier with his husband Arturo. When Emma was in bookkeeper-mode—fully dressed—she liked asking Simon about his work just to hear his down-under voice. His features were classic Korean, his accent solid Sydney.

Emma knew the others less well. There was an art teacher from the local high school and three undergrads from Silvermill's art school. A thirties-something lab-coated man who worked as a medical illustrator, a retired lawyer named Gabriela in a battery-powered wheelchair, and a pair of older women in identical Frida Kahlo smocks, mixed-media artists who shared a loft in Asheville.

Tonight was Emma's sixth time posing for the Thursday night figure session. She'd been coaxed into it back in May by Felicia when their agency model was a no-show.

"All you have to do is sit in a chair and don't move. You can keep your clothes on," Felicia added, not knowing that Emma had posed nude from middle school onward for her cousin Lucy. "We've all taken a turn at some point, posing. Clothed, nude, whatever. The main thing is, we all need a real live person to draw. Flaws and flab, warts and all."

Warts, okay, Emma thought, *but what about scars?*

After the first time, Felicia asked her to join the regular rotation. She was sweetly persuasive. "You have a lovely tranquility, Emma. So very patient. We're tired of looking at those self-absorbed bodybuilders the agency sends. All Barbies and Ken-dolls, trying to invent new positions to twist their bodies into. Just the classics, please, with no wiggling or flexing or deep smoldering looks."

Emma hesitated at first about posing in front of the same people who stopped by the office each day to discuss studio space and workshop assignments. She wasn't prudish—her body had been poked and prodded, taken apart and rebuilt by so many doctors she no long considered it truly her own—but she feared the others might find it awkward.

"Nah," Felicia assured her. "We're cool."

To Emma's relief, no one seemed to confuse Emma the bookkeeper with Emma the model.

Her last trauma therapist had urged her to discover something she enjoyed doing. You're a victim as well as an offender, he'd reminded her, and both parts need to heal. The victim needs to *feel* something good, while the offender needs to *do* something good.

Posing naked before a roomful of artists was probably not what her therapist had in mind. But when she stood in front of this group, she felt *seen*. She was no longer a ghost, stuck in the half-life of the never-healed. Expected to fade into the background because her scars and halting speech and nearly visible guilt made people turn away. Visual artists didn't care about speech or guilt. And they didn't turn away from her scars—they leaned right in for a better look.

When Jonah called the first break, Emma stepped behind the shoji screen and shrugged into her robe. In the supply closet, she pulled a water bottle from the fridge and shook out two ibuprofens from a bottle on the shelf. Swallowed, drank, massaged her right hip. Stretched everything again and returned to the classroom.

Five minutes into her last pose of the evening, she heard the distant slam of a car door. Sitting on her stool with one foot on a low rung, curly hair massed around her head and face turned toward the windows, she wondered idly whether it was someone's ride arriving early or a co-op member stopping by their studio.

Boot heels clipped sharply across wooden planks outside the classroom door. The footsteps grew louder, then paused just outside the brown-papered door with its DO NOT DISTURB sign.

The door clicked open and the room went still. Emma saw nothing and heard everything.

"I know, I'm *so* late!" A woman's voice, sounding more annoyed than apologetic. "These roads! I got so lost."

Emma flinched. Her brain stuttered and stalled, landing on one thought: *Not real. Can't be real.* It must be an auditory hallucination, a product of her still-quirky brain.

Jonah's irritation was immediate. "Sorry, this is a closed session. You're interrupting."

Someone's sketchpad slid to the floor. People shifted and whispered.

Emma shivered. Pulse pounding in her ears, she swayed and fought for balance on the stool. She could see nothing except the base of a white wall where it met the worn pine floorboards.

The footsteps resumed. Louder, coming closer.

Jonah's voice became urgent. "Please, stop there!"

"I got *lost*," the woman repeated. "It was *so* confusing when I got off the interstate. There's that new exit. I thought I knew the way. But no." Fretting, complaining. "There are literally *no* signs and how do you people drive out here? I had to turn around twice, almost went into a ditch."

The bootsteps paused behind Emma. "Oh! Hello—"

Jonah broke in sharply, "Let's go outside. Now." To the group he added, "Please continue, everyone. I'll be right back."

Footsteps receded, his heavier shuffle overlapping her crisp clatter. The woman's voice persisted, floating in now from just outside the classroom door. "I'm Lyssa. Lyssa Morales."

The four words carried an imperious subtext. She might as well have said, "And don't you know who I am?"

Yes, Emma thought. *I know you. You're my cousin Lucy. You abandoned me eight years ago, and what the holy hell are you doing here now?*

The classroom door closed with a loud click.

EIGHT

As the fat angry dude with the thin ponytail escorted Lyssa outside to the parking lot, she tried—but not very hard—to remember his name. Joseph or Jones, something like that.

When he turned back to close the barn doors, she crossed her ankles and propped her butt against the front of her rental, a 2022 Shelby Mustang. Oil-slick blue, the pimple-faced kid at the rental agency called it. She'd planned to cruise Asheville later with the top down, but now that wasn't important.

She watched the big man wrestle with the sliding doors. Denim and denim was never a good look. Short-sleeved shirt with armpit stains. Baggy board-length shorts and white socks with cheap work boots. He probably wore the same thing every day, and he wore it all ugly.

Her thoughts circled back to Emma. That was a shock, finding her here. Alive.

Nicotine always helped Lyssa think so she unzipped her plum leather crossbody and found the packet of Silk Cut Silvers. She tapped one out and lit it with a wooden match from a small gold box. Dropped the match on the gravel and watched it flare briefly before dying. The first deep inhale was a satisfying rush so she held it as long as she could, then tipped her head back and exhaled a thin ribbon of smoke upwards into the night sky.

She picked idly at one of the ripped, over-bleached threads in her skinny Givenchy jeans. She was no longer thrilled with the destroyed-denim-and-moleskin look, but she'd keep them a little longer before dumping them on Poshmark because she'd paid *mucho dolares* Canadian only a few months earlier. Just before her clothing allowance dried up, vanishing like an oil spill leaking into sand.

She'd been warned. When the Keystone XL pipeline died, Carlos told her his family was shutting down the Alberta tar sands project. Where next? His father was calling him home to the family compound, thirty miles west of Mexico City.

She said no way and Carlos said *no problemo*, they'd split. He didn't need her anymore and she hadn't fulfilled her part of their bargain anyway. Her attorney assured her he'd try to get her something, but this was the Morales family. Did she even know who she was dealing with?

Done with thread-plucking, she sighed elaborately and watched the next exhale of smoke rise in a thin trail through the pool of light cast by the parking lot's single overhead lamp.

She examined her surroundings. Half a dozen cars, a pickup, and two vans were nosed up to a pair of stone planters in front of the barn. The urns trailed purple petunias, pale green sweet pea vines, and a spray of ornamental grasses. A little too carefully arranged for her taste. She preferred the dark edges of design, with a dash of chaos to spice things up.

The ponytailed dude leaned his considerable weight against the second door and pushed it closed. His face was in shadow, his bulk lit from above by three carriage lamps mounted above the twin sliding doors. A fourth lamp, near the right corner of the barn, illuminated a human-sized passage door and the small sign hanging beside it.

Stonefall Art Center
GALLERY & SALES
HOURS: Sat 10-5 Sun 12-5
and by appointment

Crafted in the same art-deco style, a fieldstone pillar near the road held a large monument sign that read STONEFALL ART CENTER in navy on white, edged in gold. The barn was freshly painted in a trendy blue-gray, trimmed in white and accessorized with a matching pair of mailboxes on the opposite side of the road. The barn's cross-timbered doors, the carriage lamps, the urns, the sign, the weed-free gravel parking lot—everything looked new and well-tended.

In her childhood, this building was a moldering derelict occupied by rats, bats, and raccoons. The last time she'd visited, eight summers ago, there'd been several dumpster loads of trash in the yard.

Stonefall. Did the farm even have a name back then? It was always just the Gillen family farm, Uncle Jerry's summer place. The land was leased to a local farmer who mowed the pastures and pruned the apple trees. Much earlier, it was her grandparents' home but they'd died when she was young. She didn't really remember them.

The big man dropped metal pins into the concrete sill to secure the doors. He hustled toward her, moving like a human roly-poly, rocking a little from side to side like he'd just stepped off a freighter.

"Need to get those things motorized. We're waiting on the kit." He removed steamy glasses and used the tail of his shirt to wipe the moisture. "So, Ms. Morales—"

"Lyssa." She narrowed her eyes against the rising smoke and tipped her head a little sideways, appraising him.

"Okay, Lyssa. Look, we're starting on the wrong foot here." His voice shifted from casual to critical. "Like I said on the phone, the studio sessions begin right at seven-thirty. No one's allowed in after the door closes. You know how it works. The group needs quiet. And privacy." His forehead furrows deepened.

She held her cigarette away from the Mustang and tapped it with a plum-lacquered fingernail. "My bad. It was just an impulse, really. To come tonight." She added a lips-only smile, absolving him of any misunderstanding on his part. "No problem. I can stop by tomorrow. I don't think I'll get lost in the daylight. How's one o'clock?"

His frown remained. Maybe she hadn't offered enough of an apology.

"I *am* sorry," she added. "I'd forgotten it was a live figure session."

He relented. "One o'clock should be okay. I'll be busy, but Felicia can talk with you. She's on the committee, too."

Lyssa lifted a neatly drawn eyebrow. "Who is Felicia again? On what committee?"

"Membership in the co-op. That's what you asked about, right?"

"Oh, right. But I've also been visiting other places, down in the arts district. Asheville's got the edge on this place for scope and scale, and foot traffic. Out here, it's so…rustic. But I'm sure Felicity can tell me everything tomorrow." She lifted her chin toward the barn. "You'll want to get back," she added, in case he'd missed her dismissal.

She watched him disappear through the side door, then abruptly dropped her cigarette and ground it into the pea gravel with the toe of her boot. Quickly scanning the parking area to be sure she was alone, she walked briskly across the road, around a screen of bushes, and up a flagstone path to a small brick farmhouse set in a wide yard. The glow from a pair of yellow carriage lamps lit the flagstone path to the front porch.

The bushes were larger but everything else looked exactly as it had in her childhood. She figured she'd have about twenty minutes to learn if anyone was home.

***

Ten minutes later, Lyssa stumbled down the porch steps. She wanted to stop to catch her breath but she felt too exposed in the porch light, so she hurried back across the road to the Mustang.

She punched the ignition and reversed out of the yard in a small spray of gravel.

Fuck.

Fuck fuck fuck. Everything's wrong.

The Shelby was going too fast and in the dark, she almost missed the first turn. The tires slipped, then grabbed. She braked carefully.

Focus, girl. You know how dangerous these roads can be.

The visit was clearly scripted in her mind. She'd walk in and yell "Surprise!" just like old times and Uncle Frank would run to greet her, astonished and delighted. He'd give her a bear hug and swing her around, laughing. Pull out a couple of beers and urge her to sit down.

But no.

The door was unlocked and she'd walked in as planned. But when she saw the skinny old man slumped in the recliner she forgot to say "Surprise!" or anything else.

He didn't know her. She didn't recognize him for a minute, either.

There'd been a dog by his chair, barking like crazy. A little gray thing that growled deep in its throat when she went to sit on the saggy old sofa.

She'd said her name twice, her old name, and it was only when she'd repeated it and he'd startled up from his chair that she realized the frail skeleton in the barf-a-lounger was Uncle Frank.

So, two surprises. Frank fragile and sick, Emma alive and functioning instead of dead or brain-damaged or crippled.

Lyssa thought she'd done her research. What was she missing?

Eight years ago, the accident was front-page news for three days in the *Asheville Observer-Times*. Three people dead and a fourth in critical condition, after a tragic two-car crash on a mountain road outside the village of Bracken Falls, in northern Bundison County. The sole survivor, nineteen-year-old Emma Gillen, suffered life-threatening injuries. She'd been airlifted to Charlotte and placed in a medical coma.

Funerals were held for the second driver, Christine (Chrissy) Garrison, and her daughters, two-year-old Destiny and four-year-old Amber.

A month later, Emma remained in a coma. The police investigation concluded that the cause of the unfortunate accident was a rockslide triggered by a "major rainfall event." No one was charged. The insurance companies settled, the case was closed.

On the one-year anniversary, a two-paragraph update mentioned the continued poor prognosis of the lone survivor, who still struggled with memory loss and debilitating injuries.

Emma then disappeared from the local news and, apparently, the entire digital world. There was no cellphone in her name. No Facebook, Twitter, TikTok, Instagram, SnapChat, or Pinterest accounts. No voting record. She belonged to no community groups, owned no vehicles or property, and was not mentioned anywhere outside of the news archives.

Lyssa, who lived on social media and couldn't imagine a fellow Gen-Z without an online life, concluded that Emma must be incapable of using a smartphone or computer. Perhaps she was severely incapacitated. Or dead, though Lyssa hadn't found an obituary.

Emma's father Frank was easy to locate. Lyssa found his contact info on a basic people-search site. She could have called first but decided not to because that would spoil the surprise.

But the surprise was all hers. Emma was still living at the farm, doing just fine, while Uncle Frank looked like death's next breakfast and was being guarded by a vicious small dog.

Driving now along the dark country roads toward Asheville, Lyssa gave in to a fit of fury, thumping the steering wheel and yelling epithets to the night sky. She'd been cheated, again.

She forgot about cruising Biltmore Ave. She needed to buy a bottle of vodka and think about her next move.

***

Down by the creek, Chaz was lounging in his pickup with the lights off, the engine idling, and Morgan Wallen on the radio, when he saw a flash of headlights coming from the farm.

He sat up. The usual traffic from tonight's class wouldn't come by for another half hour. The last one to leave was always Jonah, who drove a rusty old Sentra. Then Chaz knew it was time to head home to his trailer by the tomato fields.

Chaz had parked his gray Ford Ranger just off the pavement by the sign for Wilbur's Cove Trail, a short creekside hike through a family-friendly corner of the Pisgah Forest. There was a picnic table under the hemlocks and space for two or three vehicles but his pickup was usually the only one there. He'd backed in at an angle so he had a good view of traffic from both directions.

The unfamiliar pair of slant-swoosh headlamps grew bigger. A low-slung car flew by and fishtailed through the next curve, its iconic triple-lit taillights flaring as it braked. A late-model Mustang with its top down.

Chaz caught a glimpse of the driver, a woman with hair bright yellow hair gleaming in the dashboard light.

A sleeve of cold French fries spilled to the floor as he reached for his seatbelt and flicked on the pickup's headlights.

NINE

She's back.

Had Emma's quirky brain fabricated a Lucy-hallucination?

No. A whole roomful of irritated artists witnessed the arrival of her long-lost cousin.

Lyssa, formerly known as Lucy.

Emma stuffed her wrinkled shirt into her jeans. She glanced in the small mirror on the back of the supply closet door and tugged a full handful of frizzy hair over the scar.

Her phone vibrated with the first few notes of a classical guitar riff, her father's ringtone.

"Emmie…" His voice rasped. "Lucy was here… She just left." An asthmatic wheeze punctuated each phrase.

"She went to the house? Damn. I'll be…right there." She propped her phone on a shelf and jammed her feet into sneakers. "How's your air? Is the ox-pen on?"

Go slow, she reminded herself. *You don't know what you just said. Go slow or you'll confuse him. Be clear.*

She heard a hiss and thrum in the background. His voice steadied. "Yeah, it's on. Lucy— She didn't knock, she just walked in. Teague went crazy. He was barking like mad, I've never heard him bark like that. Growling, too. She stayed for just a few minutes."

Good dog, she thought.

He said, "She told me she's staying at a hotel in Asheville. A Marriott? I should have told her she could stay here. Didn't say it in time."

Anger flared in Emma's gut. *Lucy shows up out of nowhere and Dad's sorry he forgot to invite her to stay? Move right in, Lucy! Instant forgiveness!*

"I'll be right there." She hung up and finished dressing.

In the classroom, Jonah was folding easels. He started to say something but she raised a hand.

"My dad called. Lucy stepped...stoppered by the house." She paused and closed her eyes for a moment. *Slow down.* "After she came here. I've got to go."

"Lucy?" His high forehead creased in confusion.

"Lyssa. Lucy. You just met my...cousin. Lucy."

"Lyssa Morales is your cousin? She never said... Is Frank okay?"

Her mouth worked, fighting for words.

"Take it easy," he soothed. "Are *you* okay?"

"Yes. He's just sure...prised. He's got his—"

"Oxygen?" Jonah dropped a handful of discarded sketches into a recycling bin near the door. "Don't worry, I'll close up. Go."

***

In the living room her father slouched in his recliner, an oxygen tube dangling beneath the deep creases of his chin. He stared at the TV on the opposite wall, where gloved players chased a bouncing ball across an impossibly green field. His cherished Red Sox were beating the Mariners so he should have been smiling, but instead he was gazing vacantly with the sound off, not tracking the action.

"Dad. You okay?"

"Yeah, I'm—" The cannula slipped from his nose so he fumbled the ear loops off. The clear plastic line trailed down to an oxygen concentrator, a squat machine the size of a small generator that whooshed and thumped on the floor beside his chair.

Emma heard a sharp *woof* as their salt-and-pepper schnauzer blasted in from the kitchen. Kneeling quickly, she snagged his collar as he tried to hurl his twenty-pound body against her chest. The little dog squirmed and made small chuffing sounds, trying to lick her face. She held him off and scratched his ears.

"Dad, tell me what happened."

He pointed to the dog. "Him first. You were gone what, three whole hours? You'd better give him some attention."

Grateful for the distraction, she raised a hand with the palm flat. "Teague, sit."

Quivering with pleasure, the dog performed a half-sit, his butt hovering just above the floor. His long undocked tail swept enthusiastically from side to side and his black beard trembled while his front feet tapped the planks. Every part of him wiggled and danced, but his rear end remained close to the floor in a qualified sit.

Her father handed her a biscuit from the box on his lap.

"Good boy…good sit. Teague, down."

The dog hurled himself downward, slapping the floor with chest and elbows. He stretched out into a frog-sploot, front legs stretched forward and hind legs splayed behind. He tilted his head, uncropped ears flopping sideways. His body stilled for a moment but the feathery tail kept swiping the air.

Teague's down was as imperfect as his sit but she couldn't fault his enthusiasm. She handed him another biscuit and he pranced away to the kitchen, head high.

Her father smiled. "A good dog is the best therapy."

He'd said the same thing every day since Uncle Jerry gave her the puppy right after her discharge from the convalescent center five years earlier.

Half-rising to lean over the recliner, she touched her lips to his rough cheek, careful not to dislodge his glasses or the inhaler tucked in his shirt pocket. She smelled his leathery aftershave mingled with warm dog and knew he and Teague had been napping together.

He found the remote and switched off the television. She sank onto the old sofa next to his recliner and took his wrist to check his pulse.

He smiled. "How am I looking?"

She loved him so she told a small lie. "Your color is good. Let's check pulse."

On the cluttered coffee table she found an oximeter and clipped it to his index finger. Ninety-two percent oxygen, marginal. When he waved off the nasal cannula, she settled back on the sofa.

Long Covid had dug its pneumonia claws deep into her father's lungs, leaving the left one badly scarred. He did two stints in an ICU and returned home with COPD. The disease also stole flesh and muscle from his lean frame. He was sixty-one but looked twenty years older.

"The oxygen helps," he assured her.

"You should...keep it in."

"I don't need it all the time."

Arguing was useless. "You used your fin sailor? The blue label."

He frowned and touched a finger to his shirt pocket. "Inhaler? Yes, right after dinner."

So far, they'd managed to avoid talking about Lucy.

"How was tonight's class?" he said. "Good turnout?"

"Fine." Time to mention the real topic. "Then Lucy came. I didn't see her, but I heard her."

"I'll bet. That girl always loved to make an entrance."

"The door was closed. Jonah put the sign up on the glass... But she just—"

"Waltzed in anyway." He shook his head but she could hear the hint of admiration in his voice, like Lucy was a clever puppy that could be forgiven for naughtiness.

"Jonah told her to leave. She's coming back...tomorrow." Emma hoped the last word was clear. Her father never gave feedback on her malapropisms and he never used the "sounds like" signal that Jonah used, the classic ear tug from charades.

She reached for her father's hand and laced her strong square fingers through his thin ones. "She's using a new name."

"Yes, she told me. But I didn't write it down. Melissa?"

"Lyssa...mortal seas." Was that right? Probably not. "Jonah said she wants to join the co-op. He didn't know she's my cousin. And...I didn't know Lyssa is Lucy." She sighed with the effort of making sense.

He coughed once, then again. As she leaned forward to hook the oxygen tube over his ears, he reached up as if to sweep the thick springy hair away from her eyes. Or maybe he meant to tug the curls forward over the scar at her temple. His hand stopped in mid-gesture and fell back to his lap, a classic girl-dad move from when it was his job to help control her wayward hair.

Her eyes filled as she watched him suck in oxygen. "I didn't recognize her at first," he rasped. "She's older, of course. She looks very—polished. Sophisticated, like she's just stepped out of a magazine."

"With all the taboos?"

"I didn't see any tattoos. Or piercings."

In college, one of Lucy's goals was to obtain more body ornaments than anyone else. She'd acquired an impressive number of holes and slots for threading metal through her eyebrows, nose, tongue, lip, ears, belly button, anything that offered a fold of skin or a bit of cartilage. Emma wondered now at the lack of skin art and hardware.

"So she's back," she sighed. "What do we do?"

"Talk to her. Invite her for dinner, at least." He paused, looking uneasy. "I gave her your phone number."

"It's okay. I'll... manage. I don't want her bothering you. It may be...hard." Emma wanted to say *difficult* or *awkward* or *contentious* or *disagreeable* or even *majorly sucky,* but she wasn't sure any of those words would stick the landing. The best words were often the big ones and those still evaded her.

She added, "You're sick, Dad. Do you want her here?"

Frank pushed against the arms of his recliner and struggled to sit upright. "Of course I want to see her. She's my *niece*. Wherever she's been, now she's back. We have a lot of catching up to do." He frowned. "Don't you want to see her?"

Silence.

He raised both hands in frustration. "Okay, okay. Yes, she should have been here for you. To help us all. After the accident, Jerry and I were like crazy people. We were out of our minds, worried about you. And worried about her, too, because we couldn't find her. Or Maggie. Then we had to sell everything up north and get this place fixed up and—"

She placed a hand over one of his, hoping to calm him. "You were…are…awe…some. You and Jerry."

He sagged back in the chair. "Finally we figured they just didn't want to be found. We never heard a word from either one."

She handed him a tissue from a box on the coffee table so he could dab at the dampness in his eyes. Held his wrist to check his pulse again. A little fast now, but steady.

Maggie and Lucy. Like mother, like daughter. Inside her head, the words flowed easily and quickly. *Do you remember, Dad, all those times Maggie took off for a new job or a new boyfriend? Or rehab, she was in rehab a lot. You and Mom always took Lucy in. Mom never complained, she'd pick us up from school and say, hey Lucy, you're staying with us tonight. Another sleepover. It's great you and Emma are in the same school, it's easy. Just come home with us.*

They'd always made room for Lucy because she'd lost the parental lottery big-time. Everyone felt sorry for Lucy, having Maggie for a mother.

Her father broke into her thoughts. "I didn't tell her about Jerry's death. I didn't think of it, and then she was gone so fast. She loved her uncle."

"Not—" Emma wasn't sure what she meant to say. Did Lucy love Uncle Jerry? She certainly appreciated him, the way she appreciated anyone who could give her things. Jerry gave her a lot. Tuition, rent, clothes, art lessons, a car. Privately, though, Lucy mocked him for being creepy and nerdy. King Jeremiah the Gullible Geek, she'd called him. Uncle Jermy, the Lord High Benefactor. The all-important Keeper of the Treasury.

"Why didn't they have someone from the model agency?" her father asked abruptly. "To fill in tonight."

Emma's antenna went up. "It saves a few…dollars if we take turns," she said carefully. "They like it when I pose."

He'd known she was scheduled to model tonight, the art center's schedule was taped to the side of the fridge. Her father was just revisiting an old complaint.

The furrow between his brows deepened. "But you don't do any drawing now, so it's not taking turns, is it? You shouldn't keep doing it. Putting yourself on display like that. Dwelling on the damage. You show your scars and that's all people think about. You can't get back to normal by dragging it all around with you."

There is no normal, Dad. That train fell off the rails a long time ago.

Aloud she said, "No one thinks about that. They just want someone to draw."

His protests had nothing to do with posing nude. He'd dabbled in art, too, before getting his engineering degree, so he knew how important live models were to artists.

What he objected to was what he called the persistent self-abasement. Picking at scabs, obsessing over her guilt. Yes, three people died eight years ago and yes, she was involved and maybe she could've done something different, but *it was an accident.* What some insurance companies ridiculously called an Act of God. And it was partly his responsibility too, right? Because he'd given her that goddammed Miata. A terrible choice for a first car, no matter how good a driver your teenager is. Your precious daughter, your beloved only child.

He often reminded her—*way* too often—how much progress she'd made on the PTSD and the nightmares. The epilepsy was under control, her speech had improved. So she needed to stop fixating on those other things, the guilt and the shame she carried around like a stupid cross and they weren't even religious, goddammit. And what about the horrible injuries she'd suffered? She was a victim, too.

She stuck a wrench in her hamster-wheeling thoughts. Her father's right hand was fidgeting, tapping a tiny drumbeat on the arm of the recliner, so she captured it with her own and stilled his restless fingers.

"I'm fine, Dad. Really."

He eased his hand away and resumed tapping. "We have to call Mark. Tell him Lucy's back. Get some advice from the legal department."

She was ready for the topic switch because of course it had to come back to Lucy. But this was much better than planning a prodigal-niece celebration.

She reminded him, "Isn't Mark on…Orkney?"

"Trout season ends soon. I think he's heading home in a few days. But we shouldn't wait."

"I'll email him. Maybe we can talk in the morning, our time. For him, that will be early afternoon, I think."

His fingers quit tapping. "What's this going to do to you? Lucy coming back. The nightmares, I mean. The hallucinations. Having her here, will that be a stress trigger?"

She wanted to say *yes, of course it will*. But she wouldn't get into that now, so late in the evening.

"We'll find out," she sighed. "It's ten-thirty. I'll email Mark before I go to bed. You need your…weevil share or the walker?"

Asking for the wheelchair meant he'd need her help getting ready for bed. Choosing the walker meant he could manage on his own.

He picked up the remote. "I'll be fine. But I'm going to sit up a little longer, I think."

Emma kissed his cheek and made the rounds. She took Teague for his evening walk, then set the security alarm. Filled her father's water glass and switched on the spare oxygen compressor in his downstairs bedroom, the only part of their nineteen-twenties farmhouse that had ever been updated. Teague curled up in his dog bed near her father's closet door and promptly fell asleep.

She typed a quick email to Mark Camerer, their fly-fishing family attorney: *Lucy's back. We don't want to interrupt the quest for the biggest trout but your sage advice is needed ASAP.*

She paced the kitchen, feeling restless and not at all tired. Should she take something to help her sleep? It was tempting, but no. She'd rather be hyper-awake than groggy.

She took her meds for seizures, depression, and pain. Then she climbed the narrow, creaky staircase to the smallest bedroom in the old house, the same room she had as a child when they'd spent summers on the farm with Uncle Jerry and Aunt Marisa.

Lucy always took the largest room at the front of the house, claiming space each June for her easels and paints and a tower of stuffed animals. Emma never minded because her single window in the small room had a better view to the east. From there she could see the apple orchard, the woods behind the house, and Mount Mitchell, the highest peak in the Blue Ridge Mountains.

The two windows in Lucy's bigger room looked out on nothing more than the dusty road and the old swaybacked barn with its sprawling junkyard of broken tractors and rotting lumber. Now, of course, the view from that room was much improved.

The four original bedrooms under the eaves shared one upstairs bathroom with a clawfoot tub and a plastic shower curtain, all unchanged from their childhood.

If Lucy moved in, where would she stay?

***

At one a.m., Emma's phone pinged her from a restless sleep. The 403 area code was unfamiliar but she knew instantly who sent the text.

> Hey cuz! U R lookn gd.
> Coffee @ Margos, 10 Fri am? L

She sat up and placed both feet flat on her worn oriental carpet, wanting to feel something solid beneath her.

Emma knew from years earlier that any message from her cousin demanded a quick response. If she didn't answer immediately, the texts would multiply and then there'd be a phone call. Or two, or six. And she couldn't just switch her phone off because her dad might call for help during the night.

Texting was way easier than talking so she tapped:

> Really? After how many years?
> You've got some f***ing nerve.

She promptly pushed the backspace to delete everything. *Spineless wimp*, she chided herself. *You've been storing up f-bombs for years. Put them to good use, spell them out.*

She typed instead:

10 is fine. CU.

Pressed SEND before her fingers could rebel by typing something else.

She checked her email, looking for a reply from Mark. It was five hours' time difference, so it must be six a.m. on Orkney. How early did fishermen wake up in Scotland?

There was no email so she placed her phone face-down on the nightstand and rolled over, pulling the covers over her shoulders and willing herself not to think of Lucy or Lyssa.

Moonlight seeped in around the curtains flanking her narrow window at the foot of her bed. The light was dim, but Emma didn't need light to see the three photos on her bureau. One of her mother kneeling in the garden, laughing up from under her sun hat as she paused in the middle of pulling weeds from a row of pole beans. Another of her mother, silhouetted in her scarlet racing suit against an impossibly blue sky, dark hair flying and skis perfectly aligned, her lithe body ignoring the pull of gravity as she topped a mogul in a cloud of fresh powder.. The third photo was a little blurry but it was still her favorite, her mom reading a magazine on the sofa as three-year-old Emma slept on her lap.

The familiar ache rose in her chest and she knew she'd never get back to sleep if she kept staring at those photos, so she turned instead to look at the poster-sized photograph on the wall by the window.

This was one of Jonah's, a tight close-up of a Cooper's hawk caught at the instant of liftoff from a dappled sycamore branch. The bird's wings were fully extended, the finger-like flight feathers etched individually against summer-blue sky. A fraction of sky was visible also below the tips of the hawk's talons, curled in the aftermath of upwards thrust.

She'd always been fascinated by that tiny sliver of blue caught between bough and bird. The negative space created when, as the hawk springs up, the branch is pushed down. Action and reaction, cause and consequence.

Jonah gave her the photo about a year after the accident, during a therapy session. He asked her to re-write the script of her most frequent nightmare. Instead of falling, he wanted her to think of stepping off a single stair. Just one down, and one up again.

Speech was still hard for her then so he'd cheerfully added that this session was a two-fer. Work on the speech, work on the fear.

She knew he wanted her to describe the bird's attempt to fly, how it needed to control the flying-not-falling effort. But she'd found herself staring at the slice of blue sky between the hawk's talons and the branch.

"Fall...falling." That wasn't right. She was thinking, *dissolving into nothingness, expanding into infinity*. But those words refused to travel from brain to larynx.

He prompted her. "She's not falling, is she? She's going to fly, not fall."

"It's...too...high."

"Yes. But she didn't just leap off the tallest tree one day and start flying. First she had to hop along the ground, then jump from a rock or a fencepost. Something small. I'd like you to stay close to the ground, too. Think of your nightmare. Now, in the daylight. Change it. Think about a step, a stair, that's just eight inches high." He held one hand above the other.

"Step up, step down. Imagine you have wings. Spread them, for balance. Step up, step down. Can you do that?"

It worked, sort of. The terrible nightmares of crashing falling screaming persisted but she began to have better dreams, too. She imagined wings. Thought of floating, then landing gently. Not on a rock-strewn mountainside in the cold rain in blackest night, but in a sunny field or a sand dune by the ocean.

Staring now at the hawk on the sycamore branch, Emma wondered what it was like to find that moment of no gravity, a place of lightness where nothing could fall.

When she closed her eyes, she stepped into a country where the hawk was forever springing up to fly, never falling. All she had to do was stay there.

***

At some unknowable time in the darkness, not sure if she was awake or dreaming—it really didn't matter—Emma heard her mother's voice.

Emma, sweetheart, your shoe's untied. Ask Lucy to help you. She's like your big sister, she can help. Lucy can walk you to the corner, hold your hand, sit with you on the bus, help you find the girls' room.

Isn't it great that Lucy's here? Lucy's always welcome. We can always make room for Lucy.

TEN

Emma woke abruptly on Friday morning, filled with dread because some terrible premonition had followed her through the curtain from sleeping to waking, but she couldn't remember either the dream or the threat.

Sunlight brightened her single window though she had no idea what time it was. She fought free of the twisted sheets but remained flat on her back, staring at a dusty cobweb hanging from the stilled ceiling fan.

The sense of alarm came with an urgency. She'd wasted time and slept too long.

Lucy.

Every morning since the doctors had brought her out of the coma, Emma's first task had been to relive the accident and remember the victims. But this morning, her mind was on Lucy.

Was this a step in healing? Or a new trigger for trauma like the high places that generated terror, or the smell of wet leaf mold that sparked nausea?

In the past, she'd have asked for Jonah's professional help, but now it would be awkward. She'd probably be crossing some line between friendship and therapy.

She wasn't seeing any therapists now. Her last one, a noted trauma specialist, had fired her eight months earlier. He told her she'd stalled on trying to resolve her moral injury, the shame that comes from acting—or failing to act—in a way that violates your ethical beliefs. You believe you're a compassionate and conscientious person, yet three people died because of you. You're certain you've violated your own moral compass but you can't remember how or why.

You need a more complete narrative, he'd told her, to find a path to healing. Hypnosis might help.

Nope, she'd said. Not happening.

She'd read the literature on false memory. She didn't trust her fragile, quirky, damaged brain to deliver an accurate reality even when she was fully conscious. How could she rely on anything recalled through hypnosis? She wanted facts, not imagined recollections.

He'd canceled their remaining sessions and she began sitting for the life classes, which was better than regular therapy because she didn't have to listen or talk or explore anything other than her own thoughts. Which always returned to the rain, a tree, a bad road, Emma's Miata, Chrissy's van. All a confluence of time and place, just shitty bad luck. Maybe it was fate but she didn't believe in fate. Just concurrences and coincidences, causes and consequences.

Then Emma's stomach clenched, remembering that she was going to talk with Lucy today.

She heard the shuffle-thumps of her father's walker on the floor below and didn't know whether to be pleased or worried by his early-morning energy. When the first wave of Covid fatigue body-slammed him two years earlier, before his pulmonologist balanced his meds, he suffered from bouts of frantic insomnia that drove him to wander the house for hours, dragging his oxygen tank from room to room. He hadn't had one of those sleepless nights for a while, but every now and then he emerged from his room at odd hours, wide awake and ready to fold laundry or start a batch of chili.

But now it was six-forty-five. That wasn't an odd hour. It wasn't even early.

As she swung her feet to the floor, she heard the rapid thumpity-thump of dog feet on the stairs. Teague galloped through the doorway and sailed onto the bed beside her, full of exuberant canine joy.

"Good morning, Blackbeard." She scratched his sturdy shoulders and floppy ears with both hands, leaning away so his flailing tongue couldn't slather her face with kisses. "You are butter than Kramer at entrancements." He looked puzzled so she added, "Shine-pelt. You're too young, you'll have to watch it in syncopation."

Nonsensical dog-speak was how she practiced talking at a normal speed. She knew several words weren't right but Teague didn't care. He valued tones, not sounds. To him, her voice was always perfect. Freed from a human audience, Emma's words could blossom in freefall.

She pointed to the floor. "Off the slip, me squirrelly matey."

It wasn't the right piratical inflection, but he bounced obediently off the bed and launched a bout of zoomies, spinning in a foot-blurring circle that rumpled the rug. Panting, he splayed his front legs and froze in a let's-play crouch. But being motionless was too hard so he *woofed* and broke away, galloping away through the open door and down the stairs.

Emma pulled on worn overalls and tied a scarf over her tangled hair, vowing to brush it properly at some later time.

She was scrambling eggs when her father appeared. He'd traded his walker for a cane, which he hung on the edge of the kitchen counter before easing himself into his chair.

She patted his bony shoulder. "You shaved. Looking good." He'd missed a few spots, but she was pleased he'd made the effort.

She said, "Sleep well?"

"Not really. Too restless."

"You've got those tests today, at two. Raylene is taking you."

"With Ian Hoskins. The pulmonologist."

"Yes. You took your meds?"

"Of course." He looked offended. His Covid brain fog had lessened over the summer, but any suggestion of confusion—even the normal uncertainty of *Where the hell did I put my glasses?*—made him anxious.

She decided not to check his pill case. His homecare aide would arrive soon and she was far better than Emma at playing the professional heavy.

She checked her phone. "Mark emailed. He'll be home early Sunday. We can Zoom that night at eight. He says we can give Lucy a copy of Jerry's will. But if she has...questions...we should tell her to call him."

Her father's brow furrowed. "Mark? He's gone fishing. What's this about Lucy?"

Emma felt a spark of anxiety. He'd gone from remembering the pulmonologist to forgetting about Lucy. *Please, Dad,* she thought, *I need you here with me. Both our brains functioning, firing on all eight cylinders.*

She held his gaze and repeated, "Mark will be home Sunday. I told him about Lucy."

He held the frown for a moment longer. Then his face cleared. "Lyssa. We're supposed to call her Lyssa now, right? Could you write that down? Her name and number. I don't have her number."

She found a pen, wrote LYSSA MORALES on a piece of scratch paper, and placed it by his elbow.

He said, "We need to review Jerry's will again. Lucy will be disappointed when she sees it."

Emma kept her mouth shut on that. *Disappointed? That's the understatement of the century. Try furious. Enraged. Seething. Or apoplectic, there's a good old-fashioned word.*

Instead she said, "Do you want to invite her for dinner? Maybe tomorrow? We can show her the will after dinner."

And for dessert, here's a big helping of nothing.

"We could have trout," he said. "There's some in the freezer. Talking about Mark made me think of trout." He paused. "This will be awkward, won't it?"

"It's already...that. She asked me to meet her this morning. At Margo's."

"By yourself? What will you talk about? Do you want someone to drive you?" He fussed with a spoon, twirling it on his placemat.

"It's just coffee at Margo's. I'll be fine," she fibbed.

He nodded and turned his attention to the eggs and toast.

Emma pulled on her barn jacket and pocketed two apples from a basket on the counter, then stepped into calf-high muck boots parked in the boot tray by the back door.

The narrow hall was Aunt Marisa's *sala de lama*, Uncle Jerry explained when Emma and Lucy were small. That's Portuguese, it means a room for mud. When Lucy opened her mouth for a question, he'd added: No. Do not try to bring in *more* mud. The dirt must always remain outside, never closer to the kitchen than the wire-brush boot scrapers bolted to the outside steps.

Whoever brings the *lama* inside, Marisa threatened them, I will swat your *rabo*. Lucy frequently tested the rule about no mud; her backside was swatted regularly.

Emma was smiling now, pleased that she'd remembered a few Portuguese words. She called Teague and clipped on his leash. They left the yard through the side gate and went along the flagstone walk to the road, the schnauzer trotting politely at her side. The morning smelled fresh from an overnight shower, and the grass by the walkway was lacy with spiderwebs the size of small napkins, each sparkling with dewdrops.

Emma went first to the chicken coop, set under a cluster of pine trees by the barn's north side. She fastened Teague's lead to a tree branch to keep him out of the way while she filled the hens' feed tub and water trough. When she unlatched the coop door, eight speckled hens tumbled down the wooden ramp into their fenced yard, flapping and rushing over her boots to snatch the corn she scattered.

The squawking hens awakened Teague's terrier heritage. He yipped and lunged against the leash. Emma told him to sit and he sat, barely, with his body rigid and his tail thumping the dirt. His yelps downshifted to a breathy grumbling as Emma tugged him away from the chicken pen.

At the pasture gate behind the henhouse, Emma used her teeth and fingers to section the apples into large pieces for the two ponies, a donkey, an old Jersey cow, and six black-faced sheep. Then she leaned on the gate for a few minutes, watching the ponies saunter away.

Uncle Jerry bought the ponies from a neighbor the summer Emma turned eight and Lucy was nine. The taller one, a black-and-white gelding named Frodo, was Lucy's. Sam, the plain brown mare, was Emma's.

The cousins were obsessed with their ponies that summer, rising early every morning to ride together. But when they went home to Connecticut at the end of August, Lucy decided to become an artist instead of a rodeo rider. The following summer on the farm, she'd barricaded herself in her room with her paints and pastels, wanting nothing to do with the ponies. Emma rode Sam by herself a few times, but it wasn't much fun alone. The ponies languished in their field, growing fat and lazy.

Nearly two decades later, Frodo and Sam were now old and slow. Emma wondered if they remembered that one summer when two girls spent every day brushing them and braiding their manes in ribbons, roaming the fields and splashing through the creeks in search of adventure.

She thought of two other little girls who might also have loved Frodo and Sam, if the past had been different. If they'd lived. But those other girls would be ten and twelve now and maybe that was too old to begin an obsession with ponies.

Thinking of the two girls who would never ride ponies or wade in the creek reminded Emma that the summer was nearly over. In a month or so, flashes of red and gold would spread through the forests. Then everything would wither into winter, bringing cold sleet and early darkness.

Dear Chrissy, I'm so sorry...

Shivering, she pushed her thoughts away from what was still months in the future and considered the more immediate problem of Lucy. The art center was heading into a busy weekend. Could she even spare the time to meet Lucy at the café?

Coward. Just do it. You want to know why she ran, why she's back, and what her plans are, right? So ask her. Maybe she'll answer, maybe not, but you won't know unless you ask.

Lucy probably wouldn't hang around for very long. She'd create drama and disruption for a week or two, then get bored and leave.

Unless she wanted to move in. Then what?

Emma must have said something out loud because Teague whined softly and tugged on his leash, pulling her back toward the house.

***

"Hey, Jonah." Emma put her phone on speaker and set it on the mudroom bench. She kicked off her boots and tugged off her barn jacket.

He stifled a yawn. "How's your dad?"

"Good. He's out on the porch, as usual. With the *Boston Globe*."

"The paper paper? I thought you got him an iPad."

"He's…older school. Likes paper, to wrap fish bones. It's a …boomer thing."

"I'm a boomer but I don't do that. Maybe putting fish bones in newspaper hits when you turn sixty." Another yawn. "How'd he react to Lyssa? Lucy. Seeing her, I mean."

"He was sur… surprised." That felt inadequate but it would have to do. She carried her phone to the kitchen table and pulled out a chair. "It's been eight years. Dad and Jerry tried to find her. They thought she was dead."

"Did you think she was dead?"

"I don't know. I didn't think about it much." A lie.

"Did she say why she contacted me first? About joining the co-op, I mean. Instead of getting in touch with family first, with you or Frank. That was odd."

"No idea. She's always been odd." Better words came to mind but she didn't feel like wrestling them into sounds. *Thoughtless, impulsive, secretive, deceptive, narcissistic.* "I'm meeting her at ten. At Margo's. For coffee. Um… That was okay? Coffee, not…coffin?"

"Coffee was fine. Just you and her? Do you want me to tag along?"

"No. But maybe you can help me think of what to say. To talk to her."

Jonah knew what she was asking: How could she hold an unrehearsed conversation?

He said, "Just tell her right up front that talking is still a work in progress for you. Write down what you want to say. Then read it out loud, or hand it to her if you think you need to."

"No time. I can't write it all."

"Not a whole script, just some notes. Show her your notebook. Explain how syllables and sounds get swapped around, so you have to go slowly. Give her some examples. Funny ones, maybe."

"How can I know that...will come out right?"

"Explain the 'sounds like' signal from charades. Ask her to cue you with that."

Emma's insides felt like twisted taffy, thinking of how the old Lucy used to pounce on weakness. She'd have exploited the ear-tug signal as a free pass for ridicule. The new Lyssa? Probably the same.

Jonah's voice softened. "Hey, you'll be okay. There's lots to catch up on. Ask her to tell you what she's been up to. Let her do the talking. You were close, you lived together when you were kids. You were roommates for a while in college. You *knew* each other, right?"

How could she explain? Living with Lucy had nothing to do with being close, not the way other people understood it.

Jonah sighed. "Okay. When she asks how you're doing, keep it brief. Talk about Jerry. Reminisce a little. Back to when you were kids, summers on the farm. You told me those were good times, right?"

"But—"

"At some point, you'll need to explain how you felt—how you still feel—about her running off, right after the accident. You felt deserted and hurt. It also hurt your dad. You're still upset. If you can say 'good to see you' and mean it, that's great. If you can't, that's okay too. Don't get pulled into talking about the co-op. We'll handle the membership thing, Felicia and me. Okay? Does that sound reasonable?"

"I guess. But...."

"What?"

"You don't know her. She'll have her own—" Emma thought about the three syllables she wanted to use. "Agenda."

"Sure, everyone has an agenda. But you won't know what it is until you talk."

"If things don't go her way, she might make...trouble."

"Trouble?"

Emma envisioned Jonah frowning and doodling on something, thinking through his face and fingertips the way he often did.

"Sorry, I don't—" Emma was going to say *I don't mean she's violent* but she then recalled all that acting-out in grade school. The simmering anger in high school, the flaring temper in college when something didn't go Lucy's way.

"Emma? You still there?"

"She's just...hard to deal with," Emma said lamely. "She takes up a lot of...."

"Energy or air?"

"Both."

"You'll be fine. You've faced harder things."

"I guess." She planted her elbows on the kitchen table and rubbed her face with both hands. "Okay, I'll just let her talk. That should be easy."

***

Emma slid her laptop into its case and added a notebook from the stack on a table by the front door. Her clothes probably held a barnyard smell but she didn't care and neither would anyone at Margo's Café except maybe Lucy.

There was a knock at the front door. Teague woofed his welcome bark, rising from under the table at Emma's feet. His feathery tail swung in large arcs.

"Mornin, Miz Emma. You still here?"

"Hi, Ray. Just about to leave."

"Hello, Mr. Teague." The tall dark-skinned woman in blue nursing scrubs folded herself down to crouch at small-dog height. Teague politely offered his paw and received a scratch behind the ears. Protocols completed, he retrieved a toy duck from a basket by the door and carried it to the sofa.

The eldest of four sisters, Raylene Pelletier had dismayed her rural conservative Baptist family by becoming a vegetarian at age ten. At fourteen, she confounded them again when she announced her plans to become a nurse. Neither choice sat well with her parents, who ran one of the few Black-owned hog farms in eastern North Carolina and was counting on her to help manage it. After high school, she'd moved to the mountains. Well away from hog country, she'd told Emma, but not so far as to completely alienate her family. Working now as Frank Gillen's daily homecare aide, she was also putting herself through nursing school at night.

Raylene's strict insistence on by-the-book care set Frank's teeth on edge at first. Depressed and angry after his second bout in the ICU a year earlier, he'd fought the dietary restrictions and physical therapy requirements. On Raylene's first day, Frank shoved a plate of unbuttered toast to the floor, claiming she'd burnt it.

Emma stuttered an apology for her father's temper and begged the aide's forgiveness.

"Not a problem," Ray assured her. "I get how it is for him. With me bein here, he's got to face what he doesn't want to. Covid's an evil disease. His brain's not workin right and he knows it. Sometimes he needs our help just to get out of bed and get to the bathroom. It's okay. Your daddy's a sweetheart, compared to some. You try movin around a four-hundred-pound market hog what's covered in pig-poo and tryin to kill you. And that pig's so pissed, he maybe wants to eat you before you can eat him. Carin for your daddy when he's a little grumpy? Piece a cake."

Emma never told her father that Raylene had compared him to a hog.

Their relationship improved a few days later when Raylene asked about the chessboard she'd found in his room. "Teach me to play?" she'd coaxed. "My grandaddy played chess. I loved that show, *The Queen's Gambit*. I wanted to learn but I always been too busy helpin the big pigs make little pigs." She and Frank had been trading bishops and rooks ever since.

Raylene slung her backpack onto a kitchen chair and called out to the deck. "Hey, boss. I got a question about Four Knights. You open with E4 or E5, and after the knights bust out, what's White's next move?"

"Bishop to B5," Frank said without looking up from the *Globe*. "But I don't like Four Knights. It usually ends in a draw."

Ray turned back to Emma. "He doin okay? He looks a little pale, even for an old white guy."

"We had a…surprise last night. My cousin showed up."

"That girl cousin, the one that disappeared after the accident? He told me a little about that."

"That one. My only cousin." Emma handed Ray her notes on Frank's vitals from the night before. "He shaved this morning. Said he took his meds."

"Okay, that's good. We got that pulmonology visit at two, right? Dr. Hoskins. I'll have them call you right after."

"Don't get lost in a chess game."

Raylene gave her a big smile. "Nah, your daddy's good for about ten moves. Then, if he still has any energy, he starts tellin stories about how hard it used to be, doin his surveyor work in some frozen swamp way up north. Or he falls asleep in the sun. I will *never* learn me a good end game. Go on now, we're good."

ELEVEN

Friday morning, nine-twenty-five. Chaz was five minutes early.

He fidgeted in the hard wooden chair outside the art center's office. He tried sitting straighter but that hitched his jeans up his shins, thinking he should've worn dark socks but his only clean socks were gray. Which didn't matter with work boots but if he got this handyman job he'd be doing more than just driving a tractor and digging post holes. He'd be around people, and they'd be judging him.

Mr. Jonah didn't seem to be the judgey type, though he'd looked kinda busy when Chaz arrived. Waved him to a chair and said back in a minute, then disappeared again. Chaz had been sitting there for at least ten minutes and now he didn't know if he should knock on the office door or what.

Working outdoors all summer, Chaz had been inside this building only a few times to use the restroom or pick up a paycheck. With the new job—if he got it—maybe there'd be a pay raise. If he kept his weekend job, too, maybe he could save a little more.

He was very careful with money but the prices of food and gas were stupid high, and now he was now regretting last night's decision to follow that Mustang into town. A forty-mile round trip, just to learn that the blonde woman was staying at a Marriott in Asheville. And that she drove too fast, never used turn signals, and had a loud, rude voice. He knew the last part because he'd heard her arguing with a big bearded dude in the hotel's parking lot.

Now Chaz really wanted a cigarette but he'd *never* light up inside a barn. Hay and straw and even the dust in the air can burn fast. But maybe this place wasn't a barn now. It looked more like a big dance hall.

He craned his head back to look up at the skylights framed into the roof, and noticed there was also a sprinkler system and three giant white fans hanging from the ridgepole. The huge wooden beams looked varnished and all the side walls were painted white. No barn he'd ever seen looked so clean and bright. If there was dust, he couldn't see it.

Long wooden benches, all different sizes, were arranged in rows to face the big doors at the rear of the hall. They looked like train station seats or old church pews, but instead of being bolted to the floor, these had felt-covered slats attached to their feet so they could be pushed around.

Along the sides, the cabinets and shelves held things that maybe were from someone's garage sale, or a museum. Ancient clocks and milk bottles, dried flowers in pots and colorful quilts in shadow boxes. A metal statue of a rodeo horse bucking off a cowboy, a foot-pedal sewing machine like Darren's grandma used. One section of wall held old farm tools—a scythe, two pitchforks, a cross-cut saw, a hand drill he remembered was called a bit and brace.

Next to all that was a glass case with real stuffed animals. A fox, a raccoon, a crow, a pair of squirrels. On the top shelf was a paper-wasp nest, twice the size of a football and still attached to the branch of a tree. It was behind glass and the wasps must have been long gone, but still that nest gave him goosebumps.

"Chaz? Hi, I'm Emma."

He jumped a little and scrambled to his feet.

She wore a thin tee shirt and baggy overalls. No jewelry. If she'd done anything to style her hair he couldn't tell because she'd tied a green scarf around her head. Sort of like Queen Elizabeth, but with the scarf worn low on her forehead and all her red-brown curls spilling out the back.

Chaz had no idea why that thought came to him except he remembered how his ma liked reading the supermarket papers, and pictures of the queen always showed her in a scarf like Emma's.

But that was years ago. His mother was dead and so was the queen, and except for the scarf Emma didn't look at all like the queen of England.

His brain stuttered and words began looping in his head: *the queen the queen the queen.* He quickly pinched the tip of his right pinky between his left thumb and index finger and hoped he wasn't blushing because the old zit scars turned red when that happened and Emma was still standing there waiting for him to say something back.

The finger-pinch worked because he managed to nod. "Mornin."

"Our office is really small," she said. "I came out so you can go in." She spoke slowly, like she was still learning the language. "Jonah's ready for you."

Chaz thought she'd be taller, or maybe he'd grown a lot because when he stood up he realized he was several inches taller than her. She wasn't exactly pretty, but he'd always liked her freckles and her gray-blue eyes. Her smile was a little crooked now but he liked that, too.

At last he remembered his manners. "Good mornin, Miz Gillen. Ma'am." His face warmed.

She smiled. "Please, it's just Emma. No Miz anything." When he made no move toward the door, she opened it wider. "There's only one place to sit. Take my chair."

He eased past, careful not to brush against her, and sat in the office chair that was still warm from her body. She closed the door and was gone.

Mr. Jacobs—Jonah, not Mr. Jacobs, they all used first names here and Chaz would have to get used to that—was sitting at a computer.

"Hi, Chaz. Just give me another sec." He tapped away, peering at the screen over wire-rimmed glasses.

Chaz was glad to have a few more minutes because he hadn't been in this room before and he needed to get his bearings. The closeness and clutter made him feel too big and sort of dizzy. There were shelves of books and files and art supplies, paintbrushes in cans and tripods leaning in the corners. Sketchbooks, stacks of paper, boxes of crayons and tubes of paint. His gaze paused on a milk crate of wooden figures, artists' manikins. His fingers began twitching, wanting to touch the life-size model of a human hand with flexible joints.

Jonah turned away from his computer and saw Chaz's stare.

"They're pretty cool, aren't they?" He pulled the hand from the crate and held it out. "Have you ever tried drawing the human hand? It's not easy."

Chaz rubbed his fingers over the smooth pale wood, then gently bent each digit at the knuckles to create a loose fist. He extended the first two fingers in a V for victory.

"That is awesome." Then he caught himself. "Sorry, sir. I shoulda said good mornin first."

"No problem. Thanks for waiting."

Chaz offered to return the wooden hand but Jonah waved him off so he held it as they talked, fiddling a bit with the joints. Jonah began talking about the handyman job, what they needed and did he think he could handle it.

"I took shop classes in school," Chaz told him. "Woodworkin, some weldin. We built chicken coops and a kids' playhouse. Did the wirin, too, so we had to learn a little electrical."

Jonah nodded. "That's good. We've got a new project, teamed up with a theater group. Right now they're performing outdoors in the park behind the high school, but they'll need an indoor space for the winter."

"They're comin here? To the barn?"

"The front hall's plenty big enough but we'll need more seating. I told them we can build more benches. And stage sets, flats and scaffolding. Pieces that can be bolted together, then struck after a performance and stored in the cellar."

Chaz frowned slightly. "I can follow plans and build things, but I ain't so good with plannin it out on paper."

"You'd be a set carpenter. They have their own designer."

"Oh. Well, yeah, I can do that. I been a stagehand a couple times, at school. We had to move the sets around. Run the lights and sound, stuff like that."

"And you took a class on security systems, right? Ours needs an upgrade."

"Yessir, I can do that."

Darren had reminded Chaz to demonstrate initiative so he added, "Maybe y'all could use a camera by the chicken coop, too, under those big trees. Keep watch for coyotes, raccoons and foxes. If you don't wanna run a wire out there, I got a trail cam I can put up. It runs off a battery."

Jonah nodded. "Good suggestion. I wasn't even thinking about the chicken coop. Let's add that to the list. But the top priority right now is getting a new camera up on the barn. There's a blind spot we need to take care of, out on the deck." He nodded toward the back door. "I've got the parts on order. If they come in next week like they're supposed to, we can get to work on it Thursday or Friday."

Jonah was talking like Chaz already had the job. He wanted to ask about pay but wasn't sure how.

"The hours are eight-thirty to five," Jonah said, "but there may be overtime. It's Tuesday through Saturday, with Sunday and Monday off. I hope that's okay? I know you've got a few things to finish up, like the sheep fence, but we'll figure that out.

"There's a fifteen percent raise from what you got over the summer. There's benefits, too. Medical, dental, vacation. Emma can go over that later with you. Sound good?"

Chaz swallowed hard and nodded. A pay raise, medical benefits. Paid vacation? He'd never had that. It made his head too busy just thinking about it.

"Great." Jonah held out a hand only slightly smaller than a bear's paw and they shook.

Then Jonah was looking at him expectantly and Chaz realized he'd missed something.

"Sorry, sir. What'd y'all say?"

"Do you have any questions?"

Chaz was still thinking about the pay raise. He hadn't planned what to ask so it just popped out.

"Those classes y'all have on Thursday nights, where everyone draws live people? I saw it on the schedule." He felt his face going warm again.

He needed to speak fast before he lost his nerve. "Can anyone come to those?"

Jonah lifted a bushy eyebrow. "Well, there's a fee. Twenty dollars a single session, a hundred dollars for six. It's open studio but it fills up fast. I'd recommend you take some basic drawing classes first. Make sure you're not wasting your money. And we want to be sure you're serious about your art. Then, sure."

He hoisted himself to his feet and rummaged in a tall cabinet. "Have we inspired you to start drawing? Here." He handed Chaz two pencils, a gum eraser, and a half-used sketchpad. "You're left-handed, aren't you? So you need the left hand for practice. Let's trade."

They exchanged hand manikins, right for left.

"Come see me," Jonah added, "if you get stuck on anything."

TWELVE

Emma backed her Jeep carefully into an end space in the lot beside Margo's Café. She released her white-knuckle grip on the steering wheel and set the parking brake. Patted the dashboard and whispered her thanks to the engineers who'd created four-wheel-drive, back-up cameras, and proximity sensors.

Margo's Bakery and Café, the older and smaller of two coffeeshops in Bracken Falls, had only a few indoor tables but the outdoor patio was large and shady beneath market umbrellas and a wisteria-draped pergola. Hoping to find a secluded table before Lucy arrived, Emma hurried along the brick path beside the café where white lattice and a hedge of purple asters separated the patio from the sidewalk.

She was ten minutes early but Lucy was already there, seated at a small wrought-iron table with her long legs crossed and one booted foot swinging.

Lucy saluted Emma's arrival by raising her white mug an inch from the table. Emma hesitated, uncertain if she should sit or stand to wait for an unlikely hug. Lucy didn't get up, so Emma sat.

Her dad was right, Lucy looked different. Gone was the chopped, spiked, bleached hair. Now she wore a smooth cap of pale gold, expensively colored and cut into a chin-length bob. Her skin was burnished to an even bronze, all the tattoos gone. The only piercings visible were in her ears, which held intricate silver hoops. Startling teal-blue eyes—maybe tinted contacts?—matched the color of the wrought-iron table.

Polished was exactly the right word, Emma thought. Lucy wore a spotless white tank top and artistically ripped jeans. Burgundy leather ankle boots and a matching crossbody bag, Italian or French leather. In high school, Lucy lusted after anything labeled Fendi or Hermès but

Uncle Jerry always laughed at the prices and said no, not on his dime. She'd apparently acquired her own dimes since then.

No more chewed nails, paint-stained knuckles, or turpentine-puckered fingers. An enormous square-cut emerald, set in a halo of diamonds, glinted from the third finger of Lucy's manicured right hand. Her fingernails were also square-cut, tipped in dusky plum. And much too long, Emma thought, for working clay or painting anything.

Clearly amused by Emma's stare, Lucy tapped a tapered finger on the table and waited. "Do I pass inspection?"

Emma felt a sudden flush of envy, not of Lucy's styled appearance but of her voice. The words flowed in a well-modulated cadence, no effort required.

"You still like mocha latté?" Lucy indicated a second white mug and a brown bakery bag. "And croissants, you used to love the croissants."

Say something, Emma reminded herself. *Anything. Just get it going.* "Hi, Lucy. Umm, no. I drink…decaf now…Or tea."

It was lame but she'd gotten it out.

In one swift motion Lucy uncrossed her legs and leaned forward, lightly grasping the sides of the table with both hands. She flashed a vivid smile. "Em, it's so freakin good to see you! It's been what, nearly six years?"

Is it too late to flee?

Emma blinked. "Eight….years."

"Well, you look fantastic." Lucy leaned back. "I like the longer hair but really, overalls and a scarf? The refugee vibe is not a good look for you. You've lost weight, I approve of that. And omigod, your freckles. The end-of-summer crop, right? You always had some, but now they're procreating."

She creased the corners of a paper napkin and rattled on. "Uncle Frank's okay, too, right? He looked so surprised when I popped in last night. Speechless, actually." This was said with a touch of pride, as if causing speechlessness was an achievement.

Emma fought to corral her thoughts, desperately wanting to get the words right. "He's... was sick. Covid. Still has it....long Covid. His lungs are bad. They're trying new... teachers."

She paused, knowing she'd fumbled that one. "Treats...treat-mouse."

Lucy's brow furrowed. "Oh. I didn't realize he was so sick. I thought he looked pretty good last night. But his dog—that was scary, I thought it was going to attack me."

Before Emma could rise to Teague's defense Lucy added, "Hey, it's been a while, hasn't it?"

We've established that, Lucy. Needing something to do, Emma wrapped her fingers around the latté she wasn't going to drink. Then she saw her own ragged nails, edged in dirt. She moved her hands to her lap and said the next thing that rose in her mind.

"It's...Lyssa? Your name."

That cued the bright smile. "Yes! Lyssa Morales. I got married five years ago and now I'm getting divorced. But I'm keeping my married name. And *this*, of course!"

She flexed and wiggled her fingers so Emma could admire the emerald. "A girl can never have enough bling, right?"

Emma wondered whether to offer congratulations or condolences. She'd settled on *sorry* because it was easier to say but now Lyssa was talking again.

"I know, it's not PC to take the guy's name but his stupid pre-nup required it. Then I decided I liked the sound of it, Lyssa Morales. So much better than Harnett. I never knew why my mother took that creep's name. She never married him and never told him I existed, right? So why should I have to own it? I figured I'd dump Lucy, too, because she's just an obnoxious cartoon character. Then I remembered what you used to call me. That title."

"What title?"

"Don't you remember? When we were in middle school. You called me the Director of Outrage and Fury. In Greek mythology, Lyssa is the goddess of anger. I googled it."

"Uncle Jerry said that... not me."

"Whatever."

How do you chase a pile of conversational ping-pong balls? Seize one, let the others escape. "Okay," Emma said. "Your name is Lyssa. I think I can...resemble that."

Lyssa's eyes narrowed. "You sure you're okay? You sound stoned. What are you on?"

Emma closed her eyes to concentrate. "My speech still gets mixed up. From the...accent. Accident. I had to learn to speak. All over again."

"Oh. Well, you sound half drugged. Definitely medicated."

"Lyssa is also ... rabies."

"Huh? What are you trying to say? That's mega-weird."

"Lyssa is the god... the goddess of mattresses. And rabies."

"*Mattresses?* What the fuck does that mean?" Lyssa grabbed her phone, ready to flee or call for rescue. "Are you calling me a slut?"

"No... not mattresses." Feeling lightheaded, Emma exhaled sharply. Beneath her struggle to speak, a bubble of laughter threatened.

Oh, that's perfect. Mattresses for madness.

But she must make Lucy or Lyssa, or whoever this was, understand that the malapropisms were not deliberate. She stifled a giggle and tried to explain. "The words I say aren't always...what I think I'm saying."

Don't fall apart. Breathe.

She tried again. "I meant to say mad...ness, not mat-tres-ses. That's a mallard proof."

Clutching her handbag and phone, Lucy scraped her chair back. The table vibrated and coffee sloshed as she turned her head left, then right. Seeking an escape route but not yet fleeing.

"That's just really freaky," she hissed. "Stop it, Em! You're scaring me."

THIRTEEN

Lyssa, the Amazonian Goddess of Mattresses and Rabies, was scared of *Emma?*

Emma hastily tucked a napkin beneath her dripping latté, then covered her mouth with both hands and choked back whatever was trying to break out. Her chest heaved with a snort-laugh.

"What the fuck?" Irritation overtook Lyssa's wariness.

Emma gulped, hiccupped, and smothered the giggles. "Sorry." She wiped her eyes with the last unused napkin.

Lyssa continued eyeing Emma with suspicion but she didn't run. "What the fuck was that?" she demanded. "Did you have a seizure or something?"

Emma balled up the damp napkin. *No, let me tell you about the seizures...*

"No," she managed. "It's just…I never thought I'd…hear it. That *I* scared *you*." A final hiccup popped out. "I'm ... I can explain. My brain thinks of a word but my voice swaps it…for another. I have to speak slowly, one sound at a time. It's called…"

Damn. She did not trust her brain on this one.

She pulled a pen and small notepad from her shoulder bag and printed EXPRESSIVE APHASIA, thinking she should have done this twenty minutes earlier.

Lyssa watched, still uncertain but now curious, as Emma wrote MATTRESSES. Drew a line through that and substituted MADNESS. Added ARMORED-DILDO with an arrow pointing to ARMADILLO.

Emma said, "I *know* the words. I can spell them. I just have ….trouble…saying them."

"That's just too freaky."

"One more." She wrote BANDERSNATCH CUMMERBUND (W/ APOLOGIES TO LEWIS CARROLL) and turned the notepad around.

Lyssa stared, struggling to keep her face straight. She lost the battle first to a chuckle and then to a peal of clear laughter.

"Ohmigod, I remember that. You absolutely ruined *Sherlock* for me! I was totally infatuated and then you mangled his name *on purpose*. I was sure I'd meet him someday and I'd go, 'Hey, Mr. Cumberbatch, I really admire your work,' but instead I'd call him Mr. Cummerbund or Mr. Bandersnatch, and now it's stuck in my head *again!*"

"I didn't...create that one." Emma admitted. "Dad saw it in a news...paper."

"But we were like sixteen! Your speech wasn't fucked up back then, was it?"

"No."

Awkward silence. Lyssa smoothed her hair and tapped her fingernails against the white mug. "Good thing you can write fast. You always got A's in spelling."

"Your name's really Lyssa? On your pass port?"

Lyssa nodded and shifted in her chair.

"Which one?"

"Canadian. I haven't changed the American one yet."

"You said you'd never—"

"Get married? Yeah. Well, never say never. A mistake, which is being fixed even as we speak."

"Any kids?"

"What, me?" Lyssa shook her head, eyes sliding downward. "Wow, no. No way. Can you see me as a *mom?* God, that would be a disaster."

She picked up her coffee mug and peered into it as if seeking the answer to an unasked question. She seemed about to say something more when a man approached their table. Late thirties, a small-town professional on casual Friday. His steps slowed as his gaze, faintly hopeful, slid past Emma and lingered on Lyssa.

He was a washed-out looking man with pale brown eyes, pinkish skin, bright copper hair trimmed short over a pale scalp, and a thin red-blond goatee.

Lyssa raised those striking blue-green eyes to his amber ones and held the look long enough so maybe he thought he should say hello. Then she cut her gaze away in swift dismissal. The man's skin went a deep red as he veered away from their table, nearly tripping over a potted Ficus.

"So that's how it's done," Emma remarked.

Lyssa produced a cynical smile and a "Duh, obviously" eyeroll.

Suddenly he was back beside their table, staring not at Lyssa but at Emma. The scolded-puppy look was replaced by a narrow-eyed suspicion.

"Hey," he muttered. "I know you."

He was staring at Emma now. She froze.

"You're that bitch was driving when Chrissy Garrison got killed." He stepped closer. "She went to our church. And her little girls, my sister used to babysit them sometimes. My sister said you must've been high on drugs that day."

A river of hot shame rose in Emma, floodwaters rising from her gut.

"You never shoulda been driving," he growled. "Stupid cunt. They shoulda locked you up."

His stare broke suddenly, swapping menace for confusion as Lyssa came up out of her chair in one fast, catlike move. She placed her hands flat on his chest and shoved. He stumbled back, flailing. Fought for balance and went down on one knee.

"Get away from my cousin, asshole," she snarled. "You white-trash piece of *shit*."

She stepped toward him again, her elegance gone ugly with barely controlled fury. He threw up both hands and scrambled away. Emma caught his backward glance, full of fear and fury.

Lyssa returned to her seat and retrieved a fallen napkin. "Well, that was interesting. What a dickwad. Ugly inside and out and couldn't you just hear the banjos?" She straightened her white tank top and inspected her manicure for flaws.

"Jeez, Em. How can you be so freakin calm? So stoic. Does it happen often?" she added. "Assholes attacking you like that."

Stoic? Calm? Emma felt her shoulders unclench. "Not much now. Most people have forgotten. The worst was right after the crash, when I was still in the...coma." Her mouth was dry. She didn't want the too-sweet mocha but it was available. She took a small sip and swallowed hard. "Dad and Jerry had to fight a lot of ...rumors. Dad won't talk about it, but I saw some of the posts."

"What rumors?" Lyssa sat very still. Anger had given way to wariness.

"That you and I were...drug users. On...meth or speed. Or I was drunk and it was all my fault. That sort of crap. They...what's the word? Doxed me. Jerry and Dad got it all taken down but..." She stared at her white mug on the teal table and blinked. "It's why I don't do...social media."

"That's ridiculous. You've always been a great driver. That's just stupid crap, bullies out for revenge because their lives suck and they've got nothing else to yap about. It wasn't anyone's fault."

She flipped open her bag and pulled out a white cigarette carton. Shifted it from hand to hand. Paused, sighed, and dropped it on the table. "Emma, this is dumb. Can we start over?"

"Okay."

"You first."

This was unexpected. Where to begin? *Begin by breathing.* "You know...Uncle Jerry died?"

Lyssa nodded. "Yeah, I saw the obit. A heart attack, right? Like three years ago."

"Why didn't you—?"

"Try to get in touch? Send a sympathy card? I only learned about it last spring. By then it was more than two years after he died."

Lyssa sounded unaffected, almost dismissive. Emma wondered if she was trying to hide her feelings about Uncle Jerry's death. Or did she really not care?

"And," Lyssa added, "I wasn't sure how to get hold of you." She twirled the cigarette box in a slow circle on the table.

Emma didn't trust herself to respond aloud. *Seriously? We're right here, Dad and me. Still on the farm, where we all spent summers and holidays for years and years.*

"Good old Uncle Jerry," Lyssa mused. "Jeremiah Gillen was one weird dude, right? He was crazy smart and he made bags of money, but definitely weird. Always talking to the birds and trees, shit like that."

Emma's brain stalled as Lyssa dredged up another memory.

"Hey, Mouse. Remember when Jerry planted all those scrawny sticks he said were baby Christmas trees? Then when they actually grew big enough to sell, he wouldn't cut them down because the birds made nests in them."

This was safer. Emma found something relevant to say and the words seemed to be coming a little easier. "That's where we spread his ashes, on the hill under the trees. We put a marker there. For Jerry and Marisa."

"Yeah, they were soulmates, weren't they?" Lyssa added mocking air-quotes to "soulmates," suggesting it was fake or slightly dirty.

Emma recoiled a little and frowned. "Yes, they were. Do you want to see where—"

"Hey, Mouse. Just *kidding*. That whole soulmates thing, it's such a cliché. And I don't really remember Marisa. We were what, eight? When she died, I mean."

"I was nine, you were ten."

"And I'll bet that house hasn't changed a bit, has it? So small and *old*. I mean, vinyl floors and plastic counters? Jerry made pots of money but nobody ever updated *anything.*"

"Some changes. There's a bedroom downstairs. And a bath. Where my dad is."

Lyssa raised an eyebrow. "Yeah, big changes," she scoffed. "And I bet you're still upstairs in that awful little room with the ceiling so low you can't stand up except in the middle. It must be like living in a holding cell."

Emma wanted to ask how her cousin would know what a holding cell was like but instead she said, "Do you need a place to stay?" She crossed her fingers under the table. *No, please say no.*

Lucy snorted. "Really? Stay in my old room, like when we were kids? And share that hideous bathroom with that rusty old clawfoot tub. For real? No way. I'll stick with my hotel room." She tipped her head a little, silver earrings swinging. "But you always liked it there. All that farm shit. Literal shit, right? Remember the chickens? And the ponies. You were well on your way to becoming one of those cringey horse girls."

Her contempt softened a little, edging toward nostalgia. "Remember when Marisa made me collect the eggs and they were dirty with chickenshit so I threw them against the rocks by the barn? Splatter art!" She snickered. "That's when that neighbor boy told me where eggs come from, out of a hen's ass. Butt nuggets, he called them." A pause. "Did you ever tell Marisa? About me smashing the eggs?"

"No."

"You always were so loyal, Mouse." She sighed. "Okay, seriously. Everything you're doing now, with the farm? I think it's great. The whole agritourism thing. You're about to catch the wave, I think. The next renaissance in rural arts and crafts—"

"That's not what we're—"

"And I know it's all been rough for you. The accident, the rehab, then Covid. I didn't realize Uncle Frank got slammed so hard by the virus. So…"

Confused by Lyssa's shift in tone—to something close to sincerity or fence-mending—Emma felt her way carefully. "Are you saying… you're sorry?"

"Hunh? Sorry? For what?"

"Leaving us." *Deserting me* was more accurate but maybe too accusatory.

"No, no. That's not what I meant. I'm just saying, I think it's awesome. Because you got hurt so bad but you recovered, right? Except you lost your memory, right?"

Emma nodded, wondering where this was going.

"And me, Em, I've had some rough times too but now I'm back. It's a new start. So here we are, together, both of us doing great."

She spread her arms wide above the table as if narrating a happy-life fairytale, or celebrating something. "Here's to second chances, right?"

"Hey," she added brightly. "Come out with me tonight. Let's go someplace fun. We'll take the Mustang, see if that place on O'Henry is still serving cheap pitchers of strawberry 'ritas."

Emma blinked. *Yeah, that'll be fun. Or not, because I don't drink. Also I won't get into a car when it's raining. Or after dark.*

Aloud then, "Sorry, I can't. Just— no."

She let that hang for a moment, then pulled a topic-shift page from Lyssa's playbook. "So you went to Canada. Right after the accent."

"Quebec." Lyssa looked annoyed, like she'd wrapped up her presentation but that irritating intern in the front row was still asking questions.

Emma persisted. "Why? And why so fast?"

Lyssa's face darkened. "Because I needed to find my shit of a mother. And art school was a fucking disaster." She leaned closer. "Your next question will be, did I find her? Answer, no. Maggie said she was heading for Stanstead, remember? I went there but I never found her. She never made it, or maybe she did but— Who the fuck knows. No Maggie, no Brad. Nothing."

Clenching a fist, she held it just above the table like she wanted to smash it down hard. Emma flinched because Lyssa's sharp nails must be cutting into her palm. Making a fist like that would leave marks.

Lyssa relaxed her hand and splayed it on the table. Sarcastically, "You remember Brad, right? The guy on the bus that she went *north* with? The day she was supposed to be coming *south* to join us for Thanksgiving. To celebrate being sober."

And suddenly Emma remembered that evening: Brad, the bus, the text from Maggie.

What did her last trauma therapist tell her? Your mind is like a sealed box of old files. Someday, a corner may break open and a few notes will slip out like scribbled Post-Its. Be ready to sort the contents whenever and wherever they fall out.

Now a few fragments fluttered free. She remembered the sound of rain on the roof, Lucy sketching. The frustration turning to anger, the anger that toppled the easel. The cracked collarbone, the trip to the ER, more rain. Days of rain.

Emma's brain switched the names back, Lyssa to Lucy. Her cousin could be Lyssa now in the present, but in the past she had to be Lucy.

More fragments came clear but could she trust them? Probably, because this was pre-crash. The hospital trip was Wednesday evening and the accident was four days later, the Sunday before Thanksgiving.

Emma continued to sort her virtual Post-Its, labeling and highlighting, as Lyssa rattled on, oblivious to what she'd broken open.

"I looked for *months*, Em, trying to find my mother." She punctuated her narrative by leaning over the table and fixing her eyes on Emma's. "I was working shitty jobs in shitty bars and hotels, in all those shitty little towns along the border. Then I met this gorgeous man, Carlos Morales. He was on his way to Calgary to set up contracts and leases in the Athabascan oil sands."

Emma tried to catch up. "He owns an…oil company?"

"His family finances explorations. They lease big chunks of land and hire engineers to go look for oil and gas. Baja California, the Gulf of Mexico, Canada, Alaska. I thought it was a sign, right? The universe telling me to quit looking for my mother and look at what was right in front of me. Carlos was my fucking Disney prince, my *really hot* prince, because the sex was mind-blowing amazing."

She grinned. "So I hooked up with Prince Carlos and a few months later we got married. In Caracas, on one of his business trips. Later I found out his father wanted him to marry a Canadian because he thought the whole Morales tribe could get Canadian citizenship if I sponsored them on the family plan. It was supposed to help their business connections. FYI that's not how it works, but they didn't know.

"That family is filthy stinking rich. They were happy for me to marry Carlos and live in Calgary, but first I needed to become *presentable*. Get rid of the hardware and the tats, the visible ones anyway. Get my teeth fixed. I've always loved ink and hated dentists, right? But they paid for all of it and the cost didn't matter because I had to look *perfect*. You have to admit the teeth look pretty good, huh?"

Her smile was large and fake and Hollywood-perfect, all the orthodontia on display. The care of Lucy's teeth in childhood was always hit or miss.

Emma made an effort to admire the dentistry so Lyssa sailed on. "FYI, Cowtown Calgary's way cooler than you think. It's got an *awesome* art scene. So for four years, everything was fucking beautiful. Then Biden got elected and bang, the Keystone XL was dead. The oil and gas contracts went belly-up. It took another couple years to wrap things up and then Carlos's dad told him to get his beautiful ass back to Mexico City. I said no, leave me out of it, I'm not living where I've gotta learn freakin Spanish."

Her tan shoulders in the white tank top rose and fell in an elaborate shrug. "We'd cooled anyway. Part of the deal was I'd produce a couple of kids, but no way that was happening."

She raised her hands beside her head and popped the fingers outward, miming an explosion. "So, boom! Just like that, I get canceled by the family. Bring in the lawyers. I decided to re-boot my fucked-up life and come looking for my family. The end."

Emma held onto her own thread. "When you left to find your mom… you never let Dad or Uncle Jerry know where you were. They thought you might be dead. Or…kid-napped. They couldn't believe you'd just leave."

Lyssa's gaze slid down. She nudged her phone with a finger. "Well—I'd lost my cellphone. That Sunday."

"Sunday?"

"The day of the accident, yeah. I got a new phone in Quebec, maybe a week later, but I'd lost all my contacts and messages. I *did* try to visit you in the hospital, you know. Before I left. Didn't they tell you? The nurses wouldn't let me in. They said you were on life support and only your dad could visit. I left a note for you at the hospital."

"In Asheville?"

"Yeah."

"I never saw a note from you." Emma pinched the bridge of her nose with thumb and finger, hoping to forestall a headache.

She wasn't sent to the Asheville hospital after the accident. She'd been flown directly to the major trauma center in Charlotte.

Her green scarf was loosening so she pulled it off her head and shook out her curls. The scar on her scalp began to itch so she rubbed it while she considered cellphones and hospitals. A side thought popped up. Back in high school, Uncle Jerry gave Lucy the money to buy the Subaru. He also paid for her college tuition. But then she quit school and took the car to Canada. She hadn't paid him back so maybe—

"Em!" Lyssa was staring, open-mouthed. "Omigod, what's wrong with your head? It's like it's been split open there. The hair's all gone!"

Emma flushed and turned away. She re-folded her scarf into an uneven triangle and hurriedly covered her head, pulling the fabric low over her forehead. "It's a scar. From surgery. They put a metal plate in there. Sorry."

Immediately thinking *Why am I apologizing?*

With the knot safely re-tied at the nape of her neck, Emma returned her cousin's direct stare.

Lyssa broke away first, glancing at her smartwatch. "Oh, wow. It's almost noon and I need lunch. I'm supposed to be at the barn at one, to talk with somebody named Felicity. About joining your co-op."

Emma scraped her chair back and stood. "It's Felicia," she corrected. "Felicia Weingardt. Eat here," she added. "The salads are good."

The patio was beginning to fill with an early lunchtime crowd. Lyssa swung her bag over a shoulder. "Nah, I'll find something else."

Margo's was a bus-your-own-table kind of place but Lyssa made no move to pick up her mug. Emma suppressed a frown and cleared their coffee mugs, saving the unopened bag of croissants for her father.

She caught up with her cousin in the parking lot. Lyssa was standing next to a purplish-blue Mustang, fishing in her bag for the key fob.

"About the co-op," Emma said. "Are you really going to apply?"

"I don't know. Yeah, I guess so. I want to get back to my art. I was good, once. Right? And Asheville's art scene is awesome." She brightened as if she'd just thought of something. "And the other thing, why I didn't contact you first? Before I came, I mean. I didn't want anyone at Stonefall being influenced by my family connection. I wanted to arrive, like, incognito. Then when I found you and Uncle Frank, it would be this marvelous reveal. Surprise, here I am!"

The Mustang chirped and Lyssa offered another dazzling smile. "And I did. I found both of you. My cousin and my uncle, the only family I've got. It's really amazing, isn't it?"

FOURTEEN

If Emma lingered long enough in the village, maybe she could avoid Lyssa for the rest of the day.

So she bought a veggie wrap from Margo's, found a shady bench beside the pond in the village park, and tossed bits of lettuce to the ducks.

Damn. She'd failed to ask any questions about what led up to the accident. Had the Miata malfunctioned, something she should've gotten fixed? Why was she driving only four days after cracking her collarbone? That last one seemed the most important. But maybe Lyssa didn't know the answers anyway.

Back in the parking lot, now packed with the lunch crowd, Emma readied herself and her Jeep for driving. She'd done only a cursory check of systems before leaving the garage earlier this morning, but now—after her car was sitting in a public parking lot for nearly two hours—she needed a more thorough inspection.

First, she crouched to examine each tire for softness or an embedded nail. Then she peered beneath the bumpers, searching for a stray cat or squirrel or turtle. Back on her feet, she confirmed the cleanliness of the windows, the headlights, the rear camera, and the proximity sensors. Inside, she searched for anything that might distract her driving—an unsecured box of tissues, a wasp or horsefly buzzing in a window.

She switched on the ignition, silenced the radio, tested the wipers. Turned on headlights and flashers. Got out again to see they were working properly.

Another car was waiting for her spot and Emma gave the driver a small wave of apology as she buckled her seatbelt. Her heart quickened, but only a little, as she released the brake and eased out of the lot.

In the village's single strip mall, she found another suitably remote space to park in. She bought a box of copy paper at the office supply store, a prescription for her father at the pharmacy, and a bag of chicken feed at the farm store.

She was thinking the whole time about the conversation with her cousin. The old Lucy would have clamped down hard on the important question about their uncle's death and shaken it like a dog toy: What had she inherited, and when could she get it?

Uncle Jerry had indeed made bags of money. But Lyssa hadn't said a single curious word about his estate.

***

Emma returned mid-afternoon to a bustle of activity at the barn. Cars were dropping off people and supplies, volunteers were hauling in tables and chairs. A landscaper's flatbed truck, loaded with shrubs and paving stones, idled next to the wire-and-wood fence enclosing the sculpture garden. The gates were propped open and Jonah was semaphoring, trying to convince the truck driver to back into a narrow space between a cherry tree and the tool shed.

"Need me?" Emma asked him.

"We're good. This guy is scared he's going to drive over our septic tank. I'm more concerned about the gates than the septic tank. Which is not even here, it's way over there by the hayfield. But if he puts a scratch on one of those gates, I'll have his head. We may have to carry everything in if he can't get closer. It's okay, Chaz is coming out to help."

The garden gates were a handsome pair of arched iron panels, installed only a few weeks earlier. Custom-crafted by Harry Felton at his blacksmith forge, the design incorporated a silhouette of the Blue Ridge skyline inlaid over square bars. The gates were each six feet wide, hung in precise balance on solid cedar posts.

Skirting the drama by the gates, Emma headed across the main hall toward the office. As she passed the open classroom door, she heard Felicia speaking.

"It says here you went to RISD. When was that?" She was using her professional no-bullshit voice, not the family-and-friends drawl.

Emma's first thought was to duck into the office and hide. Instead, she eased down onto a nearby bench, flipped open her laptop, and pretended to be working.

Lyssa's response was smooth as flan. "I took two courses at RISD in spring, twenty-twenty. It was the pandemic so of course everything was remote. One class was graphic design, relating to brand identity and the influences of social attractors. And the use of color, how it's connected to emotional response."

Emma suppressed a smile. Lyssa must have memorized that straight from RISD's website. This was not a typical membership interview. And what did "social attractors" have to do with art?

"The second course was in video production, special effects and compositing. That's my interest now, how social media can influence trends in art and design."

Felicia said, "But isn't it the other way around? Art evolves, reflecting and influencing our culture. It's social media's role to discuss what the artists are saying."

"No. Social media influences art. Instead of waiting for the critics to talk about a few new artists, everyone with a cellphone can—"

"And a clever hashtag?"

"Exactly. Everyone can share and promote new art."

"But aren't the influencers just working for their advertisers? Telling their followers where to go so they can snap a few art-selfies."

"Art-selfies are a thing," Lyssa argued. "Stonefall should be riding the wave. The most popular artist on Insta right now is a Japanese artist, Yayoi Kusama—"

"I know. She creates Infinity Rooms," Felicia broke in, sounding like someone forced to suffer fools, and not gladly. "Psychedelic fun houses. Kusama says her polka dots are a quote-unquote 'way to infinity.' She admits they reflect her own obsessive-compulsive neuroses. Is that art?"

"Well, yeah. Of course." Lyssa sounded sulky, as if her toy had been pulled away. "Kusama's got people waiting in line for *hours* to walk through her installations."

"Where they snap selfies and walk out less than a minute later." Felicia could do sarcasm, too. "It's like a cult, isn't it? The trendy followers collect art-selfies like trading cards. They don't look at a Rembrandt to understand or admire the art. They're seeing it *backwards*, reflected in their phone screens. It's all me-me-me, see how cool I am." Her voice sharpened. "That is *not* what we're doing here at Stonefall."

Lyssa's voice rose to the edge of anger. "But it gets people into the museums and the galleries, people who usually don't go. Look, I have *tons* of followers. If I say 'Come to Stonefall,' they'll come. And yeah they'll snap selfies but they'll buy stuff, too. They'll buy tickets for an experience, or buy artwork to put on the wall. That's why you need me."

"So you're not asking about co-op membership. You want us to hire you."

A pause. "Yeah, I guess." Definitely sulking.

"Then you should be talking with Emma, not me. She handles our marketing."

A breeze gusted through the barn and the classroom door swung shut.

Emma closed her laptop, feeling a little guilty about eavesdropping but more annoyed because the question of what to do with her cousin was apparently going to land back in her lap. *She expects to be hired for a marketing job that doesn't exist? Has she ever had a real job?*

In the office, she shoved away thoughts of Lyssa. Grabbed an envelope of photos and notes, found a vacant first-floor studio, and locked herself in. She'd just completed the layout for a promotional flyer when her phone pinged with a text from Lyssa. She ignored it.

Half an hour later, Raylene called. Emma answered this promptly, dread mixing with hope.

"Hey, Miz Emma. We're finishin up here with Dr. Hoskins. He wants to talk with you about your daddy. Hang on."

Emma found a pen and a scrap of paper, though she knew Raylene was already taking better notes than she ever could.

"Hello, Emma."

Ian Hoskins could deliver bad news better than any doctor she knew. He always sounded upbeat so it was impossible to tell what was coming. "I have the results of your dad's PFTs, the pulmonary function tests. I'm sorry but it's like I expected, the inflammation has gotten worse. During spirometry, he started coughing and got a bit dizzy, so we put him back on oxygen and administered a bronchodilator. We had to wait a bit for that to take effect before we could do the second set of tests, the limb plethysmography."

She envied him his doctor's voice, how easily the words rolled off his tongue. "That's where you sit in a booth." She'd been there herself, years earlier with a different doctor.

"Yes. To test the level of oxygenation in the legs. Then we did an ultrasound. It's been a long day and we've definitely worn him out." He paused. "But the good news is that he's also a good candidate for endobronchial valve therapy."

Emma felt her own lungs contract and expand in relief. "Lungs have valves?"

"Not really. Or, not yet. We're going to give him some artificial valves to help his airflow. His right lung works okay but his left has reduced function. There's lots of scar tissue, which causes hyperinflation. Meaning you can't push all the air out when you exhale. When the lung stays inflated, it pushes on his diaphragm. We'll insert three or four small valves to shut down the airflow to the damaged part of his left lung. Then his good right lung can draw in more air. It's done with a bronchoscopy so it's minimally invasive. But it does require a few days in the hospital."

"Oh. How many?"

"Three days, maybe four. The procedure takes only an hour, but he'll need sedation. Then we'll keep him a few days to rule out infection. Can you bring him in on Monday at nine? With no complications, he should be able to go home Thursday. Maybe even Wednesday evening."

"Monday? So soon?"

"The sooner, the better. I'm sending him home today with a new anti-inflammatory medication that should help over the weekend. And be sure he stays on oxygen. I've gone over everything with Raylene. She says she can stay overnight, tonight and also tomorrow, if you need her. Let's not put this off. See you Monday morning."

***

Raylene brought Frank home at six and then hovered for another hour, well past her usual end of shift at five-thirty.

"Emma, you sure y'all don't need me to stay over? I'm right close by. His new medication will help the steroids work better, but there might be side effects. If he has any nausea, vomiting, diarrhea—y'all call me immediately, okay? I got a go-bag all packed."

"I'll call if I need you, promise. Thanks." Emma stood on tiptoes to hug Raylene's big farmgirl shoulders.

"I left a bucket and some old towels by his bed, just in case. See you in the mornin."

That gave Emma pause. But surely she could manage her father's care for two nights?

Frank was exhausted and depressed by the thought of yet another hospital visit. He barely touched the pad thai Emma made and by eight he was in bed with the oxygen concentrator chugging away on the floor.

Emma switched on the call monitor and elevated the head of his bed, the same bed in the same bedroom that was hers after she'd been discharged from the convalescent home. Her father did most of that renovation himself, ripping out walls to convert the dining room and sun porch into a single large, light-filled space. The rest of the old farmhouse had never been remodeled, refurbished or re-anything, but this room was a state-of-the-art recovery suite: low windowsills, a built-in desk, and a big tiled bathroom with a wheelchair-height sink, whirlpool tub, and zero-entry shower.

He fell asleep quickly. She kissed his forehead and tucked back his hair so it wouldn't tangle in the oxygen tube. Then she curled up on the sofa with her phone and checked messages.

One text from Jonah, letting her know that Harry Felton's sculptures had arrived and would be installed in the garden early the next morning.

Three texts from Lyssa, the first sent in mid-afternoon:

> Interview was good. Many ideas for marketing! Where R U?

The other texts, plus two voicemails, were more urgent versions of the first. Emma caught her bottom lip with her teeth for a moment. It was only eight-thirty, she might as well call Lyssa.

FIFTEEN

"Omigod, Em! Finally! Where are you?" Lyssa answered mid-laugh. Background noise suggested she was in a bar.

Emma massaged a cramp in her right calf. "I'm home. Look, I forgot to ask you earlier. Can you come for dinner tomorrow night? I'll grill some trout and make a salad. Six o'clock?"

"Yeah, sure. I'll bring a white." Lyssa paused for a beat. "So Em, I'm doing a re-think about joining the co-op. Can we talk earlier tomorrow, too?"

"Tomorrow's too busy, Monday's better. Mid-morning? After I drop Dad at Mission. He's going for a— for his lungs."

"What's Mission?"

"The Asheville horseman pistol," Emma said too quickly. "You know, where—" She thought about adding *Where they X-rayed my collarbone, remember?* but changed her mind.

"Oh, the hospital. You're doing that thing again. Mangling your words." Lyssa sounded cautious, as if word-fumbles could be caught like viruses.

"Maybe. Yeah, I guess. I'm tired."

"No, Monday's no good. I need to come tomorrow, see what the weekends are like so I can learn about everything you're doing at Stonefall." There was a muted crash and Lyssa shouted, "Fuck! Watch what you're doing, asshole."

To Emma she said, "Ugh. Some redneck idiot just fell over me. Okay, so I'll be there late morning-ish. Then I can fill you in on these awesome ideas I have."

She trilled the word *awesome* like a schoolgirl.

Emma frowned. "What ideas?"

"Branding, social media, marketing. Stuff you need. Talking with Felicia was *so* helpful."

Before Emma could respond, Lyssa hung up.

Emma sighed. Why did she agree to a second visit tomorrow when the art center would be so busy? *Did* she agree? She should have said no. Wouldn't dinner tomorrow evening be enough family time for one day?

Feeling she'd been railroaded but not sure how, Emma opened her text app to erase Lyssa's earlier messages. Her thumb paused over *Confirm delete?* and she remembered what was tickling her memory about cell phones.

Texts and calls didn't automatically disappear if you lost your phone. There were lots of ways to save the data or transfer it to a new phone.

A few days after the accident, Emma's father bought her a new smartphone, trading the old Connecticut number for an Asheville one, and listed it under his name to protect her privacy. When the doctors brought her back to consciousness several weeks later, all her messages were waiting for her. Her father played the voicemails on speaker and read her messages and emails out loud.

Lyssa claimed she'd lost her phone that weekend, too. Wouldn't the replacement process have been similar? In Canada she'd have changed carriers and maybe bought a prepaid. She could have done a SIM card swap or downloaded data from the cloud and set up call forwarding. But she'd abandoned her contacts as well as her messages, left Uncle Jerry to close the old account and pay off the balance.

The larger question remained: Why did her cousin run away? Emma wasn't convinced it was only to find her mother. Maggie had spent a lifetime disappearing and reappearing from their lives.

She tried to put herself in her cousin's place. It was probably money. Lucy had borrowed money from Uncle Jerry for tuition, the Subaru, her rent, and pretty much everything else. Some of that was a gift, Emma knew, but some was a loan because Jerry didn't want to play favorites with his nieces. He'd been willing to help but he'd also expected Lucy to get her degree and pay back at least a portion of the loan after she started working.

Then Lucy quit school. She had no degree, no job, and no way to pay off the debts. The obvious solution, from Lucy's perspective, was to follow Maggie's lead and just disappear.

Why was she back now? Money again. Jerry was dead, so the debt was erased. She'd returned to see what she might gain from her uncle's considerable estate.

Emma thought the money angle made perfect sense according to Lucy-logic. But the truth hurt because for eight years Lucy hadn't cared enough about Emma or anyone else to get in touch.

***

Three hours later Emma jerked awake, gasping and clawing her way up from an indistinct terror that threatened to swallow her whole.

Twelve-ten a.m. She fought her way out of the sweaty, twisted sheets and switched on her bedside lamp. Curling tightly into herself, she heaved air into her lungs and waited for her pulse to quiet.

She hadn't had one of these paranoia episodes in months. Not a fully fleshed nightmare but more like an overwhelming sense of impending catastrophe, settling like a blanket of fog in her mind. Sometimes she heard it as an indistinct voice, a sentient alien muttering about doom and destruction. When she woke, the whispers fell silent but she knew the cloud would hover for hours.

She preferred the hallucinations. Jonah helped her identify those, years earlier. He was all about knowing and naming things. "Know them to control them," he said.

Some hallucinations occur as you're waking up, he told her. Those are probably a side effect of the anti-seizure drugs. They can seem very real when they appear but they'll probably fade when you're fully awake. If you forget your epilepsy meds, you can experience apparitions even when you're fully awake. Or you might feel only a vague paranoia, which can be sparked by a specific trigger like emotional stress, alcohol, and strong coffee.

She'd become adept at running her own reality checks. She knew she sometimes perceived images, voices, and odors that other people couldn't detect. A few months earlier while she was washing lettuce in the sink, the voice of her fourth-grade teacher reminded her to turn in her homework. Twice last spring she'd smelled dogshit and saw a yellow Labrador lying on the braided rug in the living room. The odor and the yellow dog faded a few minutes later, but the memory lingered.

In the months right after the accident, Emma's mother appeared almost daily in her hospital room. She usually stood next to the bed, dressed in her red ski suit with snow goggles pushed up like a headband and ice crystals in her long dark hair. *Come with me to the bunny slope*, her mother said. Pointing to a second pair of skis leaning against the wall.

When Emma told the nurses she'd seen her mother, they explained how hallucinations occur. Of course you miss your mother, they said. But she died years ago. It's not real. Send it away. Emma didn't want to send her mother away because if she lost that sense of loss, who would she be?

Her mother was always welcome, but the nightmares were terrifying and all too real.

Her mind skidded past those now, unwilling to dwell there and maybe summon the demons. Unable to sleep, she threw off the sheets, straightened her nightshirt, and walked barefoot downstairs to check on her father.

He slept peacefully, cannula in place and oxygen puffing quietly. No signs of distress, no need for the bucket and the towels, folded neatly on the nightstand. Emma wanted to smooth back the pale rats-nest of his hair but feared waking him, so she returned to her room.

On the top shelf of her closet, pushed far to the back behind the winter blankets, was a sturdy banker's box. She hadn't opened it in years.

It wasn't heavy. She pulled it down and set it on her bed, then used a dirty sock to wipe a film of dust off the lid. The half-dozen manila folders were neatly labeled in her father's precise engineer's writing, the same all-caps printing that he'd used for three decades to identify boundaries and easements on plats and surveys.

The POLICE REPORTS folder contained a dozen documents: Accident reports, witness and first responder statements, a summary of items logged as evidence.

She skimmed the initial incident report, awkwardly written and heavy on dry facts. "At approximately 4:30 p.m. on Sunday November 19 2015 the driver of Vehicle #1 was proceeding in a southerly direction along the private road identified as Juniper Springs Drive. The driver of Vehicle #2..."

It was a "private road?" More like a cowpath. Did she ever know its name? She didn't recall a sign. Most of the time they just called it the driveway, though after one rainy week in early summer, Lucy had referred to it as "that fetid canal of fucking potholes."

The report described how a Miata convertible driven by Emma Gillen, no passengers, was heading downhill when it encountered a fallen tree on a blind curve. A second vehicle, a Dodge van driven by Christine Garrison and carrying two passengers, approached from the opposite direction. The precise sequence of events was unknown, but it was determined that the vehicles collided. The unpaved roadbed, weakened by several days of heavy rain, collapsed. Both vehicles fell down the slope and rolled several times, striking trees and boulders and each other before coming to rest in a ravine a hundred and twenty-three feet below.

Next was a statement by Ms. Garrison's fiancé Gordon Hanks, an unemployed construction worker, who affirmed that Ms. Garrison took their daughters, four-year-old Amber and two-year-old Destiny, to an afternoon playgroup at a local church while he remained home with her two older children. He called the police to report them missing shortly after seven p.m. when they failed to return with the KFC that Mr. Hanks asked her to pick up for their dinner. By then, it had been dark for almost two hours.

The mountain search-and-rescue team reported finding them at nine-forty. Christine and her daughters were pronounced dead at the scene, while Emma was airlifted to the level-one trauma center in Charlotte.

The next folder contained a short statement from Lucy Harnett, housemate and cousin of Ms. Gillen. Ms. Harnett said she'd been at their home that evening, working on an art project while waiting for her cousin to return from shopping. A little before ten p.m., she noticed headlights and vehicles on the road. She walked down the road to learn what was happening and was intercepted by a deputy on an all-terrain vehicle. She told him she was worried about her cousin, who hadn't returned from shopping. The deputy took her back to the house and questioned her. When did the Miata leave the cabin, where was it heading, were there any passengers? Did she try to call anyone? No, Ms. Harnett said, no one. She'd lost her phone earlier that day and their house had no landline.

An investigator's report dated three days later stated that Ms. Gillen remained in a coma and was thus unable to provide details of the crash or the events leading up to it. Additional notes indicated that she'd remained comatose at two weeks, three weeks, and four weeks post-accident.

After a "thorough investigation," the final report concluded that no one was at fault. No charges were filed against the surviving driver. Case closed.

Reading this now, Emma felt the familiar knot of guilt lodge in her chest. She clutched the small stack of folders in both hands and willed some fresh insight to reveal itself.

Nothing came. The only new memories she'd recovered in eight years had surfaced this morning at the café: Lucy sketching, the text from Maggie. The broken collarbone and the trip through the storm to Mission Hospital.

Emma held on to these fragments now like rare jewels. What other memories of that day could be unlocked? If there was a key, Lucy probably held it.

SIXTEEN

First came the slow tilt and the rumble of rocks and earth...

No! This time will be different. I can stop this, I can re-write the narrative.

A hollow place opened...there was a long slide and that sickening first flip... rocks trees metal... Someone was screaming. Children were screaming.

... alone again in the darkness...

Not alone! There was someone—

People died.

It was still my fault.

Wasn't it?

SEVENTEEN

Saturday morning, nine a.m. Emma sat at the kitchen table and stared at her laptop screen, fighting to stay awake.

Waiting for the signs. Checking herself for the tingling premonition that signaled a seizure, an inner electrical storm that would send her brain into overdrive.

Her last small-scale seizures, what the doctors called focal partials, had occurred more than three years ago, but she well remembered the auras that preceded them.

The warnings often arrived first in her mouth and nose: a vile taste of rotting fish, a whiff of sewer gas. Then she'd have a vague impression of dread or fear, sometimes combined with a sense of déjà vu. Last night, she'd felt the dread and the déjà vu but she couldn't recall any nasty tastes or smells.

Her brain was an unreliable trickster.

The fear and the déjà vu were entirely logical because her car *did* fall off a cliff. She'd relived that nightmare many times. It was her own private hell, the worst *Groundhog Day* imaginable, because she could never change the outcome.

If the seizures returned she'd have to face another round of doctors and tests and new medications. Not allowed to drive until the electrical storms were brought under control.

This morning she'd moved like a robot. Fed and walked Teague, showered and dressed, helped her father get dressed. Checked his vitals, made his coffee, set out juice and cereal, brought in the *Globe*. Texted Jonah, asking him to have Chaz feed the hens and open the coop.

She should be at the barn now, helping their team on what was supposed to be Stonefall's busiest Saturday ever, but merely walking across the road now felt impossible.

And what was she thinking, rejecting Raylene's offer to stay last night in case her father got sick? She shivered and hugged herself.

"Mornin, Emma. You doin okay?"

Emma blinked back to awareness as Raylene pulled out a second chair.

"Y'all're lookin worn slap out. My daddy would say you was rode hard and put up wet."

"I feel like a Zamboni."

Raylene usually smiled at Emma's verbal slips but not this time. "Zamboni for zombie?"

Emma nodded wearily.

"What do y'all need me to do? Can I call Jonah? Leastways let me check your pulse." She held Emma's wrist in cool brown fingers and placed her other palm on Emma's forehead.

"Pulse is good. You're feeling a little warm. Any funny smells, flashing lights? You took your meds, yes? You ate some breakfast?" Raylene peered closely at Emma's eyes.

Emma kept her gaze steady. "No smells, no lights. Yes, took my meds. Gab... gaba-pentin and...that other one. Juice and an egg." That was sort of true, though she hadn't finished the egg. "Have you seen Dad?"

"He's lookin better than you this morning, out on the deck with his *Globe* like always. He's half-done with the crossword and that's a good sign. I plan on bringin him to the barn later. Get him out and walkin some. How'd you sleep?"

"Not good. Bad dreams," Emma admitted. She yawned, then tried to swap the yawn for a smile. "What's the nurse's advice?"

"What your daddy always tells me. Castle early, connect the rooks, hold the center of the board. Seriously, I think you just need a nap and a day off. Jonah can take care of things today. I'll give him a call, okay? You go on upstairs and lie down. Anybody come to the door, I'll deal with it. Teague and me."

Upstairs seemed far away but achievable. Half an hour, that's all she needed.

***

The art center was still half an hour from opening when Lyssa parked her Mustang at the back edge of the hayfield, behind a food truck advertising smoked trout and gluten-free tacos. Instead of joining the early-bird visitors hovering near the barn, she traded strappy sandals for old sneakers, tucked her blond hair under a straw fedora, and turned south along the road.

Would anyone recognize her or ask why she was wandering in the woods? It didn't matter. She just wanted to spend a little time alone, getting reacquainted with her family's farm. That's what she'd say if anyone asked.

She'd forgotten how far it was from the barn to the orchard. Half a mile at least, a solid ten minutes along the road or fifteen minutes on the winding woods trail behind the house. She walked it both ways, first along the road in warm sunshine and then back through the woods in cool shade. The trail was wide, smooth, and deeply shadowed beneath the dense canopy of trees. At night, a flashlight would be essential.

When she'd finished her hike to the orchard and back, the barn was open so she went inside, curious to see if the classroom and studios were occupied. She caught a glimpse of Felicia in the gallery and heard people moving upstairs in the loft, but the main hall and classroom were empty.

Where was Emma? It didn't matter, they'd speak in an hour or so. Lyssa already knew what she wanted to say.

Outside again, she wandered through the sculpture garden and trailed behind a cluster of British tourists. She smiled along with them, admiring the outdoor artworks. As a group, they all tipped their heads back to stare up at the long, clean lines of the huge barn's roof and cupola, broken only by a few small cameras and the music system's speakers, mounted unobtrusively beneath the eaves.

As she strolled, Lyssa hoped someone *would* recognize her as belonging here. This place was beginning to feel like home the way it never did when she was a child.

***

Emma woke two hours later from a dreamless sleep with her head mostly clear. She splashed water on her face and hustled across the road to find that she'd missed absolutely nothing.

The gallery and studios had opened on time. In the hayfield, cars were parked in orderly rows near the taco truck and Vivaldi played brightly over the outdoor speakers. Visitors strolled and chatted as a cluster of small children, mostly girls, hovered near the pony paddock, oohing and aahing over Frodo and Sam.

Today's gallery opening was clearly trending successful. Relieved, Emma settled herself in the office and pulled up the schedule for their next show, Art in Autumn, three weeks away. She sighed over the ambitious scope of the five-day event. Studio tours, live music, workshops, nature tours, expanded gallery hours. Fifty new works to be installed indoors and out, on top of what they'd just brought in for the current weekend. They may have set the bar a little high. She might need her cousin's help, after all.

The screen door creaked open and Jonah leaned in from the rear deck. "Hi. Seen any gum erasers? I bought a new box and now I can't find them."

She pointed to a cabinet by his left shoulder.

He gave a self-deprecating eye-roll. "Any closer, it woulda bit me." He pulled his glasses off and made a show of polishing them on the tail of today's shirt, a faded aloha print in green and white monstera leaves.

"Jonah, help please." Emma held up a paper template and two glossy photos. "Which image should I use for this postcard? It should be one of Harry's, but—the lady on tiptoes or the triangle mobile?"

"The shining woman." He stepped closer and tapped a photo. "No contest. It's his best work."

"It's beautiful, isn't it?" She looked again at the image.

The steel figure on her pedestal of rough-cut black granite stood nearly seven feet tall and weighed almost three hundred pounds but looked almost weightless, an elegant abstract figure of a slender woman stretching skyward in a joyous defiance of gravity.

"Done." Emma clicked *Save* on her postcard files.

Lyssa appeared in the front doorway. "Hey cuz, are you ghosting me? You ignored my texts."

She'd traded yesterday's urban couture for off-rack jeans, a black cropped tee, and worn sneakers. Tiny gold studs in her ears, no other jewelry. Today her eyes were their natural steel blue, not that artificial teal.

Reading her audience, Emma thought. *Blending in.* "Sorry," she said. "Didn't have time to answer."

Jonah tucked the box of erasers in his shirt pocket. "Hi, Lyssa. I'm on my way out. Use my chair if you want."

When Lyssa made no move to take up his offer, he shrugged the tiniest bit and left by the back entrance, catching the screen door before it slammed.

"He's kinda cute," she observed lazily. "Sort of a supersized Tevya from *Fiddler on the Roof*. Clean him up, slim him down.... But he's a little old for you, don't you think?"

Emma sighed. "Do you still see everyone as a…hook-up? Jonah's my friend."

"Joking. It's cool. Whatever."

"He used to be my therapist. He's a big reason I'm here."

"Hey, don't go all defensive." Lyssa raised a well-shaped eyebrow. "Do you mean 'here' like still-alive-here? Or 'here' as in here-at-Stonefall?"

Emma stared at her computer screen. "Both."

"He looks more like a fucking bouncer than a therapist. It's like he's protecting you. Felicia, too. Apparently she's decided I'm not a 'real' artist." Curled-finger air quotes for emphasis. "I don't think she was impressed with the work I was doing in Calgary."

"But you aren't anymore, are you? A real artist."

Lyssa stiffened.

Shit, Emma thought. *Where did that come from? I didn't intend to say that. Did I?*

The unfiltered comment just popped out, mirroring Lucy's habit of peppering everything with casual insults. But that was Lucy's style, not Emma's.

She raised her eyes to meet her cousin's furious stare. Bit her lip and looked down again. "Sorry, that was mean."

Lyssa's eyes narrowed, flat and hard. Then, just as swiftly, she pushed herself away from the door frame and moved in three quick strides to plant a hand on a stack of books as she leaned over Emma's shoulder.

"Whatcha doing?" Lyssa said. "Huh? Can I see?" Hovering like a little kid, her smoky breath warm on Emma's cheek. The playful move might have worked as comic relief except it wasn't playful or comic and Emma could barely breathe with her cousin so close.

She scooted her chair sideways and angled the laptop away from Lyssa's view.

"It's just a postcard." Emma tried to match Lyssa's fake banter. "Hey, cuz, give me some room. I need to back up these files."

Lyssa straightened and eased away. "A real postcard? Like, made from paper and mailed with a stamp? Wow. How last century."

Emma's eyes remained on her screen, looking at nothing. Her cousin had just delivered a message but what was it, a standard "fuck off" or something more sinister?

Lyssa shifted her attention to a shelf of twelve-inch-tall full-body manikins, stylized figures of black plastic mounted on acrylic stands. "One's missing a hand. And his genitals."

Emma focused on an answer. "Their hands are in a box. Tools and weapons, too. I don't know about the generals. Simon, he's a co-op member, teaches..." She paused to think and forced the right word into compliance. "Anime. He uses those for the poses."

"Simon's that skinny Asian guy, right? I think I saw him on Thursday evening. He should create an avatar based on you, Em." A sly smile. "I'll bet you're his favorite model."

"Sometimes Simon asks for something unusual." As Lyssa's smirk grew Emma added, "Once I held a skillet over my head for three minutes. He drew a four-armed space alien holding a weapon, sort of a cross between a club and a light saber."

"That's it?"

"That's it."

"So Simon *did* create an avatar of you. You should try him on, he's more than halfway hot."

"I'm sure his husband David would agree."

"Oh." Lyssa's grin vanished. "My bad, the gaydar's broken. You're not feeling thirsty for anyone?"

"Nope."

Emma closed her laptop. Enough, it was time to face the main topic head-on. "Okay. You wanted to talk about marketing?"

"Yeah, but first tell me about Stonefall. The farm never had a name when we were kids, so where'd that come from?"

And just like that, they were having a normal conversation. Emma gave herself a figurative shake.

"And Felicia said y'all've been working on this for years," Lyssa was saying, "but really it's only just opened, right? Catch me up."

That *y'all* is just wrong, Emma thought. Northerners shouldn't be playing around with y'alls. After a decade in Appalachia, had Emma herself become enough of a southerner to pass judgment? Maybe she'd inherited that along with the farm.

"Uncle Jerry named it," she began slowly. "All those rocks he pulled out of the fields. He said it was his...therapy, building walls. He was going to call it Stone Wall Farm but the first one...collapsed. He joked about it, the engineer whose wall fell down. So, Stonefall."

This was the longest speech she'd made in years. So far, so good.

"After the accident, Dad sold his house and business up north, and moved in here with Jerry. Then I met Jonah at Deerfield."

"What's that?"

"A nursing home. I was there for a year, in rehab. After the hospital. Jonah was the art therapist at Deerfield. Opening a co-op art center here was his idea." She paused to organize the words she wanted. "Using the barn for studios and a gallery, plus outdoor education and art-based therapy."

Lyssa shifted uncomfortably against the doorframe and tucked a strand of golden hair behind one ear. She circled one hand in a "hurry up" gesture. "Art therapy. You mean like basketweaving and adult coloring books?" Not even trying to hide her disdain.

"There's way more—" Why did Emma even bother? Lyssa wasn't really listening. "Like today, Jonah's doing a…directed-focus program with a group of kids who lost a teacher and two friends, in a school shooting. He's teaching them how to look for basic shapes when they draw animals. It helps them focus on something other than grief."

"Sounds boring. Sorry I asked." She ran an idle hand along a bookshelf, then noticed Emma's frown. "Hey, my bad. The farm, okay? Back to the farm."

"Jerry was already working with a land trust to protect it. He asked Mark Camerer to set up the funding."

"I remember Mark. The lawyer, right? He's helping you spend Jerry's money."

Emma frowned, then nodded. "When Jerry died—"

"Nerdy Jermy." Lyssa's laugh owned a mean edge. "But our uncle's company was a pretty big deal, wasn't it? I mean, his obit made *The New York Times*. They said he practically invented bar codes. He created a 'revolution in retail' and changed the whole fucking economy, right?"

"Jerry didn't invent bar codes. But he did make a new kind of scanner."

"Whatever." Lyssa peered into a tin can of broken crayons. "So he sold his wildly successful company and created Stonefall, then he died of a heart attack. Like, boom. While building a stone wall."

Emma shook her head but couldn't help marveling at Lyssa's ability to reduce their uncle's interesting, successful life to a brief cynical footnote.

Lyssa said, "He died in twenty-twenty, right? October."

"Yes."

"But then, the pandemic hit. Must've been tough, Zooming his funeral."

Emma bit her lower lip. "We tried to find you and Maggie. Again."

"Then it was just you and Frank. Living here, I mean."

"And Jonah. We kept working on the reservations."

"Renovations? Rejuvenations? Regurgitations? Oh, I get it. Restorations," she mocked. "What, I'm supposed to play twenty questions to figure out what you're saying?"

Slow down, Emma reminded herself. *Don't let her rattle you. Flinch and she wins.* She inhaled, exhaled, and inhaled again. "Jonah started the co-op in twenty-twenty. We opened the following summer, outdoors under a tent."

Lyssa fidgeted, touching the phone in her hip pocket. "Okay, on to marketing. Felicia said you need my help."

"Maybe," Emma said cautiously. "The arts council and the tourist bureau help a lot. *Our State* did a feature a couple of months ago."

"What's that?"

"A magazine. It's in print, and online. It's very popular."

"What about your SM?"

"SM?" Thinking *sadomasochism* but that couldn't be right.

"Seriously?" An eye-roll. "Come on, Em. Your social media, who does that?"

"I update the Stonefall web...site. And post on Facebook. We send emails. A news letter."

"Websites and newsletters? That's not SM. Facebook's bare minimum. You need to cover all the platforms, blogs and chat apps. Insta, Snap, TikTok. And X, though I'm really down on X right now."

"I— We're busy enough."

Lyssa threw her arms out, palms up. Her agitation said she needed to pace but there was no room in the tiny office. Squeezing behind Emma's chair, she pointed to the rear door. "Where does that lead?"

"The deck. It's sort of a ...balcony."

Lyssa opened the inner door and set the chunk of quartz against its base. "You need more air in here. It's claustrophobic."

Through the screen door, Emma could see a small slice of deck floor and a thin line of railing. Beyond was the far horizon, all hazy mountains and green trees against an impossibly blue Carolina sky.

Her pulse quickened. "Close it, please. It's...distracting."

Lyssa looked from the screen door to Emma and back again, her face quizzical. "Okay." She moved the doorstop rock outside onto the balcony, then closed both doors and resumed her spiel.

"You need *buyers*, not just wannabe scribblers who sign up for the old-farts' watercolor classes or the 'Hey kids, let's draw a chicken' hour. You need buyers with style and money. You need *busloads* of those people. Then you can—"

Emma rose abruptly and turned toward the main hall. "You're right, we need more air. Let's take a walk."

The small resistance felt good. She took the lead and left Lyssa to catch up.

EIGHTEEN

A sign on one of the gallery's glass doors noted the shop's hours and the usual rules: No food or drink, no photography, service animals only, no unaccompanied children.

Inside, several workers were taking advantage of a lull in the visitor traffic to re-stock. At the front counter, a boy in a blue baseball jersey fed paper into a printer. Two jeans-clad girls with identical high ponytails—one brown, one blond—were arranging ceramic sculptures and context cards on a wide shelf along the outer wall. They whispered to each other and snuck looks at the boy, who was apparently unaware that his man-bun was escaping its tether and falling apart on his shoulders.

Perched on a stepladder near the rear wall, a tall man in black adjusted a ceiling-mounted track light. His back was to Emma and Lyssa as he directed the beam at a scrap of blue painter's tape stuck to the white wall.

The only visitors were a fifties-something couple browsing a wall of misty mountain landscapes. They peered over bifocals, reading artists' bios and checking prices.

Lyssa paused by the counter. "Look, you've got a marvelous space here," she informed Emma. "But you need drama. More intrigue, some specific focal points. You need more *stories* here. We're still an oral culture as well as a visual one, don't you know?" She aimed her cellphone at the shelf where the ponytail girls were working.

"No photos!" Emma stepped forward to block her.

The three teens froze, sharing uncertain looks, and the man on the ladder turned to stare. Emma recognized Chaz.

At the back of the shop, a storeroom door opened.

"Hi," Felicia said. "Were you looking for me?" She saw the phone in Lyssa's hand, poised to take pictures. Her public-facing warmth evaporated. "Lyssa, photography's not allowed in here. That's standard gallery protocol. We've posted signs."

Eyes narrowing, Lyssa pocketed her phone and flashed her high-wattage smile. "Hey, Felicia. Emma was just telling me Stonefall's history. It's an awesome story, isn't it? Our uncle's vision for Stonefall. It's perfect for videos on Insta and Snap. I can promote the fuck out of this place."

She'd placed a slight emphasis on "our uncle."

"Videos?"

Emma bumped Lyssa's shoulder with her own. "Just some ideas Lyssa's got. Talk with you later."

As she hustled Lyssa out of the gallery, Emma glanced back through the glass doors. Felicia was gone and the teens were back at work. Chaz, however, was still staring at them. Who was he was watching, her or Lyssa?

In the parking lot, Emma kept her voice low. "Didn't you see the sign? No photos."

"No, I didn't see your stupid sign. And why can't I get video for my blog post? Everyone shoots video, all the time." She sulked. "Why are you being so pissy?"

"It's policy. People trust us to protect their work, and their privacy. And those kids? They're under eighteen, you need their parents' okay to take pictures."

"Seriously? It's a public event, right? Anyone can—"

"This is private property. You didn't even ask."

"I didn't think—"

"Yeah." Emma turned sharply, heading for the garden. Lyssa followed in irritated silence.

The wrought-iron gates stood wide, inviting visitors along a flagstone walkway into the landscaped grounds between the deck and the hayfield. Benches and birdbaths were set beside weeping cherry trees and beneath an arbor draped with wisteria vines. Violins played Vivaldi and butterflies swarmed a bed of lavender. Everything was warm and sunny or cool and shady exactly where it should be, with a backdrop of forested mountains.

"Oh!" Lyssa paused in the gateway, her sulk forgotten. "This is amazing. But isn't this where all the junk used to get dumped? Years ago, I mean. All the broken stuff, the dead tractors and old cars."

"The tractor graveyard. Engine oil, old batteries, lead paint. The EPA said it was a toxic waste site. It took forever to clean up. It's why Aunt Marisa made us stay away when we were kids."

"Yeah, I never listened. Remember when I got that horrible rusty nail stuck in my foot?"

"Your first piercing."

Lyssa was startled into an honest laugh. "Good one!" She licked a finger and mimed marking a point in Emma's favor. Then she turned slowly, arms spread wide in appreciation. "And now all this is— it's just beautiful."

They followed the sun-dappled flagstones through late-summer blooms of orange coreopsis and purple asters. Emma pointed out two of Harry's sculptures, a complicated mobile of copper triangles and a sundial of coiled aluminum that was shaped like a chambered nautilus.

At the center of a half-moon courtyard, they found the polished steel woman dancing on her black granite base, gleaming in the sun. A grove of Japanese maples and a pair of small stone benches flanked the sculpture.

"Wow. That's awesome." Lyssa pulled out her phone, then paused. "Um, can I?"

Emma nodded. Surprised and pleased because Lyssa had asked permission. *Progress? Maybe.*

Aloud she said, "Harry's cool, he doesn't mind photos and videos. But if you want to write about it, you should talk with him first. Make sure you get the details right."

"Has he named it? This piece?"

"No. We wish he would. It's featured in the ads for our October show."

"Isn't he that mega-hot babe magnet I saw on Thursday night? What's his background? Where did he go to school?"

"He didn't. He's mostly self-taught. He started in his dad's blacksmith shop, then worked in a small factory that makes custom car parts. His day job is fixing cars. His first pieces were made from ant mounds."

"Huh?"

"He collects old beer cans. Melts them and pours…that into a fire ant nest. The tunnels act like a mold. When it cools, he digs it up and washes it off. Mounts it upside down on a wooden base. It looks like coral."

"Yechh. That sounds totally grim. There's fried ants mixed in?" Lyssa sounded offended or disgusted, maybe both. "How can anyone call that art?"

Emma suppressed a shrug. "Eye of the… beholder?" She couldn't tackle *aluminum* but *beholder* sounded fine.

Lyssa looked again at the shining-woman sculpture, which bore no resemblance to an upside-down ant tunnel. "And now that guy's doing this?"

"Yes."

Lyssa turned away. "I want to show you something on my laptop. It's in the car." She waved her hand to the deck's broad patio. "Meet you up there, okay? Find us a table in the shade so we can see the screen."

"It's nearly two-thirty. I've got to—"

"Won't take a sec."

Emma sighed and climbed the half-dozen stairs to the shaded end of the deck beside the barn. Thinking she should have prepared an exit strategy, she pulled two chairs up to a small table.

Lyssa returned, flipping her laptop open as she sat. "So, let's start over. I promise not to be such a smartass."

"Can you do it in five minutes?" Emma said.

"Five minutes to not be a smartass? Absolutely. Look, here's my blog. It's called Lyssa comma Living Large. Just google it. All these posts link to my videos. There's like *dozens* of videos."

Click. "This shows how to decorate a small apartment in shades of gray, with crazy pops of bright yellow. The colors are from two years ago, but people still like it." Click, click, click. "Here's one we could use for Stonefall. Designing a room around a single big painting. See, a large piece doesn't have to sit on a big white wall. It can *be* the wall."

"People look at these?"

"Oh, absolutely! I've got almost three-K followers. They love my design ideas."

Emma wasn't sure but three-K didn't seem like a lot. "Our artists manage their own websites and blogs."

"We'll double-brand and cross-link everything. But to start with, Stonefall needs better branding. We'll need to work up a tag list. Like 'country boho chic' with an 'authentic southern' overlay. A little glam, but with a 'village vibe.'" Her plum-tipped fingers were busy, crooking all the air-quotes. "That's just a start, I'll come up with more. Then I'll pair the art with recommendations about finding one-of-a-kind furnishings from a local *brocante*. Then we'll get ad money, too."

"What's a broccoli cult?"

"Bro-*cahnt*." Lyssa gave a side-eye glance. "Are you making fun of me?"

"I'm not. What did I say?"

"Forget it. *Brocante* is French for a flea market or an antique shop. Asheville has dozens. See, you find your one-of-a-kind furniture piece, then you pair it with the perfect painting. Lots of paintings in your gallery are already trending impressionism or abstract. I can do a lot with that."

She frowned. "But *please* reassure me that no one's doing chainsaw carvings or those cringey signs that say, 'Almost Heaven' or 'Up the Creek and Down the Holler'—"

"Nothing like that."

"Well, that's a relief. So, you're probably wondering, if a platform like Instagram has billions of users posting all sorts of things, how do I even get my stuff noticed?"

Emma wasn't wondering anything like that. She was remembering that Uncle Jerry had been quite fond of the same country kitsch Lyssa was ridiculing, chainsaw carvings and barnboard signs proclaiming "You're Not in The Mountains, The Mountains are in You."

In the gardens below the deck, a pair of gray-blonde women in crop pants and sun visors paused by the copper sundial. More people gathered by the iron gates.

Emma cut into a spiel about advertising. "What does this have to do with art?"

"Zero, zilch, nada. This is brand-building. It's all about authority. Authenticity."

"You're saying Stonefall would be your client?" The sun was warm now. They'd lost their shade and were about to lose their privacy. Emma stood, wondering if she'd missed Jonah and his two-thirty pony-drawing group. She was also hoping Lyssa would move on to a wrap-up.

"Obviously. That's the whole point. You make the decisions about marketing, right?" Lyssa scowled, perhaps thinking that she'd wasted a great pearl on the wrong audience. "What the fuck, Mouse, are you even listening? You haven't heard a thing I said."

Emma flinched at the nickname. "I heard you." Not entirely true but close enough. She knew what she needed to say but it stuck in her throat.

She swallowed hard. "Look, I don't think we're ready for all this. And the co-op members have to weigh in on any changes to the marketing plans. If you write up a proposal, I'll bring it to the group. We'll see if it fits the plan. And the budget."

"What do you mean? You said it's your decision."

"Well, yes, but— Look I can't hire you just because you're my cousin. That's not the way we work. Give me a project proposal," Emma repeated, "and a breakdown of the costs."

She thought she'd held her ground pretty well. The fist behind her sternum eased its grip.

Lyssa snapped her laptop shut. "I can't believe this. All I'm asking—" She propped both elbows on the table and threaded long fingers through her cornsilk hair. A sheen of perspiration glazed her neck and cheeks.

Then her voice shifted again, swerving away from whatever she was about to say. Going smooth as glass on the surface but hinting at broken shards beneath. "You actually love this shit, don't you? Better living through art or therapy or whatever you call it. You must really love it, because it's not like you're making any money."

"That's not the goal. Making money."

"Yeah, because you don't have to. You and Frank aren't exactly hurting for cash, are you? Thanks to Uncle Jerry. So, Mouse, spill the tea. What's up with your live-model sessions? Posing nude." She made it sound vaguely dirty.

"Like I used to do for you. What's your point?"

"You're supposed to be in charge of this place. But you're not even an artist."

"Neither are you, right now."

Lyssa flinched. Her eyes sparked open, then narrowed to slits.

Emma stepped in quickly, trying to lessen the sting. "Artists need models. And Stonefall needs a bookkeeper, too. I feel useful."

"You feel useful?" Amusement combined with disbelief. "But you're way more than just the *useful* little bookkeeper, aren't you?" A lacquered fingertip twirled her rose-gold phone on the table. "You're the fucking landlords, you and Frank. And he's not exactly the picture of health so it's mostly you."

Lyssa exhaled a frustrated sigh. Emma smelled the warm cigarette breath and wondered where this was going. She was growing tired of Lyssa's verbal buckshot.

Lyssa raised her eyes to the gardens and the fields beyond, looking anywhere but at Emma. "Let's see. You have a committee that weighs in on marketing but someone has to do the actual hiring. That would be you, right?"

Emma nodded cautiously.

"And you're getting a grant from the state arts council. For marketing."

"A small one. Who told you about that?"

"You can use that for my contract, to start with."

"To start with?" Emma echoed, feeling slow and stupid because hadn't they just been through this? "I need your proposal—"

Lyssa scraped her chair back and stood. "Who else is going to fight off the social media trolls?" she said coolly. "Those assholes are gonna crawl out of the swamp again, you know they are. You need me, Mouse."

Emma's breath caught, her thoughts tangling. *Is this what we've been talking about? What did I miss?* A second thought surfaced: *She's right. She's the perfect person to go to battle when I need it.*

Lyssa closed her laptop with a snap and stood. She turned to gaze at the distant blue mountains, looking almost nostalgic.

"You need to remember, Emma, that Jerry was my uncle, too. This farm is just as much mine as yours."

The hairs on Emma's arms prickled. This wasn't nostalgia, it was an intractable determination to seize what her cousin believed she was owed.

Emma rose from her chair. "Are you still coming for dinner?"

Lyssa offered an eyes-only smile. "Of course, Mouse. I'll be back at six with a properly chilled sauvignon blanc. Something from Marlborough, will that do?"

Turning to push her chair in, Emma almost missed the look of contempt in her cousin's ice-blue eyes.

A few minutes later, the bruise-colored Mustang swerved out of the hayfield, fishtailing a little in the grass before catching traction on the pavement. It shot past the barn, brake lights flashing briefly as it veered around the gray pickup parked near the barn.

Chaz stood by the truck's rear bumper, his eyes tracking the Mustang. Then he continued toward the chicken coop, carrying a small box and a hammer.

He's fixing the fence, Emma thought idly as she walked back to the house. She hadn't noticed any holes in the chicken wire, but maybe Chaz saw a fox or a raccoon. It was a never-ending process on any farm, keeping the livestock in and the predators out.

What had Lyssa said? "This farm is just as much mine as yours."

Not according to their uncle. Jeremiah Gillen had been very clear about that.

NINETEEN

It was a little after five when Chaz set the tools back in his truck and wiped his hands on a rag, thinking that his first day at the new job went pretty good. He'd found his way around okay and hadn't broken anything. The visitors and the other kids working in the shop mostly ignored him and the work was easy enough.

First he helped Mr. Jacobs in the garden. Weeding, planting new shrubs, spreading fresh mulch. He spent the rest of the day in the gallery, adjusting lights and flattening cardboard and taking out the trash.

Now he needed to talk with Miz Weingardt. He went back into the main hall and waited a little way off as she locked the gallery doors.

She had a nice smile. "Hi, Chaz. You need something? You finding your way around okay?"

"Yes ma'am, I like the job. I think it's goin good. Though maybe I'll have to change my hours at Aldi. I been workin there on the weekends, night shift, but y'all are givin me lots of work too, so—"

He stopped and tried to rein in his thoughts. She smiled again and that encouraged him but he could feel his eyes wanting to roam the way they did when his mind raced and the words came too fast.

Start over, he told himself. *Go slow like Darren said. She's good people, she'll help you.*

He took a breath and steadied his gaze on her friendly dark eyes. "I got this letter. From a lawyer, I think. That's what Miz Buckner thought, too, though she didn't open it, a course, cause it's for me. She's my foster mom. Used to be, I mean."

He whooshed air out through his mouth and that seemed to help. "Miz Buckner took a while to get it to me because I ain't livin there no more.

She kept forgettin about it and then she had to look me up in the system. To find where I live, I mean. She brung it over—brought it—last evenin. I read it but I cain't figure it out. My friend Darren, he's in the Army now but his older brother went to the school where y'all used to work? I texted him and he said you'd be good to talk to. About the letter."

"Let's sit over here, Chaz." She indicated a church bench beside the long wall.

All day in the shop, she'd worn platform shoes and a green turban wrap over her piled-up box braids, which added inches to her height. But now she kicked off her shoes, leaving her small brown feet bare. The mass of black and gray braids hung loose and he saw she was tiny, nearly a foot shorter than him. She wore black leggings under a floaty green dress, and he liked the way she folded down gracefully onto the bench and tucked her feet underneath. She looked relaxed, just a normal adult but easier to talk to than most. He wished she'd been *his* school counselor.

He sank onto the bench beside her and held out his letter. First he'd thought it was a scam. He was going to throw it away, but then he read it again and wasn't sure. He'd folded and unfolded it so many times, it was creased and a little smudged.

"I guess I know what it says," he told her. "I just don't know what I'm supposed to do, Miz Weingardt."

She read the letter. Raised both eyebrows and read it a second time.

"You're right. It's from a lawyer," she said slowly. "Mark Camerer. It says he has information about a special scholarship. Money for college."

"But—"

"Have you called him? The lawyer?"

"No ma'am." His neck grew hot. "But see, I can't go to college. I almost didn't finish high school. They said I had a coupla disabilities, ADHD and somethin else. They said I was lucky to graduate, period." He stared at the letter in her hand. "It's gotta be a mistake. This is for someone else."

She looked again at the name on the envelope, then the letter. "Charles W. Robberts. That's you?"

He nodded, still feeling lost.

"Well, I think you should call and ask what this is about." She must have seen his alarm because she added, "Would you like me to call him for you? I know Mark, he's also the lawyer for Stonefall. We can sit together and I'll put him on speaker, or we'll do a Zoom. I'll see if Monday morning is okay. Maybe ten o'clock? If that's okay with you."

Chaz wanted to say yes, thank you, but his throat wasn't working right so he merely nodded again.

Miz Weingardt ducked her head and stage-whispered to him, like she was sharing a secret. "Monday's supposed to be my day off. But I'm planning to come in for a few hours, maybe find the time to paint. Don't tell anyone, they'll make me dust shelves or something."

He managed a weak smile. "You'll call him for me?"

"Absolutely. I'll send him a text and we'll get this sorted out. Do I have your permission to snap a picture of the letter?" She unfolded her legs from the bench and fished a phone out of a pocket in her green dress. He flattened the much-creased paper against the wooden seat so she could snap a photo.

She said, "Chaz, are you working at Aldi tonight?"

"Yes ma'am. My regular Saturday night shift, eleven to seven. Mostly I stock shelves. Sometimes I drive a truck, make deliveries."

"You look exhausted. Do you want me to give Aldi a call? I can let them know you're taking the night off so you can get some rest. It must be tough, working two jobs. You're working for us now, Tuesday through Saturday, right? That's the trouble with a place like this, it's always open on weekends. Trust me, it'll be easier in the winter. Not so busy with tourists."

She said it like she expected him to be here long-term. That was good news no matter what else happened.

"No ma'am, I'm okay. I'll sleep a few hours before I go in tonight. And tomorrow, too, after I get off. Then I'm fixin to go visit my sister Jessie in the afternoon at Miz Buckner's."

"That's important, spending time with family."

"Yes, ma'am." It was easier now to say what he'd failed to say earlier. "Thank you, Miz Weingardt. It's kind of you, helpin me with this."

TWENTY

In lieu of ice cream, Lyssa asked for a copy of her uncle's will.

Their dinner so far had been a reasonable facsimile of a pleasant family reunion, propped up with smiles, air kisses, and fond remembrances of dear old Uncle Jerry and funny old Aunt Marisa. Emma complimented Lyssa on her dress, a pale gray mini that coordinated well with her emerald ring, gold hoop earrings, and perfectly tanned legs. Frank asked what Calgary was like in the winter and Lyssa commented favorably on the design of Stonefall's gardens. For most of the evening, Emma played the role of unobtrusive host as she tossed salad, grilled trout, filled water glasses, and watched her father become reacquainted with his prodigal niece. No one spoke of Emma's accident or Lyssa's divorce or Frank's illness.

"Here you go," Frank said. "Is one copy enough?" He set the will on the table, face-down, beside his niece's wine glass.

Ignoring it, Lyssa lifted the bottle of sauvignon blanc toward her uncle. He stared at it for a second or two longer than Emma would've liked before shaking his head. Shrugging, Lyssa emptied it into her own glass.

Lyssa sat back and folded her hands on the table, waiting. Frank countered by removing his glasses and polishing them on his napkin. Emma couldn't be still so she removed a bowl of mostly uneaten potato salad and stacked plates on the counter. No one smiled.

Frank resettled his glasses and cleared his throat. "First, Lyssa, I want to say that I had no hand in writing my brother's will. I was his executor but I never saw this until after his death."

"A heart attack, right?" Lyssa said. "While he was working on the farm, doing what he loved."

He ignored or didn't hear the sarcasm. "There's not much to it. The will is basically a pass-through document. The assets went into three trusts, plus Jerry's foundation."

Lyssa gazed impassively at Frank, blue eyes unblinking, and waited for more.

"That other clause— well, if he'd shown it to me before he signed it, I'd have asked him to reconsider."

Wrist-deep in soapsuds at the sink, Emma tried to catch her father's eye. *You're saying too much, Dad. Let Mark talk with her, he's the lawyer.*

Frank reached across the table and nudged the will with one long finger, pushing it closer to his niece.

Lyssa finally picked it up and flipped quickly through the pages. "Do you have Uncle Jerry's earlier will? I think he made at least one other."

"No. Mark may have it. I believe there was one from when he married Marisa, and then an update he made after her death. I never saw those, either. This is the only one that matters, of course."

"Maggie said when I was six or seven, they wanted to adopt me. Jerry and Marisa."

His forehead creased. "Yes, we all talked about it. Jerry and Marisa drew up the papers, but then Maggie changed her mind." A pause. "What are you asking?"

She stared back silently.

Emma broke the pause by drying her hands and moving to stand by her father's shoulder. He'd gone a little pale, so she'd brought his portable oxygen pack from the mudroom and helped him position the cannula.

With her cousin and uncle's attention elsewhere, Lyssa fidgeted. One plum-tipped finger tapped the table as her eyes skimmed over the papers in front of her.

The will was only five pages long. It divided Jeremiah Gillen's considerable assets among four beneficiaries: his private foundation and three trusts, one each for Emma, Frank, and Stonefall Farm. The will also named Jeremiah's niece Lucy G. Harnett as the recipient of a private loan "for college tuition and related expenses." It confirmed that upon his death any unpaid portion of this debt was to be forgiven.

The kicker was on page three, where Jerry specifically denied his sister Margaret and her daughter Lucy from receiving any additional benefits from his estate.

When Frank's oxygen was flowing steadily and the color returned to his face, Lyssa raised cold eyes to her uncle's warm ones.

He spoke gently. "You're welcome to call Mark, of course. He took us through probate and he's the registered agent for the trusts. He was also your uncle's closest friend."

Lucy shoved her chair back hard from the table. She started to rise, then changed her mind.

"Actually, Uncle Frank, I got a copy of this from the county ages ago. What I really need is the trust documents. That's where the assets are listed, right? What did you and Emma get, ten million each? Twenty million? Jerry sold his company for more than ten times that, didn't he?"

Frank's head jerked as if he'd been slapped and the cannula dropped from his nose. Emma slid into the next chair to help fix it back into place.

Frowning, he spoke around his daughter's hands and the tube. "You already saw the will? Why didn't you say so?"

Lyssa shrugged. "I wanted to hear what you'd say about what dear Uncle Jerry left me. Which was fucking *nothing*."

She shoved her hair back, then shook her head slightly so the strands fell smoothly into place. Looking furious but also controlled, almost regal.

Frank's eyes narrowed. "When did you learn about Jerry's death?"

Lyssa held his eyes but fiddled with her emerald ring, twisting it around her finger. "About two years ago. Does it matter?"

"Why didn't you call?"

"Your phone number got changed, right? From Connecticut to here. Really, though, it was easier just to visit. So I did, as soon as I could."

Emma couldn't help but marvel at that masterpiece of a non-answer, in which her cousin managed to put the responsibility on her uncle for changing his phone number.

Frank shook his head, unable to track his niece's logic.

Emma couldn't stay silent any longer. "I'm trying to unpack this, Lyssa." She spoke slowly, feeling her way with small, simple words. "You went online and got a copy of the will, which is public. But the trust papers are not public. Which is why you want those now." She really hoped she'd said *public*, not something else.

Lyssa glared from her pushed-back chair.

Her dad picked up the thread. "Why didn't you call Mark, if you had questions? His number's on the will."

Now Lyssa's eyes skidded away. "I didn't think of that. I've been pretty busy with my own shit."

Emma struggled to keep her face neutral. *Liar. You don't want to talk with Mark. You're going straight for dear old Uncle Frank. He's the sympathetic one.*

She was about to speak again but Frank raised a hand.

"Lyssa." His voice sharpened. "What Jerry left you wasn't *nothing*. He gave you a car, paid your tuition, and covered your living expenses for years, even though the adoption never went through. I don't know how much it was, but I can guess. A hundred thousand? A hundred and fifty?"

His voice softened. "Did you know Jerry hired a private investigator to find you? Monitoring all the missing-person sites, Canadian and American. Contacting hospitals and police, posting on social media.

"He looked for three years. Then he changed his will because you abandoned Emma when she needed you. When *we* needed you. But you clearly didn't want to be found."

"And my mother?" Lyssa's words fell into the silence, brittle and bitter. "Why was she cut out?"

"Maybe for the same reason. When Jerry died, Mark and I tried again to find you because we felt you should know. But it wouldn't have changed anything, Jerry's will was probated according to his wishes. Your debt was canceled whether we found you or not."

He licked dry lips and removed the cannula to sip water. He was looking tired now, his eyes rimmed with red. He touched his mouth with a napkin and tucked the oxygen tube back in place.

Lyssa crossed her arms, sulking now. "What about the foundation? There's got to be money there. Uncle Jerry gave away *millions*."

Emma flared. "There's no reason—"

Frank cut her off, but gently. "Jerry created that foundation more than a decade ago to support his favorite causes—art, wildlife, education. Some of that money comes to Stonefall, yes, but we have to apply for grants like anyone else. Is that what you're asking?"

She didn't respond.

"I'm the foundation chairman," he explained. "One of nine board members, all professional people that Jerry selected. You're welcome to check out the tax returns on GuideStar. That's all public, totally transparent."

"But the farm—"

"Is owned by the Stonefall Trust. It's in a conservation easement so it can't be sub-divided or developed." His voice was growing hoarse. "Five trustees manage it. Mark, Emma, me, and two officers from the land trust."

"What about the family trusts? Yours and Emma's."

He sat back. "Those are none of your business."

"Well, then." Lyssa stood. "I'm done for tonight. Thanks for dinner, Uncle Frank." She did not attempt to disguise the sarcasm.

Emma picked up the will and followed her cousin into the living room.

Lyssa paused with the front door half open, one hand splayed on the side jamb. "Well, that could have gone better," she said lightly. "But hey, cuz. Let's set all this stupid family stuff aside. I'm gonna do exactly what you asked, okay? Put that marketing proposal together. So prepare to be impressed. I'm tied up tomorrow and Monday, but we should get together on Tuesday."

There it was again, her cousin's specialty. Topsy-turvy topic-shifting baked into an emotional taffy-pull. Emma wanted to yell "No!" and slam the door on Lyssa's fingers.

Instead, she held up the will. "You want this?"

"Nope. I already have everything I need."

As Emma locked the door behind Lyssa, Frank appeared in the arched doorway between kitchen and living room. He was breathing heavily and leaning on the arms of his walker, the oxygen pack slung over one shoulder.

Emma removed an issue of *Scientific American* from her father's recliner and powered on the compressor so he could switch his oxygen supply from the backpack to the floor device.

She heard a muffled *woof* and remembered that Teague was still closed up in her father's room, where she'd put him hours earlier to avoid an encounter with Lyssa.

Released, the small dog raced to the recliner. He leaped, circled, and lay down with his small body fitted into the contours of Frank's lap.

Her father rested a hand on Teague's shoulders and sighed. "What the hell was that all about? She's changed a lot."

Emma sagged into the sofa cushions. How to explain? "Not really," she began carefully. "You never spent as much time with her as I did, when we were kids. She's always been difficult. Mandible live." She felt a profound tiredness flood in. "No, that's not right." She hoped she hadn't said *mani-pedi* or something equally stupid.

"I think you mean manipulative?"

"Yes." She sighed. "It's tricky, isn't it? Talking with her. You think you're having one...conversation. But there's always a sub-text. She hears what she wants, ignores the rest. Sometimes she fakes an...emotion and watches your response, then says she's just joking. Or she turns it against you. Changes the facts and tells you her version. Pretty soon, you think her story's the right one. It wears you down so you just nod and go along."

"Gaslighting. Deny, distract, fabricate. Repeat."

"Yes. She's always been good at it but now she's better. Worse, I mean." She hesitated. "Do you want to talk more tonight or wait until tomorrow?"

"What else is there?"

"Just this. Uncle Jerry's death was late October. What day?"

"A Saturday."

"What date?"

He stared at the ceiling, thinking. "October twentieth. Almost three years ago."

"If someone wants to challenge a will, how long do they have? There's a statue of litigations, right?"

"Statute of limitations. It's three years from when the will goes into probate."

They fell silent. Frank played with Teague's ears and Emma gazed into a middle distance as they imagined what Lyssa might do to seize what she considered her rightful inheritance. And what might happen if she succeeded.

Emma said, "She's getting divorced. She needs money. And she seems to think Jerry gave us millions of dollars."

"Hah." Frank shook his head. "He gave most of his money to the foundation, ages ago. But I'm not sure how we can convince her of that. We are *not* going to open up the books just to show her." He sighed. "Anytime someone says 'trust fund,' people think it's got to be a *big* trust fund. Still, it doesn't seem fair, does it? I can give her something but—"

"No, Dad."

"She could stay here rent-free. Her old room's empty."

"I asked, she said no."

"She's smart," he suggested. "She can get a job."

"About that..." Emma explained Lyssa's request.

"What happened to joining the co-op? Getting back to her art."

"She's dropped that. Now she wants a job that doesn't even exist. I'm supposed to create it for her."

"Why does she think that?"

"Because she's family. Or because she's always been the boss of me." She flopped onto her back on the sofa and stared at the pebbled ceiling. She'd memorized its cracks long ago and they'd never bothered her before but now she saw the shabbiness of the house, its age and decline.

There was money in the farm trust that they could use for renovating and redecorating, so why did they never change anything? Because she'd never felt like Stonefall was really theirs. She and her dad were just stewards, not owners. *But isn't that true of everything? It's all temporary.*

She grabbed a sofa pillow and hugged it to her stomach, then let it slide to the floor. Teague raised his head from Frank's lap, following her with anxious eyes.

"Sorry," she said. "I didn't mean to dump that on you." She pulled her legs up, moving from flat on her back to curled on her side with hands together beneath her head like a child preparing for a nap. Teague dropped his head to his paws again as her father stroked his neck.

"Has Lyssa given you a project description?" Frank asked. "A scope of work? Ask her to write a grant application or give you a contractor's proposal, like anyone else."

"She's drafting a project proposal," Emma said grudgingly. "At least, she says she is. It may not happen. She's like a loose cabin."

"Cannon," he said automatically. "Well, maybe she can be useful. When you get it, let's all take a look. Who told her she'd be hired?"

"No one."

"Okay, that needs clarifying. But maybe we can help while she's figuring out what to do next. Give her a short-term contract, something that looks good on a resumé so she can apply for a job somewhere else."

He saw she was about to protest so he added quickly, "But only if she goes through the process like anyone else. And she should report to Jonah or Felicia, not you. Unless you'd like to be the boss of *her* for a change."

A half-smile tugged at Emma's mouth. Would that be so bad, a three-month marketing gig for Lyssa? Keep your friends close and your enemies closer. It might hold off a challenge to the will long enough for the statute of limitations to kick in.

Lyssa could keep tabs on the social media trolls. And maybe Emma could get a few questions answered about the accident.

Frank raised both hands to his temples and massaged gently. The oxygen pump whooshed and thumped in the silence.

"Headache? Or brain fog?" Emma said gently.

"Just tired." He paused. "Speaking of brain fog, have you mentioned medical issues to Lyssa? Anything that could suggest mental disability? Yours or mine, past or present."

"She knows I have a memory gap and I explained about mixing up words. I can't hide that." She thought back. "I told her you're going in the hospital Monday."

"That's okay, I think." He checked his watch. "Mark's plane should be somewhere over the Atlantic right about now. It'll be good to talk with him tomorrow night."

***

A few minutes after three a.m., Emma's cellphone came awake on her nightstand. Its volume was turned down and she was deep asleep. She never saw the pale blue glow or heard the soft pings that might have alerted her as the security cameras caught something on the prowl outside the Stonefall Art Center.

TWENTY-ONE

On Sunday morning, Emma hummed as she sliced freshly picked peaches and tried to remember the lyrics to an old Leonard Cohen song her mother loved.

Suzanne. Something something, tea and oranges from China.

When her father used to play it on his old Martin guitar, her mother always asked why the oranges had to come from China when there were perfectly good peaches growing every summer right outside their doorstep? So he changed the lyrics for her.

Kathryn drives you out to the swamp by the donkeys, he sang. *She feeds us grits and peaches that come from the Carolinas...*

Her mother preferred to be called Kit, but the song needed a name with two syllables. They took turns making the lyrics wilder and sillier until the three of them collapsed in giggles. Then her mother poked her father in the shoulder until he played the song properly, and they all sang together. Offkey, because no one could carry a tune.

Standing in the same kitchen now, paused at the sink with a knife and a peach in her hand, Emma realized she hadn't thought of *Suzanne* in years. She wondered idly where her father's guitar was, then dropped the knife and closed her eyes, feeling suddenly guilty.

No happy memories allowed.

Dear Chrissy, I'm so very sorry...

But nothing more came. She still had time. She'd finish it next week or next month and, having no place to send it, she'd tuck it away as always in her bedside table.

Emma opened her eyes to the cut-open peach on the drainboard and the knife in the sink. She rinsed both and resumed slicing small, neat chunks from the red-orange flesh. She poured boiling water over tea leaves and checked the fridge for her father's favorite Sunday breakfast, bagels with cream cheese and lox. Chopped onions, capers, lemon slices.

When she was certain her father was up and moving through his morning routine, she filled her mug with tea and joined Teague in the back yard. The little dog's extravagant beard and front paws were thick with damp garden soil. When he tried to plant his front feet on the knees of her jeans, she pushed him off with a laugh.

"You've been in the ash-pentagons again?"

He tilted his head and wagged his tail uncertainly, unsure if this was a compliment. Teague was a vegetable raider with a particular weakness for asparagus. Emma had installed a chicken-wire fence around the asparagus bed but the little terrier simply dug beneath it to pull out the entire plants, roots included.

She sat on the bottom step to check messages on her phone. Teague and his topsoil were banned from her lap so he rolled onto his back in the grass nearby and invited a belly rub. She scratched him gently with the toes of one bare foot as she scrolled and sorted messages.

Spam, spam, spam. Three wee-hour alerts from the security system but she didn't bother to open those yet. Those messages were common, as the cameras on the barn captured at least one visit from wildlife every night.

More spam. And another predawn motion alert from the cameras.

When Jonah and Frank first installed their security system, Emma carefully reviewed the new videos each morning. She liked to discover the nocturnal activity of deer, foxes, and raccoons. Occasionally, a coyote or bobcat came slinking through the gardens. Once in a while, a black bear strolled by, looking for unsecured pizza crusts and stale hamburger buns. The trash bins were kept under lock and key in the garden shed, but the bears were always hopeful.

A month after installation, the novelty of the overnight videos faded and now she often forgot to check the feed for a week or more. The cameras—five on the barn, two on the house, all hardwired into the monitoring service—continued working as designed, dutifully archiving the movements and sounds of people, animals, and vehicles.

When her father called to her from the kitchen, looking for a bread knife, Emma put her phone in her jeans pocket. She brushed off Teague's dirty feet and wiped his beard with an old towel, then went inside to help assemble breakfast.

Ten minutes later, she crossed the road to the barn, her thoughts shifting between her father's upcoming hospital visit and the previous night's unsettling conversation with Lyssa.

She froze mid-stride in the parking lot and stared. The beautiful wrought-iron garden gates, which should have been neatly chained and padlocked, looked like they'd been run over by a tank and left to hang, bent and twisted, on crooked hinges.

Her first thought was *car crash* and her second was, *But where's the car?* and then her throat caught in a small breathless whimper. Without breath, she was frozen but she was frozen anyway because it took a long minute to process what she was seeing.

There was blood, a lot of it. Splashed on the flagstone path, spattered on shrubs and flowers and a shattered birdbath.

Emma stumbled along the fence toward the gap where the gates should have been, automatically avoiding the smears of blood on the ground. She stopped at the open gateway to catch balance and breath.

Who did this? Are they still here?

Suddenly tasting fear like a copper penny at the back of her throat, she spun in place. Seeking a culprit or a threat or a witness.

She saw no one. Adrenalin easing, she tried to assess the damage but couldn't think what she needed to do.

Your phone. Get pictures.

Through the camera lens, the garden still looked like a slaughterhouse. Then she saw a gallon-size paint can beneath a weeping cherry tree and realized the blood wasn't blood, it was red paint.

Anger replaced fear because someone went to a lot of effort to destroy Stonefall's garden. And not only by smashing the gates and throwing paint in the bushes.

In the central courtyard, Harry's lovely steel sculpture on its black granite base was smeared with ugly red blotches. Someone had also attacked it with a sledgehammer or a wrecking bar, leaving wide gouges in both the statue and its stone pedestal. Nearby, the ground was pockmarked with hollows and divots as if the attacker tried to topple the sculpture, or wrench it from its base.

Emma felt her gut clench, shrinking to a safe corner where ugliness didn't exist. A familiar dark curtain loomed at the edge of her vision but she shook her head hard, willing it away.

Focus. Call Jonah, Felicia, Harry.

Finally she remembered to call the police.

***

Emma felt like she'd been shivering against the front of the barn for hours, but her phone told her the unmarked cruiser arrived in less than ten minutes.

"Good morning, ma'am. You're Emma Gillen? I'm Detective Sergeant Kendric Japanski, Bundison County Sheriff's Office."

Japanski? That's what it sounded like but the scowling brown-skinned detective was in plainclothes and she didn't see a name tag on his navy polo shirt. He pressed a card into her hand but she didn't think to look at it.

"You okay?" he added. "You think someone might still be here?"

She nodded yes to the first question and no to the second, not trusting her voice. She must have said something on the phone to the dispatcher, but now her voice refused to respond.

"You stay right here by my car," he said. "I'll take a look around, make sure it's clear." She was momentarily distracted by his voice, which was clipped and gruff and carried an unfamiliar accent. Far Eastern or Asian? Definitely not Southern.

Opening the car's trunk, he pulled on blue latex gloves and a service vest with a bodycam mounted on the chest.

Emma wrapped her arms around her own body and leaned uneasily against the passenger door of his cruiser, watching him walk slowly around the garden. He moved slowly, angling his body to capture the damage on video and snapping pictures with his phone as he scanned the scene. His right hand rested on the butt of the holster on his hip.

After the perimeter tour he moved into the garden, stepping carefully over the wrecked gates and paint splashes to photograph the paint can. He crouched beneath a weeping cherry tree, where he placed two cigarette butts into a paper evidence bag.

He returned with the paint can dangling from one gloved finger and nodded at the small camera on the nearest corner of the barn. "Your alarm, it's working?"

She nodded.

"But it didn't go off?"

"No." Her voice croaked. "I'd get a call."

"The cameras, how many do you have?"

Her shock must be easing because now she noticed his dark brown eyes, set wide beneath a low, broad forehead and a close-trimmed cap of jet-black hair. His was an old-young face, permanently creased and sharpened by worry.

She ran her tongue across her lips, trying to find moisture. "Five outside the barn. One on each corner…one on the long side.. by the deck." She wasn't sure the words were clear but he nodded and turned to look where she pointed, high up beneath the eaves of the barn.

"Some inside, too." She nudged her chin toward the house on the other side of the road. "And two there, where we live…my dad and me."

"Are they continuous feed or motion-sensitive?"

"Mosh-pen sensible." She hoped he wouldn't ask anything else that required a malaprop-likely answer. Where was Jonah?

He turned back to face her and now she saw the name on his vest, Kendric Szczepanski. She tried to remember how he'd pronounced it earlier but felt her larynx close up at the thought of all those consonants piling on top of each other. Pure alphabet soup. She fervently hoped she'd never have to ask for him by name.

His eyes crinkled the tiniest bit and her face warmed because she knew he'd seen her studying his name tag.

He said, "You should go through your video feed as soon as possible. There might be something useful, though the infrared isn't as good as daylight. Infrared's the nighttime mode," he added helpfully.

He'd closed the paint can in a carton marked Evidence and was closing the trunk of his cruiser as Jonah arrived.

"Son of a bitch!" He clambered out of his Sentra and stared at the smashed gates even as he moved to wrap a heavy arm around Emma's shoulders. His anger vibrated into her and she pulled back.

Jonah spun away from her and headed for the ruined gates.

Szczepanski moved quickly, meeting him head on and blocking his path. "Sorry, sir—"

"Goddammit, I have to see—"

Szczepanski raised his hands, palms out in a settle-down gesture. "Please. I need you to stay right here. I was just going to ask Ms. Gillen to let me in the barn. If you can do that for me—disarm the security system and open up the building—you and I can go inside. Look for a broken window, any signs of forced entry. See if anything's missing."

Tight-lipped and furious, Jonah tried to step around the detective.

"Jonah," Emma said sharply. "Jonah, please."

He stopped, shoulders sagging. He pulled out his phone, hands trembling, and found the security app. "Emma, are you okay to stay out here alone if I go in with him?"

She nodded and turned away, not wanting to watch him thumb in the code. On the third try, he succeeded.

The detective went in first, hand on his weapon again.

A soft voice breathed beside her.

"Oh my!" Felicia folded Emma into a full-body embrace. Relieved to have someone her own size to lean on, Emma returned the hug and they stood like that for several moments, holding each other up.

"Show me." Felicia kept a sympathetic arm around Emma's waist as they walked toward the smashed gates. The older woman was dressed for manual labor—or possibly battle—in an oversized straw hat and sun-faded tee shirt. She'd tucked a pair of leather gloves into the waistband of her jeans.

As they stood by the empty gateway, Felicia's eyes narrowed in confusion and sadness. "So what does someone gain from this?" she said softly, as if talking to herself. "Why go to all this trouble, to make something that's so beautiful, be all ugly? There's a whole lot of effort in that evil."

Rhetorical questions gave way to calculations. "Emma, that paint. Is it dry?"

"It must be. I saw the can, it's latex. The alerts came around three-thirty. Maybe four-five hours ago? I haven't looked at the videos yet."

"You call Harry? He's got to get here quick and figure out what needs to be done. See if he can save that sculpture."

"He's on his way."

"The rest of it, we can tackle ourselves if we get moving. Is that detective done out here?"

"I think so. He took a lot of pictures. He's inside now with Jonah." She hesitated. "What do you mean—tackle it?"

Felicia took Emma's shoulders in both hands. Her speech went inner-city Baltimore. Or as Felicia would say, Bawlimer.

"Hon, it's eight-fifteen on Sunday mornin. We gonna open at noon, right on schedule. But there's a lotta work to do."

Emma blinked. "For real?"

"For real, girl. That detective's job is to find the nasty piece of trash that did this. The rest of it's our job. You go call the insurance company. Find out what you gotta do to file a claim. Meanwhile I'm callin in the marines, everyone I can pull outta bed who doesn't mind gettin dirt under they fingernails on a Sunday mornin."

She waved a hand toward the garden. "Look, there's a lot of things that *didn't* get messed up. The punks didn't buy enough paint to get all of it. They only had a itty bit to throw around. So yeah, we'll open on time. We need a list. What can be replanted, what needs to be tossed. How much does a new birdbath cost? We need a load of mulch and a case of good old Dove dish soap. This is not my first time scrubbin off tags." She scoffed. "Hunh, latex? These're jes amateurs."

Emma was still stuck on the impossibility of opening in less than four hours. "But how—"

Felicia patted her shoulder. "Look. Those flagstones are set in sand, not cement. We'll scrub them or flip them over so the paint won't show. I'll buy a couple dozen potted plants, asters and chrysanthemums. Whites, yellows, purples. Those'll look good.

"And where's Harry? I don't want to just toss a tarp over his masterpiece and tell people to come back later. But I will if I have to."

Felicia tugged her hat lower over her tied-back braids and yanked the cord tight under her chin like a mid-fifties pint-sized warrior strapping on a helmet. She began making calls.

Jonah and the detective emerged from the barn.

"No sign of a break-in," Szczepanski told Emma. "If you can find anything on the videos, give us a call and someone will tell you how to upload it to us. You can email any photos you took, too."

She said, "What about fingerprints?"

"I've got the paint can and those two cigarette butts. If any prints turn up, we'll ask you to provide yours for elimination. But there's a lot of paint smear and they probably wore gloves. Same for the gate. It looks like they smacked that with a crowbar or a sledgehammer."

Jonah threw his hands up in frustration. "But why smash it open? They could've just climbed over."

"Maybe they were trying to steal that." He nodded toward Harry's sculpture.

"And when they couldn't get it out, they just smashed everything and threw paint around? How does that make sense?"

Szcsepanski sounded resigned. "Many things don't make sense, sir."

Emma asked, "What happens next?"

"We'll do everything we can, Ms. Gillen, to find out who did it." His voice turned apologetic. "I have to warn you, though, we're short-staffed. Unless an informant comes forward, the chances of finding out who did this are fairly slim."

Jonah bristled. "So this is what, just some random vandalism? I don't believe it." His voice rose. "That sculpture, that's an artist's sweat and tears. Why the hell was that attacked?"

"We take all crimes seriously, sir." The detective countered Jonah's anger with a practiced calm. "I understand you're upset. But please keep in mind, this is a property crime. A misdemeanor. No one's been injured. There's no swastikas or racist symbols, nothing to suggest a hate crime or a threat. That would bump it up and we'd get the state investigation team involved. But this? Probably kids getting drunk and bored on a Saturday night. They ride around daring each other to get wild, bust things up.

"And sometimes people destroy things just because they're pretty. They want to ruin what they can't have." His face softened and for a moment the surliness was replaced by sympathy.

Jonah's shoulders sagged. He rubbed a hand over his face.

Emma offered, "Maybe there's something on video."

"Maybe." The detective didn't sound hopeful. "Be sure to save any footage you think could be useful, but don't try to zoom in or edit anything. I'll call you after I've gone over it."

The radio on his shoulder squawked. "Sorry. I've got another call." To Jonah he added, "I'd recommend upgrading your security system. Get that blind spot covered, too."

Emma looked at Jonah. "What blind spot?"

He grimaced. "The back door to the office, by the balcony. I'll have to order another camera."

The detective nodded to both of them. "You can go ahead and start your cleanup. It's a shame…I hope you can get it all fixed."

Emma saw him hesitate, maybe wanting to say something more but his car radio squawked and he turned away.

TWENTY-TWO

"You haven't eaten." Raylene moved a coffee can of paintbrushes to make room for a plate with two bagels. "Jonah said you'll eat this if I wave it under your nose. Salmon and cream cheese on an everything bagel. I got one for him, too. Coffee for him, tea for you."

"Jonah called you? About the —" She wasn't sure what to call it. Attack, break-in, assault? *Vandalism* didn't sound horrible enough.

"Uh-huh. And don't worry, I didn't tell your daddy. I said you and Jonah had a small problem to solve here and you forgot to eat, so I'm bringing you over a couple bagels. I'll keep him busy, chess and baseball. But you gotta eat."

"I can't eat right now. My stomach's too…twisted." Emma was trying to find the security camera footage on Jonah's MacBook.

"I see it, your whole body's clenched up. But Frank says I gotta watch you eat. So eat." Raylene folded strong arms and propped her farmgirl body against the doorframe, where everyone seemed to park themselves for talking or waiting or supervising.

Emma swallowed first her frustration and then a small bite of bagel. "You're right, I'm starving. Thank you."

Raylene cleared the doorframe so Jonah could squeeze by. "Okay, I can go now. Jonah, your bagel's on that shelf. Coffee, too."

"Raylene, you're a saint." He sank into Emma's chair and picked up his coffee. "Okay, what have you looked at?"

"Everything from nine p.m. to three a.m. The first clip was Lyssa, leaving a little after nine."

"Lyssa?"

"She came for dinner. Tell you later." She glanced at her notes. "Then there's deer, a fox, one of the barn cats. This next one's from three-oh-seven, on camera two."

"That's the camera at the southeast corner of the barn. It shows the edge of the parking lot and the front of the garden."

They both startled as a giant white moth filled the black screen, crawling over the camera lens. Emma was about to move on to the next clip when the moth abruptly vanished and a tall human figure appeared at the top right corner of the screen. Wearing a hoodie and dark pants, the intruder moved from the parking lot toward the garden.

Emma's breath quickened and leaned forward, her half-eaten bagel forgotten.

Jonah exhaled sharply. "Shit. What's he carrying? A sledgehammer?"

"Yes. And a crowbar."

The intruder's shape blurred at the edges as the camera tracked heat in the dark. The man—Emma assumed a man, but maybe it wasn't—wedged the prybar beneath the hinges, iron against iron, wrenching them off the gate posts with quick, powerful pulls. In less than a minute, the two halves of the gate lay flat on the ground, secured only to each other by a loop of chain and a padlock.

The first video clip ended abruptly and the next sequence began. Emma recoiled as the attacker, now wielding the sledgehammer, pounded the gates that lay on the ground.

"He didn't have to do that," Jonah muttered. "It's *open*. They could drive a goddamn truck through that gap."

The next clip showed the courtyard, where the intruder was trying to break apart Harry's sculpture by jamming one end of the wrecking bar between the steel figure and its granite base. He paused, as if talking to someone, then swapped tools and used the sledgehammer as a club, bludgeoning first the pale metal and then the black stone.

Jonah turned up the sound but they heard no voice, just a series of heavy thuds followed by the raw, hackle-raising shriek of iron on steel and stone.

Emma winced. "Turn it off. Please."

On the next video, the prowler attacked the cement birdbath, smashing it with three quick swipes of the sledgehammer.

"Play that one again," Emma said. "See there? I think he's left-handed. At the birdbath, he switched his hold."

"The asshole probably pulled a muscle."

In the next segment, they saw the intruder approach from the parking lot, paint can in hand.

Emma closed her fingers over Jonah's free hand, bracing herself for what she knew was coming. The furious attack was painful to watch but for some reason, the thrown paint felt even worse. A deliberate fuck-you to everyone at Stonefall.

She sucked in breath, unable to look away as he swung the paint can in wide arcs over flowerbeds, flagstones, and the smashed birdbath before reaching high overhead to empty it over the top of Harry's sculpture. He tossed the can aside and stood for a moment with hands on hips, surveying the destruction.

The infrared camera lens captured action only in black and white but Emma's mind filled in the scene with crimson and scarlet.

How tall did someone have to be to dump paint over the top of a seven-foot sculpture? The copper-haired man in the café might have been tall enough.

She sat back and wiped her eyes on a paper napkin.

"Wait," Jonah said. "It's not over. There's someone else there."

Moving from the shadows at the edge of the frame, a second figure walked into view. About the same height as the first person but with a thicker body, arms hanging nearly to his knees. The two walked off-screen and the video froze.

The time stamp on the last recording was three-fifteen, a little over eight minutes from the beginning.

Jonah sat back. "That's it. Not one but two goddamn assholes. They didn't look drunk or high, did they? And it wasn't just a bunch of stupid kids on a random spree, trying to liven up their Saturday night."

Emma scrubbed her hands over her face, feeling exhausted though it was only nine o'clock.

"What is this about? Is it about Harry's art?" she said. "Everyone loves that piece, it's beautiful."

Jonah drained his mug of cold coffee. "His sculpture wasn't the only target. It was the birdbath, too. The whole garden. Even those gates—"

"Also Harry's work."

"Do you want me to call the sheriff's office? Find out about uploading those files?"

"No, I'll do it." She propped the card against the keyboard and picked up her cellphone. "Go on, Felicia needs your help."

TWENTY-THREE

The restoration of the garden was a marvel. One phone call from Felicia mobilized an army of volunteers that included her orthodontist husband, his six-foot-tall son, and a ten-year-old grand-niece in braces and Marley hair. Plus all of her art gallery volunteers, most of the high school football team, and several Boy Scouts.

Emma uploaded the videos to the sheriff department's file server, then joined the work crew. They scrubbed and replaced, or flipped over, all of the paint-smeared flagstones. Removed the smashed birdbath and a cracked concrete bench, pruned damaged shrubs, and spread yards of dark brown mulch donated by the local garden center. On the crimson-stained trunk of a weeping cherry tree, one of Felicia's *plein aire* painters used a fine camel hair brush to apply custom-mixed paint in shades of umber and gray. Someone with a pickup dropped off dozens of potted chrysanthemums to disguise the trampled beds of lavender and coreopsis.

When Simon and his husband Robert arrived in their Sunday morning cycling gear, Felicia introduced them to a beefy high school halfback and put the trio in charge of setting up the new fountain she'd purchased.

"On sale," she announced proudly as they unloaded four big stone slabs from the back of her Suburban. "They gave me an even bigger discount when I explained what happened. Isn't it fantastic? It's solar-powered, no plumbing or wires. A total upgrade from that cheesy little birdbath. We always wanted a water feature, right?"

"Where's Chaz?" Jonah asked. "We need to get those gates out of sight."

"I hope he's sleeping," Felicia said. "He worked last night at Aldi, remember? Today's his day off. Don't bother him, my son Sean can help."

They hid the twisted iron gates behind the chicken coop. Jonah made temporary repairs to the gate posts by facing the splintered wood with one-by-six trim boards, then sanded the edges and stained everything in dark walnut.

Emma's task was to help Harry with sculpture repairs. Which meant keeping him supplied with water and keeping everyone else at arms' length. She'd heard Felicia's stern warning to the younger volunteers: "That's one annoyed artist and he's got a foul mouth. Stay scarce."

Harry brought a wheelbarrow full of equipment and a side load of anger that had him muttering epithets and slamming his tools down into the new mulch. Emma was planning to stay back out of view, but once he'd pulled on gloves and goggles he asked her to sit nearby. He told her he worked better with an audience.

"Basically, once I've got the fucking paint off I'll use the same fucking tools to fix it that I used to create it. The contours will be different—she'll be a little trimmer, see?—because I've got to take down the surface in so many places. But the goddamn asshole who did this will *not* have the satisfaction of fucking up my work."

He began by applying liquid stripper with a toothbrush to remove the paint, wiping it off with rags soaked in mineral spirits. Next, he wet-sanded the planes and crevices by hand with successively finer grit papers.

"This grit's good shit, better than an emery board. I like three thousand."

It took Emma a few seconds to realize he was talking about a grade of sandpaper.

He buffed the steel with a polishing compound, then went after the paint on the granite base with lacquer thinner. More buffing, more polishing. As he explained each step, his foul mood improved.

Harry didn't need her help but she lingered in the shade, enjoying the sight of him rubbing the statue in long, sensuous strokes, working in the heat of the sun. He'd pushed his shoulder-length hair under an old ball cap and now several damp strands were escaping, falling over his broad shoulders. Emma had never been drawn to gym rats, but Harry's powerful body was built at a forge, not a bench press. The muscles of his forearms gleamed with perspiration and stone dust. Sweat stuck the thin tee shirt to his back and chest.

Emma grew drowsy, half-listening to his talk about steel and buffing paste. At last he fell silent.

Then she heard him whisper. At least, she thought it was Harry.

"My shining lady, she's you. Can't you see that?"

Something flared in the pit of her stomach. A small hot flame of desire, something so strange she didn't recognize it. She stared at Harry. Head down, focused on his work, he continued his rhythmic polishing.

Did he say what she heard?

"Sorry," Emma stammered. She jumped up, gesturing vaguely toward whatever pocket her phone might be in. "A call— I have to go."

He didn't look up.

She stumbled toward the hayfield but changed her mind when she saw all the cars and people there. Across the road, then, and into the woods. She found the trail to the orchard and quickened her walk. A few minutes into the trees, she stopped beneath a stand of young maples to catch her breath.

What had happened? It must have been an aural hallucination, a simple fantasy created by her exhausted mind. Not a psychotic event, not a break with reality. Certainly not a whisper from Harry, telling her she was the inspiration for his art.

***

Half an hour in the woods restored Emma's equilibrium. She combed bits of tree bark from her hair and headed back to the barn, planning to avoid Harry for a few hours. Though she suspected any awkwardness would be all on her side.

She was pretty sure Harry didn't see her as a sexual being, in or out of her clothes. None of the artists did. She was only the model, presenting an interesting challenge in form and line, light and shadow. Complexities to be rendered onto paper or board, in graphite or pastels or charcoal. Today, Harry had needed a passive sounding board while he worked and she was good at that, too, because it was a little like sitting for a long pose in a figure class.

Just remain still. Listen, be quiet, don't judge.

Sex wasn't on her table, anyway. Hadn't been for years.

Hi, I'm Emma. I'm twenty-seven. I have epilepsy. Also PTSD, night terrors, and hallucinations. Some of my bones have been replaced by steel and titanium. My speech is strange, I can't drive at night or in the rain, I'm afraid of heights and loud noises. I killed three people. I love animals and I have a dog named after a pirate. In a relationship, I'm looking for…nothing.

Lots of potential matches for that one, right?

But.

What was that strange feeling she'd felt when she was watching Harry? That small tickle in her belly, where did that come from?

Emma had had exactly one lover, a hookup near the end of her first year at Silvermill. Engineered, of course, by Lucy. A Taiwanese exchange student, he wined and dined Emma on a visit to the Biltmore estate before flying home to Taipei, to the fiancée his parents had chosen for him. Later she realized she'd been a checkbox on his to-do list for the obligatory semester abroad: improve your English, see Biltmore, have sex with an American girl.

The mystery of sex had been revealed as nothing more than a series of smaller mysteries, everything left incomplete and unanswered.

Today's moth-flutter was only that, she decided. An unexpected flicker of unreliable neurons, not to be trusted.

***

The art center was full of people all afternoon. Emma spent the next hour drifting uneasily at the edges of crowds and conversations, seeing every stranger with new eyes.

In police dramas, didn't the attacker return to the scene of the crime?

The detective with the unpronounceable name seemed to think it was local vandals, drunk or high, out for a joy ride. Emma wasn't convinced. The anger fueling those attacks felt personal.

Was Harry the target? Testosterone-forward men often sparked strong emotions in others. Certainly in his wife Sandy, a notoriously jealous woman whose husband's unexpected success as an artist often pushed her suspicion buttons.

"I know how to grill his steaks and get grease out of his work shirts," Sandy said to Emma after Harry's ant-mound sculptures earned him his first feature in a tourist magazine. "But gallery openings and champagne cocktails? Just gag me. That's *not* what I signed up for. My husband fixes transmissions, he is not an *artist* with a *fan club*. Who now tells me he needs to draw pictures of bare-assed bimbos every Thursday night, for chrissake."

Except Harry was all that, and Sandy was struggling with it. Was she angry enough to sabotage her husband's success, trying to hold him back? Perhaps, if she thought his sculpture was inspired by another woman. A naked woman named Emma.

She detoured to the restroom, needing to splash water on her face. Drying her hands on the seat of her jeans, she stared into the washroom mirror and tried to see what might motivate Harry, or anyone, to create something beautiful from damage and asymmetry. In the glass she saw only her hollow, tired eyes and the scars at her jaw and temple, topped by a wild mane of unmanageable curls.

On the plus side, she looked nothing like a bare-assed bimbo. She settled the purple baseball cap lower on her forehead and walked back to the main hall.

She saw a young boy with bright blond hair near the classroom and her thoughts shifted to Lyssa. Was her cousin the vandal? She was certainly tall enough and strong enough. She'd never handled rejection well; being denied membership in the co-op might push her to pick up a sledgehammer. But she hadn't been rejected, she'd changed her mind about the co-op and was angling for a job instead. She'd want to protect Stonefall, right? Not harm it.

What about the man who'd stopped by their table at Margo's? Emma shivered, remembering his hateful accusations and the look of disgust on his face. She hadn't recognized him but he knew her. How was that possible, after eight years? Dozens of people posted terrible lies about her while she was lying near death in the hospital. Frank shielded her from from the worst of that, but the details were easy enough to google even years later. She knew what they'd said.

All it took was one comment. Was that man clicking right now through those old rumors, reviving the lies? Shaming and doxing her? Broadcasting her existence far and wide, so the trolls could bring her fragile life crashing down.

She passed the sales gallery and considered the people whose works were showcased there. And the others, whose works were rejected. Each month, the gallery jury—Felicia, Jonah, and Simon, the same people who determined co-op membership—fielded inquiries from local artists hoping to have their work represented at Stonefall.

Emma remembered one woman who'd taken her rejection poorly after proudly presenting a portfolio of lurid sunsets and neon-green trees. Felicia was the one to say "Thank you but no," which triggered a storm of epithets and veiled racial threats. But that was several months ago and the woman moved away soon after.

And why target Harry's work? Anyone bent on personal revenge against the jury would be more likely to target Felicia's paintings, not Harry's work.

At four, Emma gave up on crowd surveillance and went home.

TWENTY-FOUR

Lyssa's Sunday afternoon nap was cut short by her bed-partner's god-awful snoring.

She heaved the big skunky-smelling dude off her sweaty legs and swung her feet to the floor, dragging along a wadded-up pillow and the tail end of a rumpled sheet. Her mouth felt thick and fuzzy, sour with cheap wine and a bitter hemp brew and maybe the taste of regret because if she regretted anything in her life it was the loss of Carlos.

She didn't miss Carlos, she corrected herself. She missed sex with Carlos.

That was epic, especially when it began with role-playing. He'd rent a room for the weekend, someplace extravagant like the Fairmont or the Hyatt Regency. On Saturday evening she'd put on a cheap wig and her sluttiest dress, no underwear and nipples pushed out to *there*. She'd go to the bar alone and flirt with three or four dudes before choosing *him* as her hookup. They'd get trashed on his daddy's sick weed and just *consume* each other all weekend long.

She missed all that now, the marathon sex and all the money—especially the money—but not the rest of it, the part where she was locked into his crazy, wacked-out family and a pre-nup agreement she couldn't possibly stick to.

Today's sad playdate with her newest acquisition had gone poorly from the start.

This one, Drew—she really should try to remember his name—was clumsy and dumb and smelly. Zero creativity in his toolbox, just a brain-numbing, body-bruising focus on the finish. Like he was dreaming, and needed to rush to get it done before he woke up.

But he'd done what she'd asked so she figured she owed him. She didn't know what she'd need him to do next, but so far he'd been useful.

"Get up, lugnut." She smacked his ass hard enough to leave the mark of her hand and draw a growl of protest.

Lyssa whacked him again. Harder, because he wasn't Carlos and this wasn't the Fairmont. He came up off the bed growling and reaching for her but she was quicker. She locked the bathroom door and turned on the shower.

"Hey!" He banged on the door. "Fuck. I gotta piss."

"Use the lobby. It's after six and I'm hungry. Take me to the fanciest place you can think of and later I'll show you some dirty pictures. We'll have some more fun."

TWENTY-FIVE

A few minutes before eight p.m., Zoom's waiting-for-host icon ended its busy spin. Emma tilted the laptop screen a little more toward her father's chair as Mark Camerer's weathered face came into focus.

She'd known the attorney all of her life. After her grandparents died, Uncle Jerry asked his good friend Mark, a junior partner in a Charlotte law firm, to help manage the estate. He'd been attached to the farm and the family ever since.

"Evening, guys," Mark said.

Emma gave a little wave. Frank said, "Sorry for interrupting your Sunday evening."

"Never a bother, good to see you both. How's the long-hauler, Frank?"

"Still hauling. My doctor wants to do a valve job on me tomorrow. I'll be three days at Mission, but then I should be good as new. Miracles of modern medicine, et cetera."

No one mentioned the oxygen cannula dangling from his face.

Frank added, "The Sicilian defense seems to be working."

Mark's overgrown mustache twitched. "You know I have no idea what that means."

Emma smiled. "Predictable and... contentious."

"Okay, that makes sense. Hey, Emma. That sounded great."

"Lots of practice. Hey, Uncle Mark, how's Aunt Hayley? How was your trip? Catch anything?" Not technically her uncle and aunt, but close enough.

"Hayley is happy and well-rested because she didn't go. The trip was great, I caught lots. Dozens. They were all *this big*." He held his arms extravagantly wide, both hands disappearing off the screen. "You can tell any fish story you want with catch-and-release."

"No pictures for proof?"

"I haven't finished the photoshopping."

Mark's post-Orkney attire included a frayed brown fishing vest and three days of gray stubble below the mustache. The whiskers were new but the vest was the same one he'd worn on every fishing trip for thirty-five years. Also on every visit to Stonefall, where he hiked happily through the hills several times a year to observe water quality, bird counts, and hybrid chestnut saplings.

On the wall behind his desk was a faded photo of three young men in gillies' hats and waders: Jerry, Frank, and Mark, laughing on the bank of a trout stream somewhere in the Scottish highlands. The image was more than three decades old and hard to see on the Zoom screen but Emma knew it well because there was an identical print in the living room.

Frank's smile faded. "We'll keep this brief. Lucy's come back."

Mark's chair began a small, slow swivel. Left, right. "Just Lucy? What about Maggie?"

"No Maggie, just Lucy. She showed up on Thursday evening. Walked in on a class at the barn, then came by the house to see me. She didn't call, didn't even knock on the door. Just walked in and surprised Teague. Nearly gave me a heart attack."

"Where's she staying?"

"Not here. At a hotel in Asheville."

Mark's chair stopped swiveling and the eraser tip of a yellow pencil appeared at the bottom of the video frame. "Well. Where has she been all this time?"

Emma answered. "Calgary. Before that…Quebec. She has a new name, Lyssa Morales." She spelled it. "She changed it when she got married. Five years ago in Caracas, she said."

"Ah. That's why we couldn't find her." He made another note, then looked up. "New name, marriage, new address. Did she say why she left? Or, for that matter, why she's back?"

"All she said was, she left to find her mother." Emma thought for a moment. "Why she came back—she's getting divorced. She told Jonah she wanted to join the co-op, but now she wants us—me—to give her a job. In marketing. But maybe there's another reason."

Frank said, "She came for dinner last evening and it got a little tense. She was pushing for answers about Jerry's will. And the trusts."

Frowning, Mark sat back and resumed chair-swiveling. Added pencil-tapping, touching the eraser to his chin. "Return of the prodigal? But I don't see you two rolling out the red carpet."

Frank sighed. "You remember what she was like as a kid, right? Always the center of attention. Impulsive and infuriating, but also smart and funny. And a good friend to Emma, especially after Kit died. We always tried to help Lucy, didn't we? To make up for Maggie's poor parenting skills."

"Maggie's poor...parenting skills?" Emma hoped she was making sense. "I'd say...*negative* parenting skills. Maggie drank and did drugs and was dealing—"

Frank cut in. "That's why we tried to help them both."

Mark stilled his chair and dropped the pencil. His eyes slid away for a moment, then back to his camera. "We all tried. I wish Jerry and Marisa had adopted Lucy. Then she'd have had some stability and Maggie could've focused on getting herself clean. But...." He trailed off in unlawyerly fashion. "What's the other reason, Emma? For her to return now."

"Dad and I have a question about the timing. Jerry died October 20, right? Almost three years ago."

"Ah." Mark's eyebrows rose. "You think she plans to challenge Jerry's will? She'll have to move fast, the clock's ticking. She's got three years from when it entered probate. Maybe she's already moving on that and we just haven't heard. Maybe there'll be a letter on my doorstep tomorrow."

Frank frowned. "Does she have any standing? Jerry specifically wrote Lucy and Maggie out of his will."

"A sympathetic judge might consider it. She's a named beneficiary because Jerry forgave those private loans. Lucy and Maggie were both included in his earlier will."

Emma said, "She asked us how the trusts are funded. Dad told her to contact you."

"Good answer. Though if the will is challenged, the judge could require me to share that information with the plaintiff. All of it—the trust documents, the size of the bequests, the value of the estate." He resumed chair-swiveling.

Emma leaned forward. "Was there ever a trust set up in Lucy's name? Something that Jerry might have…rebooked later?"

"Revoked?" Mark paused to rub a hand over his bristly chin. "Frank, did Jerry ever tell you why Lucy's adoption didn't go through?"

"No," Frank said. "Just that Maggie changed her mind."

"Jerry told me that Maggie found out how much his company was really pulling in and she got greedy. She wanted more money and fewer strings. Not just money for rehab, but a sizable lump sum for her and a savings account for Lucy, with Maggie in control of it. Jerry said no and Maggie blew up. So, no adoption."

"But Maggie did go into rehab. And about six months later, she moved into an apartment near us so Lucy could stay in the same school as Emma."

Emma spoke up. "I remember. I was in kindergarten, Lucy was in first grade. That was the first time she stayed with us for more than just a few weeks."

Mark cleared his throat. "So, back to the will. Can Lucy challenge it? Probably not. The estate's assets went to the foundation and the trusts. The farm's tied up in a conservation easement that prohibits development and commercial activity. You two have life estate, so you can live there as long as you want. You can also offer a room to Lucy if she wants to stay. The board would have to agree but the two of you, plus me, are three-fifths of the board so it's up to us." He paused. "Has she asked to move in? Are you thinking about offering her a place to live?"

Father and daughter shared a look.

"I asked her if she wanted a room for a week or so," Emma said, "and she said no."

Mark said, "Okay, we won't worry about that unless it comes up. And I'll review the files, be ready to respond if she contacts me."

The lawyer paused, listening to someone off-screen. "My wife is reminding me I have two dogs to walk." He swiveled back. "Anything else I need to know?"

"Yes," Emma said. "There was some vandalism at the barn, around three this morning. Somebody broke into the garden. They trashed the gates and threw red paint around and …damaged one of Harry's sculptures."

Frank shot her a glance. She'd told him about the vandalism but only in general terms. He never asked to see the photos.

Emma kept her eyes on the screen. "There's not much evidence. The security cameras caught it, but you can't see who it is. Jonah's installing better cameras."

Mark was making notes. "Glad no one was hurt. Is it worth filing a claim?"

"I'll get an estimate from Harry on the gates, and the cost to repair his sculpture. We bought some plants and mulch and a fountain. Everyone did a great job on cleanup. We opened on time."

"Okay, let me know about that. Let's get together sometime next week, okay? I'll come there and take you two to lunch. And hey, Emma? Whatever you're doing these days to bring your voice back, I'm impressed. You're sounding terrific."

She didn't feel terrific, but she gave him her best smile.

TWENTY-SIX

"You're just handing me over to them," Frank groused as he relinquished his walker at eight-fifteen on Monday morning. A cheerful young man in blue scrubs helped him into an oversized wheelchair stamped Property of Mission Hospital.

Emma was already feeling guilty about bringing her father back to the same hospital where he'd battled Covid two years earlier. His memories of that time were fuzzy, riddled with drug-induced hallucinations and nightmares. He'd been sedated for a month, connected to a ventilator that breathed for him and an ECMO that oxygenated his blood while doctors tried to fix his fluid-filled lungs.

She clearly remembered the FaceTime videos, the only way she'd been allowed to visit him then. Sometimes all she'd been able to do was whisper *I love you* over and over.

She did that now, bending close to his ear. Then she straightened and fixed a bright smile on her face. "At least you got to drive the Jeep."

Emma wouldn't drive with a passenger and it was Raylene's day off, so Frank strapped on his portable oxygen tank and driven them the fifteen miles to the hospital.

That brought a smile. "The highlight of my day."

"You're going to feel so much better when this is over," she reassured him. "I'll ask if I can visit this evening. If Dr. Hoskins says yes, we can watch *M.A.S.H.* and eat green Jello."

She crossed her fingers and stepped back as the orderly wheeled him away. The pneumatic doors closed with a sharp hiss of air.

***

Felicia appeared as Emma was unlocking the office door.

"Morning, Emma. Here's the mail." She dropped a stack of letters, magazines, and a chipboard mailer on the corner of Emma's desk. "How's your dad?"

"Grumpy. He'll be better after it's over." Emma plugged in her laptop. "You're here early. I don't think Jonah's here yet."

"Correct. But I have a ten o'clock with Chaz. He needs my help with a personal thing. We're doing a Zoom call. Anyone using that empty studio upstairs?"

"No, it's all yours."

Emma sifted through the mail. Picked up the large rigid envelope and turned it over. "Felicia, hold on. I think this one's for you."

The cardboard's flap was secured by a single strip of cellophane tape. There was no address or postage, just a name printed in black marker, all caps: E. GILLEN

Felicia reappeared in the doorway. "But it has your name on it."

Thinking it might be photos or artwork for the gallery, Emma popped the seal with a thumbnail and removed three large sheets of drawing paper. Each was folded once to fit into the nine-by-twelve sleeve and the ragged edges suggested they were ripped from a sketchpad.

Emma unfolded the pages onto her desk and tried to make sense of what she was seeing.

"Oh!" One hand flew to her chest. "Look, Felicia, it's me. But —"

The sheets slipped to the floor and fanned themselves out on the wooden planks, right-side up. Each bore several sketches and Emma recognized the artist's distinctive pencilwork. These were some of Simon's sketches from Thursday evening. A few were full-body nudes, but most were partial studies. Hands, feet, the curve of a leg or a breast, or hair spilling over a shoulder.

The largest drawing showed Emma lying on her left side, seen from behind, hair tumbling over her exposed neck. Shoulders, spine, torso, buttocks, thighs. A suggestion of knees and calves. Simon had created a single elegant line flowing from her right shoulder blade down her ribcage, over the sweep of her hip.

Emma moved as if to pick up the pages, then yanked her hand back as if stung and fell back in her chair.

Felicia looked closer. "Those are Simon's drawings. But dear god, Simon did not do *that*." She shoved the office door closed, then folded to her knees on the floor, next to Emma's chair.

On the first page, in the middle of the nude figure's upper back—Emma's back—a crudely scrawled hatchet was inked in red. It was sunk to the hilt beside the spine, large drops of blood trailing below the blade.

In another sketch—a classic frontal posture, seated on the stool with one foot on the bottom rung, Emma remembered it well—the figure's breasts and crotch were mutilated in a vulgar red scribble of arrows and knife blades. Dangling above Emma's head was a curved scimitar with the words DIE BITCH scrawled beside it, the letters gouged deep into the textured paper as if driven by rage.

Other drawings were marred by similar graffiti. Chopped limbs, more blood, scratched eyes, a line across the neck that suggested a beheading.

Heart pounding, Emma stared from one disfigurement to the next. She almost missed the casual doodle at the bottom of the third sheet, a childlike drawing of an upside-down car leaning against a tree. On the ground next to the car lay three stick figures with their eyes X'ed out.

Emma curled sideways on her chair, hugging her knees to her chest and staring at the maimed figures. *This isn't real. It's just another illusion. Ignore it.*

She wanted to vomit but fought it. Her mind drifted toward blankness but she caught a small detail and held on:

In that first pose on the floor, Simon didn't have time to get the feet done. Jonah's timer pinged and I changed position.

And:

Simon's work always has lovely contours, so elegant and precise.

She sat immobile. Time crawled.

Felicia's worried face came close, filling Emma's blank gaze. She grabbed the arms of her chair and blocked her view of the sketches on the floor.

"Ugly, vicious—" Felicia muttered. "Okay, we're getting that detective back in here *right now*. He didn't see any hate in that *vandalism* in the garden? He'll see it here."

Felicia's touch was gentle, her smooth hands smelling of lavender and rosemary. She held Emma's face and stared into her eyes, searching for signs of shock. Dilated pupils, perspiration, clammy skin.

From a great distance Emma tried to say *I'm okay* though she felt like choking and knew she was far from okay.

Felicia rose from the floor, rubbing the stiffness out of her knees. "I'm getting us some water. Don't you move, sweetheart. Don't you *look*."

Emma drank a little from the mug Felicia offered. Still shivering, she rubbed first her arms and then her legs, which were cold. Her insides felt like taffy pulled sideways, but worse was the feeling of her mind trying to shut down. She shook herself mentally and tried to jump-start her brain with questions.

First, the logistics. How could this happen?

Drawing sessions produced hundreds of sketches. Some artists took all their work home with them; others saved only the drawings they liked.

The art center's paper recycling bins were in a corner of the classroom, near the door. Whatever needed to be tossed—torn newsprint, construction paper, office documents, spoiled watercolors, abandoned charcoal studies—went into one of two blue containers, an open-topped bin labeled PAPER RECYCLING and a lidded one labeled PAPER TO BE SHREDDED.

Rejected sketches from the live-model sessions—all of them, not just the nudes—were supposed to go into the second bin through a wide slot on the lid, secured with two carabiner clips. If an artist needed to retrieve a discarded drawing, they could unlatch the lid and sort through the pile.

The lid was latched but not locked. Any curious visitor—a hormone-addled adolescent, say—could pluck out a naked-lady drawing.

That's how someone got hold of Simon's drawings, Emma thought. *But who scribbled on them? And why?*

She thought about the tree, the car, and the stick figures scrawled on the last page. And E. GILLEN printed on the chipboard sleeve, the words DIE BITCH hovering over the slashing knife. Whoever did this must have recognized her in Simon's sketches, knew who she was and knew who she'd killed.

Another thought surfaced: *Red paint in the garden, red ink on the drawings. The same person?*

"You okay, Emma? Your color's better. But you're looking a little lost. You kinda checked out on me for a few minutes." Felicia moved behind her chair and began kneading her shoulders. "Breathe, sister, breathe. Let it go, breathe it out. I called that detective and texted those pictures to him."

When had Felicia done that? Emma looked at the floor. The drawings were gone.

Felicia stopped the massage but kept her hands on Emma's shoulders. "I put those ugly things away in the safe, at the back of the shop. That detective, Japanski, he says he's coming right out quick to talk with us. This is more serious, he says. A direct threat, aimed at you."

Emma nodded, feeling her gut unclench. "What else did he say?"

"He said don't touch. Hold the edges and fold a tissue over. Then put the paper back in the cardboard, the way it looked when it arrived, and put everything in a bigger folder. I told him I watch CSI, at least I know that much."

Felicia crouched awkwardly beside Emma's chair again and touched her knee. "I'm so sorry, Emma. I feel like it's my fault. I'm the one asked you to pose for the figure drawing."

She glanced at her watch. "And now I got Chaz waiting on me. You okay if I leave you here? Or I can ask him to hold on for a bit."

"I'm fine. Go talk with Chaz."

Emma was very much not fine but she offered what she hoped was a reassuring smile. *How easy it is for good people to assume guilt. Agonizing over the what-ifs and the if-onlys.*

A small voice in her head echoed what she'd said to Felicia. *Not your fault, not your fault.*

But the denial followed immediately.

It's not the same thing at all! The car crash was absolutely my fault. It's true, I'm the BITCH who should have died.

TWENTY-SEVEN

"Please, Chaz. Call me Felicia."

He couldn't do that yet. To him she was still Miz Weingardt.

"Let's go upstairs," she said. "We'll find us an empty studio."

He followed her across the center hall to a pair of palm trees in big stone pots that flanked the north-side staircase. Real palms, not fake ones like in the local taqueria.

Upstairs, a long indoor balcony ran the length of the barn's north side. It had the same kind of railing as the outdoor deck, wood posts and steel cables, and it reminded Chaz of the catwalks above the stage at Bundison High. His sister Jessie got a small part in *Guys and Dolls* last year and she'd talked him into being a stagehand. He liked being up on the catwalks, swiveling spotlights and staring down at the actors. From up there, even the coolest kids were nothing more than hats and hair on top of shoulders.

Here on the second floor of the barn, he could look down at the empty church benches in the big hall. Or mind his manners, and follow Miz Weingardt past a supply closet, a restroom, and six studio doors. Small signs beside the doors told you the artists' names and what they did: oils, acrylics, photography, gemstone jewelry, mixed media. One sign said lutherie but he had no idea what that was.

A door with no sign stood slightly open. Inside he saw track lighting on the ceiling, a single tall north-facing window, a gray plastic work table, and four metal folding chairs.

"Our conference room," Miz Weingardt explained as she placed her iPad on the table.

Chaz stood by the table, one hand near his chest with his thumbnail flicking against his index finger. "You sure he'll answer? What if he doesn't want to talk to me?"

He'd seen only two lawyers close up, the ones who worked for Child Protective Services. He didn't think you could just call one up and ask questions.

"Don't worry, he'll answer. Remember, he sent *you* the letter, so he absolutely wants to talk to you. I texted him and told him I'm helping you, so he's expecting us. Besides, I know him some." She touched the iPad's screen. "You know how Zoom works, right?"

He slid a chair closer and sat. "Yes, ma'am. We had remote learning when I was a sophomore and some as a junior. That security class I took, that was online."

The last word threatened to get stuck in his brain—*online online online*—and he felt himself tense up with a need to break the headspace stutter, but before he could do something about that, the face of a man with beard-stubble and a big gray mustache filled the Zoom frame. He wore a blue shirt and a navy tie which definitely said *lawyer* but he also looked a little rumpled, like a regular guy who maybe wanted to be outdoors instead of in an office. His face was creased in a genuine-looking smile. Chaz relaxed a little.

The lawyer spoke first. "Morning, Felicia."

"Hi, Mark. You're looking well. New facial hair?"

He touched his rough chin. "I was thinking Jeff Bridges, but my wife says I've got to grow the hair on top longer for that. So maybe George Clooney. All moot, because I may never get beyond what you see here. I thought it would come in salt-and-sand but so far, it's all salt."

She half-smiled. "Every man needs a hobby."

"I heard you had a little trouble with vandalism in the sculpture garden. Night before last. Everything okay?"

Chaz felt his eyes do the rapid-blink thing. He hadn't been in the garden this morning. What were they were talking about? He half-turned toward Miz Weingardt but she made a little downward-patting motion with her hand that meant "not now."

"Somebody splashed a little paint around," she said. "Busted up the gates. But we got busy and fixed it. We opened on time yesterday and had a very good turnout."

Mark nodded as if that agreed with something he already knew, and switched his gaze to Chaz. "So, you must be Charles."

Chaz's face grew warm and his tongue got stuck on the roof of his mouth. He managed a nod.

Felicia said, "This here's Chaz, Charles William Robberts. I believe you sent him a letter, in care of his former foster mom."

"Hi, Chaz. I'm Mark Camerer. Good to meet you."

Chaz tried to wet his lips. "Yes, sir. Good to meet you. Mr. Camerer, sir." He stumbled a little on the name, which sounded like a stutter all by itself. He hoped he hadn't added an extra "er."

"I'm glad my letter finally found you. First, though, Felicia— It's always good to see you but I'm confused. How do you know Chaz? Through school?"

"He works here at Stonefall. Small world, right? He started on the farm back in May. Jonah hired him to help bale hay and build some fence. Now we've got him doing all sort of things. He's very handy, a good addition to the team. He's a little confused about your letter so he asked me to help him out."

The lawyer blinked. "That's...quite a coincidence. Chaz, do you have a sister? What's her name, please? And how old is she?"

Chaz looked to Felicia for an explanation but she only shrugged.

"Jessie, that's my sister," he said. "Jessica Robberts. She turned seventeen in June. She's still living at Miz Buckner's."

"Do you have some form of ID with you? Your driver's license? Hold that up to the camera so I can see your name and your date of birth, please."

Chaz fumbled his license out of his wallet and Felicia angled her iPad so he could get it in front of the camera.

"Thanks." Mark wrote something on a notepad. Settled back in his office chair and swiveled it slightly, side to side. "So. I'll give you the bullet points and then you can ask questions, okay?"

He paused his chair and leaned forward. "I represent a very kind man," he said slowly, "who died a few years ago. But before he died, he set aside money for you and your sister, for college. He asked me to contact you when you graduated from high school. I'm sorry it took so long to get to you—you were supposed to receive it three months ago."

Confused, Chaz stared at Felicia. He swiveled his eyes back to the screen. "But— I can't go to college. My grades weren't so good, I almost flunked history. I don't qualify for whatever this is."

What was Darren's name for it, when he felt like this? Deer in the headlights.

Felicia placed hand a lightly on his arm and that steadied him.

"Chaz," she said quietly, "you took a course from A-B Tech, right? Security systems. That was a college course."

Mark held up a hand. "Sorry, let me explain it better. This is a grant, Chaz. You don't have to pass any tests or qualify. It covers any kind of post-secondary education, not just college. And you don't have to start right away. Maybe wait a year, think about what you want to do. You can choose anything, cooking or farm management or hairdressing. Be an electrician or a plumber. Or a security systems installer, like Felicia said. You can go to any school, a four-year college or a community college or a tech school."

Chaz seized the first thought that came. "But I'd still have to work. I got rent to pay—" His eyes slid away, looking at nothing. This was crazy, he didn't understand. Was this a scam?

"Your living expenses are included," Mark said. "That's all paid, up to four years' worth. The only requirement is that you stay in school, at whatever training program you choose. If you drop out, the support ends."

"Then I'd have to pay it back, right?" Panic closed in. He placed both hands flat on the table, ready to escape.

"No. Even if you drop out, you don't have to pay it back. It's a grant, not a loan. And the same for your sister."

Chaz felt Felicia's smooth cool hand close more firmly over his forearm. To hold him there or settle him down, he didn't know which, but it worked because he was breathing again.

Felicia smiled broadly. "That's amazing. And really generous. Chaz probably wants to know how much money this represents. What the upper limit might be."

Chaz was still trying to process the part with the living expenses.

Mark said, "The amount depends on tuition costs, and the cost of living, for wherever they want to go. There's no upper limit on tuition so if they want to go Ivy League—and they're accepted—then Harvard it is. Living expenses are based on an average cost for room and board. Rent, utilities, and groceries. Wherever you choose to live and study."

"Anywhere?" Felicia asked. Her delicate eyebrows arched higher.

"Anywhere."

"Who oversees all this? Who writes the checks?"

"That would be me."

"Wow." Felicia swung her head, sweeping a pile of box braids back over a shoulder. "Did this wonderful benefactor set aside an actual amount?"

"The amount reserved for this grant is…" Mark checked his notes. "Two hundred fifty thousand dollars."

Chaz swallowed hard. "We split that?"

"For each of you."

Chaz's brain worked its way around the number. Two hundred fifty thousand each, half a million total.

"Remember," Mark added, "that's only as long as you stay in school. But yes, Mr. Gillen was very generous. And very kind."

Chaz stared at the screen. "Mr. Gillen? Miz Emma's father?"

"Her uncle. Jeremiah Gillen."

"Oh," Felicia said. "This is... through the Gillen Foundation? I've sent several scholarship applicants your way over the years. Those are usually ten grand or so. This is...different."

"This has nothing to do with the foundation. It's a special fund that Jerry set up several years ago, after the accident."

Felicia sat back and stared. She looked first at Chaz sitting next to her, then at Mark on the small screen. He waited for her to ask the obvious next question but it was Chaz who spoke first.

"It's because of the accident?" His voice steadied. "Because of who we are, me and Jessie."

"You're..." Felicia faltered, began again. "You and your sister, you're the older kids. Your mother, your two sisters— They died in that crash."

"Yes ma'am. Half-sisters," Chaz clarified. His throat wanted to close up again but now it was just a reflex, a general sort of sadness. His memory of the girls was pretty fuzzy. Back then, he was too busy keeping himself and Jessie safe. He wasn't paying much attention to the little ones.

He'd also learned to be wary of people claiming to offer help or charity. Today seemed different, though. Not charity; more like an apology.

Mr. Camerer said to Felicia, "Christine Garrison was Chaz and Jessie's mother. She also had two younger daughters, Amber and Destiny. When the accident happened, Chaz and Jessie were at home with their stepdad."

Chaz's jaw tightened. "Gordy Hanks was *not* my stepdad."

He and Jessie hadn't been home with Gordy—they'd spent the day avoiding him—but Chaz kept quiet about that.

Miz Weingardt went back to the good-news part. "This is fantastic news for Chaz and Jessie. The scholarship, I mean. But what do I tell Emma and Frank? *Should* I tell them?"

"Can you and Chaz keep this quiet for a few days? I'm driving out there on Saturday and I'd like to tell them in person. They don't know anything about this. Jerry set it up years ago and swore me to secrecy." To Chaz he said, "Jerry Gillen was a wonderful man. He would have loved to meet you and your sister. I understand Jessie's a very good student."

Chaz roused himself. "Yes, sir. She gets better grades than I did. She wants to be a social worker, maybe a teacher."

"That's great, the world needs more good people in both professions. I know this gift can really help both of you.

"Felicia, maybe you can talk with Chaz a little more, help him figure out how to take advantage of this great opportunity. Then we'll all get together and talk with Jessie. She'll get a letter like yours, Chaz, but it would be great if she could start thinking about college sooner rather than later. You're her big brother, you can help guide her."

Guide Jessie about college? Those big life-decision questions made his head spin. People were always telling him he needed a plan so he'd worked out the day-to-day part okay. Get a job or two, work hard, don't get sick. Spend Sundays with Jessie. Stay out of trouble and stay away from people who wanted his money.

Now he was being asked questions about who he wanted to be and what he wanted to do with his life. Jessie, too. Christ on a corndog stick, what should he do with that?

Miz Weingardt closed her iPad and Chaz realized the call was over. They must've said goodbye but he'd didn't recall saying thank you. Maybe he'd said it but he wasn't remembering it now.

He hoped he'd said it. He vowed to listen better.

Miz Weingardt said, "Hey Chaz. One thing I'm wondering. You obviously know who Emma is. But I'm pretty sure she doesn't know who you are, right? Christine Garrison's son, I mean."

He hadn't thought much about it but yeah, Emma probably didn't know who he was. "Chrissy. That's what my mom liked to be called. She called me Billy, but I didn't like that. Other kids called me a goat." His stomach clenched. "A stupid billy goat."

She nodded in sympathy. "Kids can be real mean. But you know what everyone thinks 'goat' means now, right? G-O-A-T, Greatest Of All Time."

Chaz half-smiled. "Too late, I guess. And I like Chaz better anyway. Ma'am."

He knew his manners slipped when he got nervous. Manners were important, Miz Buckner always said. If you got nothing else, Chaz, you always got that. As a foster parent, she wasn't so bad. Too busy with too many kids, but he and Jessie coulda done worse. They *were* doing worse, way back, but he didn't like to think of that so he tried to pay attention now to what Miz Weingardt was saying.

"Chaz, did you ever see Emma or her cousin? When you were younger, I mean. When you all lived nearby."

"Sure, a few times. Mostly Miss Emma. They lived in that log house just up the hill from us. Emma drove a Miata. That was a cool little car, I used to watch for it. Lucy had a Subaru. Now she's changed her name, right? Lucy, I mean. She's got that purple Mustang, the 'twenty-two Shelby. That's cool, too."

Miz Weingardt stood, placed her hands on the back of the chair and leaned forward a little, braids swinging. "I have a hard question for you, Chaz. You can tell me if I'm out of line, asking it."

He nodded, cautious now.

"Why did you want to come work here, Chaz? Knowing that you'd be seeing Emma every day. She's the one who survived in the accident that killed your mother and sisters." She paused. "For some people, that could make for some bad memories."

"I dunno." Chaz worried his eyes might start wandering so he stared at his hands on the table. Twisted the fingers together and forced them to go still. "I saw the ad for the summer job and figured y'all needed me." He shrugged. "I live close. The pay's okay and I like the work."

Miz Weingardt looked unconvinced. Maybe she was worried about him having bad dreams on account of the accident.

He added, "I don't get nightmares or nothing. Really, it's okay."

***

As Chaz walked across the little gravel lot toward his pickup, he felt Felicia's eyes on him and glanced up. She was watching him from a second-floor window but that felt okay, sort of like she was protecting him. Not spying on him. He gave her a little wave and she waved back.

Instead of getting in his truck right away, he went to the southeast corner of the barn by the garden and stood in the gap between the gateposts, looking for evidence of vandalism. Other than the missing garden gates, he saw only fresh mulch and a new fountain bubbling in the courtyard.

On his way back to the truck, he felt the breeze trying to lift his black baseball cap. He paused to yank it down and that's when he saw the twisted gate panels, propped between the chicken coop and the side of the barn.

He stared, fists balling against his thighs.

People can be such assholes, he thought. Trashing things just because their girlfriend dumped them or somebody'd pissed them off.

Could the gates be repaired? Mr. Felton would have to take the broken panels back to his forge, fire them into a red heat and hammer then straight. Then weld the panels back onto the frames and paint everything, one coat of primer and two coats of flat black. Make new hinges, hang them and level them on the posts. Chaz could help with the painting and the hanging. Maybe he could learn about working a forge, too. He liked learning how to fix things that got broken.

Then he turned his attention to the chickens, scratching and pecking in the dirt of their pen. He automatically scanned the fence for holes and the trees above for any sign of a predator. Before he turned toward his truck, he counted them carefully to be sure they were all there, and all safe.

TWENTY-EIGHT

Emma's mental autopilot kicked in to keep her occupied with the usual Monday morning paperwork. Sorting receipts and invoices, figuring sales commissions, checking budget figures. The mundane details of numbers and dates made the world seem normal again for a little while.

At ten forty-five, her phone pinged with a text.

Please call me before 11.
Det Sgt Kendric Szczepanski.

Japanski? If she closed her eyes against the jumble of letters and spelled it phonetically, maybe she could sound it out.

He picked up promptly and she didn't have to say it first. "Detective Sergeant Ken Shepanski."

His voice was even more gravelly than the day before, a Monday-morning kind of voice.

Should she apologize for bothering him? Of course not.

It was her turn to say something. "Detective Shuh… pan…ski? Sorry, I wasn't sure how to say it."

"Yes ma'am, I get that a lot. You did fine."

"It's Emma Gillen. From the art center."

"Yes, I remember. I took a quick look at those videos you sent over and —"

"It's not that." She collected her thoughts. "Well, yes, that. But now there's more."

"What I heard. Ms. Weingardt sent me some photos, but I'll need to see the originals. Be sure not to touch them, okay? I have a window at three today, if that works for you. If your witnesses can be there too, that'll save some time."

"Witnesses?"

A pause. "Ms. Weingardt and Simon Bell."

"Felicia got the mail. And she saw the drawings. But Simon? He wasn't here?" She hated how her voice wanted to rise at the ends of sentences.

"Ms. Weingardt said Mr. Bell drew them, the originals. So I'll need to talk with him. And with anyone else who might have information." His voice sharpened. "I understand you were the model."

Did she hear censure? Or just fatigue?

"Yes." Her voice sounded too soft. She lifted her chin and tried again. "Yes, that's me."

***

A few minutes before eleven, Felicia found Emma piling trash bags in the tool shed for the following day's pickup.

"You have a few minutes, Emma? Jonah's in the classroom," Felicia said. "I showed him the drawings."

Emma merely nodded, having nothing to add. She closed the shed doors. "I saw Chaz leaving. Is he okay?"

"He's fine. He just needed a little guidance on a personal thing. It's good news." She touched Emma's shoulder. "Come on, let's find Jonah."

When Emma and Felicia arrived, Jonah was sitting on a too-small folding chair in the center of the room, his elbows propped on a work table, hands clasped to support his chin. A large manila envelope sat on the far end of the table. It wasn't labeled but Emma knew what it contained. The drawings, the white mailing sleeve. E GILLEN and DIE BITCH.

Felicia briskly scooped up the envelope and tucked it into her tote as Emma pulled three water bottles from the fridge by the sink. As the two women sank into chairs across from Jonah, he raised his eyes to theirs. Emma saw anger there, but also fear.

Stay with the anger, she wanted to tell him. *Remember what you told me: It's impossible to hold onto fear and anger in the same moment. Stay angry.*

Jonah pulled off his wire-rim glasses, closed his eyes, and pinched the bridge of his nose between thick fingers. "Goddammit. What asshole did this to Simon's sketches?"

"We shouldn't call them Simon's," Felicia said. "He threw them away. And he certainly didn't add those ugly scribbles."

Emma wondered about ownership. If not Simon's, then whose drawings were they? Was her body still hers when it was rendered on paper? Or was all of it—her body, Simon's discarded drawings—now owned by the person who'd added the red ink?

She shivered and forced herself to focus. "That detective is coming here at three. Kendric Sheh-pan-ski. He wants to talk with us, also Simon."

Wanting to write his name down and realizing she'd left her notepad in the office, she went to a cabinet by the sink and found a sheet of yellow construction paper and the stub of a green crayon. She said his name again for practice, then wrote it twice: Szczepanski, Shepanski.

Felicia stripped off her gloves and flipped her braids back over her shoulders. "Who could get hold of Simon's sketches?"

Jonah's chair creaked as he shifted his bulk and crossed his feet at the ankles. His jeans hitched up above his hiking boots, exposing frayed white socks. He picked up the green crayon and began drawing concentric loops on the construction paper, circling the detective's names.

"Seriously?" he sighed. "Hundreds of people, everyone who's been here since Thursday evening."

Felicia shot him a dark look. "But it was someone who knew what was in the bin. Someone who knows our routine."

Emma handed bottles of water to Jonah and Felicia. Her brain was hopping again, skittering away from the sketches and landing on unrelated thoughts. *Single-use plastics. We swore not to use single-use plastics, yet here they are.*

Emma pulled out a chair and sat next to Jonah. "I think that can wait until he gets here. Shepanski."

Felicia capped her bottle and set it down with a small thud. "Okay. This other thing, then. Can we talk about Lyssa? Wanting to join the co-op."

Jonah shifted uneasily, like he was having trouble changing gears. "What about her?"

Emma rolled the water bottle between her hands. "We can relax. She's changed her mind about joining."

"Hallelujah," Felicia muttered. "Saves me the trouble of rejecting her application." She bunched her braids and flipped them over a shoulder, then chanced a quick, uneasy look at Emma. "I know she's your cousin but— You know that Toni Morrison quote from *Sela*? 'Any artist without an art form is dangerous.'"

Emma said, "I don't think she's an artist anymore. She needs money. She's asked me to give her a marketing job. Social media, blogging."

Felicia frowned. "Do we need that? And do you want to hire her?"

Emma sidestepped the question of what she wanted. "We could hire her for a few months, on a part-time contract. There's the arts council grant. She'd have to give us a proposal, like anyone else."

Felicia's frown deepened. "Do you think that's smart? She's a disrupter, Emma. From what I've seen, that's always been her go-to. Souring the milk, my mother used to call it."

"She could report to me," Jonah offered.

Emma nodded. "That's what my dad suggested. And the social media thing— She wants to blog about Stonefall anyway, so I think we need to control it. Give her stuff to write about. It could help us."

And if the trolls come after me again, Lyssa can fight them. She's good at fighting.

She hesitated, finding it hard to advocate for her cousin. Picking idly at the label on her water bottle, she wondered if it was fair to invoke her father's name again. "And...well... Dad's hoping we can give her something for her resting play." That didn't sound right. "Help her get her next job?"

"Résumé," Jonah said automatically. He crossed his arms and leaned back. "Emma, I can see Frank wanting to help her. But I'm worried about having her working here with you."

He met Felicia's frown and added, "Family history. I know some of it but it's Emma's information to share."

"It's fine. My cousin is a—" Emma paused to locate the word she wanted, the one with all those difficult sibilants. She rolled it from brain to voice box. "Narcissist."

Jonah and Felicia shared looks, deciding who should ask the next question.

Felicia took the lead. "I'd like to know a little more, if you think you're gonna hire her. Has she always been like this? Kind of a steamroller?"

"When we were kids..." Emma provided a quick summary of Lucy's unstable home life and added, "Whenever Lucy came to stay with us, my parents did everything they could to make her feel welcome. Poor Lucy, they said, she's had it tough."

She set the water bottle aside. "Lucy's a year older so...bossing me around came natural to her. My parents never knew how she much control she had over me. Lucy decided what we wore, who we hung out with. It was easier if I just ... shut up and let her take the lead. And I adored her, back then, because she was smart and funny. Life with her was an adventure. And she made me feel safe."

Felicia asked, "How did she do that?"

Emma picked at a ragged thumbnail and thought for a moment. "One day in seventh grade, I was waiting for Lucy after school. This new kid—he hadn't met Lucy yet—dragged me into the bushes behind the school and tried to pull my shirt off. Lucy saw."

Her mouth was dry so she paused to drink, then continued. "She shoved him down and held a knife to his face. Said if he ever came near me again, she'd remove his —"

She paused to think, then crooked her fingers into quotes. "Excess body parts. Below his waist. Later, I thought maybe she didn't have a knife. See, Lucy was ... scary. She could've held up a plastic spoon...and later everyone would swear it was a ten-inch switch blade. She was … fierce. She was that sort of bully."

"But she was *your* bully," Felicia said.

Emma nodded. "Afterward, she said we should be blood sisters. She swore me to silence and cut our thumbs with a real knife. The cut on her thumb was just a scratch but mine was deep.... It bled a long time. I maybe should've had stitches."

Emma glanced at the pad of her left thumb where the scar was still visible, a thin white line curving across the flesh. "Lucy…licked it. She wanted me to lick her thumb, too. But I threw up."

Felicia's dark skin paled. "Your father never noticed?"

"It was a few months after my mother died.… He was pretty busy with work."

She didn't add that for a few months her father had also been busy with a bottle of scotch.

She ruffled her hair back to front, automatically sweeping the curls forward over her left temple. Folded her hands neatly on the table and added, "Lucy always had safety nets. Jerry's money to live on, my parents' home to live in. My mom and Jerry are gone now, but Dad's still here and the money is still here. Helping us run Stonefall."

Emma saw a question on Felicia's face and realized she'd left out a key detail. "Jerry didn't leave Lucy anything in his will. He cut them off, Lucy and her mom."

"Oh." Felicia reached across the table with both hands to grasp Emma's, smoothing the blood-sisters scar with her own thumb. "I'm so sorry, Emma. I never met your uncle but I've heard he was a wonderful man and I'm sure he had his reasons. You're not responsible for your cousin. You know that, right?"

Jonah sighed. "It's hard. She's family. All you can do is try to set limits. Don't argue, keep your distance." He rubbed his chin with a big hand, massaging tension. "Emma, are you talking with anyone about this?"

"My dad. And Mark."

"I meant a therapist. Someone who can be objective."

Felicia released Emma's hands with a pat. "I agree with Jonah, you need a counselor. We all think the past will stay in the past. Because we're all grown up, right? But then a long-lost cousin shows up with all the baggage and boom, you're like ten years old again and knee-deep in all their shit. Plus your own. If you're lucky there's good memories, too, but Ohmigod, the secrets."

Jonah broke in. "Emma, you said your cousin scared you sometimes when you were younger. Are you afraid of her now?"

Emma hesitated. How to explain the dread she felt?

"Because," he added, "with a narcissist, when something goes wrong it's never their fault. They twist the facts to suit their agenda. And they can be ruthless if things aren't going their way."

He returned to doodling with the green crayon. "You don't have to answer that. But here's another question. Do you think Lyssa's behind the vandalism in the garden? Or Simon's ruined drawings?"

Their eyes met.

A shiver tickled Emma's spine. "She used to call herself the ... original poster child for FAFO. The 'fuck around and find out' approach to a problem." Another shiver. "She's ... capable. But why? It makes no sense."

TWENTY-NINE

"Join us," Felicia urged. "We're going to Margo's for lunch."

Emma shook her head. "Sorry, I can't. I need to call my dad and talk with Dr. Hoskins. And Teague needs a walk."

Felicia stood and wrapped an arm around Emma's shoulders. Hugged gently and released her. "Tell Frank we're thinking of him. Let me know if he's up for a visit this evening." She paused, peering into Emma's face. "Do you need someone to stay with you? Tonight, I mean. I can send over a niece for company, if you like. One of the quieter ones."

"Thanks, I'll be fine. Teague's good company." Emma waved them off with an assurance she didn't feel. She pulled out her phone to check messages but set it down as soon as they left.

She folded her arms on the table and dropped her head into the crook of an elbow. She'd held herself together and talked longer this morning than she had in *years*. And she wasn't done, she'd have to talk a lot more when the detective arrived. The mention of lunch reminded her that she probably needed to eat but she didn't feel like food.

Or yes, she did feel like food. Chopped and stir-fried, burnt at the edges and mushy in the middle. She pressed her face into her forearms, closed her eyes and let a few tears leak out. Just a few minutes, that's all she needed.

***

A rumble of thunder brought Emma's head up abruptly and she was back in the classroom, groggy and disoriented, folded over the table with stiff shoulders and a damp puffy face. Sunlight slanted in through the north-facing windows, reassuring her that it was still early afternoon. The nearest window framed a rectangle of pine trees and the road that followed the creek to the village.

Through the trees to the northeast, dark clouds were building and Emma recognized the signs of a front moving in. There'd be wind and rain and maybe a thunderstorm, not immediately but tonight for sure and maybe tomorrow.

How long had she been asleep? It was nearly two and she needed to call her father. She picked up her phone, propped an elbow on the table, and stifled a yawn.

He must have been holding his phone because he answered on the first ring.

"Hey, Emmie." His voice sounded rough and dry.

"How are you doing?" She flipped over the yellow construction paper with Jonah's doodles and the detective's name. Wrote the words *endobronchial valve therapy* but did not try to say it. "They did that valve thing this morning, right?"

"Okay, I guess. Did you talk with Dr. Hoskins?"

"No, I'll call him next." She hesitated. "Will you be all right if I don't visit this evening? The weather's going to be bad. Lots of rain and wind. I could ask someone to give me a ride…"

"No, you stay home. I'll just be sleeping anyway." He seemed to be already drifting in that direction.

"Okay, don't talk anymore. Love you, Dad."

She reached Dr. Hoskins' voicemail and left a message, then texted Jonah and Felicia to let them know Frank was out of surgery but resting. After a minute's thought, she sent the same message to Lyssa. That's what family did, right? They kept each other informed.

Suddenly she was hungry. A quick trip to the house and a rummage through the fridge netted her a slice of cold pizza. The gray sky was threatening rain so she folded the pizza into a paper towel and stuffed it into the pocket of a yellow raincoat, then let Teague into the backyard for a three-minute run and promised him more yard time in the evening.

Two forty-five. She went upstairs to change out of her overalls and tee shirt into a pair of navy slacks and a cream blouse. Business casual, an outfit that hadn't seen duty in years.

She couldn't find any waterproof footwear to match the rest of her outfit so she stepped into her old barn boots. Pulled the raincoat on again and belted it snugly, ready but not ready to talk with Detective Sergeant Sheh-pan-ski.

THIRTY

The wind was kicking up and the sky had gone black and gray, tinged with a sulfurous yellow. Fat raindrops spattered the ground as Emma hurried across the road to the barn.

Four cars sat in the small gravel lot. Felicia's Suburban, Simon's Lexus, Jonah's rusty old Sentra, and Szczepanski's cruiser.

Rain fell harder. The big sliding doors were closed so she hurried to the gallery entrance. As she touched the knob the door swung suddenly inward, pulling her off balance. She caught her balance awkwardly, stumbling against the detective who stood in the doorway. He held a phone to his left ear and a black messenger bag over his right shoulder.

She ducked beneath the hand with the phone and slipped through the doorway, wanting to get out of the rain. He closed the door behind her and moved several yards away to resume the phone conversation.

She stood on a mat near the glass doors of the gallery and shook out her wet jacket, spattering her legs and remembering too late that she was wearing her nice navy pants. There was mud on her boots, rain spots on the cream blouse, and squashed pizza in a raincoat pocket. She pushed frizzy damp hair off her cheeks, not even trying to arrange the snarls.

Waiting for Szczepanski to finish his call, she realized she'd mostly forgotten what he looked like. He seemed to be staring into some middle distance, concentrating on his call, so now she took a good look.

Broad shoulders, but the rest of him was slender. He seemed tall but everyone except Felicia looked tall to Emma, so maybe only five-nine or so. Despite the baked-in scowl he looked younger than she'd first thought, perhaps middle thirties. A warm brownish complexion, the color of a deep born-with-it tan. High cheekbones, small ears. He was clean-shaven wiht no hint of afternoon shadow. His short hair was a disciplined velour of tight black fuzz.

He wore a navy polo shirt tucked into pressed khakis and a black belt. Badge clipped to the left side of the belt, holster on the right. He looked slightly bowlegged, suggesting years on a horse or a boat.

He finished his call, tucked the phone into his shirt pocket, and caught her staring. She glanced away quickly.

"Sorry about that," he said. "I get a lot of calls. Many aren't so important but that one, I had to take." He shifted the portfolio into his left hand and held out his right, then hesitated.

She'd never mastered the pandemic elbow bump so she held out her hand, still damp from the rain. His handshake was cursory, suggesting he was a very busy man.

Having prepared a little welcome speech, her first words came easily.

"The office is this way," she said. "It's very small. More than two people, we … often sit here in the hall to talk. There's also an empty studio if you want something with a door."

"The office is fine. I know I said three o'clock but I got here early. I've already talked some with Mr. Jacobs and Ms. Weingardt, in the salesroom."

Conscious of her gracelessness in the rubber boots, she moved slowly. He moderated his stride to match her shorter steps.

In the office he hesitated, not sure where to sit amid the clutter of books and files and art supplies. She moved a stack of sketchbooks to clear space at Jonah's half of the desk and swiveled the two chairs to face each other.

The detective looked briefly at his watch, then sat gingerly in Jonah's battered old chair. He pulled a green folder from his bag and began thumbing through its contents as Emma hung her dripping raincoat on a hook behind the door.

She smelled pizza and remembered her uneaten lunch in the pocket. Feeling foolish, she retrieved the wad of dough and paper towel, surreptitiously dropping it in the trash basket beneath her desk.

"You should eat your lunch," he said without looking up. "I don't mind."

Her face warmed and her chair squeaked as she sat down. Her aim to be businesslike fizzled.

Done with whatever he was reviewing, Szczepanski placed a notebook and ballpoint on Jonah's desk and leaned back slightly, cautiously testing the chair's springs. "Okay. I know we talked only yesterday and some of these questions are going to be the same as before. But please bear with me."

His gaze shifted to a spot on the wall beside her. "First, I owe you an apology."

She blinked in surprise. "For what?"

"Yesterday morning, I was—dismissive. I didn't take the vandalism in the garden as seriously as I should have. So, I'm sorry."

Startled, she could only nod.

"Okay, good. So you're the office manager for Stonefall Art Collective?"

"Office manager, bookkeeper. Marking and grant-writing." They'd get to *nude model* soon enough.

"Ms. Weingardt told me you and your father—that's Frank Gillen, right? You're also the owners."

"More like caretakers because the farm is owned by a trust. Dad and I are trustees. We live here, in the house across the road."

"Who else works here? Besides you. Regularly, I mean."

Emma took a deep breath. Mentally crossing all her fingers and toes, vowing to avoid all verbal fumbles. "Full time, there's four of us. Jonah's the program director. Felicia manages the gallery. There's me. And Chaz, Charles Robberts. He started as summer help on the farm and now he's our…handy man."

"What about part-timers?"

"There's lot of those. They're compactors, not employees. Teachers, workshop leaders. Some are co-op members, too."

"How many in the co-op? Do you run background checks on them?"

"Nineteen. Yes."

Speaking slowly, she explained the two sides of Stonefall, the farm and the arts center. The shared studios and exhibit spaces, the workshops and art classes. Their roles, Jonah the art therapist and Felicia the gallery manager. The volunteers—

Detective Szczepanski held up a hand. He'd filled two pages with notes written in a small, cramped script. "Bottom line, you've got a lot of people coming in and out, plus visitors on the weekends."

"Yes."

"Seems pretty quiet right now."

"Weekends are busy, Mondays are the catch-up days. A few people will come in later today to teach classes and use the studios. Tomorrow will be busier."

"What's the usual schedule? For the artists."

"Um…they can come pretty much any time. Co-op members have their own alarm codes."

"Really? Anytime?"

"Yes. Though everyone's usually gone by eight in the evening, except when we have evening classes. The Thursday night class runs the latest, seven-thirty to nine."

He frowned. Tapped his chin with his pen and sighed. "I'll need a list of the co-op members and phone numbers. And the name of anyone else you know who's been here since Thursday, including any volunteers."

"Felicia has the volunteer list. They're mostly high school students, come college."

"What about visitors? Do they sign in?"

The rapid-fire questions were unnerving. She resisted the urge to answer at the same pace. "Only if they want to be on our email list. Do you need that, too?"

"Not yet. We'll focus on staff first."

"We've never had a problem before." She felt like she needed to defend Stonefall. "We must seem sloppy about circuitry."

She knew something had come out wrong because his eyebrow was lifting again.

All he said was, "Let's think about the vandalism in the garden. Is there anyone you can think of who'd have a grudge against Mr. Felton, or against anyone else here?"

"No."

"What about the neighbors?"

"Our family's been here for ages. Everyone loves Stonefall. They send their kids here for nature camp and art classes."

Even as she said it, Emma felt her gut lurch. *The man in the cafe was targeting me, not Stonefall. Does that count?*

Szczepanski touched his pen to the green folder. "Ms. Weingardt said there was a woman who got upset when her paintings were rejected for sale in the gallery. Miranda Graves."

Emma shrugged a "maybe," not wanting to point the finger at poor Mrs. Graves, an empty-nester with fantasies of becoming discovered as the next Grandma Moses.

He opened the folder and skimmed a page. "I spoke with Mrs. Graves. She claimed Ms. Weingardt was highly prejudiced and didn't recognize her quote-unquote 'unique interpretations.' What happened there?"

Emma felt her face wanting to smile but she needed to focus so she covered it with a frown. How to explain? She crossed her legs to buy time, then uncrossed them again because the damp pants were sticking to her knees.

"Miranda joined the landscape class," she began slowly, "after her last kid left for college. She asked lots of ... questions, but never followed ... suggestions. Felicia is very patient but Simon is not. Miranda got half-mended when Simon told her to buy a pepper."

The detective looked equal parts confused and amused. "Half? Oh, offended." His mouth twitched. "A pepper?"

"It's an art school thing." She worried an uneven fingernail with her thumb. This was way off topic but he'd asked, hadn't he? "See ... peppers have mass and texture but they aren't as confiscated ... com-pli-cated ... as humans or animals. They hold still better, too."

His eyes went wide beneath the raised eyebrows. She knew he wanted to laugh but it didn't feel like he was laughing at her.

This conversation was absurd and trivial, and she was risking verbal trip-ups, but he seemed to be listening and it felt good to talk about anything other than vandalism.

Her confidence went up a notch. "A bell pepper can look like the human body. It's cheaper than paying a model."

"You're serious." His mouth twitched.

He might have been patronizing her but she didn't care. "Every day for a week, you draw that pepper from a different angle. Slice it open, draw the inside. You can fill a whole sketchbook with one pepper. Then you can eat it."

She kept her face blank, hoping he had a sense of humor but not sure why it should matter. All she knew was that for a few minutes, she'd forgotten about everything else—the vandalism, her fears, the guilt. It felt *good*.

He nodded gravely, possibly masking a grin. "So when Simon Bell told Miranda Graves to go buy a pepper, that's like saying your work sucks and you should go back to kindergarten to learn how to draw."

"Yes." She offered a small smile.

Szczepanski's face returned to his earlier grim, unreadable blankness. He sat back in Jonah's chair. "But Mrs. Graves doesn't look anything like the person in your videos, who was dumping paint and swinging a sledgehammer."

"Not her," Emma agreed. "What's next?"

"If it's just random, someone with little or no connection to Stonefall, it's gonna be hard to crack. You could go public. Do an interview with the news media, ask for tips. Someone might come forward with information."

Emma shook her head. "We don't want to ... public-shy this. We need to find the problem, not just get someone arrested for the vandalism."

She blinked, trying to clear her eyes. "This is supposed to be a safe place. Where people can heal and be ... creative."

"Okay, it's up to you. If you change your mind, we'll handle any leads that come in."

He paused. Added, "Keep in mind it's probably out on social media already. All it takes is one teenager with a phone. If the vandalism in the garden was the only thing, we'd be looking at a single incident of malicious mischief. But now we have the sketches, and that's much more disturbing. There's your name on the envelope. An explicit threat. It's personal."

Emma pulled a tissue from the box on her desk.

Again she thought, *I need to tell him about the redheaded man at Margo's. The online slurs, the guilt campaigns. All that toxic waste.*

But again her mind skipped sideways, avoiding the shame.

He touched the green folder. "The drawings. Ms. Weingardt gave me the originals. Do you need to see them again?"

"No."

"Let's back up a bit, then. To last Thursday evening." His slightly surly voice returned. "I understand you were the model for that session. Why?"

She narrowed her eyes, hearing his censure. "Why what?"

"Why do you model? Nude." He stared, unblinking. "Seems an odd thing for the office manager to do. Or the owner."

The implicit disapproval: *What's a nice girl like you...?*

She stared back, meeting whatever challenge he'd issued. "Artists need models. Sometimes I ... volunteer, sometimes the artists take turns. Or we hire a model from the agency."

"So you know these are drawings of you."

"Of course." Her voice rose. "Who else would they be? The artist is Simon. We all know his work."

"Thursday night. How many people were there? Was it a typical night?"

"Ten or twelve. Jonah keeps a list."

"Everyone there was a legitimate artist?"

She stiffened. "What kind of a question is that? Jonah's very careful about who joins that group. You can't just show up."

"Sorry, no disrespect intended." He paused a beat. "Can you think of why Mr. Bell would deface his own drawings?"

Emma bristled again. "Don't be … silly." *Ridiculous* or *preposterous* or *idiotic* were better words but she didn't trust herself to say those. "Of course he didn't! Maybe someone wants to cause trouble for him."

"How did you feel about his drawings? Did you like them?"

"It's not— Look, how I feel— If I *like* them? That doesn't matter. I don't own the drawings, the artists do. They can keep them or throw them away or wrap up the trash, it doesn't matter. But Simon certainly did not deface his own drawings. Or write 'die bitch' on them."

"How can you be sure?"

Emma held his eyes. "Simon would never be so…hurtful. None one here would. Besides," she added, "Simon's right-handed."

He sat back, his expression a mix of skepticism and surprise. He opened the green folder and removed the sheaf of drawings in their plastic sleeves, then turned a little sideways. Holding them so he could see but blocking her view..

Emma examined her hands, which were twining themselves together in her lap. "Look at the last page. See those ink smudges to the left of the tree? That's from a hand resting on the paper. And the back slant of the letters. Left-handed."

"You noticed that?"

She stared at her lap.

"Is that common?" He seemed genuinely curious. "Left-handed artists."

On her desk, Emma located an orange fine-tipped marker and a scrap of notepaper. She wrote rapidly: PAUL KLEE, M.C. ESCHER, RAOUL DUFY, ANITA MALFATTI.

He stared at the names. "Escher, I've heard of him. I don't know the others."

Not her job to educate him. "How about DaVinci? He was ambi— He used both hands."

He glanced at her list again but found nothing to say about left-handedness so he moved on.

"The recycling containers. Mr. Jacobs said they're in the classroom, right? You don't shred every day, only when the bin is full, right? So anyone could just open the lid and grab a handful of papers."

She nodded.

The next question was important because now he was leaning forward. "Who handles the shredding?"

"Jonah, Felicia, or me. We'll probably ask Chaz to do it but he's only been working here a couple of days. I don't think he knows where the shredder is."

Szczepanski made a quick note. "Which is where?"

"The supply closet. Next to this office."

"Who delivers the mail and where is it dropped off?"

She realized suddenly how very tired she was. To buy a moment, she raked one hand through her still-damp hair, failing again to unsnarl it.

"There are two mailboxes on the far side of the road. One is for the house, the other's for Stonefall. If something doesn't fit, the carrier brings it to whoever is in the barn. Or she puts it in the parcel box, where FedEx and UPS leave packages. That's at the corner of the barn near the chicken coop."

"Is the parcel box locked?"

"Yes." Anticipating his next question. "We have three keys. One stays at the house, one is here in the office, and Felicia carries the third on her keychain."

"The lock on the box prevents package theft. But anyone can drop something in without unlocking it, right?"

"Yes, I guess."

"Is there a camera out there?"

"No. There's one on that corner of the barn, but it points toward the front doors."

"Who brought in the mail this morning?"

"Felicia."

Szczepanski tucked the sketches into the folder and stood. He squeezed past Emma's chair, heading for the door. Stiff from sitting, Emma rose and stretched her back before following him across the hall to the gallery.

Felicia was sitting on her stool behind the counter, arranging silver and gemstone jewelry on a tabletop carousel.

"Ms. Weingardt? I need to ask you a few more questions about those drawings of Emma."

Felicia's shrewd eyes flicked to her, standing in the doorway behind Szczepanski. "I see we're doing first names now," she told him, "If she's Emma, then I'm Felicia. And you're Kendric, right? Or do you prefer Ken?"

He tipped his head, assessing her. The ghost of a smile flickered. "Ken works. Okay, Felicia, what time does the mail usually arrive?"

"Eight, sometimes earlier. We're the first stop on Teresa's route. She's our mail carrier."

"Did you see her drop it off?"

"No. It was already here when I got in. Mail in the mailbox, that one bigger piece in the parcel box."

"Thanks. Is Simon Bell here?"

Emma answered. "In the classroom. I'll show you."

Szczepanski pivoted away from the gallery, then stopped in mid-stride and waited for her to catch up. He cleared his throat. "Look, Ms. Gillen—"

"Emma."

"Emma. I'm sorry. I was out of line, back there in the office. Asking why you model. It's none of my business. I don't usually—"

"It's okay." She turned away, uncomfortable with his discomfort. "The classroom's over here."

He followed her around a row of church pews, past a taxidermy owl perched on a birch limb nailed to the wall. They paused by the classroom door.

"Simon's got an after-school class in … mango. Sorry, manga. And animal … anime." She frowned in frustration. "Sorry, you've probably noticed I have trouble with words. It's from an old injury."

His face was unreadable. "That crash, back in twenty-fifteen."

"You looked it up? Why—?" She hesitated. "Oh. Do you think this— what's going on now— is related?"

The door swung open.

"Hullo." Simon looked from one to the other. "What's all this about? Sorry," he added, "Didn't mean to interrupt but I heard you talking. Felicia said you were looking for me. I'm Simon Bell."

"Detective Szczepanski. It's not about the garden, actually. It's something else. From this morning."

He turned to Emma. "Please, give me ten minutes with Simon. Then I'd like to speak with you again. And with Jonah."

Did he even hear her question?

THIRTY-ONE

Szczepanski sat with his notebook propped on one knee, cross-legged on a church pew. Jonah and Emma sat on a second bench, set at right angles. They were alone in the cavernous center hall. Light fell dimly through the skylights and rain pattered on the metal roof high above.

Szczepanski raised his voice a little to be heard above the hum of the barn's three ceiling fans, turning slowly to stir the humid air.

"Simon said he dropped several pages of sketches into the recycle bin on Thursday evening. The shredding bin," he amended. "He looked pretty shook up when I showed him the...modifications. He has no idea who'd want to target him. Or Emma."

Setting his elbows on his knees, he leaned forward a little and Emma caught the faint trace of sandalwood. Definitely nicer than Jonah's scent, she thought. Jonah usually smelled of paint thinner or dry-erase markers, which always reminded her of diesel fuel.

Before Jonah or Emma could respond, they heard car doors slam and a rising chatter of young voices. A flock of mid-teen boys with backpacks appeared, hurrying to the classroom as they jostled and flicked rainwater at each other. Behind the boys trailed two serious-faced girls, squeezing water from their ponytails and whispering together. Their eyes dropped and slid past the adults as they passed.

"It's Simon's four o'clock," Jonah said. "A group of ESL kids, all planning to become titans of the video gaming industry. They want to create unbelievable wealth and shape the history of nations by creating another *Dragon Quest* or *StreetFighter*."

Szczepanski smiled slightly. "My younger brother played *DragonQuest*. I thought the animation was done with computers."

"It is, but there's nothing to animate until you've learned to draw. You have to develop interesting characters and storylines. Can't leave that up to AI and CG, it would all end up looking the same."

The classroom door clicked shut, closing in the chatter. They heard again the white noise of the fans and the drizzle of rain. The light from the skylights had darkened to a murky gray.

Szczepanski waited a beat. "So those students, the ones we just saw—they follow the same procedures as everyone else, to throw away any drawings they don't want?"

"Yes," Jonah said. "Though Simon encourages them to keep all their work in project folders. They're doing detailed drawings, not just quick sketches."

"Were any of them here Thursday evening?"

"No. But I think a couple of them volunteer a few hours a week with Felicia in the gallery. They might have been here on the weekend, helping or just visiting."

Szczepanski sighed. "Okay. Tell me then, who should be at the top of my list?"

Jonah gazed for a moment at a taxidermy squirrel posed on a shelf beyond the detective's left shoulder. He cut a quick glance at Emma before saying, "There are two people I think you should speak to."

Emma remained still. *He's going to mention Lyssa. But who else?*

"First," Jonah said, "there's Chaz Robberts."

Szczepanski flipped to a fresh page in his notebook and crossed his legs, propping his notebook on one knee. "Chaz for Charles?"

"Yes. And Robberts, with two Bs."

Emma frowned. "Why Chaz? He seems like a good kid."

Jonah kneaded the back of his neck with one large hand, not realizing he was fretting his ponytail into loose wisps. "I like Chaz. He's a hard worker, and he's great with the kids and animals. But—" Breaking off, he turned both hands palms up. "I've seen him several times, parked down by the creek near the trailhead. Sitting in his pickup, alone. You know the place? There's nothing wrong with that. It's a nice place to eat your lunch.

But I sometimes feel like he watching us. Keeping tabs on who's coming and going."

He glanced an apology to Emma. "Also, last week he asked me about the Thursday night figure sessions. He wanted to know if anyone could just walk in off the street or if they had to sign up first."

"What did you tell him?" Szczepanski uncrossed his legs and leaned forward a little.

"Same thing I tell everyone. It's open studio, which means theoretically it's open to the public. But space is limited and we need to know you're serious about your art. Chaz is a good worker but I don't know anything about him as an artist or a student, so I gave him a sketchpad and a manikin to practice with." He paused. "He's left-handed."

Szczepanski nodded. "You said Chaz worked here all day Friday and Saturday, then was scheduled to work at Aldi that night. What about yesterday?"

"He wasn't here. He's got Sundays and Mondays off."

Emma said, "He was here earlier today. Felicia was helping him with something personal."

"Oh?" Jonah's eyebrows arched. He stood. "I'll get Felicia."

For the few minutes it took Jonah to return with Felicia, the detective kept his attention on his notes. He seemed to be avoiding Emma's eyes, so she sat on her church pew and gazed at a pottery display in a glass-fronted case at the side of the hall. Thinking about Chaz, who'd asked about the figure drawing class.

Emma scooted over on her bench to make room for Felicia, who now wore a deep-frown version of her earlier worried look.

"What's this about Chaz?" Felicia sat, resting her hands on the knees of her black leggings. Jonah stood behind both women, his hands braced far apart on the smooth wood of the high-backed bench as if sheltering them.

Szczepanski said, "Felicia, I'm trying to establish who was where this morning. Chaz arrived around ten o'clock?"

"Yes. He asked me to help him with a personal matter. A call he needed to make. We used the empty studio upstairs and closed the door for privacy." She placed a slight emphasis on "privacy."

"Was he here when you arrived earlier? Did you see him when you brought the mail in?"

"No. He came a little before ten and left right after the call. About ten-thirty, ten-forty."

"You saw him leave?"

"Yes. He has a gray pickup, a Ford Ranger."

"What was the phone call about?"

Felicia squared her small frame and tucked a curtain of braids and beads behind one shoulder, gaining a moment. "Like I said, it's private," she said carefully. "At least for now."

"Who asked you to keep it confidential?"

When she bristled, he added, "I'm just trying to figure out what happened."

Emma knew Felicia was protecting Chaz, just as she'd protected the confidences of so many students over the years.

"I called a lawyer for Chaz," Felicia said carefully. "That's who asked me to keep it private, the lawyer."

Jonah broke in. "Is Chaz in trouble?"

"Not at all. This was good news for Chaz."

"Who's the lawyer?" Szczepanski asked. "I'll like to speak with them."

"I don't see how this is—" She paused. "Can I send you a text?"

"Sure. You have my card, use the cell number."

"Is that all?" She hesitated, then stood.

"That's all. Thanks, Felicia."

"And the second one?" the detective prompted. "Jonah, you said there were two people I should talk with."

"That would be Lyssa Morales." Jonah looked away. "Emma can tell you about her."

THIRTY-TWO

Szczepanski's phone buzzed. He excused himself and Emma was left to wonder what she should say about Lyssa.

He scrolled and swiped rapidly for several minutes, then paused and frowned. Tapped rapidly, then shoved the phone back in the pocket of his polo shirt.

A long sigh. "I'm sorry, It's almost four and I have maybe fifteen minutes before the wrath of my sergeant falls on my head. Eight months on the job and they expect me to be up to speed on everything."

He sat and picked up his spiral notebook. "Sorry, you didn't hear that. Okay, who's Lyssa Morales and what do I need to know about her?"

"In fifteen minutes? More like hours—"

"Let's start with the basics. Lyssa is short for Melissa?"

"Just Lyssa." She spelled it. "My cousin. Lucy Gillen Harnett, born in Quebec. Now Lyssa Morales. I don't know what she's using for a middle name."

Emma gave him a description, realizing how much she relied on a comparison to herself: one year older, six inches taller. More slender, more fit. Pale blond hair, shorter and straighter, eyes blue but with more green than Emma's. Her thoughts added *prettier and smarter and stronger and more talented,* but she stopped herself from saying those out loud.

"Right or left-handed?"

"Mostly right. She's ambivalent." Was that right? "She uses both hands for drawing. Used to, anyway," she finished lamely.

"Ambidextrous," he suggested without looking up.

"Yes." She shifted uncomfortably.

He flipped to a previous page. "She was born in Canada. Does she have a Canadian passport?"

"She used to. Probably still does. An American one, too, I think."

"If she still has her U.S. driver's license, where's that from?"

"Connecticut? Where we grew up, before college."

"Tell me a little about that. Growing up with your cousin."

He wasn't consulting his watch now so in a halting cadence she tried to sketch life with her cousin: family members, Lucy's unstable home life, Jerry and the tech company he'd built in Boston. College.

"The only time we really lived completely apart," she explained, "was my senior year in high school, when Lucy was a college freshman. After high school, I followed her to Silvermill."

That sounded lame, she knew, but it was true. Following Lucy was just what she did, without much thought or choice. Like a scrap of newspaper pulled into the wake of a speeding car.

She went on, "The first year, I lived in a freshman dorm but we hung out together a lot. Her parties, her friends. Then Lucy rented a place off-campus so we could be housemates again. An old hunting lodge, up on Bishops Knob." She paused and took a deep breath. "That November, eight years ago—there was a car accident."

He nodded, listening closely and encouraging her the way he'd done with the weird conversation about peppers.

She told him what little she remembered about the week before the crash. Thanksgiving plans, the storm, Maggie vanishing to Canada. The crash, and Lucy's disappearance.

She shortened her own long time in hospitals and rehab to a *Cliff's Notes* version. Mentioned Jerry's death, the will, her father's illness.

Then Lucy again, returning as Lyssa. "She just opened the door and walked in. Thursday evening, when I was modeling for the figure class."

Emma was sure Szczepanski was imagining that scene, though his face was unreadable.

He said, "Lyssa's back now, but she didn't ask to stay with you? Did you offer?"

"She said she prefers the hotel. She's—hard to live with."

"In college, what were you studying?"

"Economics. Lyssa was in art school."

"You never went back? To college."

Why did that matter? She shook her head, unable to explain that sometimes she felt like her original brain had been swapped for a glitchy mechanism with undocumented manufacturer's defects. Studying economics was beyond her now; she couldn't trust her mind with anything more complex than simple bookkeeping.

He was asking another question. "You said your uncle left everything to you and your dad. I assume we're talking about a substantial amount?" He held up a hand. "No need to say how much."

She raised a hand and turned it in a "sort of" gesture.

"Okay. Why should I talk with Ms. Morales about the vandalism and the mutilated drawings?"

Deep breath, she told herself. *Here's the important part but what should I say? If the police get pushy, she'll run away again and I'll never get answers.*

"She's getting divorced and she needs money. Dad's…sym…pathetic but we also think she might challenge the will. She told me the farm belongs to her as much as me, but it's really owned by the trust—"

He held up a hand. "Hold on. Now you're getting into lawyer territory. Not my kuleana." He saw her confusion. "Sorry. Kuleana means not my responsibility. Out of my lane, above my pay grade." He flipped to a fresh page in his notebook and re-crossed his legs. "Let's back up. What could all this have to do with the vandalism? If she wants a piece of what you've got, wouldn't she want to protect it and be part of it?"

"I guess. Now she wants me to hire her." Her mind was threatening to bolt. *Think the words, then say them. Slowly.* "Social media marketing. She wants me to create a role for her, here. She got angry when I said I couldn't just hand her a job like a birthday present."

He was frowning now. "Has she threatened you? Issued warnings or hurt you physically?"

"Recently? No."

He raised an eyebrow. She knew he needed way more context, but she had only a few minutes to connect the dots for him.

She took a deep breath. "Lucy—Lyssa gets angry and kind of careless when things don't go her way. A few days before that car crash, when she was angry with her mother? She pushed over a big floor easel and it hit my shoulder. It cracked my collarbone."

Szczepanski leaned back and twirled the pen on his notepad, regarding her with a new curiosity. Did he think she was nuts? Spiteful, maybe? Or just scatterbrained?

She slumped back, feeling drained.

He thought for a minute. "That car crash. How was she involved?"

"She wasn't. Well, I don't remember. But it was my car, they said I was driving. I'm the one responsible for killing those people."

He drew back a little. "That's a pretty harsh judgment. It was ruled an accident. Why do you think it was your fault?"

Emma picked at a ragged cuticle, then wound her fingers together to keep them still. "I was driving," she repeated. "My car hit Chrissy Garrison's van." Her voice choked. "I must have done something — but I don't know what. To cause it, I mean. But I can't remember." Quickly, then: "And I *have* to know so I don't ever make the same mistake again. Whatever it was."

Leaning a little sideways, he fished a crumpled packet of tissues from a pants pocket and waited while she wiped her eyes.

He spoke softly. "The report said no one was at fault."

"There are lots of people who don't believe the report. They say I was on drugs and…" Her lips moved slightly, practicing the words before she said it. "Negligent homicide."

Then, red-faced with shame, she told him about the man who'd recognized her in the café on Friday. The accusations, the slurs. Drunk, druggie, baby killer.

Szczepanski's mouth tightened, his jaw clenching. "The trolls don't usually show up in person. Or hang around this long. They usually move on, one outrage to another." He scribbled a quick note. "Lyssa saw him? What did she do?"

Emma managed a smile. "She went after him. Jumped up, got in his face and called him a—" She thought for a moment. "'White-trash piece of shit.' She shoved him away from me and he fell down. I think she was lining up a kick to his knee, or maybe his crotch. He couldn't get out of there fast enough."

"And what did you do?"

The shame flooded back. "Nothing."

She stared across the hall toward the glass doors of the gallery, her mind stalling.

"I'm sorry," he said, though she couldn't tell if he was apologizing for asking the question or offering sympathy. He rose from the bench and walked a few steps toward the big double doors at the front of the hall. Giving her time to compose herself.

When she'd wiped both eyes with the wadded-up tissue, he turned to face her again but didn't sit. "This farm is your home," he said gently, "but it's also a legacy project. What would happen if one or both of you decided to leave?"

An odd question. "I guess...I really don't know."

"Someone else would have to manage it, right? Someone could say that the manager should be a family member. The benefactor's niece, say, who also happens to be an artist." A pause and a shrug. "I'm just speculating."

"Do I think Lyssa's capable of...sabotage? To drive me away."

"You know her, I don't. But—well, people can be real nasty when they think there's a lot of money involved." His tone lightened. "This is all off the record, of course. You'll notice I'm not taking notes right now. And my body cam's turned off."

Her eyes flew to his chest and the trim polo shirt.

He flashed a smile. "Just joking. No body cam." He grew serious. "Emma, would you like to see if there's more information in the records? About the accident."

She blinked, startled. "How?"

"I can find out who holds the case file, us or the transportation office. A fatal crash gets investigated by the DOT if it happens on a public road, but yours was on a private road. And the procedures got changed a few years back."

The damp tissue was shredding in her hands. "I have some of the reports. Copies of what went to the insurance company."

"There should be lots more. Photos, interviews, a list of evidence items. The investigators' field notes."

She didn't hesitate. "Yes. Please. I need to know. And this— what's happening now—Do you think it's connected?"

His forehead sprouted deeper furrows. Was he reconsidering his offer? Maybe he didn't believe she'd say yes. Maybe he was promising something he couldn't deliver.

He cautioned, "Maybe there's nothing to learn about the accident, and the current stuff's probably not related. Also, it may trigger terrible things you'd rather not remember."

"Things I'd rather not remember? I've already got a boatload of those. What's a few extra nightmares, a few more voices in my head?"

She'd aimed for lightness and felt that falling flat so she added, with all the force she could muster, "I need to *know what happened*."

He nodded. "Okay. I'll see what I can find."

"You'd do this, Ken? You're already so busy."

He hesitated.

I shouldn't have used his first name, she thought. *It's too familiar.* Though he'd offered it earlier.

"Nah," he said easily. "The captain tells us, use your initiative. Follow all the leads. Though maybe that's just a thing they say to make the new guy feel empowered. But instead of calling me Ken, how about you use Nakoa. Or Koa for short. It's my middle name, what they call me at home."

Very deliberately, she tried it out. "Koa. Kendric Nakoa Shepanski. Where's home?"

"Kea'au. It's one town in Hawai'i. Trust me, you haven't heard of it."

His phone buzzed again. He walked a few paces away.

"Sorry," he said over his shoulder. "Time's up. For real now."

Emma continued to sit, thinking about how he'd said the name of his hometown: KAY-ah-ow, three distinct syllables with the vowels pulled into a distinctive lilt. She'd google it later if she could figure out the spelling. How many towns could there be in Hawai'i that started with a K?

He'd pronounced Hawaii with three syllables, too. Ha-VAI-ee, with a softly slurred V replacing the W. She practiced the words silently to preserve them: Kea'au, Hawai'i. When he said "home" and "Hawai'i," she'd heard a hint of longing in his voice.

She was still turning this over in her mind when she realized he'd ended his call.

He was grim-faced now. "I've got to go. But I'll work on this tonight, Emma. I'll call you as soon as I can. Be careful."

He zipped his pen and notepad into his messenger bag and strode toward the door. A rumble of thunder rolled over the barn as he ducked his head and stepped out into the pouring rain.

What did he mean, be careful?

THIRTY-THREE

When Ian Hoskins called, Emma was staring blankly into the fridge, wondering if she was really hungry.

"Your dad's doing great," the pulmonologist told her. "He's got three new valves in his left lung. Everything went well but he needs rest, so don't feel bad if you can't get in to see him tonight. Tomorrow, we'll run some tests and see how he does without the oxygen."

Emma released breath she didn't realize she'd been holding. "Thank you. That's great." That sounded inadequate so she repeated it, wishing she had better words.

Relief gave her an appetite. She finished the leftover pad thai, then curled up on the sofa with Teague and listened to the drum of rain on the roof. She missed her father's ordinary presence in the house and now wished she'd been there when he came out of surgery.

I can't drive at night in the rain.

But she could have taken a Valium and called Jonah or Felicia to drive her to the hospital.

With a small start, Emma realized she also could have asked Lyssa to drive. But the hairs on her arms prickled in alarm. *No. Not her.*

***

"Vodka, no ice. A double." Lyssa couldn't afford more than one drink tonight. It might as well pack a wallop.

Monday evening and she was low-level furious at the way her whole day had gone.

While she waited for her drink, she shelled a handful of peanuts from a bowl on the hotel bar. She eased her short skirt up a bit and adjusted her balance on the stool so she could half-turn to gaze around the room.

We might be wide open here, her posture suggested. For the right man, of course. But a quick scan of the lounge told her she was too early to find someone to buy her dinner or the next drink or anything else.

What sad fuck sits in a bar at five-fifteen on a rainy Monday afternoon? Old farts and tourists and herself, hell-bent on a pity party.

First, there'd been the bad-news call from the local lawyer. Sorry, Ms. Morales, your uncle's will appears to be valid. You don't have cause to contest it unless you can prove he lacked testamentary capacity or duress or fraud or blah blah blah.

The next call was from Drew, reneging on his offer to buy dinner and drinks tonight. He'd sounded nervous and distracted, like he couldn't get off the phone fast enough.

Then, selling her jewelry. What a farce that was.

The engagement ring Marcos slipped onto her finger six years ago with such great ceremony—the gorgeous three-carat emerald with its attendant diamonds—cost twenty-six thousand Canadian. The ring was her security blanket, a fallback cash reserve. She'd been confident its sale would give her enough to live on for several months.

But no, the ring wasn't worth squat.

She'd driven to four storefronts, all claiming to offer the best prices for gold and "fine estate jewelry." Not one offered her more than a tiny fraction of the emerald ring's appraised value. Lab-grown, all the jewelers said. Lacking the true character, the inclusions, the saturated color of an authentic natural emerald.

The many small diamonds, by the way, were also synthetic.

Bullshit. She didn't believe it. She showed them the appraisal and the purchase receipt.

Three buyers said sorry, not interested. We only handle real gems, not lab-grown. The fourth offered her six hundred so she choked back several invectives and taken the cash before he changed his mind.

The six hundred, plus another four-twenty she got from the sale of two gold necklaces and a pair of earrings, was all she had coming in until the divorce settlement came through. Which was at least six months away and wouldn't be enough to live on anyway.

It's your own fault, Marcos reminded her when she was packing to leave Cowtown. If you just held up your end of the bargain, you'd be set for life. You'd have a big house with a pool and a staff and a six-car garage. Travel, clothes, an art studio, everything you wanted. All you had to do was keep my name, bear my children, and don't do anything monumentally stupid that would shame my family. You got one out of three right, he'd told her. The other two were an epic fail.

So I fucking failed, she raged. I don't need your family's money. I've got my own family and we've got our own money.

It wasn't really a lie. All she had to do was find a way to make Uncle Jerry's money flow her way again before her own ran out.

The bartender disappeared into the kitchen. Lyssa swallowed quickly and set down her empty martini glass. She thought about stiffing him but he knew her room number. She dropped a twenty on the bar, then reconsidered and dug through her bag to find exact change. Eighteen American dollars for a stupid glass of vodka and two olives. What a rip-off. The dude hadn't earned a tip, had barely talked to her. Let that be a lesson.

Out on the sidewalk she lit the last of her Silk Cut Silvers and exhaled a deep sigh. The damn things were expensive but she couldn't quit, she'd pack on the pounds again and none of her clothes would fit. Better to buy a cheaper brand of smokes and hang onto the Silks box for the class factor.

She'd have to let go of the rented Mustang soon. But not tonight.

It was still raining but the hospital parking garage had a covered walkway and the visitors' desk was close by. The receptionist smiled when Lyssa identified herself as Frank Gillen's niece. Visiting hours didn't end until eight so she'd have plenty of time to visit Mr. Gillen in room 756, but she'd have to wear a mask and restrict her visit to fifteen minutes because Mr. Gillen needed his rest after today's procedure.

Equipped with a map and a paper mask which she dutifully hooked over her ears, Lyssa stepped into the elevator and silently rehearsed what she planned to say to her uncle.

Seven fifty-six was a single room, crowded with monitors and instruments on wheeled carts. A ceiling-mounted TV, its sound muted, was tuned to a football game. A small table held a water pitcher, a cup, and a blue bendy straw. In the corner by the door, there was an uncomfortable-looking orange chair. Molded plastic, mid-century hideous.

Frank was asleep on the narrow bed. A clear plastic tube ran from a small wall-mounted panel to a nasal cannula, not so different from his set-up at home. A call-button cable, a bed controller, and the TV remote lay on the beige blanket near his softly curled right hand.

Briefly, Lyssa felt a twinge of affection for the man who'd helped raise her. They'd done the best they could—Frank and Kit, Jerry and Marisa. If she'd been born to either of the brothers instead of to their wacko, drug-addled sister Maggie, she'd be doing just fine. She wouldn't be standing here wondering how to convince Frank to hand over a chunk of his inheritance.

"Hey, Uncle Frank," she said softly. He didn't stir so she repeated his name, then placed a hand on his shoulder. She removed her mask, smoothed her hair, and readied a big smile.

He twitched and his eyes flew open in a confused panic, searching the room before settling on her face.

His eyes focused. "Lucy?"

"Hey. Is it okay if I sit?" She dragged the chair close to the head of the bed and perched demurely in her short skirt. Knees together, feet crossed at the ankles.

She set her mask back in place and squeezed his hand. "So good to see you, Uncle Frank."

When he strained to sit up, she found the bed controller and raised the head of the bed.

"Here. Have some water." She filled the cup and held the straw for him.

"What... are you doing here?"

"I just wanted to stop by, see how you were doing. Emma said you're here for a few days. They tell me you've had an operation."

"To help me breathe better." He managed a small smile. "It's good to see you. Thanks for coming."

"I'm glad I could make it." She patted his hand. "And, well, I wanted to apologize for the other night. I was rude, asking all those questions about Uncle Jerry's will and the trusts and all. I know you're just following his instructions, what he wanted you to do."

Frank looked surprised. He smiled and reversed their grip, his hand on top so her could pat hers. "That's okay, Lucy. Sorry, Lyssa. You surprised us, that's all. We didn't know what to say after all that time you were gone. But it's good to have you back with us."

"Uncle Frank." She pushed her sweetest smile into each word. "I'm really sorry about staying away for so long. I was so bad about not getting in touch. I was just so focused on finding my mother that I really wasn't thinking straight. I have to admit, I made some bad decisions back then but now I promise to set things right. I'm not sure how I can help our family, but I really want to try. To help out at the art center, wherever you need me."

She touched the corner of one eye with a finger, wiping an invisible tear. "What I'm trying to say is, I'd like to come home. To the farm. I'm not sure that's even possible but I'd like to try."

Fumbling a tissue from a box on the side table, Frank wiped both eyes because his tears were real. "You'll always have a home with me, Lucy. But Emma has to agree because it's her home, too. And you can't just show up demanding a job. But we'll work something out."

She hoped she sounded sufficiently contrite. "Oh, I'd love that! And I have some great ideas about how to help Stonefall, to make it really successful. I tried to tell Emma but I don't think she understands. See, I have a lot of experience with today's marketing methods. I know what works and I know I can make a real difference."

See, Uncle Frank? I can be the plays-nice kid. I can fake it, anyway.

"Please talk with Emma. Explain it to her the way you just explained it to me." Frank's words came slowly now. He was drifting away, she realized she'd have to hurry. Her fifteen minutes were almost up.

Eyelids drooping, he added, "I hate to see you two fighting. You were such great friends when you were kids."

Lyssa nodded solemnly, not wanting to go there. She clearly remembered the look of dismay on Emma's face whenever Maggie dumped her at Frank and Kit's house. Leaving her on their doorstep with a ratty old backpack, waiting for someone to let her in. She'd always been the misfit, the disrupter. The unwelcome black sheep in the Happy Family of Perfect Emma.

"I'll call her tomorrow. We'll work it out." She added urgency to her voice. "And Uncle Frank, I really appreciate what you said after dinner the other night. That if you'd been able to talk with Jerry about his will, you'd have asked him to set up a trust for me, too. And maybe for my mom."

His mouth opened as if to say something but she held the floor with her eyes and her gratitude. "And, well, Uncle Frank, I hate to ask when you're here in the hospital—so maybe we'll talk more when you're back home—but I'm hoping you can help me out with a loan like Uncle Jerry did. So I can find an apartment and get myself squared away. Build a new life right here. Near my family."

That seemed like a good exit line so she leaned in and pecked a kiss on his forehead. His eyes closed and she felt his hand relax. Did he even hear what she said?

"Thanks so much, Uncle Frank. Oh," she added, as if only just remembering. "When you get home, I'll bring you a get-well gift. You always liked your single-malt scotch, right? That peaty stuff from Orkney. Your favorite's Highland Park, right?"

His eyes flicked halfway open, accompanied by the ghost of a grin.

She mirrored his grin, made it bigger. "That's for later, okay? I gotta go now. The receptionist said fifteen minutes so time's up. I love you!"

She thought she heard a faint "Love you too" just before the door clicked behind her.

Good job, she thought. Single-malt scotch and humble pie would bring Uncle Frank around, she was sure of it. Now she just had to figure out what to do with Emma.

***

By ten o'clock, Emma had locked the henhouse and unloaded the dishwasher. She gave Teague twenty minutes in the back yard and set the alarm. Then, too restless for television or music or reading, she busied herself in the kitchen with random unnecessary tasks.

She'd rubbed beeswax into three wooden cutting boards and was using an old toothbrush to scrub mineral deposits from the base of the kitchen faucet when her phone pinged with a text. She wiped cleanser from her hands and leaned back against the kitchen counter.

Found the case file. Lots of paper.
OK to stop by 9:30 am? K

She stared at his contact ID and thought of how hard it must have been in kindergarten, a little kid learning to write Kendric Szczepanski and getting everyone to say it correctly.

She texted back:

Yes thank you. Pls come to the house. E

Another ping, another text. Thinking it was a PS from him, Emma readied a new smile.

But this one was from Lyssa and it stopped her cold.

Saw yr dad tonite, glad hes getting lungs fixed.
Looks good. TTYM 3? L

First came a wave of panic: *What does she want from Dad?*

Next, a flash of guilt. Her cousin had visited when she couldn't. She had to admit, that had probably made him happy.

Then, anxiety. Should she tell Lyssa that Szczepanski wanted to talk with her?

No. Don't warn her. She'll disappear again.

After several drafts and discards—and a google search for TTYM, which she learned meant "Talk to you mañana"—she texted back.

> *Tomorrow at 3 is good. At the house. E*

Then she texted Koa:

> *Lyssa's coming to the house, 3 pm.*
> *She wants to talk with me. Can you join us? E*

It was nearly eleven when he replied.

> *Yes. I'll drop files at 9:30 then come back at 3.*
> *Don't tell her I'm coming.*

THIRTY-FOUR

Heading out for work, Chaz locked the trailer door behind him and froze.

Thirty feet away, a brown-skinned man with black hair stood beside a gray sedan. The stranger wore trim jeans and a green windbreaker that might as well have POLICE stenciled in six-inch letters across the front. He held his phone in front of him like he was about to make a call.

Chaz wasn't expecting a visitor, certainly not at seven-thirty on a Tuesday morning. No one ever came to his trailer except his sister Jessie. And Miz Buckner, once, to deliver the lawyer letter. Jehovah's Witnesses a few times, but only on Saturdays.

He'd never been in trouble with the law. Miz Buckner kept a strict eye on all her fosters and Chaz was fine with that. His buddy Darren, however, had a knack for being in the wrong place at the wrong time with the wrong people, and he'd been questioned a couple times. Once about the theft of tools from a construction site, another time after a batch of mailboxes got blown up. Stupid kid stuff.

Darren said the best way to behave around cops was to be super-polite. Say "yessir" and "nosir" a lot and play dumb the rest of the time. He'd been on the wrong side of some situations but never did time. Darren admitted there was two things kept him out of jail, being white and joining the Army.

Chaz was white, too, so that was in his favor but he had no plans to join any army. He didn't think he'd done anything wrong but just the presence of a cop in his front yard was sending his feet sideways.

Coming down his trailer's three wooden steps, he half-tripped on the bottom one. Caught hold of the railing and barely saved himself from a fall.

The cop stepped away from his car. Held up a wallet ID and offered Chaz a card. "Chaz Robberts? Can I ask you a few questions? " He said his name but Chaz didn't catch it.

Chaz took the card but didn't look at it because his mind was already full with *A few questions, a few questions, a few questions.* He raised a hand to his head but instead of smoothing his hair he pinched a fold of skin on the back of his neck and stabbed a thumbnail into the flesh, quick and hard. That did the trick and the brain-stutter stopped.

He nodded at a large oak tree where he'd arranged what Jessie called the patio set, three upturned chunks of tree trunk and two ratty aluminum chairs with duct-taped webbing set around a big cable-spool table.

Chaz reminded himself not to look up into the oak tree, where one of Darren's camo-patterned game cameras was strapped to a high branch. The lens was aimed at the door of the trailer, not the chairs under the tree, but it might catch a short video of the cop coming or going. Not that he thought he'd need it, but you never knew.

The detective looked surprised by the offer of seating. "Thanks. You've got a nice spot here. The only one with shade."

The rust-trimmed yellow trailer was the end unit in a tightly planted line of single-wides, eighteen trailers fronting a narrow dirt driveway. The other units had one parking space each but Chaz had an actual yard beside the wide part of the turnaround. Beyond that stretched a twenty-acre field planted now in tomatoes, thousands of staked plants bowing beneath the weight of late-season fruit. Four pickers were working at the far end of the field, filling crates with ripening tomatoes.

The detective stepped around a puddle and selected the sturdiest lawn chair. He rocked it a bit, wisely testing its stability in the wet soil before trusting it with his weight. Chaz sat on the cable spool, his phone still in one hand. He slouched a bit when he realized he was sitting higher than the detective.

He was nervous of course but also curious. The cop looked vaguely foreign, not Black or Hispanic but something else. The way he held himself, too, said he wasn't from around here. He sat calm and relaxed, not scowling the way some of them did before you'd even said hey how are you.

Chaz sneaked a glance at the phone in his hand, checking the time.

The cop saw. "You'll be a little late for work but it's okay. I cleared it with Mr. Jacobs, he knows you're helping me this morning. Had breakfast yet?"

Chaz wondered about the word "helping" and tried to work some saliva around in his dry mouth. "Nosir, I usually stop at Mickey Dee's on the way in. What's this about? Am I in trouble?"

"Not that I know of. But maybe you can help us figure out who should be. Chaz, when did you learn about the vandalism at the farm? Over the weekend, when Mr. Felton's statue got damaged."

"I heard about it yesterday morning. Miz Weingardt said someone busted up the gates and splashed paint around in the garden. But they got it all fixed, except for the gates."

"That's why I'm asking questions, to find out who was behind that. Can you think of anyone who'd want to do that?"

"Nosir."

"Sundays and Mondays are your days off, right?"

"Yessir. Yesterday I went in because Miz Weingardt was helping me talk with this lawyer who sent me a letter." Chaz heard Darren's voice in his head. Telling him, *Don't volunteer info! It's Yessir, Nosir, and nothing else.* He looked down at the card in his hand because he'd forgotten the detective's name and realized he didn't have a clue how to pronounce it.

"Sorry, sir. What's your name again?"

A small smile. "It's pronounced Shepanski. It's okay, most people get it wrong."

He asked Chaz when, where, and what he'd been doing over the weekend. Now Chaz was remembering to keep his answers short and simple: worked at the barn, worked at Aldi, napped on Sunday afternoon, visited his sister.

The detective leaned forward a bit in the saggy lawn chair and Chaz knew he needed to pay sharp attention because something important was coming.

"And what about yesterday? What time did you get to the barn, to see Ms. Weingardt?"

"A little before ten." He added, "I hate being late."

"A good habit." Szczepanski nodded. "Then she called the lawyer for you, right? Mark Camerer."

"A Zoom call."

Another nod. "Because he'd sent you a letter. What was that about?"

Ms. Weingardt said they should keep quiet about it but the detective seemed to know everything already.

"He says there's money," Chaz said slowly. "For college, for me and my sister. The money's from Mr. Gillen, the one who used to own the farm. He died a few years ago."

"Why would Jeremiah Gillen leave you and Jessie money?" The detective sounded genuinely curious.

Chaz's eyes slid sideways under the scrutiny. "I dunno…I guess because of the accident that killed my mom?" He said it as a question because it still didn't make sense to him. "And my two sisters. Half-sisters."

"The same accident Emma Gillen was in. She was the other driver."

"Yessir, that's what they said. I was pretty young when it happened so I don't remember much."

The fingers of his free hand wanted to fidget so he folded them over the hand holding his phone to keep everything still.

Szczepanski was sitting back again, looking relaxed and not caring that he had to look up at Chaz on the cable spool.

"How do you feel about that, Chaz? Working near Ms. Gillen."

"Um, she's nice. I like the job." His face felt warm and he hoped the zit scars weren't going all red and ugly the way they often did.

"Do you know her? Emma."

"Yessir, she's nice." He realized he'd already said that so he added, "When I was a little kid, she was almost the only adult who was ever nice to me. Whenever she saw me out in the woods, she'd stop and talk."

"What did you talk about?"

"Trees and animals, things like that. She did most of the talking."

"You spent a lot of time in the woods back then. Doing what?"

"Kid stuff. Watching the animals. Collecting things, like feathers and rocks. I built a fort to hide in."

Szczepanski smiled. "I did that, too. Built a fort. Did you do any hunting? Deer, turkeys?"

"Nosir. My buddy Darren likes to hunt but I don't like shooting things. I just like to walk around and watch the animals."

Thinking of Darren reminded Chaz that maybe he shouldn't be saying so much.

"Who were you hiding from? In your fort in the woods."

"My mom, sometimes." He shifted his butt on the spool. "She was always getting after me to go to church with her. Mostly, I was hiding from her boyfriends. Her last one, Gordy, was a real bad sonofa— He was mean, to me and Jessie."

"Did you ever talk much with Emma's cousin, Lyssa? Her name used to be Lucy."

"That's the tall blonde lady, right? With that purple Mustang, the Shelby. Nosir. She was kinda scary-looking when I was little. Lots of ink and metal on her face. She swore and yelled a lot. I said hi to her once but she never said hi back."

"Does Emma know who you are? Chrissy Garrison's son."

Miz Weingardt had asked him the same thing so he'd given it some thought. "I always thought yeah, but maybe not. She probably remembers my nickname. When I was little my mom called me Billy. Now I like to be called Chaz."

"Okay. Is it part of your job at the art center to pick up the mail and bring it in?"

The sudden shift in topic made Chaz blink. "The mail? No, I don't know anything about that. I seen the mail truck come by some days, but I dunno who brings it."

"Okay. Just a couple more questions, then I promise you can get to work. Is it your job to empty the paper recycling bin, the one in the classroom?"

Another weird question. "Nosir. Mr. Jacobs says the artists take turns doing that. But I ain't seen anyone do it."

Szczepanski frowned a little. "What about the second barrel, the shredding bin. The one with the closed top. Who cleans that out?"

"I think Mr. Jacobs or Miz Emma does that. That's where the private stuff goes, right? Bank papers and like that. No one's asked me to do any shreddin. Maybe they will, but I'm still new there. Summer, I was workin in the fields, not in the barn."

"Last question. Did you sign up for the Thursday evening figure drawing classes? The group with a live model."

"Nosir. I asked Mr. Jacobs about it but he says I need to practice first. I took one art class last year in high school, but we just drew flowers and fruit, no people. Mr. Jacobs gave me some paper and borrowed me one of his—" Chaz didn't know what to call it. "A hand, made of wood. You can move the fingers around. He said I should practice drawin that."

Chaz worried he was talking too much but these questions seemed harmless.

"In those classes…" The detective hesitated. "Sometimes the model is nude. That's what a figure-drawing session is, drawing people. Sometimes without clothes."

This was definitely weird. Chaz's left thumbnail began flicking against his index finger. "Well, I guess that's how artists learn to draw people."

"Chaz, did you know Emma Gillen sometimes poses for that class on Thursday night? She's one of the models."

Chaz's eyes flitted away as heat rushed in. "Nosir," he stammered. "She—she's not— No, Emma's the office person. Their manager."

His voice broke. He lurched up from his chair and sagged against the tree trunk, his back to Szczepanski. His eyes settled finally on a distant tractor moving slowly through rows of tomato plants. Words looped in his mind: *Nude model Emma nude model Emma nude nude nude Emma?!*

From a great distance he heard Szczepanski's voice.

"I appreciate your time, Chaz." A pause. "I'm sorry. Sometimes we have to ask uncomfortable questions. Thank you, you've been very helpful."

***

"Detective? It's Jonah. Glad I caught you."

"Hold on." Szczepanski swung his gray Ford onto the road by the creek, heading for Stonefall.

Knowing he'd be early, he pulled over at the trailhead sign near the stream and switched the phone's audio from the car to his handheld.

Jonah wanted an update on the evidence. Fingerprints, handwriting, videos, DNA. Anything?

"Sorry, there's nothing new," the detective said, "and whatever I learn, I'm going to channel it through Emma. It's her case." He hesitated. "And I'm glad you called. I just spoke with Chaz. He's fine, no worries there.

"But I think it would be good if you could give him work that will put some distance between him and Emma, for a few days anyway. He's just learned that she models sometimes for the Thursday night classes. He's feeling pretty uncomfortable about that." Another pause.

"And Jonah, when you see Felicia, please let her know I've spoken with Mark Camerer. He's filled me in."

He disconnected and sat for a few minutes in the dappled shade, listening to birdsong and watching clear water rippling over smooth rocks, forming small cascades that pooled beneath the mossy banks.

It was quiet and lovely. It was also the perfect place to watch anyone driving to and from Stonefall.

He started his car again and drove slowly, not wanting to jostle the box of old case records resting on the back seat.

THIRTY-FIVE

Teague knew how to stay out of the way. He greeted the detective with a politely offered paw, then retreated to his cushion in the corner to keep a worried eye on his cherished human, who this morning was bouncing around like a badly worn tennis ball.

Emma fizzed from fridge to sink. "Inside or out? It's nice outside on the deck but maybe too breezy."

"Inside is fine." He set a battered cardboard box on the floor by the kitchen table and crouched to open the flaps, releasing a faint odor of mustiness and old paper. He set three fat brown accordion folders on the table.

She waved a pot in his direction. "Coffee?"

"Thanks, but no. Any more caffeine and I'll be pinballing around like you. You planning to sit sometime soon?"

Emma folded a towel two different ways and hung it crookedly on the dishwasher's handle. She'd already cleared the table by moving away her laptop and a stack of art center flyers.

She chose her usual chair and sat, then popped up again to fetch a pen and a notepad from a shelf. Returned to her seat and squared up the pad and pen with the edge of the table.

"Okay," she exhaled. "I'm ready."

His left eyebrow was already quirked. "You sure?"

She nodded, not sure at all.

He pulled off his green windbreaker and sat across from her. Flipped open the first folder, glanced at the contents, and raised his eyes to assess what? Her willingness to rip open her wounds—to freshen the guilt she lived with—just to discover the details of an eight-year-old closed case. *Yes.*

"How's your dad?" He said it like he cared, and they had all the time in the world to talk about her father's health.

Emma pulled her eyes from the open folder and focused on his question. "Good, as of last night. Dr. Hoskins said not to call until later. They're doing tests this morning." She explained the procedure. "They're keeping him for another couple days to watch for infection. Fingers crossed, he'll be home Thursday."

Talking about her father quieted her nerves. Hoping to match Koa's composure, she felt her body let go of a tension she didn't realize she'd been holding. He wasn't an imposing man—average height, compact build, nothing that pushed *ego* or *power*—but his presence filled her kitchen. It was his intelligence, she thought. Social and emotional as well as intellectual. It was a rare ability, to be still and listen.

He gave her a warm smile. "That's great. I look forward to meeting him." His face went serious and he tapped the closed folders in front of him. "Emma, before we look at this, I have a few questions. How well do you know Chaz Robberts?"

"Chaz? Does he have something to do with the vandalism?" Her voice dropped. "Or the drawings?"

He repeated the question.

She swallowed her alarm. "I've talked with him once or twice. He seems very shy, a little nervous talking to people. Jonah says he's a hard worker. That's all I know."

"Do you know his family?"

"Um, no. Should I?"

He spoke gently. "Chaz is Christine Garrison's son. Your neighbor, on Bishops Knob. When he was a kid everyone called him Billy."

She sat back. "That's Billy? But—"

"His name is Charles William Robberts. I talked with him earlier this morning. He knows who you are, and he remembers you from when you and Lucy lived next door."

"Chaz is Billy?" Her mind mind circled in confusion. "But why would he want to work here, near me? He's got to be… Why—?" She rubbed a hand over her face.

Koa handed her a tissue from a box on the kitchen counter. She wiped her eyes.

He said, "I think when that summer job came up, Chaz wanted to work here because he remembers you. You were kind to him when he was a little kid and I don't think he's known a lot of kind people. I don't think he blames you for the accident. Or if he did, he's forgiven you." He placed a slight emphasis on the word *accident*.

"And I don't think he had anything to do with the vandalism in the garden. He was working at Aldi that night, the eleven to seven shift. I've already confirmed that with his supervisor. He didn't know anything about the drawings, either. He thinks the shredding bin was for bills and bank records. And he'd make a terrible liar, he's way too nervous."

Emma snuffled again. He placed the tissue box within reach and waited while she blew her nose.

"Also," he went on, "when I mentioned that you model sometimes for the Thursday evening classes, he got embarrassed. He may have a crush on you but I don't think he's done anything wrong."

He added, "Chaz seemed to think you already knew who he was."

Emma gathered up her damp tissues and dropped them in the trash bin under the sink. She filled two glasses with tap water and brought them back to the table.

Leaning both elbows on the table, she rotated her glass between both hands and watched the liquid slosh gently. "I knew Billy and his sister Jessie went into foster care. But I never knew where, because the county keeps those files…confidential."

Her voice went soft and sad. "I think he's one of those poor kids with no one to speak up for him. The invisible ones that fall through the cracks."

"Ah. Maybe not so poor. Or invisible. Did you know that your Uncle Jerry created a scholarship fund for Chaz and his sister Jessie?"

"No. Who told you that?"

"Your lawyer, Mark Camerer. Felicia gave me his number. That's why Chaz was here Monday morning. He got a letter from Mr. Camerer and didn't know what to do with it, so Felicia helped him on a Zoom call. Mark wanted to keep that quiet until he had a chance to talk with you and your father, but then—"

"Other things happened."

"Yes." He tipped his head. "You're not surprised about the scholarships?"

"There's lots of things my uncle did that we didn't know about. Jerry's always been very generous, and Mark's always been good at keeping Jerry's secrets. After the accident, Jerry made a large donation to the mountain rescue team. He paid for the funerals, too, for Chrissy and her girls. Dad and I didn't know about that until after Jerry died. When Mark told us."

"Lawyers are required to keep secrets." He paused a beat. "Just out of curiosity, how much did Jerry donate to M-SAR? The mountain search and rescue unit."

"A hundred thousand, I think. Maybe more. I'd have to look it up."

"Ah." Both eyebrows lifted. Shifting forward in his chair, he tapped the folders. "Okay. Ready?"

She nodded. He slid the first one toward her. "This contains the accident report, which I think you already have. But there's notes, too, from the investigating officer who talked to the witnesses."

"But there weren't any witnesses."

"Witnesses include anyone who can help establish what happened before or after. Not just people who saw something happen." He touched a finger to the second, thicker folder. "The forensics reports. There's a *ton* of forensics. Lab reports, lists of items found, photos, pathology reports."

He saw the question in her eyes. "Automobile fatalities are considered unusual deaths, so a pathologist has to rule on the manner and cause."

"And the third folder?"

"Medical reports on you. Updates on your condition during the months following the accident. The final report on the insurance settlement."

"I don't need to see that."

He slid the top two folders toward her and she set the first one aside. Opening the Forensics folder, she went through the pages quickly, scanning the pages without removing the binder clip securing the pages.

There was too much, it was impossible to take in. Her mind wanted to drift, seeking a more pleasant place than this catalogue of destruction.

But until she learned everything in these dusty files, she'd be rolling her boulder up the same mountain forever. She pulled herself back to the here and now.

Koa checked the folder's index and selected a stack of transcripts from Western Carolinas M-SAR. Rescuers kept a log, documenting what they'd found and when. Their calls for extra assistance, a list of equipment, the additional units that responded in the middle of the night to rappel down a cold dark mountainside and strap her unconscious body into a rescue stretcher.

Reading the details now, she waited for her body to recoil in remembered pain but nothing came. The details of the rescue read now like the directions for a documentary, describing scenes and actions in the dry, passive voice of a set director.

She wondered about her response. Was it a healthy distance, or a troublesome dissociation?

She reached for a packet of crash scene photos and the hair on her arms prickled. The distance dissolved and she was back on that mountain, in the rain.

"I removed everything that showed the victims," Koa said gently. "I didn't think you'd want to see those."

Feeling numb, she could only nod.

Some of the photos were taken at night, the scene harshly lit by work lights. Others were shot in daylight, the next day.

Emma looked up, staring at kitchen cabinets and seeing nothing. Her pulse thudded. What was about to be triggered? There was a boxcar full of possibilities: seizures, flashbacks, night terrors, panic attacks, hallucinations.

Should she set everything aside and do this later? Wait for her dad to come home so he could sit with her?

No. It must be done now.

"Emma, are you all right?"

She hadn't seen Koa rise from the table but now he was beside her with a hand resting lightly on her forearm. Teague was there also, his front paws planted on her knees.

She hauled her mind back from its gone-away place. Threaded her fingers through the long silky hair on Teague's floppy ears, then drank from her water glass.

"I'm okay." Thinking, *Actually I'm not but I'll get there.*

Teague dropped to the floor, circled into a new lying-down spot close to her chair, and dropped his chin on her foot. She gave them both a faint smile and began sorting through the photos.

First, the nighttime shots. Most were blurry. Overexposed or underexposed, taken quickly as rescuers rushed to locate victims and save a life. She was afraid of what she might see in those images, the bodies of Chrissy or a child or her own broken self—

Koa said he'd pulled those out but maybe he missed one.

She felt a familiar whisper of vertigo, an out-of-body disorientation.

Breathe. Breathe and think. Stay right here. You can do it. The only way to the other side is straight through.

Koa stirred beside her. "I know this stuff is hard. Let me know when you've had too much."

How much is too much? How will I know?

How many other victims had he talked through a similar process? But she wasn't just a victim, she was also a perpetrator.

She hated both words: *victim, perpetrator.*

After a minute, the gut-punch feeling lessened. She took a deep breath and forced herself to examine several photos taken the day after the crash, in bright sun. Two pictures showed the fallen pine tree with its exposed roots lying on the uphill bank and its top branches sprawled over the crater in the gravel road.

She'd forgotten how small the tree was, not much bigger than a sapling. A single strong adult might have dragged it off to the side. A car could have pushed right through the thin upper branches, if you didn't mind paint scratches.

But no one pulled the tree aside, or drove through it, because then the road collapsed, taking two vehicles down with it.

The next photos clearly showed the washout, a dumpster-sized space carved from the roadbed. Tire tracks in the wet gravel ended abruptly at the gap.

The Miata's tracks.

Her throat clenched again. *Why was I driving so close to the edge? Was I trying to push through the tree?*

Shivering, Emma turned those photos face down.

The next series was of the crash scene, where the smashed vehicles looked like broken toys in a trash heap. Her beloved Miata, crumpled and missing its convertible top but right-side up, leaned against a boulder twice the size of the car. Chrissy's van, flattened and split into pieces, rested on what remained of its roof.

Orange cones sprouted from the dead leaves, indicating where the bodies—three dead, one still living—were found in the muddy, churned-up gulley. Evidence flags littered the ground like a confetti of ugly flowers, blooming on thin wire stems. Yellow-and-black police tape sagged from trees and bushes.

Emma inhaled, squared her shoulders, and focused on two pictures of her car.

A close-up of the driver's side showed the shaft of the steering wheel bent sharply sideways. Most of the dashboard was in fragments, but her keys still sat in the ignition and the parking brake lever still rose from the center console. The seat had lost its headrest and the upholstery was shredded, but the frame appeared intact.

Another photo, taken from a different angle and a few yards downhill, showed the passenger side of the Miata. The seat was nearly unrecognizable, a tangle of metal and deflated airbag.

"I've never seen these." She shuddered. "How could anyone survive that?"

"You were thrown clear on the way down. The report says the driver's seatbelt wasn't fastened."

"It was broken?"

"Not broken, unclipped."

She frowned. "I always fastened it." She looked closer at both photos. "Why did only one airbag inflate? On the passenger side."

He angled the photo to gain light from the kitchen window and peered closely. "How old was your car?"

"Twelve years."

"Ah. Did you have the airbags checked at the ten-year service?"

"I don't know. Dad bought it for my birthday, two years before."

She'd been seventeen, a responsible teenager but still a teenager. Now she felt a familiar wash of despair sweep in because she should have had the airbags checked when she got the car or when the car turned ten or—

But the outcome for Chrissy Garrison and her daughters would have been the same, regardless of what shape the Miata's airbags were in.

If her own seatbelt was fastened, she wouldn't have been thrown clear. She'd have died in the crash too and maybe the ledger would be balanced.

But she *always* fastened her seatbelt, so how—

She offered, "Maybe I got out to move that tree?"

"Would you have tried to do that on your own?"

She could only shake her head, frustrated by all the things she couldn't answer.

She examined the two photos again, looking closely at the debris field around the Miata. She recognized her sunglasses, intact and neatly folded, resting beside a smashed cell phone on a pile of leaves. Staring at the detritus of lives interrupted, she felt a lump grew in her chest. When she noticed a tiny pink sneaker and a child's backpack, she had to look away.

Koa set a fresh glass of water on the table. She drank gratefully and said weakly, "I need to take Teague outside," though the dog wasn't asking. "I'm sorry," she added. "I'm taking up your entire morning. How can you...afford to spend so much time with me?"

"You've been a bit preoccupied so you probably didn't notice, but I'm pretty good at multitasking." He held up his phone. "I've answered a dozen texts and emails in the past hour."

"But it's way later than that."

"It's only ten-thirty." He pointed to the Seiko on her left wrist. "But there is one call I've got to respond to. A barn fire in a place called Grampy's Mush. Is that a real place? Or someone's making that up, just messing with the new guy."

She stood and managed a smile, acknowledging his offer of a distraction. Sliding open the back door, she roused Teague. The small dog trotted obediently outside. He found a shady spot on the deck and promptly flopped down to resume his interrupted nap.

Koa trailed behind, still frowning at phone messages.

Emma leaned her elbows on the deck railing and looked down into the flower beds, purple chrysanthemums planted beside the steps. This old wooden deck was so much friendlier than the one at the barn. Built with a railing of solid pickets instead of invisible cables, this platform posed no threat of vertigo to provoke nightmares. And only three steps down, a comfortable height.

Though there'd been a time when even three steps had looked impossibly high.

"Mush is a local word for marsh," she said. "It's from the Cherokee, I think. There's a place nearby called Sandy Mush. I don't know Grampy's Mush, but I'm sure it will come up on your GPS."

"Uh-huh." He sounded skeptical. "Well, a barn fire's nothing to joke about. But it's probably just accidental. An electrical problem, maybe. Or someone dropped a cigarette."

She thought about explaining *spontaneous combustion*, decided against it. "Hay can burn on its own. If it's baled wet, or too green. The…curing creates heat."

"Or it really could be arson, and there goes my afternoon. They've got it contained and cooled down a bit. I'm supposed to show up as soon as I can."

He tucked his phone back in his pocket and moved to stand beside her. One hand rested on the railing near hers, close but not touching.

He said, "Do you want me to leave those files with you? I can swing by later this afternoon to pick them up."

She stared at the flowers, watching a honeybee sort through the petals of a purple blossom. "Can you do that? Leave it all here?"

He tapped a finger on the railing and thought. "It's a closed case. No charges were filed. There's no orders restricting access. It's all digitized and I'm a little surprised the hard copies haven't been destroyed. You have a legal right to the information."

"But if I requested a copy of everything—"

"It would take weeks, maybe months."

"Can I make my own copies?"

He skirted a direct answer. "Just be sure nothing disappears."

THIRTY-SIX

After Koa left for Grampy's Mush, Emma's first thought was to dig back into the folders and photos spread out on her kitchen table. But Tuesday was her catch-up day for Stonefall's accounts.

She decided to dedicate two hours to the account books, but not at the barn where it was too easy to get sidetracked. There'd be artists in and out of their studios, people wanting information about workshops, visitors asking about gallery hours and shows. All good for Stonefall, but not good for her right now.

She retrieved her laptop and set it up on a table on the deck, dragging the umbrella close for shade. From here she had a partial view of the barn. She saw Felicia carrying several wrapped packages from the barn to her van. Then Jonah's Sentra pulled in, followed by the trash haulers' truck.

No one bothered her as she recorded sales and invoices, authorized commissions and paychecks. At one-thirty, she caught up on emails. One from Jonah informing her that the new security camera for the office's back door wouldn't arrive until Friday, so the system upgrade would be delayed by a few days; another from Felicia, reminding her to order porta-potties and an extra case of toilet paper for the October show.

She felt a laugh bubbling up. Amid threats and hate messages, with her father in the hospital and Lyssa throwing herself back into their lives, Emma needed to remember toilet paper and porta-potties.

With that thought, she was done with work. Time to call her father.

Raylene answered Frank's cell phone. Sorry, her dad couldn't talk right then, he was on his way to Imaging. Then they had more tests for lung capacity. He was doing terrific, Ray added happily. Breathing better already and lordy, wasn't modern medicine great? The "lordy" made Emma smile.

"Come join him for dinner," Raylene urged her. "The roads'll be fine and dry. Food's better if you get here early."

Emma knew that wasn't true but she promised to be there at five.

After lunch, she spread out the contents of the Forensics folder again. Choosing what to copy and print, what to scan and save.

By two forty-five, she'd scanned most of the contents. She also printed copies of three photos. One was a shot of her crumpled Miata, showing the steering wheel and driver's seat; the other two were close-ups of the nearby debris field.

She'd secured the lid on the box and was washing her hands clean of archival grime when she heard the rumble of a car engine.

A car door slammed. "Hey, Em. You here?"

Damn. It was Lyssa, ten minutes early.

Where was Koa? Did she miss a message? And where was her phone?

On the table, outside on the deck where she'd been sitting earlier. In front of Lyssa, who was sitting there now.

"You got a message." Lyssa was peering at the notifications on Emma's lock screen. "Two messages. Who's Koa?"

She looked mildly offended as Emma snatched up her phone.

"So don't leave it lying around, Mouse. It's not like I was trying to open it or anything."

Emma scowled and turned away to log in. The two messages were almost an hour old. He'd be a little late, sorry, couldn't be helped. She sent a thumbs-up, closed the app and turned to face her cousin.

Lyssa leaned back in the chair and crossed perfectly tanned legs. She was continuing her country-girl theme today, Daisy Mae in thigh-high cutoffs and a pink plaid camp shirt. The shirttail was twisted up and tied above her navel, exposing plenty of toned midriff. Minimal makeup, gold stud earrings, a pink ball cap over her pale blond hair.

Her gaze roamed the yard. "Looks the same as always, huh? Asparagus beds, giant veggie garden, the peach trees."

"Yes."

"We should put in a pool. There's room over there next to the tomatoes."

"You saw my dad last night? How was he?"

"He was okay, I guess." Lyssa flicked invisible dirt off one smooth knee. "Kinda groggy. He was talking slow and breathing through that tube. Have you heard from him today?"

Emma stayed wary. "They're doing X-rays and tests today. I spoke with Raylene, his homecare nurse. She said he's doing well."

"I haven't met Ray-lene, have I?" She drawled out the name, giving it a derisive cornpone twist.

"No."

"Well. Anyway, Uncle Frank says he wants me to come home and be part of Stonefall again. And he's promised me a small loan. Short-term, until I figure out what I'm doing next. Here, sit." She patted a second chair.

Did Dad really offer her a loan and suggest she move back? Emma was struggling to hide her dismay and she didn't want to accept anything from Lyssa, not even an invitation to sit, but she sank down. "I thought you said he was groggy. So how did he—"

Lyssa arranged her face for a suitable apology. "Hey, Em, I'm sorry about trying to shoot video in the barn. Maybe you need to make a bigger sign about that."

Done with that task, her voice quickened. "And listen, I'm working on that marketing plan you asked for. For starters, we should center-stage each artist. Harry first, of course. They don't come hotter than Harry, and he's got that terrific grease-monkey background. Does he really melt beer cans and pour them into ant mounds? That's sick."

Emma squinted against the hot sun, unable to see her cousin clearly. The umbrella was tipped to favor Lyssa, leaving Emma's chair in the glare. She shaded her eyes with a hand but it didn't help. *Damn, she's doing it again. It's her script and she's got the only copy. If you try to stop her train, she's already jumped the track onto another line of lies and half-truths.*

"Let's go in," Emma said. "The sun's too bright out here."

Lyssa scowled, but it was lost on Emma who'd already opened the sliding door into the kitchen.

"You're doing it again," Lyssa groused. "You're not even listening—" She stopped short when she saw Teague in the kitchen. "There's that fucking dog. Can't you lock him up or something?"

The fur over Teague's shoulders rose. Emma heard a low mutter, the beginning of a growl or a bark.

Emma took hold of Teague's collar. "I'll take care of him." She gave him a quick pat and a biscuit before closing him in her father's bedroom, then snuck a look at her watch. Where was Koa?

"What are these, Em?" At the kitchen table, Lyssa held up the three crash scene photos.

Damn. Emma had packed away everything else but she'd left those on the table. She kept her voice casual. "I was sorting through some old files."

"That looks like your old Miata—"

There was a brisk knock at the front door, which stood open.

"You home, Ms. Gillen?"

Hiding a smile, Emma called to him, "Just a minute." *Ms. Gillen, indeed.*

To Lyssa she said, "I think it's Detective Szczepanski from the sheriff's office. He needs to ask me some questions about the vandalism in the garden. You heard about that, right?" She really hoped she'd said *detective*, not *defective*.

Szczepanski smelled faintly of smoke, moldy hay, and cow manure. One shoulder of his blue polo shirt was greasy with black soot.

He handed Lyssa his card and explained in a formal voice that he'd been hoping to speak with her, too. He was pleased to find them together. Two birds with one stone, it would only take a few minutes of her time.

Lyssa's face was closed and wary, her gaze flicking between them.

Emma indicated a third chair. "Water, coffee, iced tea?"

Lyssa said water, please. The detective asked for iced tea. "Unsweet, if you've got it. Thank you, ma'am."

Hiding a smile, Emma ducked her head into the refrigerator. How long had he been outside? She hoped he'd heard at least part of their conversation on the back deck.

As she joined them at the table, he was asking Lyssa to confirm her identity, please, and explain her connection to Stonefall. It would be most helpful, he added, if she could describe where she was last Saturday night and the early hours of Sunday morning. We're asking everyone, he added before she could interrupt. Just trying to gather information.

Lyssa sat stiffly, damp fingers wrapped around a sweating water glass. She looked trapped and, for once, uncertain. "Is this really necessary? All this for a little damage to a garden?"

"We take property destruction very seriously, Mrs. Morales." Szczepanski wore the earnestness of a conscientious rookie, pen paused over a spiral notebook like every cliché of an old-fashioned gumshoe. "Please," he added, "This is helping me a lot. You never know what details might be important."

Lyssa eased her grip on the water glass. "Okay. I had dinner here, with my family." She shrugged. "I drove back to Asheville and got a drink at that Irish pub near Pack Square. I got back to my hotel around midnight. The Marriott, in the arts district down by the river."

"Did you go out again?"

Her gaze was steady. "Not until ten or so, the next morning."

He wrote something in his notebook. "Do you know anyone who'd want to vandalize the art garden? Break open the gates and smash things?"

Her eyes widened. "No, of course not! I've been away for years, I've just come home. I don't know anyone here. Except for Emma, of course, and my Uncle Frank. I'm sure *they* didn't do it. It sounds like kids, joyriding and pranking someone. Maybe it was someone who doesn't like the artist? Or maybe he did it himself, Harry Felton. For publicity, or to collect the insurance. Sorry, I don't know how that works. It's just a guess."

"Ms. Gillen mentioned a distressing incident at Margo's Café, on Friday."

"Oh, right. That idiot. Do you think he did it?"

"Just tell me what you remember, please."

Looking bored, she confirmed Emma's account of the incident.

He seemed about to ask a new question when she flashed him an overlarge smile.

"I'm curious, Detective. Don't you guys always work in pairs? For safety. Then you've got a witness if you get accused of bullying someone. And shouldn't you be wearing a bodycam?" Her eyes slid over his shoulders and chest, clearly appreciating the body under the dirty shirt.

This was classic Lucy-Lyssa scattershot. Distraction, deflection, a little allure thrown in for fun. Emma sat back to watch.

Koa offered the merest ghost of a smile. "I'd appreciate a partner, Ms. Morales, but we're a little short-handed right now."

His tone became serious. "Most of my work is in property crime, not personal crime. It generally doesn't get violent unless there's drugs or alcohol involved. If I have to look into an assault or a robbery, then yeah, I'll get backup from the patrol team. We're recruiting, if you think you're up to it."

She shifted uneasily in her chair, not liking his challenge.

He said, "A few more questions, please. What about Monday morning? Can you tell me what you were doing between, say, six and ten a.m.?"

Lyssa shifted her gaze to Emma. "What's this about?"

He pulled out his phone and enlarged something on the screen, then held it toward Lyssa. "Do you know anything about this?"

Lyssa reached over the table and wrapped her fingers around his hand, pretending to steady the phone while she examined the image. Her nails dug into his wrist but his hold on the phone didn't waver. He waited.

When she released him, her elegant fingers trailed along his wrist a moment longer than necessary. She gave him a satisfied-cat smile and sat back.

"What's that, some kid's comic strip?"

Emma knew he'd shown her the stick-figure drawing of the tree and the car. Did she also see the writing, DIE BITCH?

"Monday morning between six and ten," he repeated.

"Six o'clock on a Monday morning?" Lyssa pouted. "Sorry, I never get up that early unless I've got a plane to catch. I was sleeping until about nine." She tucked a lock of hair behind one ear, crossed her smooth bare legs, and jiggled a foot.

Lyssa spoke casually but Emma recognized the tension. Her cousin was nervous or she needed a cigarette. Probably both.

"At the hotel?" he pressed.

"Well, yeah." She added an eye roll.

Szczepanski stood. "Okay, I think that's all. Thank you, Mrs. Morales."

To Emma he said, "Ms. Gillen, I appreciate you holding onto these boxes for me. Can you give me a hand, carrying them out?"

Boxes, plural. Hers as well as his. "Of course."

He'd already picked up his so she rose quickly and grabbed the lighter one and followed him through the living room. He propped the box under one arm, opened the front door, and motioned her through.

She joined him on the porch and balanced her box on the railing.

Stepping close, he kept his voice low. "What did she see? From the files."

"Three photos from the crash scene. I was careless, leaving them out. But I got a lot of it scanned, too." She smelled his faint stink of barnyard and smoke. No sandalwood.

"It's okay. That might be helpful." He didn't elaborate. "I'll take my box back to the archives and bring yours back tomorrow. Sorry I was late."

"I didn't see your texts before she arrived."

"It's okay. But if you talk to her again— Look, be careful what you ask. Don't accuse, don't tell her anything new. We'll talk later."

When Emma went back inside, Lyssa was leaning against the archway between kitchen and living room, her back to the wall with one knee bent and a sneakered foot braced against the trim. It was a silly cheesecake pose, shoulders arched back and breasts pushed forward into a suggestive

271

profile. Prepared to impress and distract the detective if he returned, but wasted on Emma.

Lyssa was sulking. "What was *that* all about?"

THIRTY-SEVEN

"Like he said," Emma said, "he's investigating the vandalism. And this other thing that happened."

Breaking her doorframe pose, Lyssa strolled back to the kitchen table. "What other incident? Was that the picture on his phone? All I saw was some stupid little stick figures."

"Just a hateful juvenile prank. Some jerk scribbled on Simon's drawings." Put like that, it sounded petty. She wanted a better description but didn't have one.

Lyssa was moving on, anyway.

"That cop was really lame, wasn't he? Then he said he was going to ask you some questions, but all he did was talk to me, not you. Don't you think that was at least low-key weird? And what's in those boxes?"

Lyssa plopped back into her chair at the table and drank from Emma's water glass because her own was empty.

Emma sat also. "Maybe he ran out of time. I've already talked with him twice."

"Twice? Just for that thing in the garden? Hey, Em, d'you think he's hot? He smelled like cowshit but I'm assuming that can be fixed. Nice bod, fit and flexible. Big shiny badge. He should be carrying handcuffs, too. Handcuffs are freaky."

"You can't be—"

Lyssa snort-laughed. "Just *kidding*. I can't get thirsty for a cop, not even a hot one. And he's way too serious. Positively grim." She touched the photos on the table. "This is your car, right? The Miata?"

"Yes."

"Where did these pictures come from?"

"I was going through some old paperwork and found them." Not exactly a lie.

"That's what was in those boxes? Why's he taking them?"

"They're just old police photos." Also not a lie. Or an answer.

Lyssa dropped the photos carelessly on the table and sighed dramatically. "Okay, Em. If I tell you everything I can remember about the crash, then can we *puh-leese* put this shit to bed and move on? I'm trying to figure out what I'm doing with my *whole fucking life* right now. I could use your help."

Emma's breath caught. Here it was, an offer to bargain. Information, carefully curated, in return for a welcome mat and a slice of the family pie.

"Okay," she managed, wondering what she'd just agreed to. She laced her hands together on the table like a dutiful schoolgirl, then dropped one in her lap because that's not what she wanted to be.

"So," Lyssa seemed to be feeling her way through whatever she'd proposed. "Here we go. The police questioned me for *hours* about the accident. It was exhausting, they kept asking the same shit over and over." She pulled off her pink ball cap and twirled it. Waiting for questions?

"Go back," Emma suggested. "Earlier."

"What, Sunday afternoon? There was that storm. The rain finally stopped. You took the Miata to get food, plus some gas for my car. I stayed home so you'd have more room for stuff. I was busy working on that shitty art project."

Emma pulled syllables into the right order. "Genesis and…Catharsis."

Lyssa's eyes widened. "Ohmigod, you remember that?"

"You…obsessed…it. For months."

"Yeah, I did. My bad." She paused a beat, organizing. "So you left and then it got dark but I didn't realize how late because I was working. Then I saw all these lights on the road, so I found a flashlight and walked down to see. It was real cold and windy, the trees were whipping around like crazy. This dude in a uniform came up on an ATV and said the road was closed, I had to go back. There'd been a crash. He gave me a ride to the cabin and that's when he told me they thought three people died. But he didn't know who."

To Emma it all sounded true, but also wrong and she didn't know why it was wrong. She had no way to compare Lyssa's recollection to her own experience, which was a vast wilderness of darkness and pain. *First comes the slow tilt…*

Her mind spun, landing on nothing familiar.

Lyssa was leaning forward now, her smooth face pinched with anguish and her hands turned upward, begging sympathy. "I was so scared, Em. I thought *you* died. It was horrible, I thought I'd lost you. We were like sisters, but closer."

Her eyes glistened. "I prayed for you and asked God to save you and maybe that helped keep you alive. But you don't remember anything, do you?"

Emma's astonished mind formed a single clear thought: *You prayed for me? I call bullshit. You never prayed for anyone in your life.*

"Go back further." The lump in Emma's chest dissolved and her next words came easily, sharp and clear. "A few nights before, you took me to the ER with a broken collarbone."

She remembered Koa's caution. *Don't accuse, don't tell her anything new.* But this was important.

Lyssa looked down to inspect an invisible flaw in her manicure. Any hint of tears vanished.

"Yes," she said cautiously. "That was like a week before Thanksgiving."

"Did they give me something for pain?" Emma asked casually. As if this was only a minor detail but thinking this could be the key. The bad decision she'd made, contributing to the disaster.

"Yeah." Lyssa tipped her head like she was considering a chess move. "Percocet, I think.."

Emma felt the breath leave her body because yes, that was it.

Percocet. I took an opioid, then I got behind the wheel—

Lyssa added, "But you said you were okay to drive."

Emma didn't think she could speak around the word OPIOID but a question came anyway. "Why did you stay home?"

"Well, I offered to drive but you wouldn't let me. I had a beer at lunch and you said no way you'd let me drive your precious car." Another sigh, another sort-of apology. "I never should've let you go alone but I was mad because you said I was drunk when I wasn't, so I threw a hissy fit. I said you could drive your own fucking car and I'd stay home."

Emma felt herself nod because that sounded authentic and OPIOID was no longer sitting at center stage.

"And then?"

"Then? Like I said. You left and I went back to cutting chicken wire. That stuff's nasty as fuck, my hands got all scratched up. It got dark, the guy came on the four-wheeler, he told me about the crash. That was the shittiest night of my life, Em. I didn't sleep at all."

Emma flinched.

Lyssa was busy fastening sincerity to sympathy and didn't notice. "Em, you know that crash was just shit fucking luck. Really, it wasn't your fault. The rain, the washout, that fucking tree across the road."

"When did you see it?"

"I walked down the next day. They brought chainsaws and a backhoe, then they dumped tons of rocks and gravel to build up the road again. A big-ass tow truck with a winch hauled out the wrecked cars. It was like three days before I could get my Subaru out."

The Subaru. The car we should have taken.

"How did you get gas if the road was closed?"

"The tow truck driver gave me a couple gallons. He brought me a sandwich, too, when I said I didn't have any food."

The obvious next question was, why didn't Lucy just cut through the woods? Go around the crash site and walk the two miles down to the crossroads? Emma opened her mouth to ask this but changed her mind.

Lyssa rattled on, animated now. "That morning—Monday—a deputy came by to tell me you'd survived but you were in really bad shape. He asked all his questions again but I was such a freakin wreck I couldn't think straight. And I'd already told them everything I knew."

Lyssa placed both hands flat on the table and arranged her face in a sad smile. Offering sympathy, asking for sympathy, or just indicating the end of her story? And she hadn't yet asked Emma for anything. When would that come?

Emma had her answer. She'd taken an opioid. Maybe not the cause of the crash but yes, a contributing factor.

But it didn't feel like an answer. Too many questions remained and now she was out of time.

She rose. "It's a quarter to five. I'm going to the hospital, to have dinner with Dad."

Lyssa said kindly, "I'm sure he'll be happy to see you. I can't stop by tonight but please tell him I said hi."

This was such a normal comment—normal for anyone else—that Emma paused, searching her cousin's face for a hint of sarcasm. She found nothing but a sweet smile.

Lyssa pushed her chair back and pivoted her bare legs to one side. There was a sharp *thunk* as her right thigh connected with a table leg.

"Shit." She scowled and rubbed her leg. "I'll be fucking black-and-blue by morning."

"Ice will help. I think there's a bag of peas in the freezer."

Lyssa's face twisted. "I don't need your fucking peas."

"It's just a bruise. You'll live."

"That's easy for you to—" Catching herself mid-retort, she swiftly rebuilt the smile. "Whoa. Sorry, Em. We're good, right?"

Emma turned away, not trusting herself to reply.

THIRTY-EIGHT

"All in all, I'm very pleased." Dr. Hoskins beamed over his mask as he switched off the flow of oxygen and disconnected Frank's cannula.

Emma cleared their dinner dishes and pushed her father's tray table close to the window, being careful not to disturb the travel-size chess board on the nearby counter. A few pieces remained in play on the board, suggesting that earlier in the day Frank and Raylene had been working on an endgame.

She eased down on the bed and held her father's hand as Dr. Hoskins searched the files on his medical tablet. A thickset man with a broad fleshy face and droopy down-turned eyes, the pulmonologist reminded Emma of a friendly bulldog. Dignified, but given to puppylike bursts of delight when his patients' health improved.

"Got it!" He rotated the screen and held it up. "Here's your left lung."

They peered together at the ghostly image of ribs and lungs and tiny cones suspended in three major airways of her father's chest.

"This looks great," Hoskins announced. "There's no sign of infection or inflammation. I think we can send you home tomorrow afternoon, with a few restrictions."

Frank flashed a smile. "It's working, I swear I can feel it already." He demonstrated by pulling in a deep breath. The smile widened to a grin.

His doctor grinned back. "I believe it. Most patients see good results in a few days or a week. With others, it's almost immediate. You're one of the lucky ones."

Emma squeezed her father's hand. "This is a…permanent fix?"

"We will assume so until proven otherwise. It's a fairly new procedure but it's also reversible so we can take out a valve or replace one if necessary. So I'm sending you home but there's some restrictions. Avoid stress, get lots of rest. Light exercise is okay, but no visitors for at least a week. I don't want you coming down with another virus."

The pulmonologist took his tablet away, leaving Emma to wonder about the directive to "avoid stress." Should she tell her father about the drawings? Absolutely not. What about Chaz's scholarship, the police investigation? No and no.

There was one question she needed to ask so she phrased it carefully. "Dad, what did you and Lyssa talk about? She said she stopped by last night."

His smile fading, he directed his gaze thoughtfully to the white-tiled ceiling.

"You know," he said after a minute, "I remember she was here. But for the life of me I can't remember what we talked about. I think it was a good visit, though. She was wearing a mask but then she took it off and gave me a beautiful smile. Sorry, that's all I remember."

She covered her dismay, hoping to reassure him. "It's okay. I saw her earlier today and I think we're good. Oh, and Mark's coming for a visit on Saturday. I'll tell you about that later, after you're home."

She brushed his wispy hair off his face and forced a smile. "If Lyssa calls or stops by again, call me right away, okay?"

***

Three voicemails came in while Emma was driving but she never used her phone in her car so she didn't look at them until nearly seven-thirty, after she'd fed Teague and made herself a pot of peppermint tea.

One from Koa asking her to call. Her fingers itched to respond immediately but she made herself listen to the other messages first.

One from Jonah, uncharacteristically hesitant, asking how her father was doing and how was she doing and was there any news on the vandalism?

From Felicia, informing her the flyers and postcards for the October show would be ready for pickup at the printers on Thursday. Did Emma want to pick them up or should they ask a volunteer?

Emma felt a small pulse of guilt. She'd been absent, letting her friends pick up the slack at work. She needed a shower and she needed to call Koa but she owed a response first to Jonah and Felicia. With Teague on the sofa beside her and Taylor Swift in the background, she set up a Zoom call and gave her friends her full attention for twenty minutes.

An update on Frank. He was doing great, the procedure was a success. Fingers crossed, he'd be home the following evening.

Yes, please have a volunteer pick up the flyers.

No, let's not cancel Thursday evening's figure drawing. Book an agency model, clothed, and ask everyone to take all their work home. Not drop anything in the recycle bins.

Any updates on the vandalism? Not really. Detective Szczepanski didn't seem to think Chaz was involved. Yes, he'd talked with Lyssa.

She closed the Zoom screen and turned up the music a little, admiring the agility of Taylor's voice and loving the song but also remembering how she'd hated the nickname she'd been given on the surgical ward: *The Lucky One.* As if surviving, when everyone expected you to die, was some kind of personal achievement.

The music ended. It was nearly ten and maybe too late to call Koa. She rehearsed a message in case it went to voicemail.

He answered on the first ring as if he'd been waiting for her call.

For the second time that day, Emma felt herself grinning. She leaned back into the sofa cushions and rubbed her free hand over Teague's back and shoulders. Exhaling warm dog breath on her hands, he sighed and snuggled closer.

Koa's voice was friendly but brisk. "I have news, sort of. Forensics came back on that paint can but there's not much to know. It's interior latex, Pepperpot Red by Benjamin Moore. The lid's missing so there's no information on when or where it was mixed. You can buy it—"

"Any place that sells it?"

"Yeah. It's an old can with dust in the grooves. There's three layers of dried paint around the rim. No clear fingerprints. If it was a recent purchase we could ask around but it's too old."

"Nothing else?"

"Those two cigarette butts from the garden? There's no fingerprints there, either, and no usable DNA, so all we know is that one is a Marlboro Light and the other is a British brand. A Silk Cut."

"Lyssa smokes those."

He rustled papers. "Remind me. When did she leave Stonefall on Friday?"

"Mid-afternoon sometime. I'm not sure, I was avoiding her at that point."

"And on Saturday?"

"Saturday...she was with me at the barn from about two to four-thirty or so. She came back at six for dinner with us, then left around nine."

"Lots of opportunities to drop a cigarette butt in the garden."

"Once on Saturday afternoon she went to her car and came back smelling like she had a smoke."

He was quiet for a moment and she imagined him writing notes in his quick, precise script. Her legs were going numb so she gently pushed Teague aside, swung her feet to the floor, and stretched.

"Koa, do you still have the files?"

"They're here, in my office. Why?"

She took a deep breath and told him about the Wednesday night before the accident. The storm, Maggie's text, Lucy throwing the easel, her broken collarbone, the midnight trip to the emergency room. The opioid painkiller her cousin said she'd taken just before getting in her car that Sunday.

"I shouldn't have been driving." She swallowed back the shame and was surprised to find it a manageable hurt, not the gut-clenching body slam she'd experienced earlier. One of her therapists explained the three A's of atonement: acknowledge, apologize, amend. She realized that's what was happening. Step one, acknowledgment.

"If that's true," Koa was saying, "she shouldn't have let you drive. She should have driven."

"She says I accused *her* of being drunk. That's why I insisted on driving."

"Wow. Okay, was she?"

"I don't know. But I did a lot of…designated driving for her back then."

"Emma, it was an accident. You couldn't have prevented it, no matter what you did or didn't do."

"But we don't know that, do we? I mean, they probably didn't do a tox test on me." That sounded more bitter than she intended. She bit her lip, tasting the familiar metallic tang of blood. OPIOID threatened to reappear.

"No. I'm sure other things took priority." He hesitated. "Can I ask a tough question?"

She nodded but of course he couldn't see it. "Yes," she whispered.

"Have you ever gone back to the crash site?"

"No." Her palms were sweating and everything else was cold.

"I'd like to see it," he said gently, "to get a feel for what happened. And— Well, it would help if I had your perspective, too. Would you come with me?"

She blinked hard and worried her lip, trying not to drift away. Jonah's photo of the soaring hawk took shape in her mind, beckoning. Blue sky, the space between things. *No, it's impossible. I can't do that.*

"When?" she said.

"How about tomorrow? I have the morning off. It's what, about twenty miles? I can pick you up at nine and we'll be back by noon. One o'clock at the latest."

"Tomorrow morning? No, that's too—"

Too what? Too soon, too late, too impossibly terrifying?

"Yes," she said.

THIRTY-NINE

First came a slow tilt. The rumble of rocks and earth...
It wasn't. Or it doesn't have to be, not anymore.
A hollow place opened...You fell...the long slide and that sickening first flip... rocks trees metal ... screaming.
You were alone in the darkness.
No. Not alone.
It was all your—.
No.

FORTY

Koa's car was a Toyota RAV4, sun-faded black. It had a worn, high-mileage look but it was neat and clean, freshly washed.

Emma knew it was also well-maintained because she'd noted the oil-change sticker on the windshield, and checked the pressure and tread depth on each tire. She'd also asked a bemused Koa to test his turn signals, parking brake, fog lights, and flashers before she climbed in.

He also looked freshly washed. Tuesday afternoon's lingering odor of burnt cow manure was gone, replaced by the sandalwood he'd worn earlier. The trim polo was replaced by a short-sleeved shirt with a botanical print in muted shades of blue and green. An aloha shirt, loose and comfortable over faded jeans. Untucked, it draped easily over the holster at his right hip.

Emma placed her sun hat in the back seat and latched her seatbelt, feeling like someone else entirely. A normal person, embarking on a road trip with a friend. Except she was an imposter. Unmoored and unprepared, absolutely not the right actor for this role.

"So how do you earn a morning off?" she asked him. It was clumsy, but she'd never been good at light conversation and her rehearsed list of casual topics was woefully short.

He smiled anyway. "They owe me. I did a few extra shifts and helped wrap up some auto thefts. The department maxed out the budget for overtime, so my sergeant said I should take a couple of half-day comps. My plan was to stay home, do laundry. Go to the gym, I guess. I like the gym but I hate doing laundry."

He concentrated on making the turn out of her driveway. In front of the barn, Chaz and Jonah were sliding several large cartons from the bed of Chaz's pickup.

"Looks like your new security cameras arrived," Koa said approvingly. "The sooner they can get those installed, the better."

Turning to watch, Emma caught her lower lip in her teeth, then let go because the flesh was still sore. "He lost his mother and sisters, because of me. I killed them."

He navigated a sharp turn by the creek. "That implies that you had some sort of control over what happened, which you didn't. What the shrinks call agency. I don't think Chaz is angry, Emma. I think he sees you as a victim, too. You're the one who survived. And that's a good thing."

A good thing. She didn't believe in fate or a grand design or that "always a purpose" stuff. But she definitely needed to find a way to make amends. Try to fix what she'd broken, though she wasn't sure how.

The narrow country road curved left and then right, following the bank of the creek. On one side was the new sheep pasture and on the other stretched long acres of hayfields, crisscrossed by stone walls.

As they drove over the bridge and entered the woods, Koa slowed and glanced at the sign for the Pisgah Forest trailhead. He noted the picnic table and the small parking area under the hemlocks.

"Tell me about the farm," he said. "That's the boundary?"

A safe topic, easy to talk about. "We just passed it. Now we're in a corner of Pisgah Forest." She hesitated, thinking it through. "The farm's been in the family for generations. Uncle Jerry inherited it because he was the only one who could afford to keep it. He and Marisa were living in Boston then, where his company was. He leased the land, and we all used the house for summers and holidays. When the...accident happened, Jerry and Dad sold everything up north and moved here to take care of me."

"Just your dad and your uncle?"

"Yes. Aunt Marisa died when I was eight, my mom died when I was thirteen. When I got out of the convalescent home, Jerry and Frank brought me home to the farm. Then Jerry died, three years ago."

A lot of death and disappearance, Maggie and Lucy too. Except—

Koa broke into her thoughts. "How big is it?"

"The whole farm? About three hundred acres, mostly forest. Ten acres in apples and beehives, maybe eighty acres in crops and grazing."

"But you and your dad aren't farmers."

"No. It's owned by a trust. Dad and I are sort of the stewards, and a local farmer, Jimmy Bates, rents the land for his cattle and sheep. He also manages the orchard. Uncle Jerry set it all up."

"I didn't know small-scale farming could be profitable."

"It's not. The goal isn't profit, it's conservation. My uncle made his money in high tech and it's his money that supports Stonefall." She added, a little defensively, "It sounds… privileged. But we aren't…extrapolate people."

He lifted an eyebrow and added a smile.

She grimaced. "What'd I say?"

"Extrapolate. Maybe extravagant?"

She turned to stare out the window, practicing silently. *Extravagant, extravagant.*

He accelerated onto the interstate and set the cruise control, two miles per hour below the speed limit. Did he always drive so slowly or was he being careful not to worry her?

He drove in silence. The car downshifted as they climbed a steep slope. Visible through her window, the tall peak of Mount Mitchell rose through the clouds on a wreath of wispy morning fog.

After a minute he said, "Emma, why did you want to come this morning? Won't it be painful for you?"

"Maybe. Would you have come alone, if I said no?"

"Yes." He kept his eyes on the road.

"Why? I know," she added quickly, "you asked me first."

He focused on passing a slow-moving pickup. "I can't ask to open a closed case unless I can prove good cause."

"You plan to do that? Why? What's good cause?"

"Something important that got missed eight years ago."

"Like what?"

"I'm not sure yet. Just a feeling I have." He glanced at her quickly, worry lines forming above his eyes. "Your turn. Why are you here?"

She looked out the side window again, keeping her eyes on the panorama of blue-green mountains. Ignoring the bottomless gulches and the deep, shadowy gorges below.

Because I'm still looking for answers. And I trust you. You seem to understand.

She said, "I live with this every day. Those three deaths. I need to know everything about what happened. Where I went wrong." She swallowed, trying to work more moisture into her dry throat.

Without taking his eyes off the road, Koa reached into the side pocket on his door and handed her a dented metal water bottle.

"Here. I think it's still cold."

She drank. "The therapists say I need to separate experience from identity. Let go of the shame, find something good in my life. But I can't do that without knowing more."

"Your memory has gone underground to protect you." He said it tentatively, leaving room for her to accept or reject it.

"Yes. But I think it's closer to the surface now. I can poke a stick into the crack and see something hiding there. Before, it was just blank."

"Isn't it painful? Poking at things."

"It *should* be painful." She drank again, slopping a little water on her shirt. She wiped her mouth with a hand and ignored the shirt.

Koa canceled cruise control and flicked on a turn signal for the exit. "Do you know the term 'agent regret?'"

"A kind of ... remorse."

"It's what we feel when we realize our good intentions aren't enough. Sometimes every choice is wrong. Whatever we do causes harm and we can't fix it."

She watched his hands on the steering wheel as they turned onto a county road. A road sign informed them that Chickapay Crossroads was six miles ahead.

"Every day," he continued, "we make a thousand decisions. Every decision is based on incomplete information, which is constantly changing. A deer runs into the street. Or a dog. Or a child. The temperature drops a degree, water freezes on the bridge. We never have all the information we need."

She stared at the water bottle in her lap. "Jonah says if you over-think every decision, you'll just become…paralyzed."

He nodded, letting her know she'd said it correctly.

She went on, "But doing nothing is a decision, too. Shit happens anyway."

Abruptly she turned toward him, stricken. "But—oh god, you deal with that every day, don't you? It's your job, making hard decisions. Over and over, based on partial information that's constantly changing."

"Yes." He flexed his fingers on the wheel. "It's part of the training."

He stopped at a light, signaled, and turned right. "Speaking of Lyssa."

She sighed. "Yes?"

"Is she challenging your uncle's will? You said she might."

"Not yet. Mark doesn't think she has a good case." She paused a beat. "She asked my dad for money."

"Would he do that? Give her money?"

"Probably. He still feels sorry for her—that Uncle Jerry cut her out of his will. What Dad doesn't realize is that whatever he gives her, it will never be enough. She'll keep coming back for more."

"How do you feel about it? Helping her out."

"It's…complicated. When we were kids, she was like my crazy-bossy big sister. She had my back when I got bullied. Which I did, because I was the wimpiest kid you can imagine. The girl version. Clueless, timid, quiet as a mouse. That was her nickname for me, Mouse."

"You've changed a lot, then. I don't see a mouse."

She gave him a sharp look. Was he just being kind, or did he mean it?

He seemed serious so she continued, "Something changed for her, though, after high school. She got mean and ...calculating. There was a cruel streak I hadn't seen before, though maybe I just wasn't looking. And now—she's still my cousin, but I don't know her anymore."

She thought back to something earlier. "Why did you ask about Jerry's will?"

"I'm trying to figure out what the stakes are. What Lyssa thinks she can get." He went quiet for a moment. "Can I ask a few questions about money? And you can say no, it's none of my business."

"Okay."

"I was thinking about what you said, how the farm is protected from someone selling it for development. But what about you? Your estate, I mean. And your father's."

"It's pretty simple. If my dad dies, the assets in his trust roll into mine. And vice versa."

"Any contingent beneficiaries?"

"Charities, the family foundation."

"No one else to inherit? No family?"

"Not that I know of," she said lightly. Then, more seriously, "There's only Lyssa. And Maggie, if she's still alive."

"So if you died, your father would inherit. Then— Sorry, I'm sure you've already thought about this."

But Emma hadn't thought about it, not enough and not recently. Would Lyssa try to convince Frank to include her in his estate? Or if Emma died—

Koa said, "Sorry, I'm prying. But if we follow the money into the future..."

Before she could respond he added, "My GPS says go left here. Is that correct?"

She roused herself. "Yes, at the crossroads. There should be a dollar store. It looks like a convenience store, kind of an old gas station with no gas. Or it used to. Our road—where we used to live—goes up the hill to the right."

He slowed, moved into the left lane, and waited for the green.

She said slowly, "You think it's Lyssa, don't you? Behind the vandalism. How does that fit?"

"The attack in the garden was ugly but it wasn't directed at a specific person. I think the point of that was simply to scare everyone, create some general chaos. The second incident, though—that was deliberate and cruel. It targeted you."

She shivered. "There's no proof."

The light changed and he swung the car left. "No. And here's what I don't get. Both attacks were risky. They put her under a spotlight. What's she trying to do, that she thinks the risk is worth it?" One hand let go of the steering wheel to rub the back of his neck. "Why didn't she just get in touch and apologize for running away? Your dad already felt sorry for her. All she had to do was play the long game. Show up for dinner, make amends, be the attentive niece. And wait."

Emma shook her head. "As Lyssa would say, yeah-no. It's not her style, she's never been patient. All she wants is money, as much as she can get, as fast as possible."

"Hey, is this it? Are we here?"

"This is it."

He pulled onto cracked concrete in front of the dollar store. A dented SUV and a muddy pickup with a gun rack in the rear window sat at the far side of the weedy lot. The glass door of the dollar store bore a strip of peeling duct tape that failed to cover a full-length crack.

Where the concrete gave way to gravel, a narrow dirt track sloped uphill into the forest.

Koa said, "You still okay with this? If you like, I can drop you here and drive up on my own. I have the coordinates."

Her pulse quickened but she lifted her chin. "I'm fine. Let's go."

FORTY-ONE

Koa dropped the SUV into four-wheel-drive and held it in first gear. "Off-roaders must love this," he said as the car lurched and bucked over the ruts. "Was it this bad eight years ago?"

Through clenched teeth Emma said, "The potholes are the same. Still no guardrails. But it's wider now, almost two lanes."

Instead of smiling he focused on driving, leaning over the wheel like a rider urging his horse up the mountain. The grade grew steeper, the ruts deeper. The car hugged the uphill bank on their right; on the other side, the ground fell away through dense trees and boulders.

Emma closed her eyes, clutching the handhold above the door with her right hand and the edge of the seat with her left. She tried to shut out the sounds of tree branches smacking her window and gravel spattering against the car's undercarriage.

She knew the two-mile climb shouldn't take more than fifteen minutes. An eternity.

"I think we're almost at the top," he said. "Is that the cabin?"

She opened her eyes. The track had narrowed to a one-lane trail with weeds growing between the wheel ruts. Through a thin screen of trees she saw the cabin, looking smaller and shabbier than she remembered. They'd passed the crash site a few minutes earlier.

In the overgrown yard, Koa set the brake and switched off the engine but made no move to get out. Emma felt him watching her—watching over her—as she steadied her breathing. She felt her panic subside first to relief, then to surprise. She was okay, they'd made it.

When she unclipped her seatbelt, he opened his own door and climbed out.

"The two of you lived here for how long? All by yourselves?" He sounded half admiring, half disbelieving.

In the front yard, an opportunistic grove of pine saplings had taken root among the thistles and wildflowers. No other tire tracks were visible. The cabin's metal roof wore an uneven rug of green moss and mold, and on the porch a drift of dead leaves blocked the front door.

"About seven months," she said. "I don't think there's anyone living here now."

Koa climbed the stairs to the front porch, stepping carefully over the broken boards. He rapped hard on the door but there was no response so he retraced his steps to the car.

He said, "Do you want to walk down or drive down to where it happened?"

"Walk." She didn't want his car parked there.

He retrieved a second water bottle from the back seat and turned toward the gravel road.

"Wait," she said. "There used to be a shortcut, a trail that went straight down the slope. It's a steep hike but it's more direct. A little quicker, maybe."

It was where she remembered, a rocky, narrow game trail winding steeply downward through the woods. The first step down from the clearing was a two-foot drop with an uneven landing in a rhododendron thicket. Easy enough for a deer or a confident hiker, not so simple for Emma's compromised body.

Every step is treacherous, the voice in her head warned. *Sheer cliffs and hidden gullies. There's danger everywhere.*

The voice in her head faded in the day's warmth and she became aware of other sounds: the trickle of an unseen stream, the sigh of breezes, a trill of birdsong. She remembered how much Billy loved the woods, when he showed her the secret trails and mimicked the call of the Carolina wren. Billy, who'd grown up and become Chaz.

She spotted a gap in the bushes and jumped down, skidding a bit on the landing. Koa leaped a few seconds later, his breath whooshing out as he went down on one knee in the dirt. He grabbed a branch in one hand and held the metal water bottle high in the other like he'd recovered a football fumble.

"I meant to do that." Grinning, he touched the gun holster beneath the tail of his aloha shirt, then checked his rear pocket. "Still have my phone, too."

They ducked under tree branches and clambered over around rocks, heading always downward. In a few minutes, they emerged on the gravel road, well below the first switchback.

He glanced at his watch. "Six minutes. That's gotta be a lot shorter than walking down the road."

She pointed. "The second turn is just below us. The third one —"

"Is where the accident happened."

"Yes." She started down the next section of trail, a little less steep than the first.

"Wait a minute. Here." He uncapped his water bottle and inspected it. "I think it acquired a few new dents." He wiped the metal rim on his shirttail and handed it to her.

The second leg took only four and a half minutes. When they stepped back onto the track below the second turn, Koa turned and looked back uphill.

He swatted a mosquito on his neck. "Where did Christine Garrison live?"

"There, a little way up in that clearing. But I don't see the trailer. I think it's been moved."

They walked upslope to where there might have been a driveway, now blocked with a heavy chain hung between trees. The forest was reclaiming the clearing, with young spruce and pine saplings growing among yellow-flowering goldenrod and purple-stemmed pokeweed.

They went downhill again, keeping now to the middle of the gravel. At the beginning of the third switchback, where the slope grew steeper and the narrow road twisted back on itself, Koa pulled out his phone to snap several photos.

Emma stood by a long rut of eroded gravel, her stomach churning.

"This is it." The words thundered in her head though her voice was barely above a whisper.

This is where the tree fell, where the road fell, where we fell.

She braced herself for a darkness, a vertigo. Waited for the terrible images to flood in, washing her away.

But nothing happened. Birds sang, leaves rustled. The sun continued to shine in an impossibly blue Carolina sky.

She realized with a start that she was holding Koa's hand, or he was holding hers. But she couldn't remember how that had happened. She blushed and let go quickly, stepping away.

On their right, the bank dropped sharply down into the woods; on their left, a high ledge of granite jutted out of the cliff. At the base of the ledge, water trickled down to collect in a shallow ditch.

He said, "It was like this? The water draining off the ledge?"

"Yes, there's a spring up above. When it rained, the ditch filled and it ran over the road. There's always been …erosion here."

"Here's a culvert pipe," he noted. "But it needs cleaning." He pointed to the exposed end of a stormwater drain, a black plastic cylinder at the base of the ledge. The opening was clogged with branches and dead leaves.

He found the pipe's outlet on the downhill side of the road, anchored by a pile of large rocks designed to hold the earth and gravel in place.

Emma said, "The culvert pipe wasn't here eight years ago. It must have been put it in after."

She didn't need to point out the irony: The road was in better shape now than it was eight years ago, but no one lived here.

Koa walked downhill into the tight turn of the switchback, Emma trailing behind and wondering what he was looking for. He turned and looked first uphill, then down.

He walked back to join her.

"It was late November." He seemed to be talking himself through the scene. "Not many leaves on the trees. Late afternoon but still daylight, right? The Miata's coming downhill, going slow and careful into this turn. The van's approaching the switchback from below. The drivers see the fallen tree, they see each other.

"Then what? They stop, one on each side. And then..." He paused as if realizing he was speaking out loud.

She shook her head sharply. "I'm sorry, I don't know." Tears welled. She looked for a place to sit and found a mossy log at the side of the road.

She untucked her sweaty tee shirt and bent to wipe her eyes. It was a little-kid gesture, using your shirt to wipe your face, but it was all she had.

Koa joined her on the log. "Don't force it. If you're upset because you're frustrated, because you can't dig out every answer you want, it's okay. You're very brave, to be here at all.. I hope you know that."

"I'm not—"

"Yeah, you are. When you're ready, we should go. Do you want me to bring my car down? I can pick you up here."

"Yes, thank you. But I think I'll walk a little farther down. Below this part."

"Okay. Keep the water. You've got your phone?"

She tapped the pocket of her jeans.

"I'll pick you up in maybe ten minutes. The first part of the trail was six minutes, the second part was four and a half."

That made her smile. "No way. You can't go up faster than we came down. Fifteen minutes, at least."

"Challenge accepted. Start your timer."

She stood beside the culvert and watched him climb the gravel road, moving quickly on strong legs. When he found the game trail, he turned and gave her a small wave before disappearing into the woods.

She took a last look around the place where three people died and her own life nearly ended. There was nothing left to see so she began walking downhill, moving awkwardly because her right hip had stiffened from sitting. Loose gravel threatened to roll away under her feet, reminding her to step carefully. She stopped twice to drink water and listen for the sound of his Toyota.

He found her a hundred yards below the third-from-the-top switchback.

"Thirteen and a half minutes," he said proudly as she buckled her seatbelt.

As his car crawled slowly downhill, she braced herself against the headrest but kept her eyes open, realizing she no longer needed to shut her eyes against the cliffs and gulches.

When they reached pavement at the crossroads, he switched off the four-wheel drive and they drove in companionable silence for several minutes.

Koa broke the quiet. "Have you ever heard about the places of refuge in Hawai'i? From the old days."

"No. What are they?"

"Sanctuaries for defeated warriors and people who broke the kapu, the laws of conduct. If you could get to a pu'uhonua, a place of refuge, you'd be safe from punishment. The priests took you through a purification ceremony and then everything was forgiven, you could go home again and be safe. During battles, civilians also used the pu'uhonua for shelter."

"So if you got to a place of refuge, you could be ...absolved? Like in a Catholic confession."

"Sort of, but way harder because you're probably being chased by the king's army. Anyway, there's a place of refuge on the Big Island that's been preserved and rebuilt. It's a national park, Pu'uhonua o Hōnaunau."

The vowels all ran together and she knew she'd have to ask him to write it down.

After a moment he said, "Okay, new topic. Are you okay to look at a couple of photos while I'm driving?"

She thought for a moment. "Yes, I think so."

"One of my nieces gets carsick if she tries to look at something while the car's moving. I always ask, so no one gets sick in my car."

He had nieces. And, she remembered, a younger brother who played *Dragon Quest*. She filed this information away for later.

"I might get a headache but I promise not to throw up on your upholstery." She crossed her fingers just in case.

He pulled a manila folder from his door pocket. "Here, I've put them in order. You've seen these before but I want you to take a closer look."

The eight-by-tens showed details of the crash scene, cropped and enlarged. The first was of the Miata's bent steering wheel and the bare frame of the driver's seat, its upholstery ripped away.

Emma took a deep breath and studied the photo. "What am I looking for?"

"How tall are you?"

"Five-four." She used to be, anyway. Her right leg was a bit shorter than the left and there was hardware in her back—

"And Lyssa?" he asked.

"You've met her. She's tall, about five-ten."

"And she would've been wearing boots, back then."

"Probably her Scarpas. That's an Italian brand."

"So, add at least an inch. She drove your car sometimes?"

Emma nodded, thinking. "She was always begging to drive it."

"So when she drove the Miata, she had to adjust the seat."

"Yes—"

And two memories broke free. One from Saturday, when her cousin smacked her thigh against the kitchen table. Another from eight years ago: Lucy, complaining about the position of the driver's seat in the Miata.

She worked through it slowly. "Whenever we switched, I had to pull the seat forward to reach the pedals." She looked at the photo again. "The seat is pushed all the way back."

They were on the interstate now, his eyes flicking to the sideview mirror as a tractor trailer passed in the left lane, close and fast.

He said carefully, "Maybe it got broken in the crash. Pushed back off its track."

"Maybe Lucy—"

"I checked the files," he added, "but I couldn't find where anyone made notes about the seat, or took any measurements. Both vehicles went to the junkyard, after."

"You think Lucy was driving?"

He let that hang between them for a moment. "Take a look at the next one. Anything there that catches your eye?"

The second photo showed the Miata's console and latch points for the seatbelts.

"The seatbelts aren't fastened," Emma said. "The shifter's broken."

"I forget, which side of the console was the parking brake on?"

She was pretty sure he never forgot anything. "The right. Next to the passenger seat."

"What does it look like?"

"The cover—what they call the boot—it's ripped off. Oh, I see it. The handle's pulled up. The brake's been set. But why—"

"That suggests a different scenario, I think."

She turned to look out the side window, letting her eyes rest on the the faraway height of hazy blue mountains. Hoping to forestall the travel headache that lurked now behind her eyes.

If Lucy was driving...if the parking brake was on...

When the eyestrain eased, she turned to the third photo. She saw the fallen tree, the crater where the roadbed had been. This image, taken at night, was lit by headlights or work lights. Someone in a blaze orange vest held a chain saw over the trunk of the fallen tree.

"What's the question here?" she asked him.

"How big is the tree?"

"Not very big. The trunk's only a few inches thick."

"Like a fifteen-foot Christmas tree, maybe? Small enough for a couple of people, or maybe one strong person, to drag home through the woods. If you saw a tree like that blocking the road, what would you do?"

"Maybe try to pull it away, or break back the branches. Clear the road somehow."

She looked out the side window for a minute, watching the mile markers flick past. Nibbled the corner of her lower lip and thought about "a different scenario." She slid the photos back into the folder, holding it in her lap now like precious cargo.

"If Lucy was the driver, how do we prove it?"

He slowed for the turn into her driveway. "I don't know." A pause. "Show her those pictures and ask her to confess."

When she didn't dismiss that idea, he glanced at her sharply. "You know I didn't mean that, right?"

FORTY-TWO

Koa's half-day off was over. Emma offered him lunch but he couldn't stay. He returned her box of files, which she promised to keep hidden from curious eyes. He'd kept the Toyota's engine running and within minutes he was heading for the next barn fire or car theft or whatever else was on his afternoon task list.

She stood on the porch with her file box resting on the rail and watched him leave. He drove faster now, responding to something more urgent than a leisurely hike through the woods on Bishop's Knob.

She ate a tomato sandwich. Threw Teague's ball around the yard for him, refilled his water bowl, and confirmed with Dr. Hoskins that her father was still on track for a four p.m. discharge. Raylene would bring him home and join them for dinner.

She answered a few emails and paid some bills, then remembered Koa's question about her broken collarbone and the pain medication. It was surprisingly easy to find, right there online in her patient history. She could have found it years ago, if she'd remembered that it had happened.

Her thoughts wandered back to Koa himself, marveling at how easily she'd gone with him to Bishops Knob to face her fears and find answers. She wondered if he was simply a big-hearted man who liked righting wrongs and solving mysteries, or if there was something more personal in the way he'd taken her hand that morning.

There was no immediate answer to that so she considered dinner, something easy and bland that her father would appreciate. Sautéed shrimp with steamed zucchini and rice sounded good so she moved a package of shrimp from freezer to fridge and pulled the rice cooker from under the counter.

Emma stopped in the center of the kitchen, still holding the rice cooker.

Koa had said, "a different scenario." And: "Show the photos and ask her to confess."

He'd said it jokingly, out of frustration perhaps because the evidence was thin or non-existent. And Lyssa certainly wasn't going to turn herself in voluntarily to the police. Not right away, anyway.

But would she share the details with her cousin? In confidence, as part of a bargain? She might. Because maybe Lyssa was also feeling the grief of her own moral injury. The remorse that follows when you violate your ethical beliefs.

If Emma could convince Lyssa to tell her the truth now, in confidence, maybe later she could convince her cousin to turn herself in to the police. It would be a relief, wouldn't it? For Lyssa to come clean. Not to have to lie or run away anymore.

Emma turned on the rice cooker, then pulled out her phone.

"Hey, Lyssa." Thinking *Lucy,* nearly saying it aloud.

"Em. Hey."

"I was thinking…" Speaking slowly, knowing she had to get this exactly right. "About what you said, about family. And making a fresh start. It's got to be hard for you, the…divorce."

Did this sound false? Emma hated using clichés but they were Lyssa's own words.

"Okayyy…." Lyssa made it a half-question, cautious but curious.

"You really got the short end of the stick from Uncle Jerry." Emma felt her way carefully. "From Carlos too, right? I know you need money and a place to stay. A job, too, if you want one."

"Well, yeah."

"Family should help family, right? And you can help me, I think. Like you said, I need to get past the accident. To do that, I need to remember more about it." Emma closed her eyes, willing her voice into steadiness. "So I thought it might help my recall if I went back there. Where it happened."

"Oh. Do you want me to go with you?" Lyssa sounded wary but she was still listening.

"Thanks. I'd like that, we can go together. But I wanted to tell you, I've already been. This morning."

Lyssa inhaled sharply. "No! What did you—"

"I think it helped." Emma needed now to get the words out faster because she had only one chance to say the rest of it. "I've remembered a few more things…but I'm confused. Can we talk?"

"What, now?" Lyssa's voice was low and guttural.

She's angry. And afraid. If she hangs up now, she'll vanish again and the answers will disappear with her.

Emma spoke quickly. "No, not now. Tomorrow? We can talk about what you need, too. A loan, a job. A deposit on an apartment, whatever."

She paused, debating what to say next. Yesterday Koa had said, "Be careful, don't accuse her or tell her anything new." But only one person could hope to get answers from Lyssa, and that was Emma.

"I think," she said, "I've figured it out. The photos show…I know I wasn't driving—"

Lyssa choked, "No— How the fuck—"

Shit. I said it all wrong. Wrong words, wrong time.

Then Lyssa was speaking again, her voice flat. "I meant to tell you, I'm leaving tomorrow morning. I've got to see my lawyer about the divorce. Sign some papers. So yeah, let's talk in the morning but it's got to be really early. Seven-thirty?"

Say something quickly. Don't let her go!

"Okay, sure," Emma said dumbly. "But not at the house, I don't want to bother my dad. He's coming home this evening and he'll need to rest. Instead of coming to the house, how about the office? At the barn."

"All right. And bring those photos, okay? But let's keep this quiet, just us two. No one else."

The phone went dead, leaving Emma to wonder what she'd just committed to.

FORTY-THREE

Chaz got his breakfast under control just before six a.m. He'd planned to eat while driving to the farm, but the egg-and-muffin sandwich was too sloppy for munching while steering. The only solution was to park in his usual spot under the big hemlock by the trailhead and finish the cheesy mess one bite at a time, then rinse his hands in the creek.

It was still way too early to show up for work anyway. Jonah wanted to start installing the new security cameras at eight, but Chaz still had almost two hours to kill. He was planning to use the time to text Darren, catch him up on the scholarship news.

But he couldn't decide what to write so mostly he was just sitting, listening to birds. He'd heard the *hoo hoo* of a great horned owl and now he was hoping to see deer coming to the creek for a drink.

Then a car's fog lights cut through the curtain of morning mist on the road behind him. The bruise-purple Mustang's top was up but it was moving old-lady slow. It was easy to see the driver's yellow hair.

Chaz decided texting Darren could wait. He counted to ten, then eased the Ranger from under the hemlock and followed the Mustang toward Stonefall.

When he got to the barn he panicked a little, thinking he'd hung back too much and lost sight of it. There was no Mustang parked in the gravel lot or by the side of the road. The hayfield was empty, too. Opposite the barn, a single upstairs light was glowing in the farmhouse but he didn't see any cars in the yard there, either. He drove by, going slower now.

He almost missed it. He was nearly to the apple orchard and looking for a place to turn around when he noticed fresh tire tracks pressed into the wet earth at the pavement's edge.

A muddy farm lane led through a gap in the stone wall bordering the orchard. A car had turned there, heading into the orchard.

Chaz drove past the gap and then backed in, stopping so his truck blocked the space between two stone pillars.

He grabbed a flashlight from the console, locked his truck and walked deeper into the orchard, following the tracks past rows of trees heavy with fruit. A hundred yards in, he found an open shed stacked with wooden crates and pallets. Behind the shed sat the Mustang, the hood still warm. Peering through the tinted windows, Chaz saw a suitcase on the passenger seat. Boot prints led away from the road, toward the woods behind the orchard.

Chaz sprinted back to his truck. Rummaging beneath the seat, he searched for anything that might be useful. But he didn't know what was happening or what he'd need. All he saw was pair of wire cutters, a bot of fence staples, and a can of wasp spray.

He turned toward the road and began running for the barn at the best speed he could manage. Thinking now would be a really good time to quit the smokes for real.

***

There was no moon to light the trail behind the orchard. The forest was dark and dense with brambles and branches, but Lyssa had remembered her flashlight. The path was easy to find; she'd walked it only last Saturday. As a kid, she hated Uncle Jerry's forced marches through the woods and swamps—she remembered insects, mud, sweat, and blisters—but now she was glad of that experience.

For this morning's outing, she wore black. Jeans, hoodie, backpack, and her old hiking boots, the Scarpas she'd hung onto for nearly a decade. Good footwear never disappointed.

The trail curved through the woods behind the farmhouse and ended at the road, directly across from the hayfield. Leaving the deep shadows of the woods, she jogged across the road and through the hayfield, staying well away from the security cameras that overlooked the parking lot and garden at the side of the barn.

At the back corner of the sculpture garden, where the ground sloped away down a rocky bank into the pony pasture, she climbed over a wood-and-wire fence. One quick climb up a boulder brought her to the deck's back railing and then she was on the rear balcony.

She paused to catch her breath, savoring the exhilaration of the adrenalin rush. Part exertion, part anticipation. With a tingle of risk mixed in, because who knew what would happen?

There was another factor to consider: Overnight showers had coated every surface with a slick of rain. She scuffed her boots on the planks, testing the traction. A little slippery, but not bad.

The clouds were beginning to break up and the early-morning sky carried a rose-gray hint of dawn. The air felt already warm and humid, threatening a return to a southern summer after a promise of cool autumn.

Lyssa set down her backpack and inspected her latest manicure, the short-trimmed nails now painted a look-at-me magenta. She pulled on a pair of thin leather gloves and worked her fingers into them until they felt like a second skin. She tested the fit by flipping a middle-finger salute to nothing in particular.

Thinking the gloves probably weren't necessary. Her prints were everywhere already and that was fine because she belonged here.

She still needed to figure out how to *stay* here. She had only one plan and it wasn't perfect, but it was all she had for now.

***

From the doorway of her father's bedroom, Emma used the low beam of a small flashlight to assure herself that he was sleeping soundly, his breathing steady and deep. The oxygen tank sat unused beside the nightstand and Teague lay on the bed near its footboard.

She hadn't planned to take the dog with her but then he raised his head and thumped his tail expectantly. Afraid he'd wake her father, she changed her mind and gestured *come*. Teague yawned, stretched, and dropped off the bed, his toenails clicking on the bare floorboards as he followed her to the mudroom.

Unsure of the weather, Emma pulled on her barn boots and a raincoat. Outdoors, the dim glow of almost-dawn gave enough light to see by so she switched off the flashlight and tucked it into a pocket.

She'd forgotten Teague's leash but when she asked him to heel, he took up the proper position at her left side and remained there as they crossed the road to the barn. There she switched off the alarm system and wiped her boots on the mat.

In the office, Emma directed the dog to his cushion beneath her desk. She checked her messages, half-expecting a text from Lyssa saying she'd changed her mind about their meeting.

Now, in the clarity of morning, Emma admitted to herself that she'd been foolish to think she could somehow convince her cousin to admit to anything, let alone being the driver in a fatal hit-and-run crash. The real cause of the accident—the landslide—was no one's fault. But as the driver, she'd been responsible for rendering aid and telling the truth. She'd given no aid. Instead of telling the truth, she'd lied and then vanished.

Eight years later, the stakes were still too high. Lyssa wouldn't care about remorse or forgiveness or "putting down a burden." And if she *did* confess, what would Emma do with that knowledge? Keep quiet and hold the secret forever?

Of course not. If she tells me, I'll have to tell the police.

Emma had no real power over Lyssa. She should just let her go. Send her back to Calgary and enjoy the peace and quiet for however long it lasted. Move on.

Evidence or no evidence, I know the truth. I can let it go now, right?

There was a sharp knock at the rear door.

Teague rose from under the desk, ready to greet or growl. Emma motioned him down again and opened the door.

Through the screen door, she saw Lyssa standing a few feet away on the balcony. Her back was to Emma and one hand rested lightly on the railing. She wore a dark sweatshirt with the hood up.

"H..Hey." Emma stammered, swallowed, and tried again. "Hi. I thought you'd come in the front door."

"The rain's stopped. Come out with me, Mouse. We can watch the sun come up." Her voice was low, muted by the hood that obscured her face.

Emma opened the screen door. "We won't see a sunrise from here. It's too foggy. And we're facing west, not east—"

Halfway through the doorway, she stopped in surprise. Here she was on the dreaded balcony, but the anxiety that pinned her to the wall only a week ago had disappeared. The fear was simply gone.

She closed the door behind her, cleared her throat, and began again. "My name's not Mouse. And what I said last night —"

Lyssa turned toward Emma but her eyes remained in shadow, unreadable. "Okay, not-Mouse." The low, mild voice sharpened to sarcasm. "Exactly what do you think you've figured out?"

"You were driving, not me. I don't know how you survived but—"

Lyssa jerked away from the railing and her hood fell back, revealing a face twisted in fear and anguish.

She cried, *"I can't tell you! I can't fucking tell you!"*

Emma kept one hand on the outer wall of the barn and held her ground. "I know you can't." She tried to speak soothingly. "You don't have to. Maybe— Just listen. And nod, just once if I get it right? Then I'll let it go, I promise."

They stood inches apart, eyes locked and feet braced. Emma watched as Lyssa's body sagged a little and her face eased from fury toward something close to sorrow. She stepped back to the railing and ran a gloved finger along the top of the plank.

"The driver's seat," Emma said slowly, "was pushed all the way back. You were driving and I was in the passenger seat. It was raining for days. There were potholes. And water running over the road, from that spring near the ledge."

Lyssa said nothing. Emma continued, gaining confidence. "We saw the fallen tree. You stopped the car and, I think, got out to move it. I said I'd get out, too, but you said no, stay in the warm car, you'd handle it. Then Chrissy's van came up the hill. And then it all— fell."

She paused, giving Lyssa a chance to confirm or contradict. But her cousin only tapped a finger on the railing and her gaze slid away from Emma. Looking at nothing, indicating nothing. But still listening.

Emma found herself counting breaths. On the fourth exhale, she took up the thread of her story but spoke now with urgency, knowing she was running out of time.

Searching now for some sort of closure. "Lyssa, you used to say I was the only one in the whole world who understood you. The only one who could put up with you. Do you remember that?"

Lyssa gave an almost imperceptible nod. "Yes."

Emma exhaled and sagged against the wall of the barn. *Was that enough? That small Yes? It would have to be.*

"You'll let it go now, Emma?"

"Yes. I'll let it go."

Into their silence came the sound of scratching and a low whine. It was Teague, pushing against the inside of the screen door. Emma turned, thinking to lean a hip against the door so he couldn't nose his way out.

Suddenly the door swung open, smacking her shoulder as Teague leaped out. He skidded onto the slippery deck and rebounded off Emma's legs. She lurched backward and reached out a hand to steady herself on the deck's handrail beside Lyssa.

"No!" Lyssa grabbed Emma's arm, spun her around, and body-slammed her back against the building.

A knife of pain shot through Emma's bad hip. Her head slammed against something hard as the visible world fractured into a kaleidoscope of brilliant sparks. She crumpled to the deck, clutching the left side of her head and gasping for air.

Teague launched himself at Lyssa. Growling and snapping, he snagged a cuff of her jeans in his teeth and hung on as she cursed and fought to stay on her feet. She landed a solid kick on his ribs. He let go of her pants leg, yipping and skittering away.

Emma curled herself into a ball by the barn wall and tasted the copper tang of blood. Sounds were fading by then so she didn't hear the scream when a thick stream of white foam struck Lyssa's forehead.

Just before Emma's vision faded to darkness, one random thought floated by: *Oh. Chaz came to work early today...*

Lyssa shrieked and twisted away from the hornet spray coating her face. Swiping frantically at her eyes, she slipped on the slick boards and fell to the deck but scrambled up fast, roaring in fury.

"*You fucking asshole!*"

Chaz stood a few yards away, holding a canister of wasp spray in both hands like it was a talisman with the power to ward off demons.

She rushed him then, shrieking and clawing at his face. Dancing back, he stumbled over Teague but kept his eyes on his target and his finger on the trigger. As he went to his knees, he pushed the button again.

The second dose struck Lyssa full in the mouth, choking off her screams. She staggered back against the railing, then grabbed at the cables strung below the top plank.

There was a loud *crack* as a piece of handrail separated from its post. It swung outward, tilting down over the edge of the deck. For a long moment Lyssa's weight was held by the other end of the rail, still attached to another post.

She flailed, fighting for balance.

Sprawled on the deck, Chaz dropped the spray can and struggled to his knees. He crawled to her and reached for her arm but she was already falling.

With a screech of splintering wood, the rail broke loose from the second post and fell, shattering on the rocks forty feet below.

Lyssa toppled also but the cables caught her body, stretching tight under her weight until one disconnected with a sharp *twang*. A second cable jerked free, then a third. Another post fell, dragging down a tangle of wire.

One cable snarled around Lyssa's right leg, slicing into muscle and tendons just above the knee. Another coiled around her torso, then tightened.

She dangled in mid-air for nearly an hour, screaming and sobbing, until the EMTs were able to pull her up, cut her free, and get a morphine drip started.

FORTY-FOUR

Emma woke slowly to a familiar shiny whiteness. White sheets, white ceiling, bright light streaming through white blinds. She closed her eyes, opened them again, and found a reassuring hint of color in the beige blanket tucked around her middle.

Not dead, then. Everything-white meant you were dead. All-black was how you got there, all-white meant you'd arrived.

Monitors and machines beeped and hummed nearby. Her left shoulder throbbed and her left arm was in a sling—again. An oxygen tube prodded her nostrils and something blocked the vision in her left eye.

Her right eye seemed to be working okay and she could rotate her head if she did it very slowly. She did that and looked at the man seated next to her.

His name floated away but she thought she recognized his face, anxious brown eyes below a broad low forehead and hair like black velour. A paper mask covered his nose and mouth so she focused on his eyes.

Perhaps he was an apparition. A good one, not like the big smelly dog she'd seen lying on her bed in the distant past. She tried to reach up and touch his sad worried face and found that her arm wasn't working. But he must have seen the hand move because he placed his hand over hers.

The sides of his mask stretched and she thought he might be speaking but it was hard to hear because there was a buzzing in her head. Then a nurse appeared, a gray-haired woman with cool hands who shooed away the man with the fuzzy hair and shut the white curtains around her bed with a brisk metallic snap.

***

Friday never came into focus but around noon on Saturday, Emma woke to a room full of colors and flowers.

People in green scrubs and cheerful voices checked her IV drip and removed her oxygen cannula. They disconnected most of the machines, discussed her urinary output, and removed the catheter. She discovered she could sit upright without passing out. The left side of her body from her scalp to her hip felt raw and battered but the headache was subsiding.

You've got a broken clavicle and a concussion, a cheerful young man told her. His stethoscope dangled in front of her unbandaged eye as he leaned over to check her scalp.

You got clobbered above your left eye, he added. But it's only a minor concussion and it missed the plate in your skull. You've got a spectacular shiner, really ugly, but your eyes look okay. We'll keep you another two days for observation but overall, you were very lucky.

Emma tried frowning but it made her face hurt. *How am I lucky?* she wanted to ask, but that would sound ungrateful. She knew what resided beneath the left side of her skull: Broca's area, a vital part of the brain's speech center.

The parade of visitors began at one o'clock. Jonah, Felicia, Simon, Mark. Felicia held up an iPad so Emma could FaceTime with her father and Raylene at home. Jonah brought a massive flower bouquet. Simon said how wonderfully piratical she looked in the eye patch, that she was really styling in that hospital gown—all of which made her chest hurt as she tried not to laugh. She'd seen herself in Felicia's hand mirror, and "styling" was not the first word she'd have used.

A nurse poked her head in, scowling, to say five minutes more and then she was kicking them out. Teague misses you, Jonah said. He's fine, everything's fine, we love you. We'll be back tomorrow.

After the parade ended, she slept for three hours.

When she woke again, Koa was sitting in the hard plastic chair, one leg crossed at the knee. When she stirred, he switched off his phone and dropped it into the pocket of today's polo shirt. Maroon, neatly tucked in.

He was wearing a shoulder holster and she wondered why he needed a gun in a hospital.

"Good afternoon, sunshine," he said. "You feeling better?"

"It's …relative," she said slowly. "Did that sound okay?"

When he nodded, she tried a few more words. Thinking her way into each syllable. "Hospital. Zucchini. Paradoxical Machiavellian. Please, can you say those back? So I know they came out right."

"I didn't know there was going to be a test. Did you mean to say Machiavellian?"

She nodded, waiting.

His smile faded. "You were serious?" His brow furrowed. "Hospital, zucchini, paradoxical, Machiavellian."

"I was worried I'd lost it all again."

"You sound fine. Slow and a little fuzzy, but fine."

"Good." She tried to sit up. He uncrossed his legs and handed her the bed controls. She pushed buttons until she was propped upright against the headboard.

She frowned. "No one's told me anything."

"On my orders. I wanted to talk with you first." Koa peered into her face from his seat by her bed. Dark stubble shaded his chin, the first time she'd seen him with a hint of facial hair. He smiled. "You look like you lost the first round with a kickboxer."

"How is she?"

The smile faded. "A concussion, several broken ribs. Those will heal quickly. But her right leg —" His face clouded. "One of those cables nearly cut it off, just above the knee. She was in surgery, most of Thursday and all day yesterday. They think they've saved it, but it's going to be a long time before she walks again."

Emma closed her eyes against that image. "How's Chaz?"

"He has a sprained ankle and some bruises. He's on crutches for a few days so Felicia took him home to stay with her family."

He seemed about to say more but changed his mind.

She blinked hard and shifted against the pillows. "And Teague? Is he okay?"

"He's fine. He wouldn't leave you, though. Chaz had to help me get him into a crate while the EMTs were treating you."

"You were there?"

"If I'd been just twenty minutes earlier—"

Emma sagged back against the pillow. "I should have told you —"

"I texted you that morning but you didn't see it. I was on my way to tell you what I'd learned from Carlos Morales. I talked with him Wednesday night."

"Her husband."

"Ex-husband. The divorce went through two months ago."

"But she said—"

"According to Carlos, who's admittedly biased, their marriage didn't just cool off, it exploded. He claims she was hooking up with other men and dealing drugs, and his father spent quite a bit of money covering up her misdeeds. The Morales family," he added, "is quite powerful.

"She also racked up a couple of DUIs in Alberta and lost her license for a year. Carlos said he could live with all of that, but not the abortions. Apparently, she violated their prenup."

Emma stared, uncomprehending.

He explained, "To marry Carlos and live that lifestyle, Lyssa had to agree to have his children. At least two."

"That was in her *prenup?*"

"Yes. But instead of having kids, she got two abortions. Maybe more. He's the oldest son and his father wants grandchildren. By terminating the pregnancies, Lyssa disgraced the entire Morales family."

"Wow." Emma would look for other words later but right now that was the only one that fit.

"The divorce happened fast. But I may have the terminology wrong," he admitted. "They're Catholic, so maybe it was an annulment. Like the marriage never happened."

"But...she told me she was flying back to Calgary on Thursday morning to sign the divorce papers."

"She lied about that, too. It's what she does, Emma. She lies, then she runs away." She closed her eyes and let the tiredness wash over her.

Koa's chair creaked as he changed position. "I'm going to need your statement, when you feel up to it."

She opened her eyes and saw he'd slumped forward in the chair. Elbows on his knees, hands dangling, he was staring at his shoes.

"Emma," he said quietly. "I'm so sorry. I didn't realize the danger."

"Not your fault. I asked her to meet me there."

He stared. "Why? And why alone?"

"Wednesday night, I told her I went back to the crash site. That I'd figured it out. That she was the driver. I said I'd help her get a job and an apartment."

His eyebrows rose.

She felt sheepish but she needed him to understand. "I thought I could convince her to confess. First to me, then maybe to you. But I didn't think it through very well. There wasn't any good reason for her to admit to anything, was there?"

Koa turned to stare at the window so she found other things to look at, too. The sink with its arched faucet, a box of nitrile gloves on a shelf above.

He sighed. "You thought she'd come clean because that's what *you'd* do."

She quit studying the faucet and turned to meet his gaze. "When you talked with her— Did she say anything about the crash?"

He recrossed a leg and laced his fingers over the knee as if needing something to keep his hands still.

"A little. I didn't ask her—she offered. She said you deserved to know."

"She confessed to *you?*"

"Not really. Well, in a roundabout sort of way." He thought for a moment. "Lyssa offered me a hypothesis. She said *if* she'd been the driver, she *might have* a theory about what *might have* happened. It was pretty clever, the way she talked— She was speculating, pretending to narrate someone else's story."

He shook his head. "I think she's been thinking about this for a long time. How to give you the truth, but without actually confessing. She said I should tell you that you were right about the tree. Does that make sense?"

"Yes."

"She said the car *might have* started rolling forward, with you still in it."

Emma closed her eyes. Put herself back in the Miata and willed away a wave of nausea. "My car was a stick shift. She'd have shifted to neutral and set the brake. Maybe it failed." Her eyes flew open. "I should have gotten that fixed."

"It wouldn't have mattered."

She rolled her head away and stared at the white wall. "Where was she when the landslide happened?"

"She said the *possible other driver* might have been standing uphill next to that rock ledge, holding onto the tree."

She whispered to the wall, "And after?"

"She tried to climb down the slope to the wrecked cars but the ground was still sliding away and it was too steep."

"I'd like to think that's true. That she tried."

Out of view behind her, he went on. "The driver thought about calling for help but she didn't have her phone. She thought maybe she'd left it at the cabin so maybe she ran up a trail."

"The one we took."

"Yes. This hypothetical driver might have searched for her phone in the cabin, then realized it was in the Miata." He paused to rub tired eyes. "I asked the obvious questions. Why didn't she go to Chrissy's trailer to get help? Or walk down to the store at the crossroads and flag someone down on the county road? She said she must have been in shock. Not thinking clearly. Then it got dark."

She rolled her head back toward him. He was staring out the window toward Mount Pisgah. It was out of her view but she imagined the mountains streaked blue-green in the late afternoon sunshine.

He added, "She stayed at the cabin and just— waited."

"Did she say why she lied to the police?"

His jaw clenching, he swung a hard gaze back to Emma. "She insisted she didn't lie. The police, she said, never asked the right questions."

Emma sucked in a breath. "She said that?"

He repeated it. "'They never asked the right questions.' Like she shouldn't have to do their job for them."

The fingers of Emma's right hand began trembling so she folded them over her left forearm in its sling.

He continued, "So I said, 'What were the right questions?' She looked at me like I was the biggest idiot on the planet." His voice grew thick with sadness and anger. "The police should have been more specific, she said. They should have asked questions like 'Who was driving the Miata?' and 'How many people were in the car?' If they'd asked *those* questions, she insisted she'd have answered differently."

"Do you believe that?"

He lifted both hands in frustration. "I have no idea. I guess *she* needs to believe it. Or she'd have to admit that she's a monster."

They let that sit for a moment.

Emma thought her way through this part. "She was afraid of a DUI. I know she drank at least one beer that day, probably more, on an empty stomach."

He nodded. "Makes sense. But maybe there's another possibility." He inspected his fingernails for a moment. "A darker one. If she waited long enough, there'd be no witnesses."

A chill prickled her scalp. "She said that was the … worst night of her life, sitting alone in the cabin. Not knowing if I'd survived. I thought she was afraid I'd died. But maybe she was afraid I'd live." She exhaled, sagging back into her pillow.

He picked up the thread. "She knew she'd fucked up—her words—when they told her you'd survived. She was scared you'd wake up and tell what really happened. Then she'd be charged with a felony hit-and-run and probably sent to prison. So she ran."

Emma plucked at the sheet covering her torso, smoothing a wrinkle. "Can I talk with her?"

"Absolutely not!" He shook his head sharply. "Emma, she's under arrest for assaulting you. Aggravated assault, with pre-meditation." He saw her confusion and added, "She sabotaged the railing on the deck."

"What? No. What do you mean?"

"She— Someone tampered with the hardware. That's why the railing broke. We found tools in her backpack. Screwdriver, socket wrench, pliers. Gloves."

Emma shivered, thinking of the deck's state-of-the-art invisible railing. Those thin, elegant cables she'd never trusted.

Koa explained. "Sometime early that morning, someone—the evidence points to her—replaced several bolts on the top rail. Swapped them out with shorter ones, same diameter but much shorter. She also unscrewed the cable tensioners so they were barely holding the wires. The loose cables must have been sagging but unless you were looking for a problem, you probably wouldn't notice it in the dim light."

He added, "No one goes looking for flaws on a brand new deck that passed inspection only a few months ago." His voice roughened. "I think her plan was to push you off the deck and somehow make it look like an accident." He paused there but Emma's mind filled in the blanks.

Hoping to kill me? No! Emma raised her free hand to touch the bruise on her forehead. A delaying gesture, as she struggled to wrap her mind around the malice. "But— It could have been someone else, not me. Falling, I mean. If I hadn't gone onto the deck— Jonah or Chaz or one of the kids—"

"Yes." He moved a box of tissues from the table to her bed.

"But what was the plan? Leave it like that and wait to see what happened?"

He considered that. "Maybe it was supposed to look like another random vandalism. Something that damaged your reputation and shut down Stonefall."

Emma closed her eyes again and sank back into the pillows. Then she sat up, her brow furrowing in thought. "But— When Teague bumped into me, she pushed me back. If she'd planned to...push me off... I think she changed her mind."

"What do you mean?"

"She shoved me *away* from the railing, not toward it. She changed her mind," she repeated.

He scowled, looking skeptical. "That's a lot of maybes. And we can't ask her anything about that while she's doped up on pain meds. It wouldn't be admissible in court. Just like that non-confession about the hit-and-run isn't admissible."

She still had no tears but she pulled out a tissue and wadded it up anyway, needing something to do with her empty hand.

Koa rose, stretching, and picked up two water glasses from a table by the window. He removed their paper hats and filled them from the pitcher on her bedstand. Emma smiled her thanks and waved away his offer of a straw.

She tipped her head back gingerly. Sipped water and wiped her mouth with the back of her hand. "The vandalism in the garden was her, wasn't it?"

He seemed relieved to change topics, if only slightly. "Yes, but she had help with that."

Pulling his phone from his shirt pocket, he found a photo. "Meet Andrew Kelvin."

She squinted her unbandaged eye at the image of a large man with a barrel chest and a thick, dirty-blond beard. He wore a Pittsburgh Steelers cap over what appeared to be a shaved scalp. "Was he the other one on the video? In the background."

"Yes, but Lyssa did all the damage. Kelvin works construction. They met in a bar and she asked him to help her prank someone she was mad at. A cousin who'd pissed her off."

"Well, that part's true. How did you find him?"

"A witness saw them together and remembered the license on Kelvin's pickup. When I mentioned cigarette butts and DNA, he started talking. He claims he was going to tell us anyway.

"He supplied the tools and the paint. They came in his pickup, he parked in the apple orchard. He says he got a thrill from watching her creep around like a ninja, but he got nervous when she used his sledgehammer to bash the gates."

Koa consulted his notes again. "That's when he called her a nutter and threatened to drive away without her."

Emma remembered the destruction phase her cousin had planned for Genesis and Catharsis. "But why…?"

"To create bad publicity for Stonefall. She was hoping you'd get scared and quit. Then she'd take your job and move in." He paused. "These are all his words, or hers. What she said to him."

"In college, she told me I could get ahead in the business world with a well-played… CYOC."

"Which is?"

"Construct your own crisis. Create chaos, then save the day by solving the problem that you created."

He pinched the bridge of his nose with a thumb and forefinger. "Like a rogue firefighter setting a fire, so they can be the hero and put it out."

"Yes. And she's always been envious of other people's success."

"Like Harry Felton? The car mechanic turned successful sculptor."

"Yes," Emma said. "Harry's outdoor sculpture was an easy target. It was a big eff-you to Stonefall but especially to anyone who's successful, especially as an artist."

She shifted, trying to stretch without wincing. "My legs are numb."

He eased a pillow from behind her shoulders and pressed the head-lowering button until she could lie back.

"Thanks, that's better." She thought for a minute. "Was Kelvin involved with the drawings?"

"No. And it wasn't the man you saw at the cafe, either. Margo told us who he was."

Trevor McLain was a thirty-two-year old bank teller at the local savings and loan. He'd never met the Garrisons, but his mother knew them a little from her Bible church.

When the crash happened, Trevor's mother asked him to construct a roadside shrine for Chrissy, Amber, and Destiny. He wanted to get back in her good graces after smacking her new car against a mailbox, so he fashioned a cross out of PVC pipe and decorated it with artificial flowers from Goodwill.

A weekly paper ran the obituaries for Chrissy and the girls, with a link to the funeral home's Memorials page where mourners could post their thoughts and prayers. Trevor's mom got the idea to use that, along with Facebook, to promote her theories.

Koa paused, apparently unsure how much detail he should provide.

"I can guess about her 'theories,'" Emma said. "Dad and Jerry thought they could shield me from it, but that stuff doesn't really go away. Here's one: 'Chrissy and her girls were killed by a drug-addled college kid from up north, one of those rich girls who drove around in a fancy convertible.' Am I close?"

His eyes came back to hers. "That's about right."

"And I'll bet someone else said that by paying for the funerals, my wealthy uncle as good as admitted that I must have been guilty of ..." She paused, thinking. "...vehicular homicide. And drunk driving."

Against that backdrop, it was easy for Trevor MacLain to earn back his mother's favor every time she complained about washing his shirts or buying his groceries. All he had to do was repeat a nasty slur or two and Ma was happy.

Koa's voice turned bitter. "It wasn't anything personal. He didn't know you or the Garrisons. It was just a thing he did, to keep himself on his mother's good side."

"Will you arrest him?"

"Probably. Lyssa says she'll testify about what he said in the coffeeshop. The owner saw him, too. I don't think Trevor will bother you again."

She twisted her fingers together in her lap. "But that's how Lyssa got the idea for scribbling on Simon's drawings, isn't it?"

"Yes. She found the sketches in the classroom on Saturday morning, and recognized you as the model. She says she just tucked them in a folder and walked out. No one noticed."

He poured them both more water. "Then she dropped the envelope into the box early on Monday morning."

"But if no one saw, why did she admit to it?"

"We have a video."

"A video? But there's no camera by the mailbox."

"There's one by the chicken coop."

"What? Who put that up?"

Koa glanced at his watch. "He should be here soon, if traffic's reasonable."

She fumbled for the bed controls and struggled to sit more upright. "Tell me. Who is it?"

He grinned. "Your guardian angel. Chaz."

FORTY-FIVE

The knock on the door was tentative. Chaz came in slowly, clumsy on crutches and uncertain of the strange environment.

Koa rose and held the door open. "Sit here, Chaz. I was just leaving."

Chaz leaned his crutches against the wall and lowered himself awkwardly into the visitor's chair. After a brief glance at Emma's battered face, his eyes settled on something above her right shoulder.

Her face ached from the bruises and the strain of smiling, but she didn't care. "Hey, Chaz. Thanks for coming."

"Hey, Miz Emma. They say you're doing better. Ma'am." He reddened, perhaps remembering that she'd asked him not to call her ma'am. The fingers of his left hand drummed lightly on the knee of his jeans.

"Thanks to you, I'm doing fine." She held out her good right hand. After a moment's hesitation, he took it with his left.

She said, "Detective Szczepanski says you may have saved my life. I don't know how you happened to be there at the right time, but I'm very glad you were."

She spoke slowly and precisely, not wanting to trip over the words because her heart was lodged somewhere high in her throat. This was hard for both of them and she wanted to get it right.

She knew him best as Billy, the wild-looking boy who wandered the woods on Bishops Knob. But he'd also been a child who'd lost his mother and sisters in a shared tragedy, and she didn't know that boy at all.

And now he was Chaz, the awkward young man who saved her life.

She found she was still holding his hand so she gave it a quick squeeze and let go of the hand but kept the smile. "Is it okay if I ask you a few questions? About Thursday morning."

He nodded.

Deep breath, she told herself. "You saw Lyssa arrive?"

"Yes," he said, swallowing the *ma'am* that wanted to follow. "It wasn't normal, her being there that early. I was down by the creek eatin my breakfast and she drove by so I followed her. See, I knew her from before," he added, "when you and her lived in that cabin up the hill from Ma's trailer."

He said he'd been keeping an eye out because he felt "somethin weren't right" about how Lyssa wandered around the farm at odd hours. She always drove that metallic purple-blue Mustang, the 2022 Shelby, so it was easy to follow her. Not just at the farm, but also in town.

His voice gained confidence as his story unfolded. One night he saw her with a bearded guy in a pickup truck. They'd been arguing in front of a hotel in Asheville, the Marriott down by the river. Then they drove off together and he memorized the license plate. Chaz said this a little sheepishly, like he probably shouldn't have been spying on them.

She tried to reassure him. "That was smart, Chaz."

"Maybe. But I was kinda slow to put it together."

He wasn't at Stonefall on Sunday morning so he never saw the damage to Harry's statue or the red paint in the garden, but on Monday morning he found the broken gates Jonah stashed behind the henhouse.

His fists bunched at the memory. "That was just hateful. Those gates were really cool, then some ugly fucker got in and busted them up." He blushed. "Um—sorry."

Emma smiled. "It's okay. Say whatever you need to, I don't mind."

On Tuesday, Chaz was confused by the detective's questions about mailboxes and recycling bins but he didn't thought to ask anyone about it until Thursday. Then Jonah explained about the drawings that someone dropped in the parcel box.

"I told Mr. Jonah maybe something showed up on my deer cam. He said we should take it to the police. See, I put it up on Saturday. But I forgot to check it on Monday 'cause it was just there for the chickens."

"I don't understand. What's that?"

"I borrowed these two deer cams—cameras—that my buddy Darren puts up when he goes hunting. When Mr. Jonah talked about my new job on Friday, he said y'all were gettin a new camera for the back deck but it wasn't arrivin for a few days. We walked around and looked at all the cameras he wanted to upgrade, and I said maybe we need one more for the hens, too. To watch for foxes and raccoons."

Chaz cracked a knuckle, then resumed tapping his knee and staring at the wall. "So he said yeah, let's get one there, too. But he'd already put the order in and it was gonna take a couple weeks to buy another one. So I just put a deer cam up there on one of the pine trees, for time bein. It's a little battery-powered thing, not real sharp but it works okay.

"Once I heard what-all happened with the mail, we gave the deer cam to the detective. That was Wednesday. Then I remembered to tell him about the license plate on that pickup at the Marriott, too."

Emma stared, fascinated not only by the story but by Chaz himself. The way his mind worked, making connections that others missed.

"And Thursday morning? The wasp spray."

He looked embarrassed. "I grabbed that outta my truck. I always carry some. Those cans got a good range. They work on bears, too."

She stalled a moment by rubbing a hand over her face while he waited patiently. "Thank you," she managed. "I'll remember that, next time I need to scare off a bear."

He nodded. His fingers had quit dancing and he seemed comfortable just sitting there, gazing around the room and waiting for her next question.

"Do you still like to walk in the woods?"

"Sure. Whenever I can. Jessie does, too."

She inhaled deeply, letting air out and taking it in again. "Chaz, eight years ago… the day of the accident. Were you in the woods? I thought I saw you walking along the road that day. Sunday afternoon, before…it happened."

"Yes'm. Me and Jessie were hidin because Ma wanted us to go to church with her and the babies, but we didn't want to."

"Your mother went to church often?"

"Lots." His shrug was half nervous quiver, half don't-care. "She weren't religious. She'd just go for the food, like when they had spaghetti suppers. Or there was cupcakes and juice at the little kids' playtime. That's mostly how she fed us."

There was so much in his story, she didn't know where to begin. But only one question should come next. "Did you see the accident, or hear anything? That's always bothered me, that you might have seen your mother's car go off the road."

"No'm. We didn't hear anything. And all I saw was Miz Lucy, a while after. She was walkin up that cut-through trail, headin to the cabin. Ma's van and your Miata, they'd already disappeared. I didn't know what happened until later. Jessie was cold and then it was dark so we went home. That's when we learned they weren't back yet."

"The police didn't ask you about that? Seeing Lucy in the woods."

"They maybe did, I don't remember. Jessie and me, we were just tryin to stay out of the way. Out of Gordy's way, specially. He was real angry when they said Ma crashed the van. She was supposed to bring home some dinner."

"Wasn't he upset about her death? And your sisters? They were his daughters, right?"

"Destiny was his, the littlest one. I don't remember who Amber's daddy was. Me and Jessie, we wasn't his. He didn't like us much."

His words stole her breath, describing a man more concerned about the loss of a vehicle and his dinner than the deaths of his partner and children.

"But you loved your mom, you and Jessie. You must've missed her something awful." She said it tentatively, like a half-statement. For eight years, she'd believed that she'd been responsible for destroying a whole and loving family. Now she had no idea.

His eyes shifted, slid away to examine the sink at the far side of the small room. "Yes'm, I guess. But I thought about it a lot and I think our Ma got in with the wrong people way back somewhere, druggies and losers, and she couldn't never get herself out. She did the best she could, I s'pose."

"You went into foster care then. You and Jessie."

"Yeah. Gordy left us real quick. Then a social worker took us to Miz Buckner's. Our foster mom."

"What's that been like?" She held her breath, waiting for the worst.

"Pretty good," he said easily. "People say bad things about foster homes but Miz Buckner is okay. She's been doing it a long time, she's always got five or six kids in this big old farmhouse. She was hard on us at first because we didn't know the rules. Ma didn't care if we skipped school, she never made us do chores. But Miz Buckner's real strict about that. Lots of kids get split up and bounced around, but she kept us together and we only ever stayed with her. So her place was okay. Better than livin with Ma and Gordy."

He ducked his head and his face reddened again. "I don't like to think about back then. That Gordy, he was a mean SOB." His fingers resumed their tap dance on his leg. "He was messin around with Jessie. I told Ma but she didn't do nothin. So yeah, Miz Buckner's was *way* better."

Emma took a deep full breath and felt something dissolving, a layer of shame that she'd assumed would be part of her forever.

She captured Chaz's dancing hand and felt it go quiet.

"Thank you," she said. He looked confused so she added, "For telling me. And for saving me."

His eyes skittered away but he nodded.

She let go of his hand before awkwardness overcame them both. "Have you thought about what you want to do with your scholarship? No rush," she said quickly. "We're not trying to get rid of you. You'll always have a place at Stonefall, if that's what you want."

He managed a shy smile. "A little. Hey, I gotta get back to work. The police roped off the deck, where we were supposed to do art classes today." He stood and reached for his crutches. "Jonah's takin the kids on a nature walk instead and he asked me to help identify some birds. He said he'd drive me out there, on the four-wheeler."

"Go," she said. "They need you."

FORTY-SIX

Just before noon on Monday morning, the day after the October Art in Autumn show, Emma balanced a brown mug of coffee in one hand and a yellow mug of tea in the other, trying not to spill as she crossed the road toward the barn. Teague, off-lead and behaving perfectly, trotted beside her.

She went through the still-gateless gap into the garden and up the steps to the widest part of the deck. High thin clouds coated the sky like the milky inside of a ping-pong ball. She felt a warm breeze flirt with her blue cotton skirt and ruffle the curls on her shoulders.

Selecting a teakwood table and four chairs in a patch of sun, she set the mugs down next to a pottery vase of white chrysanthemums and positioned two of the chairs for a good view of the gardens.

She motioned Teague into a down, and tapped the floor with a foot to suggest a spot beneath the table. The schnauzer circled twice before settling into his lion pose, with his head above his front paws, gray beard trembling and black-spotted pink tongue dangling in a rhythmic pant. She kicked off her sandals and rubbed his furry back with a bare foot, waiting.

A car door closed and footsteps crunched on gravel.

They'd talked on the phone several times but she hadn't seen Koa for three weeks. He was dressed for court, minus the tie and jacket, in a pale gray shirt and navy slacks, accessorized with the ever-present sidearm and polished badge. He carried a long white mailing tube beneath one arm.

The detective set the cardboard cylinder on the seat of an extra chair, bent down to greet Teague with a neck scratch, then sat beside Emma and lifted the coffee mug in a small salute. "I don't think I've seen you in a skirt before. Are we celebrating?"

It was an innocuous comment but then he added a warm smile and she was completely unprepared for the way her insides lurched, everything turning warm and soft. Dissolving into a puddle, even as she felt the freckles on her face brighten.

He noticed and quickly deflected her discomfort with a different question. "How's your dad?"

Emma felt a strange and sudden urge to grab his hands. Or his shoulders. Or some other warm and lovely part of him she hadn't even considered before that very moment.

What had he said? She returned his warm smile with a wobbly one of her own and made herself assemble a few words.

"My dad?" she managed. "Umm... he's great."

But his question deserved more attention than that. She concentrated and amended her answer.

"Physically," she said, "he's doing well."

"But?"

"But he's still a mess about Lyssa. One minute he thinks she's pure evil, the next she's the victim of Maggie's bad parenting. He blames himself for trusting her, and he still feels guilty about Jerry cutting her off. Jonah's found him a good therapist."

"It'll take some time to process. None of us realized what she was capable of. I'm the detective, I should've seen it."

Despite the sun's warmth, she shivered. "You were in court this morning."

"Yes. The deal held, she pleaded guilty to aggravated assault. She admitted to tampering with the railing, but she insists it was only meant to scare you. Not...make you fall."

She nodded. "Not kill me."

He seemed about to protest, then cut his gaze away and began tracing the rim of his coffee mug with an index finger.

"The lesser charges were dropped," he said. "The vandalism in the garden, communicating a threat with the drawings. I wasn't happy with that either but it wasn't my call."

"When's sentencing?"

"There's no date set. But she got a tough judge. I think your cousin will do some serious time, once they figure out where to put her." He saw the question she was about to ask. "She'll be wheelchair bound for a while, and then who knows? The state prison system isn't known for its great physical therapy programs."

Emma nodded. "Dad wants to arrange for additional care. Like I said, he's got a lot to work out." She plucked a chrysanthemum stem from the vase and twirled it. "What about the hit-and-run?"

"The DA's office says there's not enough to open the case. And what Lyssa said in the hospital, her hypothetical non-confession? She didn't actually admit to anything. Her attorney also reminded us that she was barely out of surgery, loaded up with drugs."

He offered an ironic smile, touched with admiration. "That's a good time to get something off your chest, if you're planning to deny it later."

"I'll remember that." Emma dropped the wilted flower and sat back. "But now I know what happened. She gave me that, at least."

"Oh. And something else, too. I nearly forgot." He reached beneath the table and retrieved the mailing tube from the third chair. "We found this on the back seat of her car. She said you should have it."

Emma frowned at the cylinder and reluctantly popped off an end cap. "Not more of Simon's marked-up drawings, I hope."

She pulled out a tightly furled roll of paper. Koa moved the mugs and flowers, making room on the table, as Emma struggled to uncurl a charcoal drawing. Together they held down the edges and stared at a larger-than-life portrait.

It was a three-quarter profile of a young woman. Delicate shadings of gray described her softly rounded mouth and wide eyes, while white highlights emphasized the high cheekbones, straight nose, and strong chin. Swirls of wild dark hair in blackest black created a contrasting frame for the serene face of a confident young woman.

"It's...from that night in the cabin," Emma said slowly. "She kept it. She must have finished it later and fixed it."

Koa leaned in for a closer look. "Fixed it how?"

"Sprayed it with fixative so it wouldn't smudge. That means she thought it was good enough to keep."

"It's you, at nineteen."

"Yes, but—" She tried again. "It's me but not me. Not how I remember me at nineteen."

"It's beautiful. She's really captured your strength."

"Strength? No, I was a mouse." She touched a finger to the portrait's forehead. "I think she drew me the way she wanted me to be."

"And here you are," he said simply.

Emma felt a sudden warmth and hid it with busyness, rolling the drawing back into its tube and setting their mugs back into place.

Those small tasks completed, she sat back and crossed one leg over the other. Began to swing her foot and wonder how to move the conversation forward but having no idea what *forward* might look like.

Koa shifted uncomfortably in his chair. "There's another thing. I may have news about Lyssa's mother."

Startled, Emma uncrossed her legs and sat up. "Someone found Maggie? Where? Are you sure?"

"I'm sorry, that was abrupt. I didn't say it very well." He paused to regroup. "We've found a…body. We're still waiting for DNA results, but there was a wallet with her ID in it. A park ranger found the remains, way up north in New Hampshire near the Canadian border."

"Remains. How long ago—"

"Years. Just a skeleton."

Emma closed her eyes as tears welled, borne on a sudden flood of chaotic memories and the pain of what could have been. Her father's baby sister, the original wild child of the family. Maggie the party girl, the absent alcoholic mother. The aunt who failed to step in with love and guidance after Emma's own mother died. How different all their lives would be if Maggie had managed to make a few good choices.

She blinked away the wetness. "You told Lyssa? How did she take it?"

"Hard to tell with her. I think she was relieved."

"Should I tell my father now? Or wait until you're certain?"

"Up to you. I'll come with you, if you like."

She gave him a grateful smile. "Maybe we should wait until you're sure. No sense getting him worked up if it's not her."

He nodded. Now he was the one shifting in his seat, stretching his legs and straightening the creases in his slacks. He peered beneath the table to be sure he hadn't disturbed Teague, still snoring softly and twitching with dog dreams.

Koa offered the hint of a smile. "How was the art show?"

"Great. Well, mostly great. It rained Saturday night and on Sunday, all the cars got stuck in the hayfield. Chaz was busy all day with the tractor, pulling everyone out of the mud."

She lifted her chin toward the hayfield, where deep ruts scarred the grass.

"And we're losing Harry Felton," she added. "He's decided to work on his art full time, but not here. He's joining a new metalworkers guild, a group that's setting up a maker's place in an old warehouse. In the downtown arts district."

"Will Stonefall be okay without Harry?"

Emma finished her tea, now cold. "They will do just fine, with or without Harry."

He quirked an eyebrow. "You said 'they.' Not 'we?'"

"I'm not sure what I'm going to do now. Go back to school, maybe. Though it's been so long, I'll probably have to start over."

"Economics?"

"If my brain can handle it."

His left eyebrow quirked. "How will they manage without their star model? And just when I was thinking of taking up art."

She wrinkled her nose at him. "I'll buy you a pepper."

He laughed, then sobered. "Seriously. You said you found it satisfying, modeling for Stonefall's artists. A sort of meditation."

She was quiet for a moment. "Remember when you told me about the... Puʻuhonua o Hōnaunau? The place of refuge, on Hawaiʻi Island."

Both of Koa's eyebrows climbed. "You've been doing research."

"Where the priests—"

"Kapuna," he supplied.

"The...kapuna performed a ... purification ritual, for people who committed crimes. Then they were forgiven, free to go."

He nodded.

"So what if your purification ritual is to stand naked before your community and ask for forgiveness? Ask them to find you worthy to rejoin the world."

His mouth curved. "Have they?"

"I think so."

The smile widened. "I think you should travel a little. Get off the farm, literally."

"Step out of my safe bubble? Leave my place of refuge?" She pulled a wilted chrysanthemum from the pottery vase and twirled it by the stem. When a few petals fell to the table, she pushed them into a small pile of pale slivers.

"So this is me, thinking out loud," she said. "A month ago I'd have said absolutely not. But now, I'll consider it. Maybe, if I take it in small chunks. So, yes."

He threw back his head and laughed. "Are you sure? It took a while for you to get to 'yes.'"

Emma plucked another chrysanthemum from the vase. It felt good to be sitting in the warm sun with an interesting man.

This is flirting, she thought with a sense of wonder. *That's what we're doing. I think.*

She bought a few minutes by rubbing a foot gently against Teague's shoulders. Beneath the table, he sighed and rolled onto his back.

"Tell me about your home," she said. "In Kea'au."

He blinked in surprise. "You remembered the name."

"What are the beaches like?"

He gave her a wry grin and shook his head. "Ah, for sure, no beaches in Kea'au." He shifted a little in his chair, getting comfortable. She stopped mutilating the chrysanthemums and stilled herself to listen.

"It's an old sugar town," he said. "Used to have a cane factory and a railroad. Closest beaches are in Hilo, little ones. Black-sand, pocket-handkerchief size. There was a great snorkel place, lots of rocks—is that a beach, without sand? Kapoho tidepools, maybe twenty miles southeast. Then Kilauea volcano erupted in twenty-eighteen and buried Kapoho, plus a few hundred homes."

She liked the subtle change in his speech, revealing the rhythms of his homeland. "But that's stopped now, right? The volcano."

"Ah, no. Kilauea, she's on-again, off-again. Just a matter of time to the next one. The volcano goddess Pele is always busy, creating new land. That's how all the mountains were made, like Mauna Loa and Mauna Kea. They're so tall they have snow in winter."

He gave her a mock scowl. "And do not say 'land of fire and ice.' That's what we used to say before *Game of Thrones*, but now it's a tourist cliché. It's a true thing but a bad cliché."

"A land of magic, then. And the Place of Refuge?"

"Kona side. Eighty-ninety miles, maybe two hours away. Nice beaches in Kona."

"Wow ... How big is the island?"

"About the size of Connecticut."

"Oh. That's ...big." Feeling a little foolish but wanting to keep him talking, she searched for something else to ask about. "Your family's been there a long time?"

"Some of us, yes."

"But— your name. Szczepanski is Polish, right? You don't look—"

"I don't look Polish? Because I have black curly hair and my skin is brown like a mac-nut shell, instead of pale like a blanched almond?"

She opened her eyes wide. "Am I a blanched almond?"

"With freckles. The freckles are maybe trending walnut." His smile was playful. "There's lots of ethnic humor in Hawai'i. We make jokes about ourselves and everyone else. So the bigger the mix, the more groups you make fun of. Maybe you're Chinese-Samoan-Irish-Icelandic and you marry a Portuguese-Hawaiian. Lots of Portuguese in the islands."

"Are you? Chinese-Samoan-Irish-Icelandic?"

"Chinese and Portuguese, yes. Also Hawaiian and Korean. My dad's dad was Polish, a refugee from World War Two. He married a Red Cross lady, Hawaiian-Korean. My mom's family is Chinese, Portuguese, and more Hawaiian. You?"

"Um… Mostly Scots, some Irish."

"Haole, then. Plain-vanilla white lady. But strong and very brave, so maybe some Viking?"

She had no words. No one ever called her strong or brave.

The warm-insides feeling rushed back and she blinked hard, struggling for composure but failing in the nicest way possible.

His eyes crinkled. "And my mother has her own theory on our name. The Hawaiian language uses only eight consonants. There's no S or Z or J or R sound, and every word ends with a vowel. The vowels get a lot of exercise. But the missing letters, all those consonants, they had to go somewhere, right? She says they found a home in Poland. So it makes sense to bring all the Polish sounds, those hard consonants, back home to Hawaii. Balance the vowels."

He'd given her time to recover her wits. "That's the best explanation possible. All the lost consonants traveling around the world, searching for their missing vowels."

"Exactly."

"So how'd you end up in North Carolina?"

It was a casual question but she'd touched a nerve.

He looked away, the smile fading. "Ah. That's a long story."

"Is there a short version?"

He propped his elbows on the table and leaned his chin on folded hands, thinking. She waited patiently, not staring at him but instead watching a bumblebee sort through the small purple florets of a butterfly bush.

He dropped his hands to the table and met her eyes. "My first job out of college, I joined the county force as a patrol officer. Not a popular career path in my family. Half of them ghosted me, the other half wanted me to fix their parking tickets. I asked to work Kona side of the island, so less conflict with family. But still not good. Right after I made detective, I had to arrest two cousins and a nephew for selling drugs. My uncle said I betrayed the family and I should leave."

"That's not fair," she protested.

He shrugged. "It's what happened. He told me to go off-island at least. Better, the mainland. No one argued with him, so—" He looked away. "North Carolina seemed far enough."

She inched her chair a little closer and rested her fingers lightly against his forearm. "I'm sorry. That must have been hard for you."

"Not the hardest thing I've done. But yeah."

She offered a wry smile. "And here I thought I'd written the book on self-exile. You must miss them."

"My brother. My sister and my mom, yeah. The others, not so much."

His phone pinged on the table between them. She withdrew her hand from his arm and glanced away.

Ignoring the phone, he took both of her hands in his and drew her eyes back to his. "The long version of my story is very long."

"I have time." She felt her heart leap in hope and happiness.

His small smile broadened. "How about I tell you a little more over dinner? I know this new place downtown, in an old warehouse by the train tracks. They do a wicked huli-huli chicken."

She began nodding at "dinner." Added a smile and kept nodding.

He raised an eyebrow. "Are you feeling brave enough to drive us?"

She tried to copy his expression, knowing she had little control over her left eyebrow or the good warm feeling flooding her whole body.

To her surprise, the right words came easily. "You'll be my first passenger in eight years. Question is, are you feeling brave enough to ride with me?"

He laughed. "I'll chance it."

FORTY-SEVEN

November 21, 2023

Dear Chrissy,

I'm so very sorry about everything that happened eight years ago. Every day, I still think of you and Amber and Destiny. Every day, I wish with all my heart that I could go back in time to warn you about the danger that was waiting for you. For all of us.

But we couldn't have known. The storm arrived, the rain fell, and the road collapsed. We happened to be there, so we fell too.

I can't change the past but I can tell you about your other children, Billy and Jessie. I know you'd be very proud of the wonderful people they have become.

Billy prefers to be called Chaz now. He has grown into an outstanding young man, smart and kind and brave. Two months ago, he saved my life.

I'd like to tell you about that....

ACKNOWLEDGMENTS

This book was made so much better by the special attention generously given by my dear friend and brilliant editor, Joan Weston. Her insights and thoughtful comments on the cover design as well as the manuscript were spot on.

I'm grateful also for the enthusiastic support of my friends and talented colleagues in the Weaverville Writers' Workshop. Thank you to Sandy Mariaskin, Mel Kelley, Jarie Ebert, Dan Ward, Glen Miska, and Diana Morley. A huge thank you also to my beta readers: Rich Valcourt, Patty Tracey, Mel Kelley, Jarie Ebert, Beth Siegel, Rachel Graham, and Jessie Gifford. Your feedback has been invaluable!

Developmental editor Annie Mydla (Winning Writers) provided much-needed assistance with her insightful comments and sage advice, while always remaining positive and enthusiastic about this project. Author Angel Khoury also gave generously of her time to explain both the joys and challenges of launching a novel into the world.

ABOUT THE AUTHOR

A New England farmer at heart, Sarah P. Blanchard also lived for several years in Hawai'i and North Carolina, where *Drawn from Life* is set. Rural life and the natural world have strongly influenced her writing, as have the works of writers Barbara Kingsolver, Charles Frazier, and Ron Rash.

Sarah holds a B.A. in English literature and an M.B.A. in marketing. Before turning her attention to writing poetry and fiction, she worked for many years in communications and marketing. On side journeys, she has been a volunteer firefighter, radio news and talk show host, magazine editor, website developer, horse trainer, and facilities supervisor for an astronomical observatory. She taught English and communications for several years at the University of Hawaii-Hilo, and also taught fiction writing in the College for Seniors Program in the Osher Lifelong Learning Institute at the University of North Carolina-Asheville.

In her writing, Sarah is drawn toward flawed, compassionate characters who believe they must battle their demons alone, and complex antagonists who think they have nothing to lose. Many of her short stories, poems, and essays have been published in magazines and literary journals. She was a finalist for the 2021 Doris Betts Fiction Prize and the 2024 Porch Prize for short fiction. Her short story collection, *Playing Chess with Bulls*, was published in December 2023.

Follow the author on her website, social media and blog.
Website and blog: sarahpblanchard.com
Facebook: SarahWritinginWeaverville
Instagram: sarahpblanchard
X: Sarahs_Lexicon
Tiktok: sarah_p_b_author

Book Clubs

Looking for a Discussion Guide for this book?

Scan the QR code or go to Sarah's website:
www.sarahpblanchard.com/readers-guide-drawn-from-life